MW01168987

ONCE UPON HER VEINS

THE IAOMAI CHRONICLES

RACHAEL KATHARINE ELLIOTT

Copyright © 2023 by Rachael Katharine Elliott
All rights reserved.

No part of this book may be reproduced in any form or by any electronic
or mechanical means, including information storage and retrieval systems,
without written permission from the author, except for the use of brief
quotations in a book review.

This is a work of fiction. Names, characters, places, and incidents either
are the product of the author's imagination or are used fictitiously. Any
resemblance to actual persons, living or dead, events, or locales is entirely
coincidental.

Edited by:
Anne J. Hill
Crystal Grant
Sarah Harmon

Cover art by JV Arts
Book art by Reba Cochran
Book map by Cartographybird Maps
Internal formatting by Michelle M. Bruhn

ISBN (paperback): 979-8-9879675-0-8
ISBN (hardback): 979-8-9879675-2-2
ISBN (ebook): 979-8-9879675-1-5

To the doctors and nurses at Comer Children's Hospital,

who saved my life.

TABLE OF CONTENTS

PART TWO: EARTH

PART THREE: LIGHT

UTARA
KINGDOM

THE LAUTEN SEA

DOLOK'S
HAMLET

DANAU
KINGDOM

LEMBAH

ALANG
KINGDOM

THE CAPITOL CITY
OF LIGAS

HUTAN
KINGDOM

DIKIT
KINGDOM

RIMBA

KUCOR

SELATAN
KINGDOM

◉ MAJOR SETTLEMENTS

◉ MINOR SETTLEMENTS

THE SAMUDRA OCEAN

◉ TASHNI

KOTA ◉

◉
KEMA

BIAYA ◉

ELAOMAYN
KINGDOM

PULAO SEA

PULAO
KINGDOM

PRONUNCIATION GUIDE

Iaomai: EE-oh-my

LOCATIONS:
Dolok: doh-LOCK
Utara: OO-tarAH
Alang: ah-LANG
Elaomayn: L-oh-main
Ligas: li-GAHs
Lembah: lem-BAH
Kema: KEY-ma
Tashni: tahsh-NEE

CHARACTERS:
Mzia: mZEE-ah
Tariq: TAR-ick
Anuva: ah-NEW-vah
Yulia: YOU-lee-ah
Lila: LEE-lah
Ezhno: eh-ZEE-no
Aasim: A-some
Orinth: OR-inth
Ishtar: ish-TAR
Grinith: grin-ith
Kaisar: KAI-zar

PART ONE

SKY

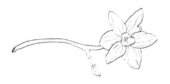

CHAPTER 1
THE SECRET

THE WORST PART OF being a healer was telling the truth. Mzia only told it when she absolutely had to. When there was no other way around it—when she had tried everything else only to end up back at the truth. The horrible, empty, ugly, killing truth.

"Healer?" Sari, mother of two, stood holding her youngest son on her hip just inside the small examination room. Sari's traditional ankle-length dark blue skirts swished as she rocked back and forth to keep the toddler from fussing.

Mzia completed her examination on Sari's oldest son and set down her stethoscope. The boy, Ethik, at only six winters old was all arms and legs and clumsy movements. Mzia had seen him shoot through the streets in front of the clinic with the other boys his age, laughing loudly and covered with dirt.

But today he sat almost completely still on the examination table, his eyes dull and lifeless, and his skin an unnaturally light shade of brown.

"Healer?" Sari prompted again.

"Still waiting on those test results." Mzia forced lightness into her voice. She didn't need the test results to know what was wrong with Ethik. She had seen these symptoms time and again. Nobody knew the source of the illness. Even research doctors—whose scientific papers she read late into the night—had no answer. Sometimes the illness would just pop up in the Utara Kingdom, take hundreds or thousands of lives, then vanish for several years. Most doctors disagreed about how it passed from person to person, causing the more superstitious to blame it on spirits or Caouete, the god of rain. Something to do with an old belief that one could catch cold from the rain.

And this illness wasn't the only one the doctors disagreed over. There were more incurable sicknesses every year, so many she lost track of all the names.

A good healer would tell Sari the truth. A good healer would send the boys from the room and sit the mother down and tell her that her son had something that only Iaomai, a drug grown in the Alang Kingdom, could cure, which in a poor mountain town where nobody could afford such a drug because the government had a monopoly on the supply grown, was the same as telling Sari that her son would soon die.

Yulia, Mzia's mentor, would tell Mzia it was her duty to tell the truth. After all, they were healers and only the truth would make the people trust them.

But Yulia wasn't at the clinic today. So Mzia smiled easily and said, "I wouldn't worry about it; I saw another little boy just last week come in with the same thing. I think they are eating some of those berries growing by the temple."

Sari relaxed a little, adjusting her headscarf after her youngest tugged it out of place. Most women wore them out of convenience instead of tradition because of the sudden winds and dirty life in the mountains. Sari lowered her voice. "You really think so? Because when he didn't want to eat this morning, I thought that maybe . . . maybe it was . . ."

"I don't see any cause for concern," Mzia said, giving Ethik a pat on his bony leg. Just then, her handpad buzzed and Mzia quickly picked it up off her desk. Her eyes scanned through the results of the blood test she had taken not half an hour before. It was as she suspected.

A normal healer would have to tell the truth now. Would be unable to lie because even if they did, Ethik would die in just a few weeks without the Iaomai.

Mzia deleted the test in one tap and smiled up at Sari. "It is as I thought, all negative. It must have been those berries."

Sari sagged in relief. "Oh, healer, thank you. I was so worried."

Mzia adjusted her own headscarf and set of goggles that she was never without and ducked her head. Without looking up from her pad she said, "I am just going to give him a shot to help his immune system, and then I will send you home with some herbs to help his stomach. Nothing but broth and bread for two days, even if he begs for something else."

"Yes, healer." Sari smiled and kissed her youngest on his cheek.

"Why don't you take your little one and wait for us in the front room?" Mzia suggested. "I find siblings don't like watching others get shots."

"Good thinking. This one cries at the drop of a leaf, don't you?" She kissed her youngest son again and walked out.

Mzia turned to her patient. It broke her heart to think what would have become of this boy if he hadn't been brought to Mzia.

"I will be right back," Mzia said, and left through the second door into the lab and storeroom. The cool back room grew with one wall against the mountain itself. The walls were lined on one side with ancient books on uneven shelves and the other side with baskets of herbs and tools and a door to the stairs going up. A center table held various medical equipment Yulia had been able to scrape together over the years. Such a lab was considered very outdated, especially when compared to the modern hospitals in the Alang Kingdom. However, this clinic was perhaps the best within a day's travel.

Mzia got to work collecting the herbs for settling a stomach and portioned them out into little bags which she then labeled. These she would send home with Sari to help provide a cover for the real cure.

With a quick glance over her shoulder towards the examination room, Mzia snatched a vial she had filled earlier that day from the bottom of a basket of tek moss. The moss was a rarely used ingredient due to its many side effects, which made it a perfect place to hide things she didn't want Yulia to find.

"What's that?" a voice asked from the stair door.

Mzia whipped around to find Anuva on the bottom step, one hand on the open door. "You shouldn't be down here!" Mzia hissed, walking over to shut the door. Thank goodness the girl at least had her headscarf on.

"What's that?" Anuva asked again, gesturing to the vial in Mzia's hand.

"Nothing. Now go back upstairs before someone sees you."

"If it's nothing," Anuva pressed, "why did you hide it in the tek moss?"

Mzia sighed. At eleven winters old, Anuva let Mzia get away with nothing.

"I can't tell you. But I can tell Yulia you were breaking rules if you don't go back upstairs right now."

"You won't tell on me," Anuva said evenly. "Because I will tell on you."

"There is nothing to tell," Mzia insisted. "Now go."

Anuva frowned. "It's your blood, isn't it? That's what you were hiding?" Her eyes widened. "Are you going to heal someone? Can I watch? Please!"

"No and no!" This was getting too far out of hand. Mzia sighed. "I will tell you everything tonight if you go upstairs right now."

Anuva nodded, satisfied with that answer, and pulled the door shut. Mzia waited until she heard little feet pad up the steps before returning to the examination room and Ethik. Mzia talked to him kindly as she fitted the vial on a syringe. "This might hurt a little," she told him as she tightened a band around his upper arm and searched for a vein in his inner elbow. "But it will be over fast."

He didn't respond, and her heart broke a little. Not that she needed any validation to do what she did, but it was comforting to know that she wouldn't have to supply his mother with the traditional incense at his funeral.

Mzia pushed the dark liquid into his vein and removed the band from his upper arm. "There, all done. Not so bad was it?"

She lifted him down from the table and walked him out to his mother. He would be his old self by morning, having no idea how close death had brushed him. He would grow up to be tall and strong like his father and probably never even remember this trip to the healer. As it should be. As it was with all those she had cured.

EVENING STOLE IN AROUND Dolok's Hamlet as the sun sank behind the hills to the southwest. Mzia locked the clinic door to walk down to the market as she did on many nights. The main road of the town zigzagged away from the clinic down the mountain, with buildings half-grown, half built up many years ago.

The process for growing homes always fascinated Mzia. Long ago it had been more of an art form, myths told one had to sing the tree-like plants into the right shapes to live in. But now it was all genetically coded into the house plants; they needed only the right growing conditions and homes would take shape in a matter of weeks. Taller buildings, ones that reached the clouds, grew in the Alang, or Central, Kingdom. It took a few years to reach such heights but even that time was being shortened constantly by new and better technology.

In the Utara Kingdom where she lived, and particularly in mountain towns where wealth was in short supply, some were so impoverished that they built parts of their home out of the earth. Mzia only saw this poverty as an added reason to justify what she did. But she couldn't think of that now, because then she would have to think about what she would tell her adopted sister when she returned to the clinic. And it was simply much too beautiful of an evening to dwell on that.

She passed the meeting hall grown with its shallow roof and open walls. Wide and flat, the town used it for holidays and solstice dances and sometimes market stalls during the rains. Tonight, a group of girls skipped rope inside, and the popular rhyme about a princess in her tower reached Mzia as she walked by.

The sky turned a dusky pink as she entered the lower market. Because nights were so long in the winter months, people learned to live in the darkness. Even now in mid-spring, bioluminescent lamps were brought out to drive off the night for a little while longer. Mzia had her own little lamp, swinging at her hip. Not because she needed it. Her *condition* gave her what Yulia called "impossible vision" and let her see nearly as well in the dark as during the day.

Mzia paused at a bend in the dirt road to look down on the hilly lowlands to the south. She could see the blue and green glows of the larger cities near the swamps. There were even more amazing things happening in the other kingdoms. And beyond them, the other nations of the world. So much life happened just out of reach. But with things the way they were, Mzia couldn't leave the mountain side. Her condition made it too dangerous. For most of the twenty-two winters she had been alive, Mzia's life was confined to this mountainside.

The air crisped as twilight stole over the land, so Mzia turned from her thoughts and made her way to one of the food stalls.

"The usual, healer?" the older man, Kip, face deep-set with wrinkles, asked. At her nod, Kip flipped the flat rice breads on his wide thermal stove. Metal that big was rare and had been passed down for many generations. Such things were considered primitive by modern standards. In a poor town, however, it was necessary.

As Kip wrapped the rice breads up, he asked, "Will you be leading the solstice dances again this year? My granddaughter has talked of nothing else for weeks."

"Wouldn't miss it for the empire!"

"They say it'll be a special celebration this year because it's feared to be Emperor Kaisar's last. He is soon to follow his wife to the stars." His eyes became unfocused, distant. "I remember the last few they did for his father, very grand." Then he returned back to reality. "I swear you fly across the ground you move so fast! Nice to see the young people 'round here so engaged, keeping old traditions alive."

"You flatter me." Mzia smiled, "And I love the dances. They are fun." She took four of the flatbreads and tried to pay, but, as usual, he waved her off. "You saved Bire's life. For you, anything."

"You won't make any money this way." She forced a little laugh, hoping he didn't brag about her to everyone. "I was just doing my job."

"No, others do their jobs; you are gifted by the Starbreather."

Mzia forced another laugh. "You flatter me, Kip. I hope you don't spread such rumors around or people will be coming to me for miracles."

"As far as I am concerned, you have worked me a miracle."

Mzia thanked him again and ducked away before anyone could

overhear. She wouldn't trade the lives she had saved for anything, but to hear others even joke about her having a special gift sidled uncomfortably close to the truth.

She purchased a few more items, including some sweet tea and a surgery puff for Anuva, before climbing the road back up to the clinic.

After going up the back steps into the upper rooms where they lived, Mzia shed the headscarf and goggles she always wore. This was the only safe place to go without them. She shook out her long braids and felt them slap against her lower back. Maybe Anuva had forgotten about what she saw in the clinic. As they sat down to dinner, her first words to Mzia were, "So how often do you give people your blood?"

Mzia sat on a cushion by the low table and crossed her legs. She busied herself with pouring the tea for both of them, but Anuva didn't touch the food, waiting for an answer.

At last, Mzia looked at her sister. The girl had also taken off her headscarf revealing the white hair they both had in sharp contrast to their tawny skin. Though Anuva was never supposed to leave the upper rooms when anyone else was around, Mzia and Yulia often took Anuva into the woods on herb gathering excursions and picnics so she wouldn't get bored shut away in the upper rooms of the clinic. But it was just too dangerous to let her out alone.

So, just as Mzia had been hidden until she turned thirteen, Anuva would remain a secret until she was old enough to keep the *great* secret. The secret that kept them hidden away in this mountain town.

Mzia folded her hands—it was time Anuva understood the whole truth.

CHAPTER 2
SET SAIL

T ARIQ SHOOK HIS HEAD in disbelief. Could it really be true? The datapad he held said as much, but he still couldn't quite wrap his head around it.

An adult Iaomai Child. How could one possibly evade capture for so long? Their odd hair and eye color made them impossible to blend in without drastic measures, in addition to the common knowledge of what they meant to the empire. Their bone marrow contained the only thing that could cure one addicted to Iaomai. Parents with any sense of decency would give the child up the day it was born because of the potential. The possibility of helping find a cure to the addiction. It was a great honor.

An adult. Tariq had to reread the report several times over to gain every detail, but it sadly lacked specifics of how the Iaomai Child managed to survive so long. He had his own suspicions. Not that he would ever voice them—that wasn't his job.

The multi level skyship bay bustled around him as the workers loaded the needed equipment onto his skyship, the *South Wind*. Tethered to the landing field beside and below many other military skyships, the *South Wind* boasted the latest and best fittings the military could produce. It stood at 100 feet in height, not including the noot flotation balloon, and 250 feet in length. Shaped to vaguely resemble the seaships that brought their ancestors to this continent thousands of years ago, they now sliced through the air with modern engines at speeds only dreamed of just 20 years before.

Tariq enjoyed the preparations going on around him, the sounds as familiar as the sound of his own breathing. He worked in and around skyships from the moment he chose his training path. Military service of some sort had been required, given that he was a Marked One, but which direction he took depended on what strengths and talents he showed.

His wristpad vibrated with a message from his second.

Everything on schedule, sir.

Tariq sent an acknowledgement back and was about to check with his helmsman when his wristpad vibrated again. This message came from command. *Report to headquarters immediately. Room 234.* The lack of explanation told him enough, and he turned and headed to the tram that transported soldiers up and down the field. The tramcar came moments after he called it from the platform and only minutes later, he entered the headquarters. This building grew only one level high so as not to impede landings, but it made for long halls to traverse down. The architecture consisted of smooth walls with a few grown flourishes and glow lamps placed at exact intervals for best lighting. It was sturdy and simple, like the army. He didn't need to double-check the building map before heading to the southwest corner. He had been to Room 234 before. Several times.

A slight uneasiness overcame him as he approached the doors. The palace guards stood on either side. So, it was as he suspected. Tariq straightened his uniform and stopped before the double doors.

"Skycaptain Tariq, reporting as ordered."

"Tariq, is that you?" A voice from the slightly ajar door called.

"Let him in."

Tariq knew the speaker before the guards could open the door. Stepping inside the room, much too grand to be titled a conference room, Tariq was met with the sight of his eldest half-brother. Prince Orinth leaned on the projection table in the middle of the room, his silk robes reflecting the table lights. He waved Tariq over.

Tariq saluted before coming over to join him.

The table showed in three dimensions a rendering of a mountain range and a village on the south side foothills marked *Dolok's Hamlet.*

Prince Orinth straightened and gestured at the projection. "You know where this is?"

Tariq regarded the mountain range more closely for a few moments; they were tall and jagged, the peaks capped with snow and the lands to the north quite hilly. It ran from east to west. "The Northern Mountains," Tariq said. "Is this the final destination for my mission, Your Majesty?"

"It is. The crew will be told as little as possible until the targets are acquired."

"I am sorry, Your Majesty. Did you say *targets*? I was under the impression—"

"Yes, the briefing lacks all the information. Apparently, the reason we are dealing with an adult is because my dear sister has finally tracked down that rebel doctor from 20 years ago. You were a bit young then to know, but I assume you have read the report?"

Tariq nodded. Doctor Yulia on the government research team had stolen an Iaomai Child, just under two years of age, from the lab. It had been a great scandal, and to this day, they were not sure how she did it. Some whispered she had help from separatists who opposed the empire and who wanted the kingdoms to be independent again, but nothing could ever be proven. At least, not with the information Tariq was privileged to.

"Then you know," Prince Orinth went on, "what importance this is to the emperor. It would mean a great deal to the royal family if we were to recover both the doctor and the Iaomai Child."

"I understand, Your Majesty."

Prince Orinth lowered his voice. "I have a . . . personal interest in this mission. It is important to me that the Iaomai Child is recovered, and quickly."

Tariq nodded again. He suspected that the prince knew who would be cured, but he didn't voice the thought. Instead, he said, "I will take all necessary precautions."

"Yes, about that." The prince rubbed the back of his neck. "I didn't just come here to wish you well. I came to warn you: Princess Ezhno will accompany you on this mission."

Tariq nearly lost his composure. "The princess, Your Majesty? I don't understand—"

"There isn't room for discussion." Prince Orinth sounded rather bitter about it, as if he had already tried.

Tariq tried to phrase his next question carefully. "I know Her Highness's role is head of the Iaomai research team, so her expertise is invaluable in that area. What role will she be performing on board the skyship?"

"I am afraid you are not going to like it." The prince looked a little rueful, and this set Tariq on high alert. Prince Orinth didn't normally pull his punches. "She has convinced the emperor that her private team is the best to extract the targets. You and your men will act as assistants only on this mission."

Tariq kept his face neutral. "If those are my orders, Your Majesty."

"They are," the prince said, but he didn't sound any more pleased than Tariq about it. Then he smiled a bit, relaxing, "This could be it, Tariq. The mature bones of the Iaomia Child could be the answer to . . . to everything. To the cure."

"I'll bring it back safely, Your Majesty."

"I know you will. That's why you were chosen for this. You have been a loyal soldier in many difficult missions. It hasn't gone unnoticed. Great things are in your future, Skycaptain."

CHAPTER 3
A BROKEN WORLD

MZIA REGARDED HER ADOPTED sister's eager and open expression. Yulia really should be here to help explain. But Anuva probably knew or at least guessed most of it. That was the best place to start. With what she already knew.

"Anuva, why do you think you can't go out and play with the other children?"

Anuva held up one of her white braids, "Because of this."

"And why do the two of us look like this?"

"We are Iaomai Children," Anuva said simply. "Our mothers were addicted to Iaomai flower when we were born."

"And why is that rare?"

Anuva frowned. She fiddled with her star pendant necklace that she was never without—a summer solstice gift from a few years back.

Mzia tried again. "What I mean is, why aren't there more like us?"

"Oh, because mothers can't have babies when addicted. The

drug doesn't let them."

An oversimplification of the drug's effects, but accurate. Pregnancy, let alone carrying to term, was almost unheard of while addicted. The Iaomai was a miracle drug in many ways, curing everything from colds to cancers and cuts to broken bones. It had its limits, but those addicted lived nearly pain-free lives. But one of the consequences was the inability to have children; the unborn were attacked like another virus the drug might find in the body.

The other consequence took the form of an unbreakable addiction. To stop taking the drug equaled a death sentence and just one dose was enough to addict a person for life. And it wasn't always a long life. Everyone on the drug had an expiration date. Nobody could predict how long—could be 10 years, could be 40. But one day, the drug would stop working no matter how much they took. This change was marked by tremors of the hands and a purple-green rash. Once a person exhibited those symptoms, they would die in a matter of weeks.

Mzia shifted in her chair. "So that brings us back to the original question: why do we hide ourselves away?"

"The emperor wants us dead."

"The empire wants us silenced," Mzia corrected. "Yulia isn't sure how deep the corruption goes, but she knows many in the government are aware of our true gifts and keep that from the public."

"But why though?" Anuva asked "Why do they hate us? We could cure so many people! Why doesn't the emperor want that?"

"That," Yulia said from the door, "is a complicated question that involves a lot of economics and politics."

Mzia tried to explain. "Yulia, she asked and I—"

Yulia held up a hand, looking tired. She set her large bag on the floor by the doorway and pushed her headscarf back to reveal streaks of gray in her black hair. Mzia never really considered how old Yulia was. Her mentor always had enough energy for the both of them. But just now, after a few days' travel, her age at last began to show.

Yulia pulled off her shawl and hung it on the hook over her bag. "It's all right. It was about time Anuva understood. After all, she is about to become nearly as powerful as you."

"I am?" Anuva bounced eagerly. "When?"

"Soon," Yulia said, crossing the room to the biolights. "You both forgot to turn on the lights again." She tapped on the lamps and the room alighted in a green glow. Then she came over and knelt at the low table to plant a kiss on Anuva's brow.

Anuva wrapped her arms around Yulia's midsection. "So why does the emperor want us dead—er—silenced?"

Yulia smoothed down Anuva's hair. "Well, it is like this: the emperor is the only one who controls the growing of the Iaomai flower crop. He knows that it is the only cure, if only a temporary one, to all the illnesses that keep popping up. The people of all kingdoms on this continent are eager to stay in the Empire because they want access to the Iaomai and—"

"Why can't you help people without Iaomai? Isn't that what healers do?"

Yulia and Mzia shared a pained expression. If only it were that simple.

"There once was a time when healers could solve nearly everything except for the gravest of illnesses," Mzia said. "But that was hundreds of years ago, before all the strange new illnesses we have now. We have fallen behind in our understanding. And for many, the Iaomai is their only hope at life."

"Now." Yulia pulled away from Anuva so she could look her in the eye. "What do you think would happen if there was another cure? If the kingdoms didn't need access to the Iaomai?"

Anuva wrinkled her nose, considering. "I don't know,

maybe . . . I don't know."

"Come now, I taught you history. Why did the kingdoms unite in the first palace?"

"To find a cure for addictions and illnesses and . . . Oh!" Anuva's eyes sparkled with excitement. "If they didn't need that anymore, they would leave! And it would be like it was before, separate kingdoms!"

"Yes, I think that is precisely what the emperor fears. It isn't quite so simple as that. There is a lot of money and a lot else at stake not just for him, but for his children. And it doesn't hurt that having all these odd diseases makes the other nations want as little to do with us as we do with them."

Anuva looked rather pleased with herself for figuring out the correct answer and she looked over at Mzia with a smile.

"But wait . . ." Her brow wrinkled. "Why can't we just tell people the truth about us?"

Yulia gave her daughters a sad smile, "I tried . . . once." Mzia had been just older than Anuva, but she remembered. "Once Mzia passed through puberty and the healing properties of her bone marrow spread to her blood, I gathered all the information and sent it to Princess Ezhno. Even then, she was in charge of that branch of research. I thought, well, hoped, that she would be pleased. I was willing to let her take all the credit for the discovery if only it meant that Mzia and other Iaomai Children could share the cure." She gave Anuva's hand a squeeze. "Not a day later the government released a statement claiming those who said adult Iaomai Children had healing quantities in their blood and not just the bone marrow were merely conspiracy theorists. There were official documentaries made with fake science explaining exactly how my tests couldn't be true."

"So . . . we have to hide forever?" Anuva asked.

"Not forever," Yulia said carefully. "But we must do all we can to stay hidden away until the right time."

Mzia felt Anuva's eyes on her. Anuva knew what Mzia had done, that she had risked it all to heal. However, Anuva said nothing to Yulia. Secrets were one of the few things the Iaomai Children could claim for their own.

AFTER DINNER, WHEN THEY had cleaned and put away the few simple dishes they owned, Yulia and Mzia went down to the workroom. Yulia opened up her pack and took out all she had bought from her journey to the closest trading city. She embarked on the three-day round trip twice a year. Mzia always looked forward to her return, where she got to look at all the new herbs and ingredients from all over the empire. There were spices from the Alang Kingdom, where the seat of the empire sat, dried cati from the Gao Desert on the eastern side of the continent, herbs from the grasslands in the south, and flowers that only grew above a certain elevation in the Central Mountains.

As Mzia marked each ingredient on her handpad, her mind returned to Anuva's question. *We have to hide forever?* A forever of people dying when she could save them.

She stowed each ingredient and as her fingers brushed the precious stock, her mind's eye saw each of the places they were from. In her youth, she had kept files and files of the digital images, wondering what it was like to live in the places that looked so different from her own. She would fall asleep and dream about the harsh sun of the desert, the warm Pulao islands, and the icy sea at the tip of the northernmost part of the continent.

All the places she would never experience for herself. The secret was too precious. It had to stay hidden until the right time.

"Yulia?" Mzia said slowly. "When will the time be right? You know, for us."

Yulia stopped filling the jar with herbs and sighed. "If I knew that, I would tell you."

"You don't even have a guess?"

Yulia shook her head. "In truth, what we need are allies." Yulia had spoken of this before. Of the potential backers they could get. Those willing to stand up to the empire were few and far between.

We have to hide forever?

"I know you say they are dangerous," Mzia prodded. "But surely if the separatists helped us before, to hide us here, surely they could—"

"We have been over this." Yulia shoved the basket of herbs onto the shelf. "If they knew what you were capable of, they would take you both away and start a war they couldn't win." Her mouth set in a hard line. "They are powerful, yes, but their leaders don't have the support they need. And their main goal is to unseat the emperor, which would cause a lot more death than you could ever help cure. I don't want to be responsible for starting a war, do you?"

"Of course not," Mzia said. "How could you ask that?"

Yulia softened. She opened her arms and Mzia stepped into the hug. Yulia took a deep breath. "I know you mean well, my star. I know you just want to help everyone. But this is how it is. To share the truth is to die."

Mzia nodded. She had to stay hidden. Well, mostly hidden. What did mountain folk know of healing anyway? Was anyone going to complain when something cured faster than it should? No. She wasn't exposing the secret. Nobody suspected a thing beyond good luck, and they never would. Not in this out-of-the-way town in an out-of-the-way province of the Utara Kingdom, a kingdom known only for its lack of remarkability.

Nobody had found her in the twenty years since Yulia had brought her here. And nobody would come looking.

CHAPTER 4
OFF COURSE

WE SHOULD REACH THE second drop site just after dusk," Skycaptain Tariq reported. His voice clear and loud over the hum of the skyship's engines. The briefing room they stood in had low ceilings like a majority of the ship and slightly reflective walls of the new alloy they built most skyships out of. "Your men are in position?"

"They are." Princess Ezhno sat in a chair by the projection, her white dress made of a fabric so thick she appeared to be sitting with blankets over her legs.

Princess Ezhno looked up at the table projection and smiled. That was the first time on this two-day trip from the Alang Kingdom that Tariq saw her smile. And it wasn't pleasant. There were very few things about the princess that anyone might call pleasant. She set every man and woman in his crew on edge just by walking into the room. She had an oiliness in her countenance, as if she always knew something about a person they didn't want her to. The crew understood she deserved respect and honor of her rank, but none of them were quite sure just *why* she was here. Tariq knew, but the knowledge didn't make it any easier.

Tariq turned to the table which held a three-dimensional projection of a mountain with a small village, Dolok's Hamlet, near the base. The glow mushrooms on the walls dimmed so he could see better. He zoomed the projection into a spot on the southern side. "My scouts reported their clinic to be high in the town, about here." He pointed.

"Yes, the team has been briefed."

Tariq would never say so, not out loud, but he disliked her team. He disliked the whole idea of someone other than the army, than his men, extracting fugitives. But he had no say. He had his orders. The prince's orders.

Tariq gazed across the table projection at her. The other nations of the world might think it uncouth to let a princess go out on secret and dangerous missions. However, Ezhno was middle-aged and well past caring about appearances of any sort. Most of the empire revered her as the lead scientist on the Iaomai Project, the only hope for the deadly drug addiction sweeping the continent. And she was the second born, so she wouldn't inherit the empire. Tariq secretly thanked the Starbreather for that.

Tariq gathered himself and continued his report. "The *South Wind* will stay well out of sight, as planned. When your men have obtained the targets, they will signal—"

"Target, Skycaptain," the princess corrected in a drawling voice. "We are only to bring back the Iaomai Child. The rebel doctor is to be eliminated."

Tariq pulled up his handpad and frowned. "When did the orders change?"

"Last night." Ezhno dismissively waved a hand without looking up from her own handpad. "I didn't think you needed to be bothered with such a detail since your men aren't helping with the extraction."

"True." He fought to keep his voice neutral. "But I would've liked to be informed before they brought back only one prisoner to be transported. Were you going to tell me before then?"

"Of course, Skycaptain," she said in a way that made his title sound like a mockery and not a hard-earned position. "I wouldn't keep such important information hidden."

Tariq turned away and pretended to be checking something on the handpad. Apparently, the briefing he had been given three days ago with Prince Orinth was just that: brief. There was more going on than they would say. Tariq was used to the government and secrets. That wasn't what was unsettling him. It was the absolute authority Ezhno exercised. His study of history taught him that legitimate children of the emperor never enjoyed the kind of freedom or authority that Princess Ezhno did today. Prince Orinth was the heir, so he had some excuse to do most things in the name of training to be emperor. But he didn't abuse his authority the way Ezhno did.

The skycaptain shook his head. These were matters for those with the pure bloodline. He shouldn't interfere.

Tariq turned back to the table. One of his men entered and saluted, fist to hand with a nod of the head. Tariq saluted back. "Report."

"We're near the first drop point, Skycaptain."

"Good," Ezhno said. "I will contact the alpha team. Tell the beta team to prepare."

The man didn't move. He glanced at Tariq.

Tariq paused for just a moment. "Tell the team to ready, soldier. Dismissed." They saluted each other again and the man left the briefing room. Tariq tried not to look pleased as a frown formed at the edges of Ezhno's mouth.

With a wave of his hand, he closed the mountain projection. "I will be needed on the bridge, Princess. Please let me know if you require anything."

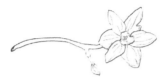

CHAPTER 5
INTO THE WOODS

"THEY FOUND US?" Mzia struggled to keep her voice calm and soft, unheard by her patients in the front room. The pad she held with the data on her latest patient slipped from her fingers and landed with a soft thud on the red mossy floor. She blinked, fighting for focus. "Are you sure?"

Yulia only gave Mzia a nod. The older woman stepped forward, an odd calm in her features, and clasped Mzia's hands. "The farmers said they saw soldiers in the southern rice field. There is only one reason they would be here. You need to get Anuva to the safe house. Take the western path we tried last summer; it is less known. I will see to your patients and close up."

"What? No, you can't stay. It is you they will recognize. I look just like everyone else with this headscarf and goggles. They wouldn't—"

"Mzia." Yulia pursed her lips and closed her eyes. When she opened them again, they were lined with tears. "I need you to do this for me without question. I have to stay here so nobody will be suspicious and to delete data. We both know the information is too precious—" the word caught in her throat. "Your place is with Anuva. And if I shouldn't make it—"

"Please don't—"

"And if I shouldn't make it, you know what to do. The contact information is all at the safe house."

Mzia shook her head, fighting tears of pain and panic. "You are going to make it," she whispered. "You will."

"Go," Yulia urged. "Get Anuva. Tell her as little as possible. I don't want her to worry."

Mzia nodded. She hastily undid her healer's apron and hung it up on the hook by the bookshelves. She scrambled to gather up her medical bag and stowed her goggles inside. She set it by the back door before stumbling up the steps.

"Anuva?" she rasped. "Anuva?"

Anuva entered the kitchen. "What is—" She stopped when she saw the tears clinging to Mzia's face. Her tawny skin paled. "We . . . have to go?"

Mzia nodded, unable to form words.

Anuva didn't hesitate to run back to her room. Mzia heard the girl shoving the few things she owned into a pack and forced herself to pack a bag with food. She didn't need to pack clothes for herself as they always kept a spare set at the safe house. Her midnight blue dress she had on would do well for the journey tonight.

Mzia took her sister's cold and clammy hand to descend the steps. They paused at the door at the bottom of the stairs out of habit. Both of them wore headscarves but no goggles as the evening swept in and such things might impede their eyesight.

Mzia pushed open the door to find Yulia bent over her computer screen.

"We are ready," Anuva announced.

Yulia straightened. "You two go on ahead. I have some things to take care of here."

Yulia should've known better than to lie to Anuva. The girl's shoulders slumped; she understood.

Mzia held back tears as Anuva and Yulia embraced. Was this the last time she would see them together? No. She couldn't think like that. She had to get Anuva to safety.

Only when Yulia hugged Mzia for the final time did she let a few tears escape. "I am proud of you, my star." Yulia kissed Mzia's teary face. "May the Starbreather guide you on the path you need to take."

"And may he light your way to the end," Mzia managed to get out.

Mzia took Anuva's hand again and slung the well-traveled healer bag over one shoulder. She paused on the threshold to the side door, throwing one last glance back at Yulia. Their mentor didn't look their way, busy at the computer, erasing files.

Mzia bit back the sob threatening to rise in her throat, and left, pulling Anuva into the evening air.

They stumbled up the back path and into the woods where twilight was already well established. She remembered, despite her distress, to tuck her skirts up into her belt to keep from stepping on them in the steep path. The trees and underbrush soon obscured the village lights from view and they were truly alone in the gathering dusk.

They didn't stop until night had fully settled. Mzia dropped Anuva's hand and leaned against the rough bark of a tall oak to catch her breath. A deep ravine to the left of the path sent the sound of the stream floating up to them. Neither spoke—there was nothing to say. Mzia set her jaw. It would be no good to distress Anuva any more than she already was. It would only worry her sister if she saw just how scared Mzia felt.

So Mzia adjusted her headscarf, took a deep breath, and continued up the mountain path, Anuva at her heels. They had only gone a few paces when a small animal went scurrying along behind them. She paused and Anuva ran into her from behind.

"What—"

Mzia put a finger to her lips. Something wasn't right. She was sure she heard . . .

A twig snapped.

Faster than she could think, Mzia grabbed Anuva's arm and leapt into the ravine. The two of them scrambled down to where the ferns grew waist-high and pressed themselves to the cool, damp earth. Mzia didn't need to tell Anuva to be silent as they waited.

An owl hooted and took flight. Then nothing. Mzia began to wonder if she had dirtied her dress for nothing when the distinct sound of not one, but two sets of footsteps.

The pounding in Mzia's ears grew louder as two dark shapes appeared on the path where they had stood just minutes before.

"Shouldn't we have seen her by now?" One of them said in a harsh whisper.

"This is the path the food seller said the healers take up the mountain."

Had Kip unknowingly sold them out? Did he tell the passing travelers where the healer's clinic was and where they might go looking for herbs themselves? This part of the path was used by many people before it split off into the secret way to the safe house.

The men moved on without another word. Mzia caught snatches of their dark uniforms between the leaves of the ferns. Soldiers. The nightmare she always told herself wouldn't happen was happening.

Once she was sure they were far enough away to not be heard, she roused Anuva and took her hand once more. She brought them down to the shallow creek at the bottom of the ravine, as its banks were impossibly steep to walk along. Wet shoes would be regrettable, but she didn't so much as pause before splashing into the middle of the rocky water, with Anuva right after her. The freezing water from the mountain snows seeped into her tight-laced shoes almost instantly. From past summers exploring the mountain, Mzia knew the gorge to be narrow and took sharp turns if she went back the way they had come—a good place to lose someone who might be following.

Her feet were numb when she rounded the first corner, but she stumbled on, soaking the back hem of her skirt as she nearly ran through the ankle-deep water. Anuva kept pace just behind. There would be no tracks for these men to follow if they doubled back.

Only when she was certain she had gained enough of a distance did Mzia wade to the edge of the creek and, being as careful as possible not to step on the muddy riverbank, pull herself out onto the side of the gorge. She turned and helped Anuva out, and they scrambled up a spot that was a little less steep than the others.

"Starbreather, protect us." She prayed this plan was clever enough to confuse their pursuers. They climbed out of the steep banks and back up into the woods. The men looking for them would go much farther into the woods before deciding to turn around.

Mzia paused just long enough to get her bearings before turning and leading them west—away from the safe house. She would take no chances of going that way unless she was certain they were alone.

Reaching a grove of aspens, she stopped to catch her breath, bent over her knees. Anuva huffed with exhaustion and between the darkness, Mzia could see her sister's distress. No sooner had she straightened up again than the dreaded footsteps sounded. Growing up in these woods taught her to know the signs when someone approached, especially someone who did not know the forest.

Panic gripped her as the reality of the situation set in—she wasn't going to get away from them even with her advantage of knowing the landscape. The quaking breath she took next steadied her for what would be her most important task—to keep them away from Anuva.

Mzia regretted not preparing the girl for the possibility that she would have to go on alone. And now there was no time.

She took Anuva's hand and they were off again at a run, summoning up the energy to move on from somewhere deep within. Down a steep incline and through underbrush, she put what she hoped was enough space between them when she entered an ancient grove of white spruce where they had picnicked last summer.

She paused at the base of one of the ancient trees that she and Anuva liked to climb. Taking both her sister's hands she had only the breath for one word. "Climb."

Anuva's mouth wobbled even as she gave a sharp nod. She understood. Mzia slung the food bag she had gathered off her shoulder and onto Anuva's. But Mzia kept her medical bag, she refused to give up all hope just yet. Anuva stifled a sob with one hand as Mzia crushed her into a hug.

It began to rain.

Mzia breathed in the lavender scent of her sister's hair, forced herself to step back, and shoved Anuva towards the tree. "Stay up there until tomorrow at nightfall. I will meet you at the safe house."

Mzia was never more proud than when Anuva, not even looking back, swung herself up onto the first branch, and then the next.

Mzia stayed only long enough to see her sister to a good height before she turned and ran. The wind began to pick up. A storm was coming. Perhaps that would hide both of them.

Rain pelted her face and lightning cracked the sky. Thankfully, all of these trees grew close, and she slipped between well-known trunks and underbrush. The tangled mess of branches must have obscured her enough because she still saw no sign of her pursuers. But every now and again, she heard them. And as much as it frightened her that they were following, that meant that they were not looking for Anuva. If the Starbreather truly guided her path, they would never know Anuva existed. The night was dark, the clouds blocking any moon or starlight that might have given her pursuers help. The ground became rather soggy, and she kept slipping in the underbrush.

The lightning had moved off, rounding the mountain to no doubt come again in the early hours before dawn. And these were her woods. She had grown up in these shadows. She chose paths that nobody taller than herself could follow.

But she could still hear them. The night birds and the trees themselves told her they were coming. Now that she had gotten them away from Anuva, she had to find a way to shake them off her trail so she could sneak back.

She slowed to a walk, pulling off one shoe and then another. She ducked behind a large oak tree, pressing her back to it, catching her breath. They were still coming. She forced herself to wait, to be patient. She calmed her breath to listen to the forest. When the forest told her they were close, she threw one of her shoes as far as she could. To her left. Her pursuers paused.

They were too far away to see and could only hear what she had done. So, she threw the second shoe. The men, three or four now it sounded like, headed in the direction her shoes had landed. They had no headlamps with them, so it might take them some time to discover her deception.

When they passed her hiding place, she took off as quietly as she could at a right angle up the mountain. Her adrenaline kept her on high alert when she entered another pine grove, her bare feet slipping on a bed of soggy pine needles. Distant thunder rumbled. She had to get away from there as fast as possible, find out if Yulia had somehow escaped, and get back to Anuva.

Mzia could neither see nor hear the men behind her. So, she

turned and dashed for what she hoped was a direction her pursuers were not. Her feet pounded on the muddy ground and for a time, that became the only sound above the patter of the rain. She turned about and saw nothing. The forest was quiet. Unnaturally so. The hair on her neck pricked.

A green light blasted from above. Shielding her eyes, she looked up and found a skyship hovering just above the treeline. Ropes dangled down all around her and, before she could make up her mind which way to run, soldiers in blue uniforms slid down the ropes and surrounded her. They had strange looking guns, short and sleek. Flashlights on their helmets shone in her eyes and made it hard to see in contrast with the dark.

Breathing heavily, she threw up her hands in defeat. No part of this could be good.

CHAPTER 6
END OF THE ROAD

YULIA DIDN'T LOOK UP when heavy boots thumped into the front room of the clinic. She didn't run or bolt the door. An odd calm settled over her and sharpened her focus just like twenty years ago. The memory washed over her . . .

The air was crisp and the lights bright. She came into work like any other day. She smiled at the receptionist who had no idea what actually happened on the top floor of the hospital. Yulia had only learned a few months back and been granted access just weeks before.

The Iaomai Project. The hope of the empire. The only solution to the drug wars and the staggering amount of people who were addicted. Her parents, had they still been alive, would have been so proud of her achievement. And now, the latest research showed there was even more hope. Ezhno wanted to wait a few more years, run a few more tests. Find a few more Iaomai Children to be sure. Yulia was so pleased to be part of the process she didn't bat an eye at agreeing to wait a little while longer. It was unfortunate that more Iaomai Children would die, but if it meant finding a cure? She would be a part of bringing an answer and changing the world forever. What were a few lives compared to that?

Yulia took the elevator up to the highest floor and stepped out into the hall.

It was designed like most other floors: a central station in the middle and rooms branching out in all directions like spokes of an ancient wheel. Yulia walked to her desk to begin her work. Then a sound cracked through the air. A cry. A child's cry. Yulia froze. There were never children on this floor unless . . .

She spun mid step: drawn to the sound like moths to a light. She pushed past another doctor who tried to say something to her. She ignored everything and entered the room where the cry was coming from.

There, on an examination table turned crib, lay a tiny Iaomai Child, almost two years old. She was naked, her white hair a frizzy mess, her bright eyes red from crying. She was strapped in place so she wouldn't pull out her IV and the numerous other wires taped to her skin. The world slowed to a crawl as Yulia crossed the four steps over to the examination table. The world narrowed to just the child, this beautiful, helpless child.

Yulia had known, of course, since she began to specialize in this area several years back, what Iaomai Children looked like. It wasn't exactly common knowledge as they were so rare and lived such short lives. As part of her doctorate, Yulia had studied drawings made by those who claimed to see them. While their skin was the same beautiful, tawny shade as the rest of the people on the continent, they did not share the same eye or hair colorings. And to see a shade lighter than brown was . . . unnerving. And the eyes. At first she was sure they were all white, but the child looked at her when she came closer and in the white was a flash of gold.

'Otherworldly' was the only way she could describe the Iaomai Child. Like she had somehow fallen off a passing star.

Yulia didn't think. She didn't pause as she reached forward and touched the toddler's arm. The Iaomai Child's cries hushed in an instant and the girl blinked up at her with watery eyes. Her face smoothed and she whispered, "Mama?"

And the whole damn world crashed down around Yulia.

So, she had stolen the little Iaomai Child away to the Utara Kingdom. To let her grow up and prove her theory right.

The only problem was now, nobody would believe them. And

it was too late. She had waited too long. In her attempt to be thorough, in her fear of losing the best thing she had ever found, she had waited too long.

The entire memory was only a moment, a second between heartbeats. So when Yulia looked up calmly from her handpad and saw the soldiers enter the back room, she greeted them with a bow. With one flick of her finger, she sent the separatists a distress call. They wouldn't get here in time to save her, but they would save her children. The girls didn't stand a chance, not against the empire's army. How foolish she had been.

If this was to be the end, she would leave this world knowing that she had, at the very least, done her best. Her one regret was that she wouldn't live to see the dream fulfilled.

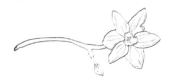

CHAPTER 7
BEFORE THE DROP

THE MEN SAID NOTHING. One of them moved forward and cuffed Mzia's hands together in front of her. Another fitted a harness around her and before she could take in what was happening, she launched into the sky with the rest of them. *How had they known to look for her in the woods? Did they know about the safe house? Had they found Anuva?*

Before she could finish the thought, she entered the belly of the skyship and the bay doors closed below them with a *thud*, cutting off the pattering rain. Each man dropped and began to unclip from the thick harnesses. There were sharp lights everywhere and feet stomping. Two soldiers came over and detached Mzia from the overhead pulleys, and a third removed her harness. With one on each side holding her upper arms and several behind, they marched her out of the bay room.

She was taken down several halls, brightly lit with mushrooms and spotlessly clean. The floor was slick under her feet. They rounded a corner and came into a large room full of complicated equipment covering the walls. They stopped in the middle of the room where everything seemed to glow and the computers only added to the brightness.

The men dropped her arms so she stood on her own.

Three people approached with an air of importance. The woman on the left was clearly of high rank as she wore a well-tailored, supple white dress and her ebony hair with silver streaks swept up into a bun with no head scarf but instead a silver circlet. Mzia knew Princess Ezhno only by reputation. Yulia had whispered her name on the rare occasions when she recounted the escape story. Of how Mzia had cheated death. In her deepest nightmares, Death had the face of Princess Ezhno.

A thin twitchy man stood slightly behind her. He carried a data pad, and wore goggles that obscured most of his face.

The man to the right was dressed in a blue uniform with cords and pins to designate his rank of skycaptain. Everything about him was crisp, as if his attire had been pressed on him. His facial features were strong and smooth, all firm lines and angles. Despite his air of authority, he looked too young to be a skycaptain: the rank supposedly unachievable until the age of thirty-five.

As the three came to a halt a few paces away, the skycaptain looked Mzia up and down. She became aware what a disaster she must look with her drenched, torn blue dress and muddy bare feet. Like a Utara street urchin.

He clasped his hands behind his back and met Mzia's eyes. "You're rather short to have caused so much trouble." He used the Utaran dialect almost flawlessly.

"And you're rather young to be a skycaptain." Mzia's words flew out in retort before she could stop them.

The skycaptain only smirked at her remark and turned to the princess, who, from the blank look on her face, didn't understand the conversation. "Well, Your Highness," he switched to the Alang dialect, "It seems you have met your rival. Your 'expertly trained' reconnaissance team was no match for this young woman and some trees. Luckily my ship and men were here to provide assistance, or she would have gotten away."

Ezhno's face twitched as if she suppressed a frown. Or the urge to slap him. "She is here, isn't she? So the mission is complete. Sekcio," she snapped at the thin man beside her. "Take off that scarf. She looks too ordinary when her hair is covered. I want the images we take to be clear."

Mzia fought to keep her face wary but blank as he approached, so they wouldn't know she understood them. She flinched as Sekcio ripped the head scarf off, revealing her two white braids that uncoiled down to her waist—the only thing besides her eye color that marked her different from them. Mzia had to bite her lip to keep from crying out when he grabbed her arm, shoved up her sleeve, and stuck a needle into a vein in the crook of her elbow. His vial filled up with her blood and he withdrew the needle and stepped away.

Ezhno examined Mzia's overall appearance for a moment. Her eyes lingered on her pack, but after a moment she redirected her gaze to enter something into her handpad's touch screen. The bright light from the screen lit her face from below in a ghoulish fashion.

"Everything in order?" the skycaptain asked, sounding for all the world that he could care less if she found things to her satisfaction.

The princess nodded. "They are bringing in the equipment now."

"We have security cameras that have already captured the whole thing." He pointed out in the same restrained voice.

"The emperor wanted it to be properly documented," she said with a dismissive flick of her hand. "Now take your place. And do try to be more charming when the cameras pan onto you."

Mzia felt her already high anxiety levels spike at the word "camera." Of course they were going to film this moment, to record for the world the novelty of her. Of an adult Iaomai Child. None had lived to adulthood in recorded history, and that wasn't due to any fault of their own.

The skycaptain took up a spot behind Mzia and to her left. She saw from the corner of her eye that he stood at attention close to her with the rest of his soldiers behind. She glanced over her shoulder and caught the skycaptain's gaze a moment before turning away. An emotion had flashed there. He didn't want to stand before the cameras either. He didn't want to be here. So why was he? But something else, much more important, was wrong so she couldn't dwell on the skycaptain's motives. There had been no mention of Yulia or Anuva to anyone. And she dared not ask.

Just moments later, a camera crew emerged with fancy looking sound equipment. The crew nearly scraped the floor when they bowed to Ezhno. Mzia watched the whole fiasco and determined quickly that the princess must have thrown her rank around at everyone in the most unkind way. The crew, soldiers, and the man she called Sekcio, tripped over themselves to set everything just how she wanted and nearly cowered when she focused her direct attention on them.

They were running lighting tests, and Mzia looked about as if a way out would somehow just offer itself up to her. But instead of focusing on escape, her mind skipped from one thing to another. Forcing her to notice everything and nothing at once. Her eyes locked onto the soldiers in one corner looking at her and whispering, then skipped to the closest wall panel where she read all the posted directions for what she realized was a ship-wide intercom. She peered over her shoulder again and found the skycaptain watching her. He cocked an eyebrow as if to invite a question. But exactly what sort of question could she ask him? It wasn't like she could say, "Why are you okay with killing me over a lie?" But if this was to be her last few days free . . .

"Skycaptain!" Ezhno snapped. "Tell that Iaomai Child to face forward."

The skycaptain leveled a stare at the princess. "You could ask her yourself, Your Highness; she understands Alang."

Mzia whipped her head back to him before realizing what she had done—he had been speaking in Alang and not Utara.

"How do you know that?" the princess asked.

He nodded to the intercom on the wall. "She mouthed the words while reading the directions on that panel."

Mzia ground her teeth in frustration. Were none of her secrets safe?

A hand grabbed her chin and forced it forward. "That's better," the princess said as she released her bruising grip. "Now, keep your eyes lowered and say nothing unless I ask you a question. Understood?"

When Mzia said nothing, Ezhno scoffed. "Have you suddenly gone deaf?"

Mzia opened her mouth but the skycaptain cut in. "Surely Your Highness has better things to do than argue with the Iaomai Child?"

"Stay out of this!" Ezhno snapped. She looked back at Mzia. "Well?"

For the first time in her life, Mzia felt the overwhelming urge to spit in someone's face. Before she could, the skycaptain said, "The camera crew are ready for you, Princess."

Ezhno kept her eyes locked with Mzia's. "Well?"

Mzia lowered her head to the ground.

"Good." Ezhno turned away and prepared for the recording.

The princess prattled on to the camera about the mission being a success and the Iaomai Child that had escaped them all those years ago had been found. "We are planning to run some tests before we harvest the bone marrow to cure someone," she explained. "These tests will be the next great step in reproducing a cure for everyone else, and I am proud to say I have been a part of it."

Lies. Mzia was sure that parts of the recordings would be shown on a broadcast to the empire while she was secretly kept alive in a lab where her blood would be used only to heal those the royal family chose.

She was only half listening, her brain refusing to let her focus on the words. Princess Ezhno turned to a man, a soldier in black. "And Doctor Yulia? She has been eliminated?"

"Yes, Your Highness. Her body was properly disposed of as you asked."

Mzia heard herself say, "You killed her?"

Ezhno glared at her, "Don't speak—"

Mzia turned to the skycaptain. "Why did you kill her?" He opened his mouth to respond, but she screamed, "You killed her!"

Her head spun. Her vision blurred. The floor rushed up to meet her. The world would never know the truth.

Yulia was dead.

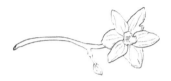

CHAPTER 8
A TIME TO CONFESS

THIS PERSON WAS NOT what Tariq expected of a "dangerous fugitive of the emperor" to be. The wisp of a thing had stared them all down with defiance in her white-gold eyes. Even captured, she somehow looked undefeated—until she realized they had killed the one who had stolen her all those years ago.

Tariq caught her a moment before her head struck the floor. She writhed a second and then went completely still. Even dripping wet she weighed almost nothing. As he held her limp form, he made a decision.

"I want the ship's medic to check her," he said. "You two!" He called over two of his men. "Take her to the sickbay. I want a full report from the medic." When they came to lift her from the floor, he stood and straightened his uniform.

"I appreciate your concern, Skycaptain." Ezhno studied her data pad. Her speech over, she basked in her victory. "But she is under my supervision and I am—"

"Not the skycaptain," he said. "Everyone aboard this skyship is under *my* supervision."

She finally looked at him, ice in her eyes. "I have orders from the emperor—"

"As do I, Your Highness. And those orders are to get you all back to the capital *alive*. She will be placed under medical supervision until *my* medic deems otherwise. If you cannot accept these terms, by all means, feel free to find your own way back." He didn't give her a chance to argue and left.

One point to me. Finally.

The bridge flurried with activity, readying for the return trip home. Most of the crew understood the reasons for the journey now that they'd captured the Iaomai Child.

Tariq looked up from his controls, a long panel of screens waist high that spanned in a slight curve in the center of the bridge. "Lieutenant?"

"Yes, Skycaptain?" The man saluted.

"How long until we are ready for departure?"

"We are scheduled to depart in half an hour."

"Very good." Tariq bent over the screens on his control panel. Something was off about this mission. It wasn't often he got such an inkling, and even rarer still that he let it progress beyond a thought. Most things were not supposed to be questioned. There wasn't just the matter of the Iaomai Child, it was also the rebellious doctor's death. The more he considered it, the more he certain he became that he would have been informed by *someone* if the details of the mission had altered from an extraction to an elimination. That was something he should know as skycaptain. If not by the grand prince's direct line, then through him in some way. If communication had come to his skyship in flight, he should have known. When Princess Ezhno had first told him of the change, there was no way to argue against information he didn't know existed.

He could hear the admiral he had served under for many years telling him to second guess big decisions when the time wasn't urgent. *Act first in times of crisis*, the admiral would always say. *But always reflect in times of peace so you can act better next time.*

He wished he could discuss this with the admiral now, and ask his advice. But it was very late and unlikely the retired man would know about this government secret. There was one person, however, who somehow always knew more than he did.

Tariq straightened. "Jonti?"

His first mate saluted. "Skycaptain?"

"You have the bridge."

"Aye, Sir!"

Tariq left for his private quarters, taking halls and a spiral stair down to the starboard side of the skyship at a jog. The skycaptain's quarters were large and luxurious compared to even the first mate's. However, what he enjoyed most was his own private computer. Being one of the air force's flagships, the *South Wind* needed to have covert ways of communicating with the government. Only a select number of people could even detect the signal put out by the systems, and each was grown with unique parts so that anyone receiving a signal knew who was sending it. Tariq understood very little of this, and so he sat down to contact one of the people who had helped the government design the system in the first place.

Tariq tapped out the code. He was unsure if she would be awake at this hour. He had to know if the signal had been sent to his ship in flight. But perhaps it would be better not to pry into such matters . . .

The screen flashed on. A woman appeared with chin-length hair and a headset. She reclined on a chair in a small, dark room filled with computers.

"Tariq?" She didn't take her eyes off the screen next to the one he was on. "It is awful late. Mother says you need your sleep. You know, because you are off defending the empire and all that rot. She would be angry if—wait . . ." She looked at him at last. "Aren't you still on that super-secret mission to the Utara Kingdom?"

Tariq ran a hand through his hair. If he had been worried about explaining the situation to Lila, that wasn't an issue any more. She always knew what went on in his life. Even if that involved covert operations for the emperor.

"This just can't be." A mischievous smile played across her lips. "There is no way my brother has contacted me just to chat in the middle of the night on a secure channel. Could it be?" She clapped a hand over her heart with pride. "Is my perfect baby brother breaking rules?"

"Lila, I am not breaking any rules. I can contact you whenever I like. And I am only two minutes younger than you."

"Discussing our age difference is most definitely a sign you are hiding something. Do tell me. No, wait!" She held up a hand to stop him. "Let me guess!"

"Lila . . ."

"You are second guessing your life choices and think you should have gone into house growing instead?"

"No, it's—"

"You are ready to admit at last that I am the smarter of the two of us and that school tests don't really prove—"

"Lila, would you just—"

"No! I have it!" She grinned in triumph, "It's a woman! She has caused your dereliction of duty!"

When Tariq just blinked she leaned closer to the screen. "No comeback? Is it possible I have struck upon a truth?"

Tariq rolled his eyes. "For all intents and purposes, it does, technically, involve a woman. But not like that!"

It was too late. Lila pumped her fists in the air. Tariq tapped his fingers on the desk, waiting for her celebration to finish as she wiped a fake tear from the corner of her eye. She leaned forward, her chin on her hands. "If this is about a woman, dear brother, you'd better tell me everything."

CHAPTER 9
A BROKEN PROMISE

WHEN MZIA AWOKE, SHE was alone. The room was dark except for some luminescent blue light that swept from under the bed across the floor. It was small, a quarter the size of her bedroom at home. Beside the bed stood a low table with several medical supplies including gauze and empty vials.

The lone window above the bed was round and small and had darkeners so she could not tell what time it was. Groaning, she pushed herself up a little. An IV line tugged at her arm. She traced it to a large computer attached to the wall beside her bed. Clearly it affected her in some strong way because she had no greater desire than to go back to sleep. And she couldn't just take it out because the IV had a second green wire that would send out an alert if taken off.

And Yulia was dead.

Mzia shook her head. Something they had given her dulled the pain of it all. She should be upset enough to cry but she couldn't. The inability to mourn as she should consumed her until a vast emptiness opened up inside.

Her healer's bag was nowhere in sight. She had nothing but the slightly damp clothes she had been wearing when they took her.

Yulia was dead. In her worst night terrors about being found, Yulia was always imprisoned. But to kill her without even a trial? Or a chance to say goodbye?

With a despondent sigh she rolled over. Nothing hurt as bad as the ache around her heart. The emptiness. And what about Anuva? The girl was probably going half mad wondering why they hadn't been in touch. Would she ever know what had happened to them? Would she think they abandoned her?

Mzia closed her eyes but did not find peace even in sleep.

Yulia was dead.

MZIA WOKE TO INVADERS in her room. Princess Ezhno and Sekcio were muttering about counts and charts on their pads. Some back part of her brain told her to be on alert, to guard herself while this woman was in the room. But she couldn't keep her eyes open for more than a few moments at a time. And she struggled to focus her vision. Her heart gave a panicked flutter. Her eyesight was always perfect.

The drugs were getting stronger. They would soon overtake her altogether.

"Why is there food here?" The princess's strong voice pierced the fog around her mind. "She should be fully sedated by now." She checked something on her pad. "Stars above, this isn't enough to keep her under. Sekcio, I want an extra dose . . ." This was followed by a string of medical jargon that Mzia's brain was too tired to translate.

She could feel herself slipping away and panicked. With a moan and all the concentration she could muster, Mzia forced herself to sit up. She blinked blurrily at the princess and Sekcio, who both appeared only mildly surprised at this development.

Mzia bit out, "Why did you kill her?"

Ezhno ignored her and checked the dosage on the IV computer.

"Answer my question." Mzia clutched the edge of the bed, forcing her legs over and her feet to press against the ground.

Ezhno arched an eyebrow and turned to her at last. "You mean Yulia never told you the story?"

Mzia knew she was being baited, but asked anyway. "What story?"

Ezhno dismissed Sekcio with a wave of her hand. When her assistant left, she squared off with Mzia. "You know what we do with Iaomai Children, don't you? We harvest their bone marrow to cure someone. Did you ever think to ask who you were supposed to cure? Did you never think that perhaps Yulia was murdering another by taking you away?"

"Well, I—"

"No, of course you didn't, selfish girl. You probably never once considered it. But you, at least, can claim ignorance. Yulia cannot. She knew full well who she was leaving behind to die."

"Who?" Mzia whispered.

"My son," Ezhno spat. "My only child was born with a heart defect, and only an Iaomai addiction could save him. But his life was an hourglass, as are all those who are addicted. The cure from an Iaomai Child was his only hope of living a normal life. Yulia knew all this and took you anyway. I trusted her, and she let my son die!"

"Princess, I—"

Ezhno cut her off again, her voice dropping to a deadly whisper. "He was only seven when the Iaomia drug stopped working. He died on his eighth birthday. All because that selfish woman took you away."

"So, you killed her?" Mzia shook her head to try to clear the medication, but it didn't work.

"She brought this upon herself," Ezhno corrected. "She deserved what she got." Her eyes cut as she leaned close. "As you deserve what is coming to you."

Before Ezhno could say more, Mzia shoved her away, grabbed the tray of food from the side table, and flung it at that horrible woman. The door opened and Sekcio walked in.

Ezhno ragged, "Why you little—"

Sekcio threw a small object which attached itself to Mzia's forearm.

"What—" a jolt of fire surged through Mzia. She screamed and collapsed onto the floor, writhing in pain as they just stood over her and watched with mild fascination. "That," Princess Ezhno sniffed, "is only a taste of what is to come. Nice work, Sekcio. One more jolt will keep her down the rest of the trip. But not at full strength; I still need her alive."

Mzia was mid-scream when the door opened again.

CHAPTER 10
MEDICAL ADVICE

TARIQ TOOK IN THE scene quickly and before anyone could speak, he knelt and ripped the device from the Iaomai Child's arm. She curled up on the floor, sweating and shaking. He stood and pointed the device at Ezhno. "What do you think you are doing? I don't even know where to begin. Wait, yes I do." He dropped the disk, and before it could stop rattling on the floor, he crushed it under his boot.

Ezhno looked far more concerned for her pain device than any concern she had shown before. "That was—"

"Illegal." He removed his boot to reveal the smashed device. He bent again and helped the trembling fugitive up to perch on the edge of the bed. Her skin was clammy and her breathing labored. He looked again at the princess. "If I find you have another one of those, Your Highness, you won't just have to find your own way to the capital. You will have to find your own way to the ground!"

"Is that a threat, Skycaptain?" She almost laughed at the words. "The power has gone to your head. May I remind you that you were only promoted so early because your skycaptain failed to follow procedure and was killed—"

"Careful, Princess." Tariq straightened his uniform. "Your words and actions will be reported *accurately* in my log and my dispatch to the emperor. You know, the one I deliver to him personally when we get back? Now get out. She is to have no more visitors until we reach the capital. I will be posting a guard."

"I will not be ordered about like some common—"

"Luica!" He called to his man outside who appeared a second later.

"Yes, Skycaptain?"

"Escort the princess to her rooms."

Ezhno narrowed her eyes. "This isn't over." She drew herself up to her full height and walked out with as much dignity as someone covered in food could muster. Sekcio followed.

Two points to me. Tariq smiled grimly.

He turned his attention back to the silver haired woman, who clutched the edge of the bed and fought to keep her head up. "Are you all right?"

She didn't look at him. "I will . . . heal."

Tariq nodded. "Good."

"Skycaptain?" She lifted her tired eyes, white-gold and endless in their depth. "The princess isn't going to . . . it isn't what you think . . ." She tugged uselessly at her IV. Frustrated tears welled up in her eyes. "You . . . you don't understand . . . Please . . ."

Tariq stepped back. He had a duty. He had always known what this mission involved. The prince was counting on him. He knew this Iaomai Child was only found to be experimented on and killed. Her bone marrow would mean the cure to someone who was addicted. It would mean furthering the research to find and replicate the cure. A sacrificial lamb. All this he had known and accepted from the start.

But until then, she was a person on his skyship under his supervision.

"Lay back down," he urged softly. "You need rest."

"But it's a lie," she protested even as she obeyed, slumping sideways on the bed and pulling her knees up to her chest. "It's a lie and I don't—" She gave a frustrated huff.

Tariq pulled the blanket back up to her shoulders where her silver hair tangled and splayed across the pillow. Her brow wrinkled. She was unhappy even in sleep. He watched her, debating what to do next. The princess's reckless actions only added fuel to the small fire of doubt he had allowed to kindle in his mind. He confirmed with his sister that no transmissions were sent to his ship once they took off. Which could only mean the princess got the orders before . . . if she ever received them at all. But why would she lie about something as trivial as when she was granted orders? It just didn't add up. And if he couldn't trust her with telling him the truth over something so simple, he most certainly couldn't trust her judgment about something as important as the Iaomai Child.

He called in the ship's medic, Doctor Grett.

The older man examined the Iaomai Child, checking her pulse and heart rate.

"Well?" Tariq asked after several minutes of silence.

"She seems healthy, no damage done."

"And?"

Grett chuckled a little. "You know me well, Skycaptain. I only wish to give caution to the princess." He waved a hand at the IV computer. The screen showed her dosage of sleep medication. "The sheer concentration she has the patient on is, shall we say, medically ill advised."

"It could hurt her?" Tariq asked. How far should he push this issue?

"I honestly don't know for sure. I have never dealt with such a patient."

"But in your professional opinion," Tariq hedged, "it could

cause harm?"

"I cannot guarantee one way or the other, but if you are asking my advice . . ."

"I am."

"Then the dose should be lowered. You said you would post a guard? I don't see why she has to be on medication at all."

"Then, on your medical advice, doctor, I order a lowering of the dose."

"Very well, Skycaptain."

CHAPTER 11
THE SKYSHIP'S HALLS

S OMEONE CAME IN AND cleaned up the mess Mzia had made with the tray, although most of its contents had landed on Ezhno. They gave her several more pillows. As if that was supposed to help. She remembered bursting out in anger over something, and pain, and then it got all fuzzy. The skycaptain had been there . . . maybe. But that didn't make any sense. Why would he come to her room? Didn't he have a ship to run? Maybe she had just imagined that part. It was the drugs. They were affecting her more than she wanted to admit.

It was many hours later before Mzia found her head clearing. She sat up and the room only tilted slightly. A glance at her IV screen told her that her dosage had been altered. And more importantly, there was no red light for the security setting. No alarm would sound if she unhooked herself.

I trusted her and she let my son die!

Sorrow stabbed her afresh. First Yulia and now this. Of course her harvested bone marrow had been meant for someone, but Ezhno's own son? It was almost too much to contemplate. It threatened to consume her whole as her body shook with sobs. The only thing that pulled her out, that kept her from losing herself completely to the pain, was Anuva. Her sister needed her, needed her to be strong. Needed Mzia to stay alive and get back to her. She could cry later.

Footsteps sounded outside her door. She laid back down and pulled the covers up over her face in a slight panic to hide her crying, just on the off chance the low dosage was an oversight. The door opened, and the guard walked in, did a round of the small room, and left. Mzia pushed off the covers and stared at the ceiling, trying to think. She let the grief sharpen into anger. The anger kept her grounded. The guard couldn't see her, but he knew she was there. He hadn't bothered to dawdle because it was clear she was in her bed. An idea started forming in her mind.

Mzia crept out of bed and began pulling cabinets and drawers open. As suspected from her own clinic experiences, extra medical supplies were left behind, including several unopened syringes. Mzia examined the IV computer again. The flow was set so low it wasn't enough to make her or anyone else sleep unless the patients themselves wanted to. Surely, her captors knew that. She frowned. Who had changed the dosage? Wait. The skycaptain had said something about that. There had been a doctor too. Maybe. She shook her head. There was too much to sort through. For now, escape had to be her only focus.

With one motion, she pulled the needle from her vein. No alarm. At least, not here. She stood on wobbly legs, arranged the pillows to resemble a person, and covered it all with the blanket. She tucked the needle end under the blanket so it would complete the look. She needed the guard to think she was in the bed just long enough to take a few steps into the room.

Finally, she took out an empty syringe. Poking the smallest hole just above the liquid line, she extracted from the top of her IV bag enough of the harsh drug to knock someone out in seconds. It was more effective in a vein, but she doubted she would have time to find one. She drew a second vial full.

She pressed into the only dark corner by the door and waited. Sure enough, the guard soon came into the room to check on her. With his back to her, she struck, plunging the syringe into the side of his neck. He cried out and tried to push her off but instead collapsed to his knees. She stayed just long enough to guide his body down to the floor and ensure that he wouldn't hit his head. Even though he should wake in a few hours, a little voice in her screamed how wrong this was. Her oath to do no harm pounded in her head. The amount she had given him was dangerously high and could have lasting effects.

But Yulia. They had killed Yulia. And Anuva. Anuva was all alone.

It was easier than it should have been to get up and leave the soldier. To not dwell on what she had done. To leave the room and dash down the hall. The passage ended in a four-way split, and she chose the one on the right. Seconds later, she came upon another hall to the left and sprinted down that one.

Voices sounded around the corner and she tried the door to her left.

Locked. The voices came closer.

The next door was also locked. She slammed into the third door in the hall and it gave way, opening so fast she tumbled in and it closed behind her.

Even with the low floor lighting, she could see that she was alone in the storage room. She held her breath as the men passed by in the hall. They didn't stop. Hand to her heart, she breathed freely again, looking more closely at the room around her. Sacks and shelves holding everything from computer equipment to seeds covered the four walls.

"Starbreather, help me," she murmured. Where did she go from here? They would find her missing soon enough. Why was this a good idea again?

She stood and walked the room, looking for anything that might help her. She ran her fingers along the growing cords of a complex computer part and halted. Over the edge of the shelf just above her head hung a strap that looked familiar . . . But it couldn't be . . .

Without much hope, she tugged the strap. Down into her arms tumbled her medical bag. Stunned, she laughed out loud. What were the odds . . . but maybe the Starbreather really did intend to guide her.

She slung the bag over her shoulder and went to the door, listening to be sure she was alone before stepping out into the hall again. Left at the fork, and that hall ended in a spiral stair which she climbed. She meant to get off at the first landing, but she could hear voices beyond the door. The next landing was the same. So up and up she went, brushing her fingers along the cool mossy walls.

The stair ended in a narrow, empty hallway. The air was damp and the low ceiling sloped down to the right. It wasn't flat but rounded and not made of metal like the rest of the ship. The light here was dimmer, only a few glow mushrooms along the ground for light.

Mzia stepped into the hall. Out of instinct, she put a hand up to touch the curved ceiling that was muddy green in color. It was warm and soft and felt . . . alive. She gaped—she must be touching the noot plant, responsible for lifting the skyship. It kept the ship afloat even if the engines failed. The idea had only been proposed a few generations back, when smaller versions of the plant naturally were found to be airtight.

Mzia felt a smile forming—in awe of what she experienced here, what she never thought she would see for herself. The reason

ONCE UPON HER VEINS

anyone could travel far and fast in an empire covered with mountain ranges, swamps, and deep ravines was all because of this plant. She brushed her fingers along its length as she walked, captivated by the idea that someone could see a growth and think of flight. How wonderfully beautiful. How Anuva would have loved to see this with her. The girl was fascinated by skyships and had recently started spewing facts to Mzia about them any chance she got. It was how Mzia knew the skycaptain looked too young for his rank.

A rumble shook the hall slightly. The noot flushed a pale gray, its taut surface forming wrinkles. She withdrew her hand in surprise. A loud alarm sounded overhead, and a voice boomed, "Emergency! All crew to stations!" The alarm continued to sound, and the warning repeated once more. Running feet pounded below. The door just a few steps away at the other end of the hall opened.

Another soldier appeared. "I found her," he said into his comm.

Mzia turned and sprinted a few steps, but he caught her arm from behind, forcing her to stop.

"No!" she protested, struggling weakly against the soldier's firm hold. It couldn't end like this. She couldn't end like this. She stabbed him with her second vial in his chest.

He cried out and let go of her. She hadn't paced it well and didn't inject all of the liquid before he fell away. But it was enough to send the soldier to his knees. The alarm still blared.

She ran out the door he had come in and down a straight staircase that ended just one level later. This hall had many doors and several halls. She searched behind her to make sure nobody saw her as she rounded a corner—and collided with someone coming the other way.

The other person kept their footing much better than her. She fell back, tripped, and landed on the floor, breath knocked from her lungs.

The skycaptain eyed her in confusion, "What are you doing here?" he asked before coming forward and pulling her to her feet. He didn't let go of her wrist once she stood.

"What do you think?" she spat, trying and failing to wrench free.

The skyship shook beneath their feet, and the skycaptain's wrist pad beeped.

"I haven't time for this," he said. "Come with me."

She gave up fighting only so he wouldn't pull her arm from her shoulder. The drugs had made her even weaker than normal. He took her up the stairs at the other end of the hall. The ship kept dipping and swaying unexpectedly.

The door at the other end of the hall was wider than the others and slid open when they approached.

Ahead a set of bay windows showed a raging storm alongside several large screens with numerous readings that meant nothing to her. Many other screens and equipment covered the other walls and people sat at the computers or else stood and entered data on their pads. In the center of it all stood a wide control panel. Lightning flashed and illuminated the panic on everyone's faces. Something was very wrong.

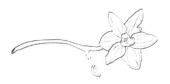

CHAPTER 12
BUMPY RIDE

TARIQ STEPPED ONTO THE bridge. Another huge crash shook the ship and the engine started making high pitched squeals. "Jonti, report!"

His second didn't look up from his screen. "Something has punctured our noot, sir. We are losing altitude."

"Can it be patched?" he asked, walking up to his control panel and bringing the Iaomai Child with him.

"The location is impossible to reach in this storm, sir. We have to land."

He leaned over to inspect a screen to his right. The readings were unusual even for a thunderstorm. He glanced at the Iaomai Child standing at his side. She shrank from the lights in the bridge and the people in the hall as if they burned her. Her silver hair fell loose from its braids down her back. It outlined her form in a glow of light, like her own personal halo. It was almost too extreme to be real. It must be a trick of some sort.

She looked back at him with defiance. He didn't have time for this. "Stay right there," he said, dropping her wrist and pointing to the spot on the floor where she stood. Not like she could leave this room without help. The doors wouldn't open for her.

The ship took a sharp dive to the left as more lightning slashed the sky. The Iaomai Child threw out a hand to stop herself from bashing into the control panel. Tariq tapped on his screen and switched a few dials. Another violent shake of the ship knocked everyone except Tariq from their feet.

"Is that supposed to happen?" she whispered, rubbing her elbow as she pulled herself back up.

"No. Quiral, more lift on the starboard side!" He compared data, again unusual and falling towards dangerous, and ordered men to go aft to fix yet another issue. Lightning had fried a sensory panel on the port side. Rain pounded the windows and several more minor shakes followed in quick succession. That was not good.

Tariq flew between the controls. The screens started to glitch out, freezing and going dark. That was not good either. He scanned the room, taking in the chaos of the bridge, the fear of his men. He had been in this situation before with a skyship in danger of crashing, but not as skycaptain.

Now it was up to him. And they were flying blind.

Only one thing left to do.

"Initiate separation sequence!" Tariq ordered his helmsman. He hated to try something so risky with the storm, but he had little choice—he would have to split the engines and bridge from the rest of the ship. The engines being the heaviest bit would mean that once separated, the majority of the ship with the noot would sink down to the forest floor, everyone unharmed.

"All non-essential personnel off the bridge!" Tariq ordered. The men jumped to obey, working quickly to separate the bridge and engine from the rest of the ship. The rest of the crew exited back through the open doors.

Another crash of lightning. Sparks flew from a ceiling panel.

"I said non-essential personnel off the bridge!" Tariq barked. "That means you, Iaomai Child."

The ship swayed. Another loud explosion shook the bridge. The helmsman cried out and collapsed. Tariq moved to check on him, but the healer beat him there. Blood poured from a deep gash on his side. The healer didn't hesitate to yank his ruined uniform over it and apply pressure.

Another tremble crossed the floor. She couldn't be here. She needed to survive; that was his mission.

"Leave the bridge!" he ordered, rerouting the control of the ship to his own panel.

"If I stop, he will die!" she shouted over the chaos.

Tariq had bigger problems, like how he was supposed to take down a ship when he hadn't flown one in over a year. The memory of the last time this happened flashed across his mind. The last time he had been on a skyship that crashed. Only then he had been over a city.

A loud grinding noise was followed by several loud pops. What was left of the skyship went into a sharper dive.

"Separation successful, Skycaptain!" a soldier reported through the intercom.

"We are going to run aground!" someone else warned.

"Release the drag shoot and brace yourselves!" Tariq ordered as he took hold of a wall rail made especially for this purpose. The healer ignored him again, digging around in her bag for something while keeping pressure on the wound. None of her efforts would matter if they crashed. And the mission would be a failure if she died.

He let go of the rail and tumbled more than ran across the floor to her.

"He will die!" she shouted up at him.

Despite her objections, he pulled her away and back to the wall rail.

"You will die!" was his only response as he caged her in with his arms against the wall, clutching the bracing rail once more. He had hoped to separate the bridge from the rapidly destabilizing engine, but they didn't have the distance. Just like last time. Emergency parachutes were deployed, but the ground approached. Just like the towers had been. The flames. The screams. It all came back in horribly perfect clarity.

Much too soon, the skyship struck land.

A hissing filled the cabin. With the bridge located near the engine, one of the biggest issues in the event of a crash was a possible leak.

Tariq pushed himself up off the floor despite his body's protest. He must have been flung from the wall during the crash. He didn't remember. Darkness. Only darkness swam across his vision. And not the darkness of night. He was alive . . . somehow. He touched his face and found something warm and wet covering his forehead, left eye, and cheek. He swore violently and reached out to try and feel where he was. Nothing but floor.

"Skycaptain?" The healer's voice trembled. But she was alive. Stars above, they had survived.

"My crew? Who else is . . . ?"

"They, they aren't moving." Her voice wavered then strengthened. "I don't think . . . Skycaptain, I don't think anyone else will survive."

If nothing else, he trusted her judgment on that. So, it was just the two of them. The engine sputtered and fuel vapors mingled with smoke. "The engines are leaking." He blinked. Still darkness. "We have to go, but I can't see anything. Can you stand?"

A hand touched his shoulder and she helped him rise to his feet. He allowed her to lead him to the door. Her footsteps felt steadier than his own. Heat told him there was fire nearby but he couldn't see it. It was difficult to stay upright. The world tilted under him even with her strong shoulder to lean on. The hissing grew louder.

Most of the ship had separated in flight, taking what was left of the noot. Meaning the doors to the bridge led now to the open air and not a hall. They pried open the doors with little trouble because of the emergency release and crawled out of the skyship. The night air mingled with the smell of fire and smoke, making his sightless eyes burn.

"Faster," Tariq urged even as he stumbled forward, each step filled with pain. It was too early to know the extent of his injuries, but that could be tended to later. "We have to get away. The engines are unstable."

Stumbling through the dark and into what he presumed was the forested mountainside, the Iaomai Child did her best to keep him upright. Stronger than she had looked, it seemed. They half slid in their mad dash down the side of the mountain, the hissing growing louder at their backs.

A clap like thunder rocked the earth. Knocked clear off their feet, Tariq felt the fall in slow motion as he tumbled into the dark. Like before, he saw the end. Yet unlike before, he swore he could hear the call of *Glory Glory Glory* . . .

The stars were calling them home.

CHAPTER 13
THE PRINCE

L ILA DIDN'T WANT TO believe it. But her information was never wrong. She checked and double-checked and triple-checked the signal. Dead air. No response. Which could only mean . . .

She shoved her chair back and checked another screen. Flashing through tabs as she searched for possible other reasons in the manual for the computer. The manual she had written. But no, she knew the answer before she got to the paragraph about fail-safes and backups. No response could only mean one thing.

On a third screen, she dialed her bodyguard.

His image appeared. "Yes?"

"We are going out. I need to talk to the grand prince."

"Lila, it is three in the morning. I don't think—"

"This is an emergency, Aasim!" She shoved her handpad into her bag while checking traffic patterns to the palace. "The highest priority!"

"Perhaps if we just sent a message for his majesty to see in the morning—"

"This can't wait that long!" Lila snapped, locking down her computer so nobody could tamper with it when she was away.

"Please, you know that the palace guards won't even let us in unless—"

"Tariq's computer isn't responding!" Lila said, stopping long enough to glare through her screen. "So unless you want to tell the grand prince tomorrow that the ship carrying the princess probably shipwrecked over the Central Mountains, but we didn't think it important enough—"

"All right, fine!" her bodyguard gave in. "But surely the military will inform him soon that they lost contact with the skyship?"

"Yes," Lila said with a wicked grin. "But won't it be grand if I get there first?" She closed the screen before he could protest and bounded out of her room.

The lift took an agonizing twelve seconds to arrive, and she impatiently tapped the screen for the eighth floor. If she knew Aasim, he would have a tram at her building's rail before she could get there. Bouncing on her toes impatiently in the lift, the only thing keeping her from going everywhere at once with worry was that she might just beat the navy general to the prince. And the look on his face would sustain her until she learned what had become of Tariq.

Aasim waited with her emergency tram, looking for all the world like he didn't get paid enough. He stood tall and intimidating, as a bodyguard should look. His dark hair combed neatly back around a clean-shaven face with a uniform that was rumpled and wrinkled and told he slept in it to avoid having to change for just such times as these.

"If we are going to see the grand prince, you might want to run a comb through that hair," Aasim said mildly as they entered the tram.

Lila rolled her eyes but looked at her reflection in the window. She looked like she had been awake for the past 48 hours. Which she had. But Grand Prince Orinth was used to her by now. He had watched her grow up, took special interest in her training as he had with all those who were to bear the Mark of the Emperor. He had spent more time with Tariq, naturally, when they were growing up, as they both shared the mind of a strategist. Lila was sure that if Orinth had also been a Mark Bearer instead of Grand Prince, the emperor's eldest, he would have gone down the same path Tariq had with the military.

Between the towering growths of the capital city, Lila saw the hill on which the palace stood flick in and out of view in the blue glow of the city lights. The ancient building's base was several stories high shaped like a ring made out of stone. It was built when the empire was just one of the many kingdoms on the continent, before it had grown and conquered and expanded into what it was now. Before they had learned to grow their dwellings from trees instead of building them out of bits of earth.

Atop the original granite palace stood eight mighty towering trees, one for each of the eight kingdoms. On the ground in the middle of it all was the original courtyard, holding regular sized trees and plants from all over the empire. It got plenty of sun between the towers, except for the hours around high noon. At the top of the enormously grown towers, branches larger in diameter than she was tall reached inward, forming a canopy above and below the uppermost room in the massive building: the throne room. Clear webbing stretched between the branches, reflecting the sunlight and moonlight like a huge multifaceted diamond.

Lila had been in the throne room many times. The first was six years past when she and Tariq had come of age and been presented to the emperor for his service as Marked Ones. And every year since at the Summer Solstice celebration. A place to be seen if nothing else. As a Marked One she had to be seen, whether she liked it or not. Parties were all well and good, a time to show off her fancy clothes and learn the latest gossip, but the parties thrown at the palace were not her favorite.

Lila huffed a little as the tram transferred to the line that would take them to the front gate. The tram lines ran on bridges several stories above the waters that ran below. Boats were used for pleasure and slower transport and the trams for quicker access.

When they entered the palace's shadow, she slipped on a mask of calm and shrugged off her jacket to be sure the tattoos across her shoulders were showing. The Marks of the Emperor forever inked onto her body. They told of her loyalty and dedication to the emperor and empire before all else. Her blood ran with royalty she could never wield but was forever bound to.

The tram stopped at the first guard tower, for no line led directly into the palace. Lila stepped out into the warm night air. Spring was getting on. Lila frowned at the starless sky; they approached the end of their wet season, so rain was common at night.

The palace guard came out to meet them. From the casual way he strolled over to their tram at three in the morning, Lila assumed Aasim had called ahead. When he stopped before them, he ran an eye over her marks before saying, "You have business with the grand prince?"

"Yes. And if you don't let me pass it will be on your head he didn't hear from me first."

The guard was unfazed by her taunt. Perhaps she had dealt with him before or he had been warned, for he just gave a sharp nod and said, "The Marked are always allowed into the palace, but to see the grand prince you will need to speak to his personal guard."

"I am well aware of protocol. Now would you be a dear and ring me in?" Lila forced casualness into her voice. If the prince's personal guard tried to stop her—well, she would burn that bridge when she got to it.

THEY DIDN'T TRY TO stop her. Apparently, they took her seriously enough, and she didn't have to wait long to be let into his personal chambers. His rooms were only a few hallways and a lift ride up one of the eight towers. She was the first to reach the prince. In the time it took the prince to be up, dressed and ready to receive Lila, there was still nobody else there, which was a little odd.

"You are sure?" Prince Orinth was doing that annoying thing Tariq did. He called it "gathering all the facts," and it made her blood boil that he wouldn't just act sometimes instead of trying to see it from every angle.

She forced a smile though. Frowning would get her nowhere. Through clenched teeth she said, "I designed those computers, Your Majesty. I grew parts of them myself."

"I didn't know Tariq had told you about this mission," the prince said without looking up from his tea.

"He didn't."

Orinth waited for her to go on. She, naturally, didn't divulge just how she knew about this mission or the six Tariq was on before that. So the prince cleared his throat, "The issue is, that this is a rather delicate matter."

Tariq had told Lila of the Iaomai Child. The prince was acting odd towards the one person who was supposed to be so important.

Orinth went on. "Until I have more information, I am afraid I can't send a rescue party."

"What?" Lila forgot to check herself. "What do you mean you can't send a rescue party? Their ship crashed. Tariq could be dying. The princess could be dying."

"Do not imply I don't care about their lives." His voice was even but his eyes cut. "Tariq has been an indispensable Mark since his training completed. I would hate to lose him. But the delicateness of this mission, you see . . . ." He frowned and set down his tea cup. "There is just too much at risk. I must wait until I have solid evidence of what happened before informing the local authorities."

Lila dug her nails into her palms until they threatened to draw blood. She couldn't tell what she was angrier about—Tariq's endangerment or the fact that her evidence wasn't good enough. Her brother had been right to question things about this mission. Maybe he should have questioned them sooner.

Part of her wanted very badly to hurl the closest chair at the prince. But that would get her nowhere. She bowed, fist to palm, and said, "As you wish, My Prince."

"You will tell no one of this, do you understand? Our conversation doesn't leave this room."

Lila nodded and bowed once more before leaving the room.

In the hall, Aasim was wise enough to wait until they got back into the tram before asking her what was wrong. Well, his exact words were, "What has put you into such a murderous rage this time?"

"They aren't sending a search party."

"What?"

"You heard me. He says it is too delicate a matter to tell the local authorities about it."

"But your computer—"

"*Not enough evidence*," she mocked in the prince's voice. "*There is just too much at risk.* Well, I will show you risk."

"I have to advise against whatever it is you are planning."

"I know. And I have to ignore you." She leveled a look at him, "So the real question is, are you going to help me track down my brother, or are you going to get in my way?"

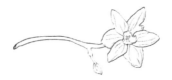

CHAPTER 14
HEAL WHAT HAS BEEN HURT

*M*ZIA?

Yulia called her name; she must be dead. Then the world refocused and she moaned. Daring to open her eyes, she found the world bathed in an orange glow. The rain had stopped. Somewhere to her right there stoked a huge fire. Burnt metal and ash filled the air. She sat up slowly, her back stiff. Everything about her hurt but nothing appeared broken. An odd stillness blanketed to the forest around the crash, broken only by the crackling of the fire.

She had to get away from there. They would surely come looking for the crash site come day break. They would come looking for her. She got to her feet, glad to find her medic bag still with her like a faithful friend.

Only a few steps away lay the skycaptain, sprawled on his back. If she left him, they would probably find him in the morning. But only if he lasted the night. Part of her, the part with the strong self-preservation bit she had long cultivated, told her to leave him. He would turn her in as was his duty, and she would end up dead in a lab. Plus, there was that small detail that he killed Yulia.

As Mzia turned to go, he let out a low moan. Before her vengeful survivor self could stop her, she went and knelt at his side. She hadn't saved him from the explosion and fire only to let him die of exposure on the mountainside. "Skycaptain?" She shook his shoulders gently.

He moaned again. "What happened?"

"You have a good gash there on your forehead. Can you see anything?" She pulled bandages out of her pack and began to bind his head to stop the bleeding.

He blinked open his eyes and brought his hand up to his line of sight. "N—nothing," he admitted. "Why do I smell smoke? The skyship is burning? The engine?"

"Yes."

"My crew? They didn't . . . they didn't get out, did they?"

Mzia took a deep breath, debating what to say to someone in his condition. She finished securing the bandage to his head and sat back.

"Go on," he said flatly. "Tell me I'm right."

"I didn't see anyone else get out." She brushed the dirt from her hands. She didn't tell him that before he had woken after the crash, she had checked on his crew. They all were either without a pulse or bleeding out too fast. Survival. Survival had to be the first thing. They could die of exposure and injuries just as well as die in a crash. Well, he could anyway. "Can you get up?"

"I think so . . ." He sat up and pulled himself into an unsteady standing position, heavily favoring his right leg.

"Does it hurt when you put weight on it?"

"Yes."

"Then here. Put your arm around my shoulders. We need to get somewhere out of this rain."

He obeyed without hesitation. They shuffled on in silence for a time, the fire at their backs cooling and disappearing behind the many trees. Mzia tried to figure out their general location by the plants she found growing, as she had only gotten a brief glance at the positioning system on the skycaptain's control panel. The rain drizzled out into nothing.

"Where are we?" she panted, trying to keep them both upright.

"Central Mountains, along the border." He caught his foot on a root and was on his knees before Mzia realized he had let go of her. She huffed.

"I am trying to keep you from hurting yourself further," she said, kneeling down beside him.

"You weigh half what I do," he said through gritted teeth. "No need for us both to be hurt more."

Mzia ran an eye over her stubborn patient. In addition to the long cut across his forehead, he had several tears in his jacket over his shoulders and back, revealing more cuts, and his right knee swelled. He probably had a concussion, and he felt warm as she helped him walk, possibly a fever starting. They were both wet from the earlier rain, which didn't help anything either. She shouldn't be making him walk, not in his condition. But they had little choice if they wanted to survive. He needed proper medical care and a dry place to sleep. And she needed to not be anywhere near the crash come morning.

"Can you . . . can you see anything now?"

The skycaptain shook his head. Mzia sat back. He appeared disoriented from the trauma. It was hard to picture this man ordering, or at least overseeing, Yulia's death. What she wouldn't give to know what went on in his mind. He didn't look like a killer. But what did she know of that?

"What am I doing?" Mzia asked nobody in particular. The skycaptain looked her way but said nothing. Finally, she went for it. If this man would ever tell his secrets, it would probably be now.

"Why did you kill her?"

He bent his head and for a moment he looked like he would say nothing. "My orders," he spoke softly. "My orders were to bring the princess here so she could take you both back to the capital. I didn't know about the death order until we got here."

"And that is supposed to comfort me?"

"Those were my orders from the emperor," he said tightly, as if that was a perfect explanation. "You are not really in a position to question my motivation seeing as . . ." He swayed and put out a hand on the ground to steady himself. "Seeing as you have hidden away your whole life just to . . ." The skycaptain collapsed onto his side.

She went to him for the third time that night.

His face dripped with sweat despite the coolness of the night. "I—I feel remarkably unwell."

"I'll say. Can you stand back up? We need to get you to some shelter."

"West." He muttered as they struggled to their feet. "The closest village is to the west."

"All right, good. You just concentrate on walking." They made slow and slipping progress down the mountainside. Mzia didn't stop for more than a moment to adjust her grip. They came across a stream that snaked its way across their path. They were forced to turn and follow it for a time so that she might find a way around the icy water. Mzia kept glancing at the skycaptain's head wound. He still bled. She should have used something besides bandages to stop the bleeding.

He slipped and she knew the moment he hit the ground, he was not getting back up again. It was all she could do to roll him onto his side, into the trauma position with his knees bent. She shouldn't have pushed him to walk so much. He needed healing. The sort that required a hospital at the very least or maybe even Iaomai or . . .

Mzia lifted her head to scan the stars as if they could provide some direction for her next action. If only she could talk to Yulia. But the sky was clouded over and Yulia was dead.

She bowed her head, so unsure and unsteady. She was used to the feeling. When someone came to the clinic and had an injury or illness that only Iaomai could cure, the need would well up inside her. The need to fix the bad and restore balance.

But they were innocent people and this was a soldier willing to bring her to her death.

It was risky. In his state, he wouldn't remember her helping him. He wouldn't believe her even if she told him what she had done to cure him. Why should he believe her? In his eyes, she was a wanted fugitive who would do anything to survive.

But he was still a person. He needed healing and she was a healer.

Once she made the decision, her hands moved of their own accord, pulling out the things she needed from her pack. She would save him. And if the Starbreather continued to watch out for her as he had her whole life, then the skycaptain wouldn't be her undoing.

CHAPTER 15
AFTER THE FALL

DARKNESS. ONLY DARKNESS. Then . . . a gentle voice. A cool touch. Birds singing.

"Drink this."

A cup to his lips. He drank. The water soothed his dry throat. The hand that held his head up set it back down on . . . the ground. He was on the ground. He was outside, on the mountain where—

Tariq sat up so fast the healer gasped. "Careful!" Her hand pressed to his shoulder. "You are still recovering. You need to move slowly with a head wound."

He blinked, but still only darkness covered his vision. He rubbed his eyes. "Why . . . why can't I see?"

"I—I am not sure." Another hand angled his face slightly. He could feel her close, examining his eyes. "If I had to guess, I would say the head trauma. You need to see a specialist. I'm afraid I am only a mountain healer."

"You saved me."

Silence.

"I was taking you to your death, but you wouldn't let me go to mine."

Still silence.

"Tell me the reason—no—tell me your name first."

He heard her shift away. "How do you not know it already? Wasn't it in some information you were told or read of me?"

"I was told very little about you before I came on this mission," he admitted. "And the princess has been less than forthright about information since you came aboard. Though, I am sure she has her reasons."

"I am sure she does." The healer made no attempt to hide her scorn. She sighed. "I suppose since we will be traveling together you might as well know. My name is Mzia."

"Mzia? Like the star?"

"You know about it?" Surprise caught her voice.

"All skycaptains know the heavens." They were the guides when all else failed.

She didn't reply.

"Well then, Mzia, Healer of the Utara Kingdom, will you tell me why you saved my life?"

She was quiet for a long while. He was afraid that she wouldn't respond at all when at last she whispered, "I took an oath, as a healer, to do no harm."

He could hear in her voice that it wasn't the whole truth. He cursed his lack of eyesight, for he was used to being able to read people, learn their tells, and understand them. To gather all the relevant data and make predictions and plans. What was she thinking? Did the healer have a death wish? After staying hidden for so long, she had had many opportunities to leave him, and yet she stayed. "What aren't you telling me, Mzia? Why am I alive?"

She placed a cup in his hands, "Drink. You need more water."

"Are you not going to answer me?"

She shifted and next her voice came from above. "We need to get you to a village, preferably a temple, because they will take in strangers without question. They can send for help. You seemed at least mildly familiar with the area last night. Do you perhaps know which direction to go?"

Tariq drank his water and rubbed the back of his neck. He contemplated lying, wondering what answer would keep her with him the longest. In the end, the truth won out as it often did, "As I think I said last night, west is the best bet. There should be people and perhaps a village near here down on the plains."

"Good. When night comes we will go. I will leave you at the temple, where the healers will find you. I am sure if you tell them who you are, you will get help soon enough."

"And you? Will you disappear again?"

"You know why I can't be found."

"That doesn't mean I understand your reasons."

"There are things you don't need to understand." She was being evasive.

He tried again. "Maybe if you explained them to me."

"I don't think you would believe me, even if I did."

"Well, there is really only one way to test that theory."

She was silent again.

"Tell me." He failed to make it sound like a command. Like those above him in rank, this healer would never fall under his authority—she lived in an arena all her own.

"We are both alive because the Starbreather bids it so. Perhaps that is not for us to question."

He ground his teeth, "That is not an answer and you know it."

"It's the only answer I can give you."

CHAPTER 16
TIDYING UP

THE SKYCAPTAIN ASKED SO many questions and she didn't want to part with the answers. He was observant too; even injured and without his eyesight, he saw through her partial truths. She did not understand why she had saved him. It was true that she took an oath to do no harm, to help those who came to her or that the Starbreather brought her way. But perhaps it was more that she was done with death. Enough people had died around her in her years as a healer, and she was done looking at it.

But Mzia still did not trust the man for many reasons. Just as there had been many reasons she shouldn't have healed him last night. Yet once again, all those reasons dropped away, slipping through her fingers as water in a sieve. The fact that he was hurt and she was a healer trumped all other reasons.

She watched him for a time as he fingered the rips in his uniform from the crash and subsequent dash through the woods.

Mzia crossed her arms. Her self-preservation side was once again screaming this is a bad idea. Yulia had always said they could trust no one. There had been plans made in the event that they were discovered and forced to go on the run. But none of those plans had involved finding herself alone with her kidnapper. A blind kidnapper who needed her. The rules had changed and she would have to adapt to survive.

The main issue was that he didn't understand the truth. She could heal his eyesight now to persuade him, but that came with many risks. His eyes only didn't heal the night before because injuries were tricky things, often needing topical application. The blood she had given him the night before was too busy keeping him alive to do much else.

But everything inside her screamed that healing this soldier further was a bad idea. If his eyesight returned, he could force her to go back with him. His current handicap was the only thing giving her an upper hand. He struck her as a by-the-book type of person, and they were not easily persuaded. If he was as loyal as he appeared, healing him wasn't just a bad idea, it was a crazy one.

But she couldn't leave him to die. What was the point in having a power like hers if she just left him blind in a forest? As backward as it might seem, she would need to save her kidnapper. She closed her eyes, sure the image of him, blind and huddled on the forest floor as he had been last night, would haunt her to the end of her days. Those she had refused to help or had been unable to back in the village still plagued her nightmares.

Her mind made up, she said, "I am going to go back up the stream a ways. I need to wash some of this mud off."

"You should get rest," he protested. "We'll be walking most of the night to reach the foothills, if I remember our position right."

She ignored him and asked, "Do you want me to wash that uniform jacket?"

"Is it as bad as it feels?" he said with a wry smile, his fingers working to unbutton the double-breasted front.

"Worse," she said in just above a whisper. Yet she chuckled a bit as he finished opening the front. She took the jacket from his outstretched hands and felt over the material. It was a durable, strong kind that reminded her of her work apron. Practical. Only the medals pinned onto the front and the cords denoted his rank. Spot washing would help, but it wouldn't take care of those rips.

"I will be back in an hour or so," was all she said when she left him with one of her water jugs from her pack. She followed the stream back a ways to where it ran shallow and swift.

The afternoon she spent washing her outer dress as well as the skycaptain's uniform jacket. She sat on the bank of the river in her underthings and stitched closed the rips in both of their clothing. Once again, her healer pack proved useful. If only there had been food inside as well. She kept her mind on her work and didn't let it slip as the millions of questions bubbled up inside her. Didn't let herself think about Yulia or the empire chasing her or of Anuva being all alone in the woods. Because she would not cry again. She wouldn't think about whether Anuva made it back to the safe house all right. About how far of a trip it was back to their mountain from here.

No, she wouldn't consider such things.

She would not.

Only the forest witnessed the flood of tears that followed.

CHAPTER 17
THE FOREST SPEAKS

THE HEALER HAD WALKED off into the woods with his jacket, presumably a rather far distance. Who was this woman, saving his life and now washing his clothes?

Some time passed, and he felt the shift of the tree's shadows. A sound echoed off the mountain side. At first, he didn't know what to make of the sharp noises, rough and irregular between the sounds of the forest. A bird? No, an owl? While he couldn't give them a name, the bursts unsettled him. They tugged at an odd bit of memory. He frowned and sipped some water, trying to master simple movements again without his sight.

The sounds grew louder and more pronounced. Cries? No, sobs. The guttural, primal kind that knew no hope or reason.

Tariq passed a hand over his brow. In his darkness, the faces of his men appeared. His second in command, his helmsman. They were but one week out of port; his newest assignment. He had captained a skyship before; for the past year, he had been sent hither and yon by the emperor and the grand prince. But then he moved to a new ship, the *South Wind*, with a new crew, for this mission. And while he hadn't known them well, their deaths were on his head. Not in the same way as the lives he had taken during the last great drug war, but these still marked his soul.

His only consolation was that the part of the ship that held most of the crew should have landed with nothing more than a few bumps after it separated. The weight of the engines made them go down so fast, and once detached, the majority of the ship would have landed softly amongst the trees.

The crash had come completely out of nowhere. It could not have been the result of instrument failure or human error. They had struck something as they flew. Nothing else should have been in the sky on such a stormy night. Civilian skyships would not have flown into such a storm and there were no government crafts in the area. But something had caused a rip in the Noot. He had encountered something like this once before. During the drug wars, he had been the first mate on a skyship that went down. So he knew the signs. This was no accident; no act of nature would have brought down the skyship like that.

The healer's sobs grew louder still, scattering birds and hushing the frogs in the stream. She cried for Doctor Yulia, the one Princess Ezhno had killed.

When her footsteps returned, an evening breeze blew up from the mountain side. She came close to him and sat down with a huff. He again silently cursed his lack of eyesight. He looked in her direction but she was silent for a long time. When she did speak, her voice was soft and tired. "Did she suffer?"

Tariq didn't need to ask who, but still he hesitated. He could lie. He could say no, Ezhno was a professional, that she would kill as ordered. That he hadn't seen the gleeful vengeance in her eyes when she was told of Yulia's death. But he couldn't. Mzia deserved the truth.

"I don't know," he said, flexing his fingers. "I didn't get to question the team before the crash." He left out the fact that he had put it off. That every time he considered it, all he could see was the horror in Mzia's white gold eyes when she learned. How helpless she had looked, unconscious on the floor. Yulia had been more than the woman who stole Mzia away; she had been her friend and mother.

He had killed her mother.

CHAPTER 18
THE JOURNEY FORWARD

REALIZING SHE SPIRALED INTO sorrow again and not wanting the skycaptain to hear her cry, Mzia asked, "Where did the other part of the skyship go? When we crawled out of the bridge, it was gone."

"Separation protocol," Tariq said. "In the event of a malfunction, the bridge and engines, the heaviest parts of the ship, can detach and allow the larger part to stay connected with the flotation device."

"Seems rather extreme. Is it used often?"

"I've had to do it once before."

"When?" Mzia had to keep talking about something other than what was. She had to.

"Two years ago. A show of force gone wrong. We were only supposed to intimidate, not engage, but . . ." He shook his head. "Lost a lot of good men that day, including my skycaptain."

Mzia vaguely recalled something the princess had said about this man being promoted early because someone had died. She took him in again, sitting in his smoky and dirty uniform and yet somehow still every inch of him spoke authority. She couldn't tell him. He believed in his cause as much as she believed in her own.

"You saved my life," the skycaptain said, startling her. "And you still haven't told me why."

"I gave you an answer. You just didn't like it."

"No, I didn't understand it. How can my life mean anything to you when you let so many others die?"

"It isn't so simple as giving myself up."

"Isn't it? The Iaomai supply is dangerously low all the time, and only those with enough money can afford to live. And even those have a death date looming over them. In addition to the horror of the drug wars, I have seen people sell themselves, sell their own children to buy Iaomai. And the addicted don't have a kind death. It is painful and slow. It takes weeks."

"I am a healer," she spat back. "Don't speak to me about addiction and death as if you somehow know them better."

"Then how is it you don't understand? I was told that maybe, just maybe the answer, the solution to all the violence, lies in sacrificing the life of one person."

"Two people," Mzia argued.

He threw up his hands. "Two, a hundred! What does it matter if you can save thousands? Millions even! Tell me how you can call yourself a healer and keep the best chance the empire has hidden away—"

"You know nothing of my life."

"No, I don't," he agreed, matching the edge in her voice. "For someone who claims to do no harm you seem rather determined to keep a cure from the empire."

"You don't understand what you are talking about."

"Then tell me!" he challenged. "Tell me why you kept yourself hidden all these years. You know what the marrow of your bones can do, don't you?"

"Of course I know." She fought tears. How dare he.

"Then why? How can you justify your choices? Maybe when you were younger you didn't have one, but now you do."

Mzia crossed her arms. She couldn't tell him the truth. He wouldn't believe her anyway. Why should he? The empire had lied to him all his life. Told him only one thing about Iaomai Children. Finally she said, "The best choice is not always the most obvious, Skycaptain."

"And what is the best choice, healer?" When her silence stretched on, he asked, "If you didn't want to deal with me or my questions, why didn't you just let me die?"

Her mouth was unable to form around the anger coiling in her soul. The pain she felt whenever she saw one afflicted. When she longed to help but could not. Who was he to judge? What pain could he possibly know that compared to her own?

He sighed. "You saved my life, and I don't understand why, but I'm grateful. I need you to know that, at least."

Mzia sighed and shook herself slightly as if to shake off the feelings. Considering what he thought to be the truth, this wasn't completely his fault. They were talking in circles. She held out his jacket. "Here, I washed it for you."

He reached out and took it from her. With some awkward motions, he managed to pull it on. He ran a hand over his shoulder, feeling for the tears. "You fixed it?"

"Nights can get cold on the mountains. I didn't save your sorry life just to see you die of exposure."

He smiled a little as he finished buttoning up the front, then he felt the empty spots where the rank pins and cords had been.

"I took them off," Mzia explained before he could ask. "Without them, the jacket looks ordinary enough. You will forgive me for not wanting someone to recognize you."

Tariq frowned but he didn't argue.

She cleared my throat, "So I think we will go faster if we walk as we did last night. You can put one arm around my shoulders and I can guide you. But it should be much easier because you aren't as injured."

"What about you?"

"Me?"

"Were you hurt at all?"

"Some, nothing serious."

"Are you sure? It was a bad crash. I wouldn't want you to strain yourself."

"How about we get started walking, Skycaptain?"

"The sooner you can be rid of me?" A ghost of a smile appeared as he brought himself to his feet. He tested his right leg. "It feels . . . much better."

"Yes, odd how that worked out," Mzia said easily. Taking up a place beside him, she guided his arm around her shoulders. This felt a little different from the night before, where the rush of adrenaline was not there to guide her.

They headed southwest, down the mountain along the creek and towards easier terrain. Tariq told her this was the closest way to a village or some kind of civilization. Once the stars came out, she could be more specific in her direction. Most of their conversation consisted of her telling him what the next step would be like.

"Rock on your left. There it is. Now roots, so set your foot slowly. Good. A few more steps of flat ground. Sorry, slight dip there."

Tariq struggled, even with her directions, to walk well. And even though she was there to stop him from falling, he rarely leaned on her fully. They were into late evening when he slipped on some damp underbrush. He let go of Mzia and fell hard on his hands and knees.

"What did you let go for?" she asked, guiding him up.

"I would have taken you down with me." He winced and dusted the dirt from his hands. "I am pretty sure we established this last night."

She tried to look out for berries or edible mushrooms as they traveled, but this forest and plants were as unfamiliar as the situation she now found herself in. If they didn't make it to a market soon, they would be in big trouble. Water wasn't a problem, however. The mountain side was covered with springs and creeks.

They stopped several hours later to drink and refill the bottles from the stream.

"What time is it?" Tariq asked.

Mzia frowned and looked between the sparse canopy of trees. "The Dragon is sinking nearly to the horizon, so it should be—"

Together they said, "Just past midnight."

"Oh, right," Mzia said. "You know the heavens."

"Part of my profession. But not yours. Unless healers are very different in the Utara Kingdom."

"No, we are mostly the same. Our knowledge of local plants may differ, though."

"So why do you know the stars so well?"

Mzia sipped her water. How could she explain to him that the stars were her one comfort growing up? The one, solid constant in a world of so much uncertainty. Her reminder that even in the darkness, the Starbreather made beautiful things.

"What?" Tariq prompted. "Some trade secret?"

A partial truth would do. "No, it's just . . . I don't think you know what it is to grow up with nothing. Children in my village have so little, no toys or newest gadgets to entertain us. So, we look elsewhere. I happened to look up."

"What is your favorite constellation then?"

For some reason that felt like an intimate secret. Perhaps because nobody had ever asked her before.

"My favorite is the River," he offered. "Are we facing south?"

"More or less,"

"Then it should be about there." He lifted his arm to point.

"You are close," she said, taking his wrist and guiding it slightly to the right. "My favorite is the Aster, which is about here." She pulled his arm to the left and slightly down.

"I will be glad to have my eyesight back," Tariq whispered. It was followed by a sort of unspoken thought, *if only to see the stars again.*

Mzia let go of his wrist. "We should keep going."

The night grew old, and the star she was named after rose before she called a rest. Mzia knew Tariq was tired though he would not admit so. He fell asleep before she had finished building a lean-to shelter with some fallen branches and leaves. Not waterproof or anything, but it would have to do for the time being.

CHAPTER 19
A MATTER OF PRACTICALITY

TARIQ COULD HEAR HER teeth chattering. In the early dawn, a downpour had rudely awakened them. They huddled against the tree trunk and managed to keep out of the worst of it. But rain during this time of year would go on for hours, and soon there wouldn't be one inch of them that remained dry. And with the rain came the cold mountain air. If he had his vision, Tariq was sure he would see his own breath clouds.

They now sat back-to-back, one shoulder to the tree trunk. Every few seconds her body shuddered. He felt he should say something, ask how she was, but beyond the brief conversation about stars, they hadn't really been speaking, just surviving together. She was understandably angry with him for everything he had done, and his pointed questions the day before didn't do anything to ease matters.

The clothing the healer wore was not waterproof. But his uniform jacket was. He might get a little cold from the rain and wind, but Mzia? If she were anything like his sister, she could shiver from a summer's breeze. Something needed to be done.

He loosened the buttons on his uniform.

He fumbled with the last button, and only as he moved to shrug it off did she ask with chattering teeth, "What are you doing?"

The air was cool on his shoulders as he pulled off the jacket, but not cold. Not to him. Years of training involved sleeping in all sorts of conditions to harden him.

He turned slightly and held out the jacket, still warm. "Here."

"Oh-h-h, n-n-n-no. I'm f-f-f-fine . . ."

"I'm blind, not deaf. I can hear your teeth clacking. Take it."

She said nothing.

"This is purely selfish of me. I don't want my only chance of survival to die. Take it."

A sigh. She took it. Her hands brushed his. Her fingers were ice.

"Th-th-thank you."

They said no more and resumed their positions. From the way she settled, he guessed she had draped the jacket over herself like a blanket. After some time, her breath slowed to normal, and the shuddering stopped. She shifted about, leaning her head on the tree. Soon her breath was long and even. She had fallen asleep.

MZIA SLEPT DEEPLY FOR some time. The showers ended as quickly as they began, and the bright midday sun woke her. She teetered on the edge of sleep, her mind replaying over and over her last conversations with the skycaptain. Something bothered her. It felt off.

She jerked awake and pushed off her blanket only to find it wasn't a blanket. It was the skycaptain's jacket. Her face softened. She looked over her shoulder; he appeared to be sleeping peacefully in the warm afternoon and leaning mostly on the tree trunk as she had been. His wet shirt was almost transparent, and now the tattoos across his shoulders and upper back were visible. The white ink sprawled across his tawny skin in symbols and patterns that looked vaguely familiar. Something she had buried too deep to call up now. Tattoos were rare, and ones that large and intricate were only given for acts of bravery and symbols of loyalty. To whom was he loyal?

Mzia rubbed her face and sat at the sunny entrance of their cobbled together shelter. She fanned out the bottom of her skirt to dry, then sipped some water. Hunger started to gnaw at her the way loneliness had as a child. To distract herself, she took in the view. Between the trees, she could make out the plains far below as the rain cleared away. She remembered seeing images of this place, the middle part of the Alang Kingdom, but pictures didn't really show the scope and strangeness of the area.

While plains or wide-open spaces were common enough in the empire, none were quite like those here. The rivers cut deep grooves into the land, slicing it up with valleys and gorges so steep and deep that sunlight never touched the bottom. Travel on the plains had been precarious until a few hundred years before the empire, when their king had ordered the construction of bridges. Before that, there were only a few places where one could travel down to the rivers and back up again. This cracked looking landscape went on to the western horizon line.

Her stomach growled again. She glanced back at the skycaptian. Still asleep. But if she was hungry, he must be ravenous. And to recover fully, he would need food. Determined to find something for the two of them, she got up and trudged out into a bit of forest that was more open with less underbrush and older trees. Keeping the direction of the river in mind, she scrambled around rocks, up and down steeper terrain.

A songbird called to her from the treetops. In a story she told Anuva, songbirds taught humans which berries were okay to eat and which ones were poisonous. For lack of better options, she followed the sound up the mountain for several minutes.

A whole flock chirped at each other in the branches above her. And under different circumstances, she would have been delighted to watch and listen, but now she was too hungry. There were no berries. Just as she was about to move on, a blue flower caught her eye. *Wild carrot!* She scrambled over and found a host of the plants, all growing where an old tree had fallen and made a break in the canopy. Mzia used her hands and a piece of bark from the fallen tree to dig up as many plants as she could; the roots were thick and healthy. She was so hungry she nearly bit into one there but managed to abstain, heaping them into her skirt to carry back to the stream.

She scrambled back down the mountain and thankfully found the stream again without much trouble. She had to follow it back up a ways to find where they had made camp. The skycaptain was still asleep.

Using her palms and nails, she scrubbed away the dirt in the cold water. Unable to wait any longer, she ate the first root she finished while she cleaned the second. Then she ate that as well before regaining her self-control. She washed the dozen or so more that she had left. The roots ranged in size from the width of her hand down to the span of two of her fingers. She hoped they would be enough.

The skycaptain muttered something in his sleep. Mzia turned around to see him blink his eyes open. He rubbed his face then slowly stretched out his hand back to where she had been sleeping. When his hand felt only ground, he whispered, "Mzia?"

She couldn't help smiling a little. "I'm here. And I found some food."

"Food?" He crawled toward her voice. "Where did you find that?"

"On the mountain." She sat beside him near the entrance of

the branches where she had left his coat. "Have you ever had wild carrot?"

"No, I can't say I have."

She placed one in his hands and he felt it over before taking a bite and then quickly eating the rest. She gave him another and another. Mzia found herself satisfied, at least for now, with just four of them. Tariq ate the rest and perhaps would have eaten more, but he didn't say.

Once they had finished eating, he asked, "Are we close? Can you see the plains?"

"Yes. We should reach it by nighttime."

"Good. And thank you for the food. I must admit I haven't felt that kind of hunger since my training days."

Mzia didn't know what to say. First the stars, and now this. Were they making small talk now? Like people meeting for tea? Unable to think of a reply, she placed his jacket in his lap, "This is . . . yours."

The skycaptain tugged it back on but didn't button up the front. "Thanks." He kept frowning and blinking. So his eyesight had not improved at all.

After the uncomfortable silence stretched into several minutes, Mzia stood. "We need to keep moving."

"Yes, right." He got cautiously to his feet. He said nothing as she took up her spot at his left side, putting his arm around her shoulders. The food didn't make him any chattier, to her relief, and they trudged down the mountainside in the same near silent way as before.

CHAPTER 20
A SECRET MISSION

ASIM LEANED ON THE rail of the boat next to Lila as they snaked their way through the valley. The boats were made of much the same materials as skyships but were sleek and narrow to navigate the many twists and turns of the river. This boat on which they had managed to secure passage was a wide-roofed cargo ship that curved down at the edges to catch the most rays to power the turbines and push them along against the current.

"I still think this is a bad idea," Aasim said.

"Then why did you come?" Lila asked indifferently as she checked her handpad. She tried to decrypt the information the princess had uploaded before the crash and as yet was unsuccessful. Normally she liked to take her time, feeling out the code and learning its nuances before turning the key to its secrets. Time wasn't a luxury she had. She didn't know for sure that the information gathered from Doctor Yulia's lab would be helpful, but she also couldn't say that it wouldn't be. With so little else to go on, she might as well start somewhere.

It had been a laughably easy thing, once Tariq had unknowingly given her an approximate time and location, to find the new data the princess had obtained. If Lila wanted to know more about this crazy mess, and she always did, then this information would be a good place to start. It had to be connected to why the prince refused to send a search party for Tariq.

"I came because you carrying out a bad idea alone is much worse than when you have supervision." Aasim had that edge to his voice when she pushed him too far.

Lila rolled her eyes, "You sound just like Tariq. You ever notice how the other Marks our age don't have bodyguards?"

"Yes, I did notice." He placed his hand on her pad, forcing her to look up at him. "Which you should consider as to why your brother and mother think you need one."

Lila's eyes narrowed. She was taller than average and only had to look up slightly to meet his eyes. "Well, whatever the reason, either you are doing a terrible job, or this idea isn't that dangerous because then you wouldn't have let me go."

"Don't patronize me. We both know you would've found a way to sneak off without me if I had forbidden it."

Lila allowed a small smile, and the tension broke. "That's true. You're really more of a glorified guard dog."

Aasim sighed but didn't deny the allegation.

Lila went back to the data on her handpad and pulled up again the information on Tariq's skyship crash. The computer let her know the moment of the crash. But that would only help her find the ship, not her brother. The decision to open up another tab and start hacking the database came as easy as breathing.

"Do I want to know what you are doing on there?" Aasim asked after several minutes of silence.

"Nope!" Lila said with her most cheerful voice. "You are just along for the ride, here to make sure I don't hurt someone."

"Or yourself."

"Sure."

Lila quickly became absorbed in her work. She set one of her programs to hacking the new files and went back to the second task, which she considered more urgent. The day slipped into night and their cargo boat slid into valleys so deep the sky was only a sliver of dark blue far above.

CHAPTER 21
THE CEMETERY

A S DUSK FELL, MZIA and the skycaptain walked at last out of the mountains proper and into the sloping foothills. The land that appeared so flat from up above was not so at all. Beyond the deep valleys gorged by the rivers, the ground held low sloping hills, and the lands between the rivers rose at varying levels, forests intermixed with open fields.

When they started walking through what appeared to be a field of heather, the horizon was quite close, but no matter how many little hills they climbed, she couldn't see more than a few hundred yards at a time, either blocked by another finger of the forest or a hill. With the night came the light of the nearly full moon to guide them.

There was no sign of a village or even a house, and Mzia began to get anxious. So much so that the skycaptain asked, "Are you . . . all right, healer?"

"Fine," Mzia said shortly.

The skycaptain frowned. "I may not be able to see, but I can . . ."

"Hear. I know." She tried and failed to keep the ire out of her voice.

"Well, if you are not going to share with me what is going on, I will have to guess."

Mzia huffed and took his arm off from around her shoulder. "The ground is flat enough here. You can just hold onto my arm."

He was silent for a few moments as they readjusted to this new position. But as soon as they started moving again, he asked, "So are you concerned about the weather? Because we have already had rain for the day and the air doesn't smell of it anymore."

She didn't answer, straining to see over the next low hill.

"Is there someone nearby you don't want to see us? Because I haven't heard anything else."

They crested the hill and Mzia saw at last a road that led down to a bridge to the left over one of the river valleys. "Finally," she breathed.

"What?" he asked.

"There is a road. I am sure if we take it, we will find a village."

The road took them to a bridge. Even though they were both exhausted, they continued over the deep ravine and onto the next chunk of woods. There was a small hill to climb before the land flattened out for a bit on either side of the road.

In this area, the grass was low, growing out to the trees in the distance that bordered three of the four sides of the mostly square space. The river valley they had just crossed made up the fourth border. Every two steps or so was a large, square stone about the height of a knee. These were set at even intervals all over the flat area and up on the low hills on either side. Around each stone, a circle had been furrowed in the ground. The rising moon cast everything in its pale glow. For a moment, Mzia didn't know what to make of it all. They looked kind of like . . . She gasped.

"What?" the skycaptain asked.

"It's a cemetery."

"Oh." He let out a little laugh. "You sounded so worried there, I thought it was something serious."

"I have just never seen one so large. And the grave mounds all look the same. Large, square, and single pieces of black stone."

"Ah. That would be an addiction cemetery then."

"An addiction cemetery?"

"You know, because so many die of the Iaomai addiction. Many don't have money, so the emperor started a program that granted proper burial for . . ." He tilted his head. "How is it you, as a healer, don't know this?"

Mzia shook her head. Then she remembered he couldn't see that and said, "I guess I maybe heard about it. We must have them somewhere in my kingdom, but I didn't exactly travel around . . ." She couldn't stop looking at the rows and rows of square stones. "There are just . . . so many. And we are so far out from a city. Why would they put it here?"

"There is space here," the skycaptain said. "And when you are getting a free burial, you don't get to decide where that is."

Mzia was silent for a time. Her hunger and other immediate problems were forgotten. She understood the statistics. How more and more people were becoming addicted every year. She saw the growing number of deaths. She knew how big the addiction problem was. But standing here, faced with the unending rows and rows of tombstones, it appeared she didn't understand the numbers at all. It was one thing to see them counted on a screen. It was an entirely different thing to see them lined up to the horizon line. This was not balance; this was an imbalance if she ever saw one.

"So are we going to keep going or . . . ?"

"Oh, yes." Mzia shook her head. "We will need to keep going. Maybe there is a temple nearby. They often put cemeteries on temple grounds."

"Yes, maybe." The skycaptain didn't sound hopeful, and she didn't feel that way either.

While the idea of walking through a bleak cemetery at night had always frightened Mzia a bit, there was nothing creepy about this graveyard. The quiet that filled the space was like the revenant silence of a temple at prayer time. The shadows thrown by the moon didn't shift or hide things, they held firm as the mountains far to their left, bold and still. Mzia didn't want to hurry along but to walk through with respect and calmness. There wasn't anything to fear here, but a good deal of sorrow hung in the night air.

She could make out the dates of the closest stones as they passed. Some were so young, many barely her age. They had cemeteries in Dolok's Hamlet. They had one by the temple just outside of the village where her clinic was. But it was small. And since she had been secretly helping people, the last few years there had been very few deaths not attributed to old age. Her eyes landed on a grave just beside the road. She stopped so abruptly that the skycaptain nearly tripped.

"What is it?" he asked.

She ignored the annoyance in his tone and slid her arm out of his hand to kneel down before the closest grave. The dewy grass soaked her skirts as she brushed her fingers along the indented stone. The dates were just eleven winters apart. That's how old Anuva was.

"Healer?" the skycaptain called. Exhaustion edged his voice.

Tears slid down her face, startling her because she didn't feel them form in her eyes. She was tired of this. Of traveling. Of losing Yulia. Of not knowing what would become of Anuva. Of not knowing what would become of herself. Of children dying. Of everything.

She turned and curled up next to the gravestone. Her face in her hands, she wept. It didn't matter who heard her.

The skycaptain gave a tired sigh. He inched his way over to the side of the road and crawled through the short strip of grass to sit beside her. "Am I right in thinking we are not going further tonight?"

Mzia managed to sniff out a confirmation.

"All right then," he said. "I guess we'll sleep here."

Mzia dashed away tears. How selfish she was being, crying over people she never met when they were both slowly starving. She looked across the sloping hills to the place where the cemetery met the uncleared tree line. Someday maybe that too would be cut down to make way for more headstones.

This was ridiculous. They had to keep going.

She took a deep breath and prepared to force herself to her feet again, to press on toward finding a way back to Anuva. A shadow moved near the tree line. A group of people were moving closer to the open ground of the cemetery. A chill crept up her spine when she made out the half gray, half black uniforms worn by only one group—Separatists.

There was no way these people could know she was here. The odds of this being coincidental were next to nothing. They couldn't have known she was kidnapped unless . . . Unless Yulia had told them. In her desperation or wisdom, Yulia must have feared the worst for Mzia and Anuva. She must have called for aid. How the Separatists figured out she was on the skyship that crashed was a mystery for another time.

"Skycaptain."

"Hmmm?"

He was almost asleep. How long had she wasted pulling herself together? Her chest tightened. Only one thing was certain—she didn't want to face this dangerous group alone. And now she and her kidnapper had something in common. "Skycaptain, I need you to trust me."

"Trust you with what?" he asked, sitting up.

"I need to heal your eyes."

"What are you talking about?"

"Lie on your back. I can heal you."

"Mzia, what are you—"

"Just trust me!"

"I don't understand—"

"Lay. Back."

Perhaps it was the tone of her voice that finally convinced him, or just his complete lack of other options. But in either case, he laid back on the turf.

Mzia worked quickly, taking out first her syringe and then the eye dropper. As she drew blood, she scanned the tree line.

"What are you going to do?" he asked.

"I am going to put some liquid in your eyes." Mzia said, drawing blood from her inner arm. She drew too much. Only a few drops were needed, but she hadn't the time to be precise.

She filled the dropper as the people in the tree line started circling. Surely the Separatists in the trees could see her and the skycaptain out in the open among the headstones, but maybe they didn't know she could see them. Carefully, Mzia knelt beside her captor and tilted his face towards the sky.

Starbreather save her; there was no time.

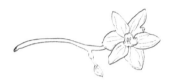

CHAPTER 22
SEPARATISTS

TARIQ BLINKED THE WARM liquid from his eyes after Mzia took her hands away. He stared up into the endless night that was his existence. This was ridiculous. What could the healer possibly give him that in a few drops would—

One large light and blurry pinpricks of light appeared. Tariq blinked and rubbed his face. Squinting, the lights started to distinguish themselves into smaller lights. He sat up and looked around. The world around him was a fuzzy gray mass, and the light was the moon and stars. He put out his hand and saw a lighter shape slowly start to come into focus. He laughed. The exhaustion was finally catching up with him. Surely this was only wishful thinking and he couldn't possibly . . . he couldn't possibly be healed?

All at once, the world snapped into razor sharp focus. Tariq turned about, drinking in the night landscape with every ounce of his being. The grass, the headstones, the sky. At last, his eyes landed on the silver-haired woman who sat next to him. Her hair nearly glowed in the moonlight. Who was this healer? What had she done to him?

"I can . . . see." He looked down at his hands, his uniform.

Relief and joy mingled in ways they never had. "You healed me? How?"

Mzia looked away, the light catching the streak of tears glinting on her face. Her shoulders slumped in weariness, dark circles under her eyes. She had hidden well just how much of a toll the past few days had taken on her and looked more defeated than when she had been kidnapped and taken to her own death. Or even when she learned of Yulia's death.

She passed a hand over her brow and spoke at last. "Would you believe me, if I said just a few drops of my blood did that? And that it could do so much more than that?"

"Your . . . blood?" He shook his head, "I don't understand. That's not possible."

"And yet here we are." She shifted her gaze to the tree line. "But I healed you for a reason, Skycaptain. I can see Separatist rebels in the trees."

Tariq looked, but the night shadows prevented him from seeing anything past the first few trees. Tariq would indeed question her later about how she saw anything in this night, but for now there was a more pressing issue. "Where exactly did you see them?"

"To the east," she said, having enough sense not to point.

"And how many?"

"At least a dozen but . . . wait, I think there are more."

"And you are sure they are Separatists? They could be wandering pilgrims or—"

"Not unless pilgrims wear black and gray uniforms. Look, they are here for me, but I would rather not go with them. Yulia says . . . said they are dangerous and not to be trusted."

"She was right. We need to move."

Men, a dozen from each of the three sides of the cemetery, appeared at the forest line. They stepped out into the moonlight so even Tariq could see them now. He stood and helped Mzia to her feet. Their options were few, and he flew through them as he looked around. They could run back over the bridge, but Mzia didn't look well enough to try even a panic-induced flight. They could fight, but even with another trained soldier on his side, they didn't stand a chance against so many. That left only negotiation.

But what had they to bargain with?

The groups all started to move in together. Not with the clean march of the army, but trained men just the same. As they approached, it became clear they had weapons, staves, and projectile munitions like firearms. Again, not as good as the army gave, but still formidable. And he had nothing, everything burned with his skyship.

Tariq stepped closer to the healer, placing her slightly behind him as if he could protect her. They were out of time and options. She put a hand on his arm, and he looked over at her. She was afraid, certainly. Yet just like their first meeting, a defiance colored her stance, the set of her jaw. A bit of the exhaustion slid from her shoulders as she stood ready to face another unknown. For that moment, they were united in a cause.

MZIA FOUGHT HER EXHAUSTED body into stillness as the strangers came to a halt just a few paces away. They moved to surround them fully, and one stepped forward. A woman in gray armor-like clothes that matched the others with a braid down her back came to stand before them.

She looked them over before turning to Mzia. "It is good to see you unharmed, Iaomai Child. You don't have to hide from us. It isn't as if the empire could or would protect you anyway."

"What's your name?" The skycaptain asked.

"I could ask you the same thing, Tariq of the Alang Kingdom, but your reputation precedes you, Mark of the Emperor."

So that was his name, Tariq. And Mark of the Emperor? That term was familiar to her but she couldn't remember what it referenced.

"Do I know you, madam?" Tariq inquired.

"Not yet. But I know you. Was it not your skyship that crashed in the south just two years ago? What an interesting coincidence to find you have survived a second crash." Her eyes turned to Mzia. "I wonder if the Iaomai Child would have saved you if she knew who you are?"

"It doesn't matter who he is," Mzia snapped. "It isn't any of your affair. I am fine on my own. I don't want anything to do with—"

"With what?" The woman practically laughed, "With the empire's politics? With the Separatists? Look at you. Your very existence is part of my affair. You are only alive because of us. The payoff Yulia promised us years ago is finally here."

"I don't know what Yulia told you, but I don't want—"

"I don't care what you want. We are talking about the future of the empire here. Or its lack of future, I like to say. Now you are coming with us to the meeting point," she eyed Tariq, "But the real question here is, do we take the Marked One with us or just leave his body here?"

Tariq kept his cool. "You claim to know who I am, so you must know what killing me would mean."

"It wouldn't be the first time I ended one of your filth," the woman bit back. "But if someone found your body this close to our meeting, it could lead to investigation. It's settled then. Sargeant," she snapped at the man just behind her and to the right.

"Yes, ma'am?"

"Take out his tracker."

"What are you doing?" Mzia demanded when two men stepped forward and pulled Tariq away from her. Another Separatist soldier blocked her when she tried to follow.

"All Marks have a tracker in their forearm," the woman in charge said without taking her eyes off of Tariq. "The empire knows exactly where you are right now."

One man pulled out a rather large knife.

"You can't use that!" Mzia protested.

"He gets his tracker thrown in the nearest gully, or we throw all of him in."

"Well then, let me do it. I am trained."

"You have made poor choices lately." She gestured to Tariq. "So you will forgive me if I don't trust you." To her soldier she said, "Do it."

One soldier yanked off Tariq's jacket and tossed it aside. It landed near Mzia's feet. They forced Tariq to his knees beside the headstone of the girl Anuva's age.

Mzia failed to get past the man blocking her as they made Tariq place his forearm on the headstone. One man held his wrist while the other held his shoulders in place. Horror closed her throat, and she couldn't look away as the knife started to carve the flesh off his inner arm. In a proper facility, tracker removal was a painless process. A fifteen-minute minor operation.

These people did not care to use the proper tools.

To his credit, Tariq didn't fight. He didn't flinch or pull away as the knife sliced skin and muscle. He did swear. A lot. Mostly under his breath, and it drifted over to where Mzia stood helpless. Blood trickled down the front of the headstone, and drops pooled in the words carved there. A gruesome defilement of the resting place.

"Ah, there it is." The pseudo surgeon plucked from Tariq's mutilated flesh a dark piece of tech the size of a thumbnail—the tracker. The soldier did a hasty job of binding up Tariq's arm. They really should have used a sealant or stitches along with cleaning the wound. Tariq could easily get an infection with just bandages.

Mzia, needing to do something useful, bent down and picked up his discarded jacket. She held it out to him as they pulled him to his feet.

He shook his head, his face pale. "Keep it. You look cold."

His kindness confused her, and she pulled it on. As they bound up his hands behind his back, Mzia couldn't help remembering when she had stood before him on the skyship, her own hands tied. These Separatists did not tie her hands, but she was just as much a prisoner again.

The entire time Tariq was having his arm sliced open, the woman in charge conferred in whispers with several other soldiers. She spoke up when it was all done and said, "We move to the meeting point; we must get there by dawn. Move out."

CHAPTER 23
THE STARBREATHER TEMPLE

A S THE EASTERN SKY paled for the coming dawn, the woods grew thick around them and there wasn't a clear path. The group came abruptly to a trench in the ground that sloped down into the earth at a slight angle. A huge, stone doorway opened up at the other end with carved stone pillars and no door to block the entrance. This place, this underground building, was the oldest structure Mzia had ever seen. The stones looked hand carved. Sentries stood on either side, dressed in a grayish green to match the stone behind them. They each had a sword strapped to their backs—which was oddly archaic—and a small firearm at the belt.

The woman led them down the incline into the ground and halted before the sentries. "Has the other scouting party returned?"

"Yes, ma'am." The guards both saluted her, fist to palm.

"Good. And Akrosa has arrived?"

"Yes, ma'am. About two hours ago. Shall I tell him you have returned?"

"Yes." She stalked past them and the rest of the group followed her into the dark mouth in the earth. Crossing the threshold enveloped them in even colder air and entombed them in stone. A hallway with an arched ceiling stretched on ahead with passages breaking off every few paces. Small, bluish mushrooms pushed through cracks and lit the walls with a soft glow. The floors and walls were smooth, made of large cut pieces of granite. Water dripped somewhere unseen.

"Take the Marked One to one of the eastern rooms and set a guard," the woman told her second in command.

They took Tariq through a passage to the left before Mzia could protest. They had only a moment to lock eyes before he disappeared. Tariq seemed to be impressing caution to Mzia, but he needn't have bothered. Caution pulsed through her veins and pounded in her ears.

"Where are we going?" Mzia asked, as she was ushered along with the six remaining men following the woman.

"Akrosa will want to see you for himself," she said without turning around.

Ahead, there was more yellow glow of natural light. The hall gave way to a large room. Circular in shape and two stories tall, in the middle of the room was a large round pool of water built up out of the floor. On the ceiling directly above the pool was a skylight. Several paces out from the pool were stone pillars forming a second circle. Arched doorways branched off in many directions. One doorway dropped off into darkness, and from there came the sound and slight reflections of running water. An underground river.

The six men vanished down a passage to the left, and Mzia had a feeling they didn't go very far. As the woman and Mzia approached the pool in the center of the room, the sky reflected in the pool, showing off the brightening stratosphere and the last few stars. Around the stone rim of the pool scrawled an inscription. Written first in a loopy script that she couldn't read and followed by words in the Alang dialect: *He determines the number of the stars and calls them each by name.*

"Where are we?" Mzia dared to ask.

The woman didn't look at her, her gaze on the pool. "We are in a Starbreather temple, built several dynasties ago. Here in the Alang Kingdom, several such places still survive from the old times when we built things instead of grew them."

Mzia frowned. "Why are we here?"

"Don't play dumb, you know who I am."

"You are a Separatist. One of the people who helped Yulia escape when I was a child."

"Correct. My name is Danu. And we are here because Yulia sent us a very urgent call a few days ago that she had been found out. I was sorry to hear she didn't make it." Danu didn't sound very sorry. "And yet her work lives on." She gestured to Mzia. "Time to tell the truth."

"About what?"

"I told you not to play dumb. You know very well what. The little secret you and Yulia have been keeping all these years."

Mzia crossed her arms. "You are going to have to be more specific."

"You are just like Yulia with your secrets. She only bothered to contact us and say she had succeeded when they were taking you away. But she was vague and rushed, and I want to learn all the details from her Iaomai Child. If she had bothered to ask for our help sooner, maybe she would still be alive."

"Don't speak about her so flippantly!" Mzia flashed. "She didn't trust you and neither do I."

"I wouldn't be so quick to judge." A male voice sounded from across the room.

The man walked towards them from the other side of the pool. He was tall like Danu, with the same high cheekbones and calculating look. He wore brown trousers and a tunic that buttoned up the front. Mzia was unsurprised when Danu said, "This is my cousin, Akrosa."

He appraised her from head to foot and frowned, evidently not pleased with what he saw.

"You are a difficult person to find, Mzia," Akrosa said dryly. "Even when we shoot a skyship down looking for you."

"What." Mzia couldn't make it sound like a question. They did *what.*

"That's right, we have the power to do such things. No matter what lies the empire feeds people, we are rather influential and you would do well to align yourself with us."

"*You* shot down the skyship? People died! I could have died—"

"Weren't you going to a kind of death anyway?" Danu pointed out.

"But you killed those crew members who didn't get out of the bridge."

"Ah yes," Akrosa interrupted. "How interesting we find you here with your kidnapper, the skycaptain. And a Marked One at that." He frowned. "Is that his uniform you wear?"

"Marked?" Mzia clutched the jacket closer. "Do you mean his tattoos?"

Akrosa shook his head. "The skycaptain bears the Mark of the Emperor. He is none other than one of many image bearers of the emperor. To put it delicately, illegitimate children."

Mzia blinked. "He is a son of the emperor? No, he is a skycaptain—"

"But you must have heard of the tradition? Emperors and kings as far back as time itself have done it. It isn't hard to find them if you know how to look. And you always know if you meet one because of the tattoos like the skycaptain has. They are marks of loyalty to the emperor. They swear undying allegiance and that they or their children will never try to take the throne."

Danu seemed to enjoy Mzia's confusion. "He is one of the emperor's favorites."

Mzia shook herself, "I don't see what his birth has to do with anything. I am a healer, and I saw someone in need of healing. And I don't really understand why you are telling me all this."

"Because," Akrosa said with mounting impatience, "You, like Yulia, don't seem to understand what we are up against here. People are dying and you are keeping the cure from them!"

"The time wasn't right! The emperor would have killed us if I had cured anyone." Mzia said.

"Stop lying to us." Danu crossed her arms, "I saw the unnaturally low death numbers from your village. I knew you were all up to something. That was probably how the empire found you out."

Mzia felt a wave of nausea sweep over her. She placed a hand on the edge of the reflecting pool to steady herself. Her worst fear was a reality. She had hoped it a coincidence that the empire had found her when they did. She had been so careful and still Mzia had led the empire and now the Separatists right to her door. It was all her fault that they had been found. That Yulia was dead. That Anuva was now in danger. She might as well have given them a map and painted a large red X. Without Yulia's permission, she had cured people.

What under the sky above had she done?

CHAPTER 24
WAITING IN STONE

M ZIA DREW HERSELF UP, "What exactly is the plan here? If I cure people, won't the emperor find me again?"

"You will know of our plans when we want you to know them," Akrosa said flatly. "At present, all you need to know is that everyone close enough is gathering for a demonstration and discussion."

"Demonstration of what?"

"Of your abilities, of course. Yulia led us to believe the cure now resides in your blood and not just the bone marrow. This is true?"

Reluctantly, Mzia nodded.

"And how much is necessary to cure one addicted or sick?"

Mzia hesitated. How much did they need to know?

"Obstinate girl!" Akrosa stalked toward her. "Do you want the empire, who has hunted you all your life, to possess you? If you are of no use to us, then we have no problem turning you out—"

"Akrosa," Danu cautioned. "We agreed no violence."

"We are well beyond violence," Akrosa snapped. "This is war. And we are stuck with this fragile flower that Yulia raised, not the key to the rebellion as I was promised. Yulia promised us a weapon, but just look at her." He gestured to Mzia, who indeed felt fragile at that moment. "What could she possibly do for us? The council is all but assembled, and I have nothing but a spoiled child to show them."

Danu threw up her hands. "Starbreather save me. Akrosa, I told you, it isn't what she is, but what she represents that matters."

"They all look to me. How can they rally around someone who won't even tell me the truth?"

"You will leave that part to me," Danu said. "I will make her presentable to the council. She won't speak. She won't have to."

"But the plan—"

"Plans change, Akrosa," Danu said. "Trust me with this."

Akrosa looked hesitant. "I don't know . . ."

"Trust me."

"Fine. But she will heal someone."

"Of course," Danu soothed. "Have I ever let you down?"

"No. You know better than to." He stalked out.

Danu turned to Mzia. "You've had a few hard days. I think after a little rest and food you will be in your right mind to see our side of things?" She phrased it like a question, but Mzia knew it wasn't.

The six men reappeared and Danu ordered them to escort Mzia away. "To the northwest room with the sleeping mat. Post a guard."

MZIA REMEMBERED LITTLE OF the next few hours. Only that she was shown a large, mostly empty room with a simple mat to sleep on. There was a bathing chamber with running water attached but no window.

They took her healer's bag but let her keep Tariq's jacket after an inspection. She fell into an uneasy sleep with a guard at her door. She had traded one captor for another.

She dreamed of Anuva, alone and afraid. Then she woke, still exhausted, some hours later to voices outside her door. She had a second of panic and touched her bare head, still not used to being around anyone without her headscarf. She felt indecent without her coverings, like somehow her soul was laid bare. A young woman in a grease-stained apron brought Mzia food and water. Her hair plaited into a swirling bun, and she had a slight limp. She smiled faintly at Mzia but said nothing, setting down a plate of food that sent echoes across the walls. She hurried out before Mzia could ask any questions.

Mzia hugged Tariq's jacket tighter and felt rather guilty eating the food brought to her. It was simple and unseasoned, unlike the food she was used to, but it was the first real food she had eaten in days. Had Tariq been given something to eat? He was just as starved as she. Even enemies deserved better than starvation. Even illegitimate princes.

That last idea sent her mind spinning in ways she didn't care for. She had traveled with, cared for, the emperor's bastard. He was one of many, dozens, if the rumors were to be believed. It all made sense now. His authority, his rank for one so young. How unintimidated he was by Princess Ezhno. A week ago she couldn't have imagined keeping company with someone with such high connections. Tariq wasn't what she imagined a Mark to be like. But then, what could she know of such things? She was just a village healer.

Mzia fingered a new tear on Tariq's jacket. She would need to fix it again. The woods had not been kind to their clothing.

The same girl came again. But now Mzia noticed she favored

her left arm as she walked in and picked up the plate off the floor. Wincing slightly, the young woman put a hand to her shoulder as she stood back up.

Mzia wasn't planning on saying anything to her food deliverer, but the young woman gasped a little in pain as she turned to go.

"You hurt yourself," Mzia said.

The girl blushed. She glanced out at the hall before whispering, "Just being clumsy. Fell off a chair reaching for something on the top shelf in the kitchen. Landed wrong on this arm." She rubbed her left arm.

"What's your name?"

"Kimya."

"Have you any arnica in the kitchens?" Mzia asked.

Kimya eyed Mzia with suspicion. "Why?"

"If you mash it into a paste, it can help with soreness. That and an icy bath."

"Oh, that's . . . very kind of you." Kimya spoke cautiously. Mzia wondered what they had told Kimya about her.

"It's my job," Mzia said. "I'm a healer."

Kimya frowned. "You were a healer? But I thought you could just . . . cure people?"

It was Mzia's turn to frown. "That's what they say."

"So why would you learn all that complex healing stuff if you could just . . . not?"

"It's . . . complicated."

Kimya peered over her shoulder before whispering in a quieter voice, "Is that why you helped the Marked One? The skycaptain? Because you are a healer?"

Mzia shook her head. "One shouldn't need an excuse to help someone, Kimya. I would have offered help to you even if I wasn't a healer."

Kimya bit her lip. "That kind of attitude will get you

overshadowed in most places." She left without another word.

Restless, Mzia stood and paced the small space. She didn't like this place. Not at all. She found herself wishing she was still climbing down the mountainside with the skycaptain. He was better company than these Separatists.

CHAPTER 25
A CERTAIN SLANT OF LIGHT

LILA HAD BEEN TRACKING him for several days now. It was simple, almost too simple at first, to follow the signal once she found it and use her mobile positioning system to plan a direct route. The river took her most of the way, all the way down to a quiet town at the top of the river valley. They spent a night at a quaint little inn where the owner made her and Aasim the best soup. She had complained at the delay, saying they were so close, but Aasim insisted that it was necessary to get some proper rest.

Before the sun rose, they set off towards Tariq's signal, leaving the little town behind as they entered the foothills. His signal hadn't moved in a while, which worried her a lot. Survival training taught them to keep moving if they were going to leave the spot of the accident. He should have stayed with the crash site for three days, as was protocol. But he had left almost immediately according to her data. What need or madness had driven him out of the mountains? Breaking protocol was not something Tariq did.

She would wring the answers out of him when she found him. Along with a few others. The data she had found about his secret mission was heavily encrypted. She had been casually trying to crack it open before news of his crash came and was yet unsuccessful. Normally, she loved to take her time; fiddling with the codes and trying to find a backdoor was the best part of her job. But now, in light of his disappearance and odd actions, this information could be helpful in some way. She set her home computer to run an algorithm of her own making, one that was sure to break into any files people didn't want broken into. She kept checking on it almost compulsively every few minutes.

Normally she only set the algorithm on projects she didn't care to do herself. But this time she didn't have much of a choice, being away from her lab and all her lovely tech. Pure nature was nice, of course. Different from the uniformity and cleanliness of city life. Yet she missed the touch of her keyboard and the gentle hum of her many information towers. The soft blinking lights were constant reminders of why she chose this profession. They were the anchor for the chaos she created for herself.

Tariq had always been the one to love field work, she recalled, trudging up yet another slope with Aasim at her heels. Tariq had excelled in their survival and combat courses. His gift of strategy did not go unnoticed by their instructors, earning him praise for his forward thinking. Lila, on the other hand, had been mediocre at best. Only in their technology courses had she pulled ahead, quickly surpassing even her instructor's knowledge and developing programs that the military still used today, albeit the updated versions. Which she had also created.

Lila checked the signal again on her pad. He still hadn't moved. And she was close now. She scanned the countryside and saw nothing but sloping hills. The day fell to evening when she stopped by a tree to rest. She frowned at Tariq's unmoving signal. Pulling up the topography of the landscape, she couldn't see anything that would make him stop there. Maybe there was something she was

RACHAEL KATHARINE ELLIOTT

missing?

Pulling up building permits and land plots, she learned that there was a cemetery not far to her north. But no records of where Tariq was. Topography showed an underground river close to his location that fed into the closest river valley. But again, nothing helpful.

So she tapped into the latest surveillance footage for the twelfth time since his signal stopped moving. Nothing. Hills. Grassland. Nothing that would indicate—she gasped. There was a dark mark she hadn't noted before. It could just be stone, but when she zoomed in closer, the darkness was shown to be a crescent shape. She looked at the time stamp on the image. Taken in early afternoon. When the sun was at an angle. Which would give a perfectly circular hole a dark crescent shape at the bottom. And there was only one reason people made perfectly circular openings that wide across.

Lila grinned at her pad. "Gotcha."

CHAPTER 26
SIDES DRAWN

EALER?" KIMYA'S VOICE came out shy and hesitant. "I, uh, wanted to tell you the salve you suggested to me is working well." The girl had brought in another plate of food.

Mzia forced down all her worries and put on a smile. "I am glad to hear it. Just don't overwork your arm for the next few days and you should be fine."

Kimya stood twisting her hands in her skirt.

"Is there something else you needed?"

"Well, yes, sort of. If it isn't a bother, Lukus—he is one of the soldiers here—has this rash on his arm? Only if it isn't a bother," she added quickly.

"No bother. Is he waiting outside?"

"Yes, he has been guarding your door. I told him to ask you. It has been so long since we had a healer."

"It's no trouble. Tell him to come in."

Lukus came in looking a little sheepish. "I told Kim not to bother you. I don't think I should be talking to you at all."

"It can be our little secret. Now, let me see your arm."

Lukus rolled up his sleeve to show the red, patchy skin on his inner forearm.

"How long have you had this?" Mzia went through all the standard questions about diet and exposure to try and find a cause.

They discovered he had been sent to a different watch than his normal area and that he may have encountered some new plants. She gave him a list of things he might try, and he thanked her profusely before returning to his post.

"Thank you, healer," Kimya said.

Mzia again felt the reward of warmth about her soul. This was why she did this. Why she pressed on. She brought just a tiny bit of balance back to the world. It wasn't much. But it was all she had.

Danu came by not long later. "How are we feeling, Iaomai Child? In a good state of mind to answer questions?"

Mzia rubbed her face. "What is it you wish to know?"

"How much blood is needed to heal?"

"It depends." That was not a lie. Injuries often took more than illnesses or the addiction.

"Don't be coy. How much is needed to heal someone addicted to Iaomai?"

"Less than a vial." Also not a lie.

Danu, nodded, satisfied. "The people are gathered, so you need to know what is expected of you." Danu turned to the door and called, "Kimya!"

The girl brought in a bundle of white fabric. She shook it out and handed it to Danu. A dress.

"This is . . ." Mzia shook her head. "This is far too fancy for a gathering in a cave."

"We are making the decisions here, not you," Danu said. "Turn around, and I will help you into it."

The dress was white gossamer silk, nearly transparent but for all the layers. It reminded Mzia of the ones the dancers wore at the summer solstice. Mzia set aside the skycaptain's jacket and shimmied out of her grimy dress. Her under layers were in just as horrible shape, but they would have to do.

"You are not to say anything." Danu laced up the back of the flowy gown. "Unless myself or Akosa ask you a question. Is that understood?"

Rebellion rose inside her. She wanted to say no, to demand a voice in this madness. To demand . . . equality. Yulia's many years of advice about staying hidden were pounding against her mind. To side with these Separatists was crazy.

Mzia looked down at the layers of dress that fell about her feet and trailed behind her. What if this, this revolution, was her chance? Her chance to change the world. Her one shot to help those addicted. The empire was certainly not going to do that. Maybe these people were crazy. But maybe this world needed a little crazy.

IN THE LATE AFTERNOON, they gathered in the cathedral chamber, around the reflection pool. Mzia stood just out of sight in the shadows of one of the archways, waiting with Danu for her cue— whatever that would be. The gown offered little protection against the chill, and her bare toes curled on the cold stone. Thankfully the chamber was warmer in the daytime, and she wasn't completely freezing.

Fourteen men and women had assembled, all uncomfortably shifting from foot to foot around the pool. Light streaming in from above, Akrosa stepped forward. The room quieted.

"I have called you all here today to celebrate a victory. We have discovered a cure for the addiction to Iaomai." He gestured to Mzia, and Danu had to nearly shove her forward.

Gasps flared across the room as Mzia stumbled into the light. Danu prodded her forward until she stood just beside the pool in the center of the room.

"Can it be true?"

"Iaomai Child!"

"The legends are real."

"Starbreather save us!"

"Iaomai Child!"

Mzia crossed her arms and refused to look at them. What was she? An item on display in the street market?

"As suspected," Akrosa went on. "Our emperor knew and kept the cure a secret. He has consistently found and killed the Iaomai Children, making sure they could never reach adulthood. In fact, the accounts of adults are more of a myth than the cure itself, none of the sightings being confirmed in the past century. But they are no myth." He gestured to Mzia.

Mzia lifted her head at last, not to look at anyone, but instead to focus on the hazy sunlight that separated them all. The sunlight was the only thing familiar, the only thing known at this moment.

Akrosa continued. "This is the Iaomai Child that Doctor Yulia stole from them all those years ago. Unfortunately, they were found and Doctor Yulia was killed. The Iaomai Child was captured just a few days ago to be brought back to the emperor to be used in secret or killed."

"How did you get her away from them?" an older man asked.

"With a little help from an old friend," Akrosa smiled dangerously. "We were able to track the skyship she was on, and then it was a simple matter of taking it down."

Murmurs spread across the ring of people. Mzia dropped her hands to her sides and looked at Akrosa for the first time. He had taken down Tariq's skyship. He had caused the deaths of Tariq's crew. And he didn't care. He didn't care how many lost their lives to further his cause.

No matter who she sided with, there was death.

Akrosa spoke again, and Mzia fought hard to focus on his words. "She can cure with only a small amount of her blood. Dozens could be cured right now with no effect to her health."

Hundreds, actually. Mzia had done the math.

"We control the cure now. The emperor will have to listen to what we have to say. The time to act is now." He searched the faces in the room. "What say you?"

A middle-aged woman with silver streaks in her hair spoke. "These are brave words, Akrosa. But they are just words. You expect us to stake everything we have built on this one discovery?"

Several nodded in agreement.

Akrosa uncrossed his arms. "I knew you would say that. And you have every right to question me. So how about a demonstration?"

Akrosa turned and gestured to the shadows behind him. Feet scuffled on stone and two of his men emerged from a nearby doorway, pulling Tariq forward between them. He had been stripped of his shirt, revealing the stark white lines of sprawling ink across his shoulders, upper arms, and back. His hands were bound behind his back and a gag firmly tied around his mouth.

People gasped and stepped back as Tariq was forced to his knees beside Akrosa. Hissing whispers skipped about the hall. Tariq looked little like the proud young skycaptain the day he and Mzia met. Unwashed and unshaved, his eyes unfocused and hollow above dark circles. How long had they kept him like this? Had they fed him today? Given him water? Let him rest?

As he knelt beside the pool just a few steps away from her, Mzia saw that the loopy script around the pool was similar to the tattoos on his back and shoulders. The style matched, and yet instead of just writing, the marks took on shapes and patterns that might add another layer of meaning. If she hadn't seen his marks next to the pool's, she might not have known his tattoos were words at all.

And something else caught her eye, something she had missed. Maybe it was just the stark lighting, but Mzia swore she saw, under his tattoo markings, some very old, faded scars. They were more like memories of scars than scars themselves. So faded that she was sure she was the only one to notice them now.

"You were always one for theatrics, Akrosa," the woman spoke again, startling Mzia out of her observations. "We know who this bastard child is. But just what sort of demonstration did you have in mind?"

"It is a simple one, Thrisha." Akrosa gestured to the man just behind him and was handed a small, narrow box. Akrosa stepped forward and set the box on the stone rim of the pool. He opened the box and withdrew a vial filled with a milky-white liquid. "This," he said very calmly, "is Iaomai." Without pause, he turned and stuck the needle into Tariq's arm.

Even louder murmurs than before broke out, hiding Mzia's soft, "No." Her body started to move, to go to him, to stop this madness. But Danu grabbed her arm, nails digging into her skin. She gave Mzia a sharp look to stay put. Mzia teetered helplessly as she watched Akrosa inject the entire vial into Tariq's arm.

Several voices in the room questioned the ethics of this choice, but Thrisha said loudest, "Can you cure him with your blood?"

Mzia froze—Thrisha was talking to her. All eyes again swung to the Iaomai Child. And in the center of her being she knew that she could cure Tariq. She could cure anyone—had cured so many. But she wanted to say no, to throw doubt and sow confusion. She wanted to run away. But as a healer, she always faced danger. Always looked at death and went into battle without flinching.

She summoned that courage now, fighting to not fight. To give into this battle in hopes of winning the future war.

"Answer her question," Danu demanded.

Mzia nodded. Just once. But it was enough.

Conversation rose and fell like a flash flood.

Nobody bothered to consult Mzia, the only true expert there, on what would be best. They debated for what felt like hours on how long to wait before having Mzia cure the skycaptain. Several days? A week? Should they let him progress into the final stages of the withdrawal to be certain the cure really worked or just until he started showing the first symptoms, such as trembling hands and a rash? This felt like a decision that should have been made before injecting the skycaptain, but evidently Akrosa hadn't bothered to inform anyone of this plan except maybe Danu.

Mzia felt everyone moving and talking around her, and their individual voices blurred together into a dull roaring. She fought to control her own breathing and the urge to rush over to the skycaptain. She didn't understand the pounding in her ears, the shortness of her breaths. She was angry at him. For keeping things from her. For participating in Yulia's death. And most particularly, she was angry because she was a healer and he was in need of healing.

Her mind snapped back into focus from her inward spiral. Had anyone noticed her staring or the distress that was sure to be clear on her face? She kept forgetting she didn't have her goggles and headscarf to hide behind.

A quick glance around told her that most were much too engaged in the debate to pay attention to her. Only a single set of eyes looked back at her from a dark doorway. Kimya. The cook glanced at Tariq then back at Mzia before slipping into the shadows of the hall.

Mzia started listening to the conversation again when one man said, "Why don't we just let him die?"

Thrisha rolled her eyes and crossed her arms. "It is as if you haven't been listening at all. We are trying to prove a point here. The Iaomai Child needs to cure him first. We can kill him later."

"Thank you," Akrosa said, and most people hushed. "All this talk of revenge is well and good. And we shall have our retribution later, on the emperor and the Marked Ones who blindly follow him, but for now I propose the following.

"We wait five days. That is when withdrawal will be clear enough to see, and the rash will appear. Then we shall inject him with the Iaomai Child's blood. Once we are sure it works, we will start giving it to those we know who are in need and documenting the results. The people will see we are right and will rally to us too quickly for the emperor to stop them. We will let the anger of the people do the work for us. And while they are rioting and demanding satisfaction, we will come forward with our solutions." He gestured to Mzia. "And since we will control the cure, they will do our bidding."

Cheers and general agreement rose from the crowd. Then more conversation that Mzia was unable to follow.

Night came on. The stars were out in full force, a small mercy from the Starbreather. He must have known she needed the encouragement for the task ahead. How could she possibly call herself a healer now? How could she keep to her oath to do no harm when everywhere she went, harm was all she caused? A rebellion? Separating the empire? What had she done? A shaky breath was all she could manage as she prayed for guidance. She looked down into the pool and traced with her eyes the constellations that reflected back at her.

A small shadow blocked the stars at the pool's rim. She looked up to the sky to find it gone. It must have been a whiff of cloud in the otherwise clear night.

Decisions were made all at once. The people dispersed. Tariq was taken away. Akrosa and Danu left in full discussion with a few of what Mzia had learned to be Separatist leaders. Some were related to the last kings and queens of the kingdoms before joining the empire.

A man showed up to escort Mzia back to her room. She went without comment because here her opinion didn't seem to matter anyway. She was just an object. A means to an end. They were all off discussing what to do with her and never once asked what she thought was best.

Halfway back to her room they were stopped by Kimya in the hall. She addressed Mzia's guard. "Akrosa wants you on the south watch. Kuit hurt himself in training. I will take the Iaomai Child back to her room."

The man looked about to argue when Kimya cut in again. "Do you want to leave the south watch empty? Akrosa will be very put out if something should happen. Besides, where is she gonna go? It's not like every exit isn't guarded."

The man still didn't look like he believed her, but he stalked off anyway, deciding it wasn't worth the risk.

When the guard was out of sight, Kimya pulled Mzia into a side room lined with shelves of food and supplies.

"What are we doing here?" Mzia dared ask.

Kimya checked to make sure nobody came down the hall. "I don't trust Akrosa to keep your skycaptain alive."

"He's not my—"

"Just listen. I heard them talking in the side rooms. Akrosa knows others who are addicted. He can just let the skycaptain die and let you cure someone else. They have taken other Marked Ones before. And they never left them alive. So even if it isn't now, it will be soon." She took Mzia's hand. "I had to tell you because I saw your face when Akrosa injected him with the Iaomai."

"My face?"

"You looked so . . . angry. People may not notice me, but I

notice them. And I saw you couldn't stand the idea of him being hurt." She looked down at their joined hands. "I don't know what you can do about this, knowing that Akrosa will let him die. But I figured you would want to know."

Mzia's mind jumped directly to the default she always fell back on. She tightened her grip on Kimya's hand. "I have an idea. But I need your help."

CHAPTER 27
A TURN OF TIDES

SHE COULD HEAL. Tariq wrestled with the concept that went against all he had been taught when the Akrosa's needle pierced his skin. As if all the humiliation hadn't been enough. He had been stripped bare to the waist and forced to kneel on the stone floor until his knees went from pain to numbness to somehow both. All the while, he listened and tried to piece together the new information, to learn if anything would help him get out of this.

And the healer, she was there with them. Mzia had stood there in a white dress, truly looking like a fallen star or the Iaomai flower that coursed through her veins. He felt her eyes on him, and was careful not to look back. Once assessing she was fine physically beyond looking as tired as he felt, there was nothing else to be done. Maybe he had only imagined it, but when they had injected him with the Iaomai, she had stepped forward, as if . . . as if to stop them.

Why hadn't she just told him sooner she could cure people with her blood? If she hadn't waited until they were found by the Separatists, he might have been able to help her. Was she afraid he wouldn't believe her? That he would insist on turning her in anyway?

Even now he doubted Prince Orinth could be so cruel as to allow such a thing as these people were accusing. Ezhno he had no doubts of; she was mean down to her bones. But Orinth? Orinth was nearly twice Tariq's age and more like a father than a half-brother. The man could be strict but he was always fair. Always had time for Tariq. Had taught him about loyalty and duty and . . . Was it all just a lie?

What did these rebels know of cures? They were not doctors. And as much as he disliked Ezhno, she was the leading expert in this field.

It was decided. He would need to hear this from Orinth's own mouth before he would believe this madness. He would have to find a way to contact the prince. If he survived, that is.

When they yanked Tariq to his feet and made him march on numb legs, he was more determined than ever to see this through. To learn the truth. He plotted all the way back to the room they kept him in, recounted the steps it took and the turns that would need to be made. He was fairly certain that he remembered the way out.

They unceremoniously pushed him against a wall and he, rather ungracefully, slid down to sit. There wasn't much he could do with his hands bound behind him and his mouth gagged.

Some silent minutes in the dark passed before there was a slight commotion at the door. His guard argued with someone.

The woman had a soft voice. The guard huffed something sharply that he didn't catch, and then the sound of retreating footsteps.

The light was dim, but he didn't need much to know who the glowing figure was in the doorway.

Mzia came forward, knelt, and pulled the gag out of his mouth and down around his neck.

"Mzia?" His voice was a bit hoarse and his throat dry.

"Shhhhh," she hushed. "We don't have much time."

"What are you doing here?"

"Being stupid."

"That doesn't answer my—how did you even get in here?"

"Kimya sent both our guards on fake errands so I could cure you."

"Why would you do that?"

"I told you—I am being stupid. And apparently, I can't live with myself knowing someone is hurting and I can help. Even if that person kidnapped me. Now, do you want the cure or not?"

"Of course," he said, the only words that he could get out.

She pulled a syringe filled with dark liquid and a small pair of scissors from somewhere in the folds of her dress.

"Now scoot away from the wall."

He obeyed and turned so she had access to his arms. Cool metal slid between the ropes and his wrist. With a few snips of Mzia's scissors, the ropes fell away. Tariq brought his arms forward and rubbed the blood back into his hands. He felt human again. She took his right arm, her fingers like ice, and straightened it. The needle pricked the skin of his inner elbow.

"You can actually cure me with just a vial?"

"A few drops, really, but I thought I would be safe."

Several empty seconds passed and Tariq tested the waters. "Your dress looks nice."

"Don't patronize me," she said, but there was a hint of humor in her voice.

There were millions of other questions lining up to be asked in his mind—questions about her abilities and if her efforts could really help. Their time together was limited, so by the time she withdrew her needle, he had the questions lined up in order of importance.

"Won't the Separatist leaders find it odd that I am not going into withdrawal?"

"Only if you are still here." Mzia stood. "Our guards will

realize their fake errands soon. I need to leave."

"Why are you doing this?" Tariq asked again. "You know who I am."

"And now you know who I am," she flashed, "possibly a very foolish girl who just wants to help people and is willing to go to any lengths to see it done. I can't live with myself knowing you—yes, even you—will die when I can help."

"Mzia!" a woman called from the hall. "He's coming back!"

Mzia looked at the doorway then back at him.

He sighed. "Mzia . . . if things were different—"

"But they are not different. I have my life and you have yours. So go back to it." She handed him the pair of scissors. "Now your one job is to get out of here. If you want to do me a favor, never come looking for me again. Now go."

"Mzia!" the woman in the hall hissed again.

Mzia went to walk out of the room but paused in the doorway. Over her shoulder she said, "And maybe don't kill anyone on your way out. Not everyone here is a mad revolutionary."

She ducked out seconds before footsteps sounded in the corridor. His guard had returned.

TARIQ REPLACED THE GAG around his mouth then sat back at the wall with his hands holding the rope. The guard came in to check on him and, not finding anything amiss in a brief glance, returned to his post just out of Tariq's line of sight.

Now the issue was timing his escape. He remembered the way in, but the front door seemed a dangerous way to go. There was the underground river he had seen just off the main cathedral chamber, but without equipment or knowledge of how long underground it ran, it was as good as suicide. That left the skylight above the reflecting pool. Surely there were other ways out, but Tariq couldn't waste precious time finding them. To climb out, he would need equipment of some sort. They had passed a supply room when they first brought him here.

He mentally traced out the route he would need to take and assessed two possible backup plans. He had hoped they might bring him food or something soon so he could build up a little strength, but they appeared to have forgotten about him. All the better.

His plan firmly set, he was about to make his first move and call the guard in when a scuffle echoed in the hall. A grunt followed by a sound he knew all two well—a body hitting the floor. He held his breath and a woman appeared in the doorway.

"Lila?"

CHAPTER 28
A PRICE TO PAY

W HAT HAVE YOU DONE?" Akrosa thundered, a
storm brewing behind his dark eyes.
Hours had passed and it was late evening. Mzia had
gone back to her room, wondering if and when news would come of
Tariq.

He seethed in anger as Mzia stood. She leveled a cool glare at
him, masking her anxiety. "You're going to need to be more
specific."

"Don't play dumb with me!" He grabbed her shoulders and
pinned her into the nearest wall with enough force to knock the
breath out of her. "The Marked One is gone, and you helped him
escape!"

"How could I do that?" Mzia gasped, trying to wrench herself
free of his crushing grip. "I have been here under guard this whole
time!"

"The men tell me otherwise." He shoved off her with bruising
force, took a step back, and called, "Bring in Kimya."

A tall soldier yanked Kimya into the room by her upper arm.

Mzia got the sinking feeling as when the skyship had found her in the woods. But she kept her cool. This was no longer about her own safety.

Akrosa pointed to Kimya. "This kitchen witch sent two of the men away on fake errands. Why else would she do that if not to aid you in helping the Marked One escape?"

Mzia folded her hands. "Kimya needed to speak to me on a personal matter, that's why she sent my guard away."

"What personal matter?"

"A woman's complaint. Would you like to know the details?" It gave Mzia no small amount of pleasure to see Akrosa blink and look distinctly uncomfortable.

He recovered quickly, however. "That doesn't explain why she sent the Marked One's guard away."

"I wouldn't know about that." Mzia shrugged.

"Don't think just because you are an Iaomai Child that I will be lenient in any punishment I decide to give you. I understand you recover fast, and I am of mind to test that."

Mzia remained silent. She had only enough time to flinch before he struck her so hard she fell to the floor. Still, she said nothing.

"Stop!" Kimya begged, starting to cry. "Please, she didn't do anything!"

"Silence! I know you are both hiding something, and I will learn what it is! Secrets kill people. *My* people."

From her spot on the floor, Mzia saw her guard, Lukus, in the doorway. He seemed distraught. "Sir, maybe this isn't the best—"

"Are you in on this, too?" Akrosa reeled on him. "How deep does this deception go?"

"Sir, I only meant that she is valuable. Perhaps Danu could—"

"You will keep your opinions to yourself. Now return to your post."

Lukus hesitated a moment, locked eyes with Mzia, then vanished into the hall. She wasn't enough for him to break orders. She was an outsider, a suspect, and Akrosa was his leader.

Akrosa shouted some more and Kimya again begged him to stop. He struck her as well and left her whimpering in the corner. Even then, Lukus did not come back, which left Mzia wondering if she had been wrong about their relationship.

Akrosa made Mzia stand back up only to strike her again. The pain came to her as the flash of a dying star. Whereas most people might experience pain over the course of hours, it lasted only minutes for her as her cells knitted everything together at hundreds of times the speed of a normal body.

While nothing was broken, Mzia's face was sure to be red and swollen for a few hours and her eyes bruised for at least a day. The skin there was so fragile. Keeping stock of the injuries as if they were someone else's helped her keep her head until someone entered the room.

"Starbreather save us, Akrosa, what have you done?" Danu marched into the room followed closely by Lukus, who was out of breath. So that is where he had been.

"She helped the Marked One escape!" Akrosa seethed, not checking his anger. "And she has the nerve to lie to me about it."

"I don't care if she heals the *emperor* in front of you, you don't shout so much that I can hear you from the front entrance!" Mzia peered up and when Danu saw her face, she threw her hands up. "They are going to lose faith in you when they see this! They will think you are unstable! Some of them already asked me on my way here . . . Stars save us, I leave for one minute to check the perimeter!"

"Don't lecture me like I am a child! You haven't seen the destruction I have. You don't know—"

"I know enough to see when power is slipping from your grasp.

These people are going to go back and tell everyone that you are unstable and you will be replaced. Is that what you want?"

Akrosa made a sound between a growl and a yell. "I will get an answer out of her!"

Danu took a steadying breath. "Do you or do you not want to lead?"

"Of course I want—"

"Then act like it, dammit! Use your head! You will get nothing out of her tonight. Tomorrow you can try again, but we have other things to worry about. A skyship was spotted."

Her words snapped Akrosa out of his rage, at least momentarily. "Where?"

"The eastern perimeter. It isn't scheduled. It might be a coincidence, but I doubt it. We need to make plans to move again if necessary. And I have other things to discuss with you." She glanced at Mzia. "But not here."

Akrosa stormed out and Danu followed.

Lukus went to Kimya and helped her up. "I am sorry, healer," Lukus said. "I did what I could. I didn't know he would—"

"I will be fine." Mzia waved him off. "Take Kimya. I need to be alone for a while."

"Yes, healer." Kimya clutched his arm tightly and together they left.

CHAPTER 29
THE CHOICE

TARIQ ONLY HAD JUST enough time to catch his breath when they got back to Lila and Aasim's temporary base before he asked, "Status update."

He still couldn't quite believe that not only had they found him, but they got him out with minimal casualties. Now they stood in a wayfarer's hut, built along ancient paths that pilgrims took. This one was very old, mostly cobbled together with moss and rocks between the roots of an ancient tree. Tariq told Lila and Aasim most of what had happened on their dash here, as it involved a lot of stopping and checking the area for anyone. Tariq felt useless without his own gear. He had managed to escape with nothing more than his clothes minus his uniform jacket, which he presumed Mzia still had.

"Status update," he asked again.

Lila grinned. "Well, I am kicking it with my first field work in years and I think I look fabulous in this new suit I got for the occasion, but next time I think I'll go with a grayer color to really bring out—"

"Not you." Tariq waved her off. He didn't have time for her

shenanigans.

Aasim cleared his throat and looked up from his handpad. "I have made contact with the capital to report your rescue. I expect a response back within twenty minutes."

"Twenty minutes?" Tariq frowned. "Why aren't you using an open line?"

"Well, about that . . ." He looked at Lila. "Would you like to tell him?"

"Oh, I think you should. You do it so much better. In fact, I was just telling Quinn the other day—"

"Lila, please!" Tariq rubbed a hand over his face.

"Okay fine, they didn't exactly send us to rescue you."

"You came without backup? Unsanctioned?"

"They wouldn't send anyone!" Lila protested. "I went to Prince Orinth the moment your computer stopped responding, and he said there would be no official search! Something stupid about it being too sensitive of a matter to tell the local authorities about and a bunch of other nonsense that I was too angry to remember. So I . . . decided to come myself."

"Aasim." Tariq groaned. "We talked about this! What did I even hire you for if you are going to let her do things like this?"

"Don't take this out on him!" Lila snapped before Aasim could respond. "We both know I would have come without him, and this way I am much safer. He is such a loyal guard dog. Don't be mad at him. Actually, you shouldn't be mad at me either, I just saved your life."

"At the expense of your own!" How was he born with so much common sense and she with none?

"You risk your life every day." Lila crossed her arms. "Like it or not, that is what Marks do." She reached for his face. "We are going to need to talk about this facial hair choice—"

He swatted her hand away. "Don't change the subject. We can

discuss your actions later when we are all safe. Aasim? What is the withdrawal plan?"

Aasim's handpad buzzed. He tapped a few things on the screen. "Looks like Prince Orinth is most anxious to talk to you. He is calling on a secure line." He reached into his pocket for the earpiece and held it out to Tariq. "Lila and I will set up the next phase."

Tariq accepted the pad from Aasim and put in the earpiece.

The prince appeared on the screen. "Greetings, Your Majesty."

"Tariq, you had us worried. Glad to see you survived not only a crash landing but a kidnapping?"

"Yes, sir. I am afraid there were casualties both times. I—"

"No need to give details now," Prince Orinth said. "Soldiers will soon raid the compound where the Separatists are hiding. Your tracker has led us right to them."

"Very good, sir."

"But tell me, the Iaomai Child, did she survive the crash?"

"Yes, sir. She stayed with me in the woods until the Separatists found us."

"Good, then we may recover her yet. I assume you didn't believe any of the lies she fed you while you were alone?"

Tariq shifted. "Lies, sir?"

"Yes, I understand from my sister that the Iaomai Child boasted of enhanced abilities. She didn't try to persuade you, did she?"

He knew. Stars above, the prince knew. Tariq schooled his face into neutrality. "No, sir, we didn't have much time to discuss anything beyond survival." Tariq looked up at Lila and Aasim who were watching him. Tariq swallowed. "We didn't speak much at all."

Lila looked at Aasim, who appeared as confused as she did. Tariq had lied and they both knew it.

"Good, good. I was concerned that after such an ordeal you

might be . . . vulnerable to lies. You are sure she told you nothing?"

"Nothing worth recalling." Tariq could hear his own heartbeat.

"Wonderful. It is all working out better than expected. The raid on the Separatist hideout will proceed in the next two hours. Report to command when you return. I want your account by tomorrow morning."

"Yes, sir."

"Oh, and tell Lila that if she is going to sneak off, next time at least ask for backup. I knew she would go after you the moment she left my room, but I thought she would bring more than her bodyguard."

Tariq stammered out a goodbye and ended the call.

"What just happened?" Lila asked as Tariq handed the pad back to Aasim.

"I am not . . . sure." He frowned. "Do either of you have a blood reader?"

"Yes, but what has that to do with—"

"Just let me use it."

Lila sighed but pulled out Aasim's medical pack. After digging through it, she handed him the handheld device that was smaller than his palm. He pricked his finger, then waited.

Lila tapped her foot. "Do you think you're ill?"

"No," Tariq said after a moment. "Not exactly . . ." The device beeped. Tariq looked at the results and swore.

"What?" Lila looked ready to jump out of her skin. Well, more than usual.

Tariq handed the blood reader back to Lila, and Aasim read the results over her shoulder.

"This makes no sense," Aasim said. "For these results to be accurate, you would have had to have been addicted to Iaomai and then . . ."

"Cured?" Tariq finished.

Lila shook her head. "Who did this to you?"

"The Separatists injected me with Iaomai to experiment. They wanted to prove that Mzia could cure me with just her blood, and well . . ." he gestured to the blood reader.

"That's impossible!"

"So I thought too, yet here we are. And I'm afraid it gets worse." He dug the heels of his hands into his eyes. "Our grand prince knows. He just tried to tell me that the Iaomai Child would lie to me about this and I shouldn't listen to anything she said. Yet this is the third time she has cured or healed me."

"What else did he say?" Lila asked.

"That they are raiding the compound soon, now that they know the Separatists' location. They are going to find her."

"Is that why you lied?"

"I didn't—" He shook his head and dropped his hands. He looked at Aasim. "I may have omitted things, but Aasim, he knew about Lila. Prince Orinth knew Lila would try to come for me. He even suspected the Separatists had something to do with this, and he let her go . . ."

Aasim let out a breath. "I expected better. He knows she's a flight risk."

"Hello! I am right here!" Lila said.

They ignored her. "I . . . I don't know where we go from here." Tariq ran a hand through his hair. "Could everything I heard the Separatists say really be true? Is it all just a power grab? And at the center of it all is Mzia." His eyes unfocused as he stared into the middle space. "What do they mean to do to her?"

"I know that look," Aasim said. "You want to go rescue the Iaomai Child and keep her away from the empire, don't you?"

Tariq frowned. "How could you possibly—"

"Because I have seen that look before."

"When?"

"On Lila. Every time she's about to break the rules, she gets that same look. So naturally, I see it four or five times a day."

"Hey!" Lila gave Aasim a shove. "You really need to warn people before you start pegging them with such deadly accuracy." A mischievous grin spread across her face and she turned to Tariq, "Are we really going after her?"

"*We* are not doing anything. You are going to stay here with Aasim—"

"I will not!"

"Lila! Let me finish! I can't have you risk—"

"Risk what? Getting caught? Dearest brother, you think you are in your element, on a mission. But this is different. You are about to enter my realm. And if you don't want to face a court martial, then you are going to need my help. Breaking rules is something I do very well."

Tariq let out a breath. "Fine. You can be ground support. And when I get back, the three of us are going to have a chat about your boundaries."

Lila laughed. "Please, like boundaries mean anything to me. Now, before you get upset, just tell me what you need for this treason we are about to commit."

Feeling nearly a physical pain at the word "treason," Tariq said, "I need a map of that underground river."

CHAPTER 30
THE RIVER

MZIA HAD TREATED her injuries calmly. Everything was going to be okay. She was already healing. Her split lip had scabbed over, not much more than a faint scar. The swelling and redness had reduced drastically, and her bruises were fading from purple and blue to yellow.

Nobody had come to check on her. In the hall, Lukus shuffled about when she emerged from the bathing chamber, but nobody interrupted her. She sat on her bed mat and tucked herself into Tariq's coat, which still smelled of the woods. And of him. Some minty scent she couldn't name, probably from his soap. She wished she could get out of this ridiculous dress, but her other dress, while in need of cleaning, had disappeared when she was brought back to this room.

More than her dress, she missed her medical bag. It had the sort of familiar items she wanted to run her hands over—her last ties to home.

Emptiness encircled her. How had everything become so very wrong? Was it really just over a week past that she had been giggling with Anuva about some silly thing she heard in the market? Nothing would ever be the same.

A shuffling sounded outside the door, and Mzia looked up, expecting Kimya.

But it was Tariq. Tariq, who she had risked everything to help get away. Tariq, who had promised not to come back.

"What are you doing here?" she hissed.

"Breaking my word and over a dozen other laws I would rather not mention," he said, coming further into the room.

"How did you even get back in here without getting caught? Surely my guard—" She gasped. "You didn't kill him did you?"

"No, just knocked him out. But—"

"I didn't save your life just so you could come back here!"

"I'm breaking you out. Let's go." He held out his hand.

"Tariq, I don't want to go to the princess. Surely you know that."

"I can't explain everything, but the empire is about to storm this place, and you need to come with me right now so they don't find you."

Mzia blinked. Akrosa must have knocked loose her brain because it sounded like . . . "You aren't going to turn me in?"

"No!" He said it with such force she was half convinced. Half convinced that this illegitimate son of the emperor had really returned for *her*. That he had thrown away everything for *her*.

"How can I trust you?"

He dropped his offered hand. "You can't, only—" He frowned and stepped closer. "What happened to you?"

Mzia touched her face and longed for the protection of her headscarf and goggles. "It's nothing. In a few hours—"

"It's not nothing." He knelt beside her to get a closer look. "That's some serious bruising. Who did this to you? Akrosa? I thought you were valuable to them. Why would he . . . ?"

Understanding flooded his features. "He knew you helped me."

Mzia refused to look at him.

"Starbreather, what was I thinking, leaving you here?"

"I wouldn't have gone with you. It isn't your fault."

"Isn't it?" He shook his head. "You tried to tell me how it was, and I didn't really believe you. Well, I have seen my blood reading and heard the grand prince lie. I'm sorry that's what it took."

Mzia passed a hand over her face. Could she trust him any more than the Separatists? *Starbreather, guide me, what should I do?*

"Isn't a chance with me better than a certainty of this?" He gestured at her face.

A chance. A chance to get away from here. A chance to get back to Anuva.

Tariq held out his hand again, and this time she took it.

SHOUTING ECHOED OFF THE stone walls. Mzia checked on Lukus as they left her room to find him indeed unconscious, not dead. One truth from Tariq. She stuck close to the skycaptain's side as they ducked in and out of passageways. Tariq never hesitated, weaving them this way and that through the halls of the ancient temple as if he had lived there all his life. More than once, they stepped into a room or alcove just in time to miss someone rushing past.

"How far away?" One woman asked another as they ran past the room Mzia and Tariq had slid into.

"Less than ten minutes out," the other panted. "Hurry, before . . ."

They turned a corner and her words were lost.

So, Tariq wasn't lying about the empire coming. Nothing else could've this place in such an uproar. Two truths from him.

Only when they entered the main cathedral room with the reflection pool did Mzia question what the plan was. They neared the center of the temple. Why were they here?

Tariq took one look across the space before sprinting ahead, aiming for an archway on the other side. They were just passing the pool when Mzia saw where that archway led.

"Skycaptain!" she hissed, "That's—"

Footsteps pounded, and across the pool, Ezhno entered the room from the main archway flanked by three of her soldiers.

Tariq grabbed Mzia's wrist and they paused. He whispered, "When I say, run."

Run? Run where?

Ezhno looked surprised but only for a half second. Her eyes took in Tariq's stance and his hand on Mzia. "What's this?" The laughter in her voice echoed across the walls. "I thought you were supposed to be leagues away from here, Skycaptain."

"That's strange, I could say the same of you." His voice held that lethal calm that he had used before on the skyship. "The grand prince didn't tell me you would be on this mission personally, what with you still recovering from the crash."

"I am afraid my brother and I do not communicate so well as you two do," She glanced at Mzia, and back to Tariq. "Did he send you back here? That was unnecessary. Bring her to me and I will take her back."

There was a flicker of uncertainty in Tariq, which Mzia didn't have time to analyze before he said, "I am afraid my orders are not to be interfered with." He started walking again, towards the archway.

"This is madness!" Ezhno snapped, calm finally lost. "How could you think Orinth meant for you to ignore me? It isn't as if he doesn't trust—" She stopped herself and smoothed out her features. "It matters not, all will be sorted when we reach the capital. Now be a good little soldier and—"

"Run!" Tariq jerked her forward and Mzia barely kept her feet as they hurtled toward the opening.

Ezhno shouted. Mzia tried to slow before they entered the doorway, "Tariq, I can't swim!" Her feet slipped on the damp floor. She collapsed through the doorway after him into the dark waters of the underground river.

PART TWO

EARTH

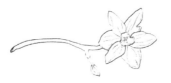

CHAPTER 31
RIVER VALLEY

ER LUNGS BURNED. The night called. Sweet, lovely blankness as she had never encountered wrapped around her and invited her deeper. Deeper where the pain was less. Where the fear was gone. Deeper and yet somehow higher. Pinpricks of soft light called to her in the night. And laughter like a pink dawn brushed her cheek. She wanted to stay, to go deeper still. To find the source of the laughter and light. To understand the voices calling. What did they say? *Glory, glory, glory* . . .

A stab of pain. Then it was like someone wrenched her from behind, yanking her back. The laughter and light faded. No! She wanted to stay. She wanted—

A heaving cough escaped her mouth. Pain as she had never known stabbed her chest, urging her to cough again, to dispel the water in her lungs. Someone thumped her back, and held her arm above her head.

Tariq's voice. Close, just above.

Mzia coughed and gasped and moaned. The Separatists. The temple. Tariq. They had jumped into the—

She forced her eyes open. "The princess?" Her voice croaked.

"Just breathe," Tariq soothed. "She won't find us before we move on. She has the Separatists to deal with, and Lila should be at the fork soon. The underground river let us out far enough away."

Mzia pushed herself up to sit, only half taking in his words, as her breathing was still punctuated by coughs that burned her lungs. The banks of a river within a gorge rose up around them so deep she was sure the direct sun wouldn't reach them even at noon. For now, she could only see a small strip of stars far above. Tariq steadied her with a hand on her back.

"Thank you," she managed, hoping he knew it was for more than just helping her sit.

"Can you stand?"

Mzia nodded, but when she went to push herself up, her legs refused to hold her up. Trembling and weak, she fell back on her knees. She shook her head and dashed away the tears the coughing had brought up. "I can't," she sputtered and cried some more. "I can't."

"I'll carry you then," Tariq said.

"No—" cough, "just—" cough, "leave me."

"Seriously?" Tariq knelt beside her. "You think I just saved your life and openly declared rebellion to my emperor and country just to leave you here for that witch to find you?"

Mzia looked at him for the first time and understanding settled on her. He had made a decision. Princess Ezhno had been right there. He had pulled her into the underground river to save her. He had chosen a side. *Her* side. Blatantly declared his stance in a way that could not be taken back. She wanted to laugh and cry all at once. This, unfortunately, only made her cough more.

Tariq pounded her back until she gestured for him to stop. "Better?"

Mzia nodded. His uniform jacket was like a ton of bricks on her shoulders in her fight to breathe, so she shrugged it off.

"I can't swim," she said.

"I didn't consider that variable."

Mzia pushed the wet hair from her face, dreading the tangled mess she would have to brush out later. "What about me saying no? Did you consider that?"

"I did," he admitted. "But you came with me."

"I might not have if I knew it involved nearly drowning." Each breath still hurt.

"Didn't take that into account." He muttered as if he was quite disappointed with himself.

The silence of the night rolled in with only the river splashing at its banks. They were here, away from the empire, away from the Separatists, away from everything like before. Only now he knew who she was and he chose to stay with her. Chose her. She would need to get the details from him when she could breathe again.

"What happens now, Skycaptain?"

"Why?" He smiled in that disarming way. "You have somewhere you need to be?"

She forced a smile, but his joke came unnaturally close to the truth. Obviously, he must know she didn't consider him a friend yet. An ally, maybe, but not yet a friend. "Only away from everyone trying to use or kill me."

"Well, you are in luck, for that I can help you with. However, before we move on, I need you to cut out my tracker."

"What?" The world still spun a little.

"My second tracker, I need you to cut it out for me."

"You have a second one?"

"Standard procedure for Marks. It's how Lila found me and helped me escape the Separatists. It's how the empire found them as well. There's also one in my uniform jacket. It's how I found you in the temple."

"Who's Lila?" Mzia asked, suddenly wary.

"My sister. You needn't worry about her, she assisted in your rescue. As did Aasim."

Mzia put her hand to her temple.

"Are you all right?"

"No, it's just . . . it's . . ." It was so much. So fast. And had she just nearly died in the river? Was this what her life was now? One near death experience after another?

"Hey," he spoke softly. "You are not alone now. For better or worse, we are in this together."

She blinked back tears. "Really?"

"It isn't as if I can go back," he said with forced lightness. "I have broken about twenty—no—twenty-one laws. Not to mention a few dozen military regulations."

She nodded. Right. For him to turn back now would mean a slow death or, at best, life in the prison mines of the south. Which was, upon reflection, another type of slow death.

"But I need your help to break one more," Tariq said. "I need you to cut out my second tracker."

"I don't have my healer's bag anymore."

Tariq pulled out a scalpel from his satchel. He held it out to her, total trust in his eyes. "It is just under the skin above my left shoulder blade. It isn't hard to find once you know where to look."

He pulled his shirt over his head and twisted to sit with his back to her.

Other worries fled as she fell into a familiar role. Mzia pushed up onto her knees behind him and leaned in, one hand on Tariq's shoulder, to examine the area more closely. Not only did she find the tiny incision, but her early observations about old scars were true. They crisscrossed his back. Dozens of them. From the smooth way the ink of his tattoos lay, she surmised they were made before he had been Marked.

She prepared for the first cut. To keep Tariq's mind occupied, Mzia asked, "Where did you get these scars?"

He stiffened. "You can . . . see those?"

"It might just be my healer's eye," she allowed, making her first cut between two swirls of ink. "I doubt someone who hasn't seen as many old cuts as I have would spot them."

"It's a long story," Tariq said after a pause. "For another time."

She nodded and kept working. Though her mind wandered through many things, her hands were steady. As always, her goal was to inflict as little pain as possible. She found the tracker with little trouble and needed only two cuts to get it out. The remarkable little device was no thicker than a leaf and about the size of her thumbnail.

Mzia quickly dabbed away the extra blood with the sleeve of her dress. Tariq said thanks and tugged back on his shirt. She handed him the tracker, and he frowned down at it. "As soon as it leaves my body or I die, it stops working. Now everyone will know what I have done without question." He set it down beside him on the river bank with an odd amount of ceremony, like he was setting aside his old life.

He took back the scalpel and tucked it into the satchel. He retrieved his uniform jacket, and after pulling out the tracker from the lining and smashing it, he gave the jacket back to her, as she still had so little to wear. After scanning the horizon, he offered her a hand. "You ready?"

Her lungs burned a little less, and she was able to get to her feet.

"Where are we going?" she asked when she again found her breath.

"Somewhere safe."

CHAPTER 32
GREETINGS AND MEETINGS

LILA CHECKED HER PAD. He should have shown up by now. She stood in the tiny bridge of the watership at three hours past midnight waiting for her brother who was never late. The ship was a smaller, sleeker version with a roof and a shallow hold down below. On deck, only two small rooms were usable: the bridge she now stood in, set near the stern, and the other room of small sleeping quarters set in the aft. Between them was only an open deck and rails.

She set the pad down next to the helm with the navigation controls and felt a twinge in her left shoulder blade. Aasim had been as careful as he could have been when cutting out her tracker, but he was no healer. The pain was enough to rub her nerves raw on this night.

"He'll be here, Lila." Aasim came up and stood beside her as she watched the fork in the river.

"You don't know that," she snapped.

"It's only been a few minutes."

"He's never been late before."

"He's never broken so many laws before," Aasim said dryly. "Perhaps that takes longer than he thought."

"Oh, shove it." She crossed her arms.

Aasim put a hand on her shoulder. "He'll come, Lila."

Despite her irritation with her bodyguard who had the emotional range of a tree, she was calmed slightly by Aasim's touch. He had always been there to dig her out of whatever scrape she got herself into. He didn't hesitate to join them in this treason, even though it would mean a lot of uncertainties, including money.

"You will pay me back some day," she had heard him tell Tariq, before the mission. He had said, "I will keep track of what you owe me."

Lila had liquidated all her assets and made sure she had enough to pay Aasim for the next few months. As loyal as he might be, she wouldn't blame him if he decided to take his talents elsewhere.

Picking up the pad, she checked the time again. It had only been a minute since she last checked. He was another minute late.

She bounced on the heels of her feet and schooled herself to wait. Nothing irked her more than waiting.

Her pad buzzed. She snatched it up too fast and had to force her eyes to focus. "He's nearly here! Aasim, get the—"

But Aasim was already gone to let down the gangway. Lila scanned the river valley for any sign, unable to see in the darkness below, and she dared not turn on another light than the soft glow of the bridge controls. Nobody could know they were there.

Footsteps treaded on the gangway—Tariq had arrived. She started up the engine and dashed out the door.

Her brother stepped aboard the ship's deck, and Lila threw her arms about his neck—only to instantly yank back. "Are you wet?"

"You remember the plan involved swimming, right?" Tariq sounded weary, but he was whole.

"And you're late." She smacked his arm. "Do you have any

idea how much Aasim worried?"

"Lila, I was fine. Just ran into a few snags that slowed us down." He turned and Lila beheld the Iaomai Child for the first time.

Even in this little light, her hair was clearly white and in two long, messy braids. She wore the tattered remains of a white dress and Tariq's uniform jacket. She hugged herself and looked up at Tariq with anticipation. And maybe just a little fear.

What had Tariq gotten himself into?

"I am not sure my clothes will fit you well," Lila said. "But anything is better than this mess you're in. Who told you white was your color? It completely washes you out." She moved forward and threaded her arm in the healer's before she could protest and turned back to Tariq. "Well, aren't you going to introduce us?"

"Lila, Aasim, this is Mzia. Mzia, this is Aasim, a friend. And this rude woman is my sister."

"Older and *wiser* sister," Lila corrected. "And as such, I claim use of the quarters to dress."

"Lila, perhaps Mzia—"

"Needs female company after being with you so long?" Lila sniffed. "I know I would if I had been alone with you for several days."

Lila knew she had won this when he rolled his eyes. As she pulled the Iaomai Child along, she called over her shoulder, "Oh, you can find dry clothes on the bridge."

She led her new charge back to the cabin room. Once the door shut, she dared to turn on a dim glow light that wouldn't show from the outside.

Mzia looked at her with eyes that were unsettlingly white. Lila might have called her slight and perhaps fragile, and yet Lila saw in her the determination of a survivor. They could be dangerous. *Brilliant.*

"Let me help you out of those things. I never like to be in wet clothes, it reminds me of the winter rain storms we had to train in."

Mzia said nothing she dressed. Thankfully, Lila had packed one dress that was on the shorter side, and so it only fell to just above Mzia's ankles. It was a bit large in other dimensions, but its matching cape hid that well.

"About your hair," Lila said, turning to her pack. "I think I might have something . . . yes, here's a scarf." What she pulled out didn't match the outfit, but that couldn't be helped. Mzia took it and mumbled a thank you, her first words to Lila.

Lila crossed her arms. "You might say something else than that, healer. I did, after all, play a vital role in saving you. Or did Tariq neglect to mention that?"

Mzia gazed at her with an unnatural calmness.

Lila felt her skin itch. "What are you doing?"

"Why . . . why did he come back for me?"

Lila shrugged. "My brother always has his reasons. Some disgustingly honorable code he lives by. Makes him no fun most of the time, but you, from what I hear, you are quite the heroine yourself. The Separatists, his eyesight, the skyship." She had another question, or a dozen, she wanted to ask. "Have you healed many people before? Addicted ones?"

"Um, yes. Some."

"And it's really in your blood? Like you can just give people your blood?"

"Yes." The healer tugged at her headscarf.

Lila opened her mouth again, but Mzia cut in. "So are you and Aasim . . . together or . . ."

Lila snorted. "Please. I would be with someone much more attractive. No, he is just my loyal bodyguard." Lila crossed her arms. "Speaking of connections, there seems to be some *tension* between you and Tariq."

Mzia frowned. "Of course, there is tension between us. He

kidnapped me."

Lila barked out a laugh. This girl was funny, even if she didn't mean to be. It might also be that Lila hadn't slept in 24 hours, but it felt oh so good to laugh again. When she recovered, she shook her head. "You're all right, healer. I think we'll get along just fine."

"I DON'T LIKE IT," Tariq said, pacing the bridge while Aasim ate a very early breakfast. "I don't like any of it."

"To be fair, you did sort of pick the most difficult path possible," Aasim said.

"What choice did I have?" Tariq challenged. "Who knows just how deep this corruption goes? Is it just the royal family? The royal council? The governors?" He leaned the heels of his hands on the control panel. "The empire I thought I was serving doesn't . . . exist."

Aasim squinted out the windows into the early pre-dawn hours.

"Go on, tell me what you are thinking."

Aasim shrugged. "I mean, is it really such a surprise to you that the government is corrupt?"

"I'm not stupid. I knew it had its flaws, its blind spots. I guess I foolishly hoped that it was only a few evil souls and most wanted good for the empire, for the people." He waved a hand in a meaningless gesture. "Maybe I *am* stupid."

"It isn't stupid to be optimistic," Aasim allowed. "But you did choose me, private security, to watch your sister and not government bodyguards."

Tariq rubbed his temples. "Perhaps a part of me always knew. But something else is bothering me. Something Princess Ezhno said about the prince, back in the temple. Their rivalry goes deeper than I thought." He relayed to Aasim the encounter.

"That is strange," Aasim agreed. "It sounds almost like they are competing for the Iaomai Child."

"Yes, it does sound that way, doesn't it?"

"How much do you think the emperor knows?"

"With how much power they have now, I can't imagine he is in good health, or he would never allow this."

"I hear things," Aasim said.

"And what are the rumors saying about our emperor?"

"That he is dying."

"Of what?"

"Old age, I expect. Doesn't that happen often to people over ninety?"

Tariq shook his head. "Perhaps the prince and princess feel the coming power vacuum. That could be why Ezhno acts the way she does, gaining the power she can now."

CHAPTER 33
SAFE HOUSE

MZIA WOKE IN CONFUSION. She felt the rocking sensation of the boat before she was fully awake. Someone breathed nearby, and she opened her eyes to daylight. On the opposite side of the small room, Tariq lay on his back, one arm slung over his eyes, his right leg bent, and one knee propped against the wall beside him.

He stirred as she sat up and then gasped fully awake. "They were supposed to wake me!" he said to himself as he rolled over to push himself up. He was nearly standing before he noticed Mzia. "What time is it?"

"I just woke up." Mzia yawned. The bandage on his arm from where they had cut the tracker out had fallen off. "Let me see your arm."

"It's fine," he said without glancing at his arm. "I have to go check in with Aasim."

"It will only take a moment." Mzia searched for the simple medical kit she had seen the night before. Tariq looked ready to argue more, but she found the kit, knelt down, and patted the floor next to her. He begrudgingly sat beside her as she took out a cleaning solution.

She pushed up his sleeve, and examined the incision. After several moments, he asked, "Well? What's the diagnosis, healer? Will I live?"

"Maybe," she said gravely. "But I prescribe no more skyship crashes and Separatist kidnappings."

He chuckled a little, and she felt herself flush. What on earth was she doing? She reached for the cleaning solution and began to dab away the bandage fibers that still clung to the area.

"That may be a hard prescription to follow, seeing as I am now hiding the empire's most wanted. Also, I have survived two skyship crashes. What's a third or even a fourth?"

"When was the first one?" She didn't want him to stop talking.

"Back when I was first mate. It was . . ." He frowned. "Oh, three winters ago? There was an uprising in the south. Kucor. Do you know it?"

"I have seen it on the map. A large city."

"Yes, well, the people were rioting and the army was called in. We were only supposed to be crowd control, scare them enough to stop the looting." He rubbed his neck. "Nobody could have guessed the violence to come."

Mzia's inner eye was filled with images she had seen on the live broadcast about riots turning violent. People became desperate when years of particularly bad illness swept through. The one he spoke of, if she remembered right, had taken the very young and the old but left all the mothers and fathers alive. The city of Kucor was still rebuilding.

Tariq returned to a lighter tone as she began to bind his arm. "So, like I said, I have survived without your prescription." He cleared his throat. "But there is something else I have been meaning to speak to you about."

"Yes?" Mzia didn't look up from her work.

"I know you have no real reason to trust me, or any of us for that matter. Is there anything I could do or say to make you believe that I want to help you?"

Mzia thought for a moment. "Tell me where we are going."

"An old friend lives in the city we are headed for. He will take us in without too many questions."

"And . . . after that?"

"We hide. We go somewhere the emperor and the Separatists can't find you. Eventually we could build allies, try to gain support. I think there might be some family connections I could call on. After that, I think our best bet is if you heal someone publicly, somebody important and notable enough that we can't be ignored." He shifted. "I know it isn't much of a plan, more of a shadow of one, but the instant I have more, I will tell you."

She nodded. She believed him. He would not turn her in after his actions in the temple. And his plan was much better than anything she could come up with. He had resources, connections. Yulia had things like that, even besides the Separatists, but Mzia didn't know how to get in touch with them.

"If nothing else," Tariq went on, "you must believe me when I say I will do everything I can to keep you safe."

Mzia didn't know what to say as she clipped in the end of the bandage. But she made the mistake of looking up at him and found him looking back. There so much unknown stood between them. The question she had asked Lila the night before threatened to bubble up again.

Why did you come back for me?

The door to the cabin swung open and morning light nearly blinded them both. The river must have been facing directly east-west here to catch the sun's rays.

"Good morning!" Lila said, leaning on the door frame.

Mzia checked to make sure her headscarf was in place out of habit.

Tariq stood up. "You were supposed to wake me hours ago!" He picked up his uniform jacket. Mzia had been careful to set it out to dry the night before.

Lila rolled her eyes. "Relax, nothing is happening. And you two looked more tired than pilgrims crossing the mountains, so Aasim agreed to let you sleep."

"That wasn't your call to make." Tariq brushed past her into the sunlight.

Lila appeared unfazed by his brusqueness and turned back to Mzia. "He claims to be a morning person, but he is rather curt this early."

Mzia tucked away the first aid items and stood to replace the medical bag back in the stack of supplies.

"Come on," Lila said. "We are about to approach Lembah."

"Then maybe I should stay here," Mzia said. "I don't have my goggles."

"Nonsense. Nobody will be able to see your eyes from inside the bridge."

Mzia hesitated only a moment more before following Lila across the riverboat's deck and into the bridge. Tariq glanced up from the controls in surprise to see her there but said nothing about it.

Pretty soon, they passed another watership, rounded a bend in the river, and the city of Lembah appeared. The river valley widened just a bit here to accommodate the city. On both sides of the valley, houses were built right into the stone from the riverbank. The topmost houses appeared to be set in the sky itself. Mzia had seen pictures of such things, but to be there in person was another matter. The fronts of the houses and buildings were a combination of grown and carved stone. Between those were sets of steps that were nearly as steep as ladders. An elevator system of some sort transported people to the upper levels and several personal pulleys led right to buildings' doors. Bridges spanned the valley from one side to the other, footpaths mostly, and a wide one across the very top for a train.

The water port buzzed with early morning activity; hundreds of people and goods moved about the pier. Tariq docked them on the end in an empty spot and shut off the turbines. All four of them stood in the pale light on the bridge of the ship and Mzia chewed her lip. What came next? Lila brought out her handpad and scrolled through a few screens at lightning speed. "How much hush money do we owe, Aasim?" Lila asked, not looking up.

Tariq shifted and sighed. "I wish you wouldn't call it that."

"Exactly what am I supposed to call it? Bribe money?"

Tariq grimaced. "That's somehow worse."

"Well then, just pretend it is a normal, legal transaction if that helps you sleep at night."

Tariq made a noncommittal grunt and crossed his arms. Evidently, that wasn't going to help him sleep at night. Mzia glanced between the siblings.

Tariq's clear discomfort at doing something illegal made her question why it wasn't making her uncomfortable. She broke the law just by existing, so paying bribe money was rather trivial in her world. For a flash, she was almost envious of Tariq, of a life he could live that was legal and considered morally right. What would that be like? To have society approve of your actions? Mzia would never have such a life.

Lila left with Aasim to let the owners of the boat know she had brought it back. Tariq and Mzia stood in silence on the bridge as they watched them disappear into the bustling port. So many people. Mzia tugged at her headscarf.

"People only look for what they expect to see." Tariq broke the silence. "Just keep your head down and nobody will notice you."

She nodded and hugged herself. This was it. The first real test. The wilderness and the boat were one thing, but could Tariq keep her safe with people around? Why was she relying on him anyway?

Because she had nowhere else to go.

Tariq checked the time on his pad. "It's time." He tucked the pad away in his shoulder satchel and led the way out of the bridge.

Mzia followed him down the gangplank. Everything went fine until they entered the crowd of people. Mzia dared not look up but she found herself bumping into people and muttering apologies. The air felt damp and close by the river. So many people. This city was so much bigger than her little mountain village.

A baby screamed somewhere on the dock. The air smelled of fish and damp wood. Birds squawked and fishermen shouted their wares. Barefoot children, thinner than they should be, begged for food. One approached her, boney hands outstretched in supplication. She was forced to turn her head away and brush past to avoid making eye contact. Maybe this was a bad idea. Maybe she should have insisted he leave her—

Tariq slipped his hand into hers. Mzia grabbed his forearm with her other hand and walked half behind him as he parted the crowd for her. He didn't seem phased by the blatant poverty.

"Are there always so many?"

"Sometimes more," he said. "The Iaomia crop was good last year but the prices keep going up. Makes new orphans every day."

The air was difficult to breathe until they climbed off the docks and into the narrow streets of the city proper.

Tariq only let go of her hand when they met up with Lila and Aasim again. The skycaptain then led them all up several steep sets of steps, then into an elevator. This one took them up many roads to a narrow way by several grand houses covered in purple moss and much fewer people walking about.

"How much further?" Mzia whispered.

"We're nearly there."

They slipped back up a narrow stair that looked private and down a path between a building and stone wall wide enough for one person at a time.

Tariq rang the intercom. After a moment, a polite voice asked, "Can I help you?"

"Please tell Admiral Grinth that Skycaptain Tariq is here to see him."

The door opened and a servant ushered them inside. It was a large hall, reaching towards a front door on the street side. Welcoming arches of stone opened on either side of the room to another set of rooms and light poured from the many windows in the wall directly across from them that faced the river valley. Their footsteps echoed on the blue stone floors, and yellow vines covered the walls. The leaves on the vines swayed to a phantom breeze in a wave-like pattern from floor to ceiling.

Mzia wanted to admire and look more but there were footsteps at the top of the spiral stair, so she quickly directed her gaze downward again.

"Tariq?" an older man asked. His feet came into view. "This is an unexpected surprise." He sounded pleasant enough.

"Admiral." Tariq said. "Sir, I apologize for dropping by unannounced."

"I am retired now, Skycaptain; no need for such formalities." The older man embraced him. "And you are welcome any time." He turned to Lila. "And this is your sister, if I remember right from last Summer Soulstice?"

"Lila," she reminded him. "And it is my pleasure to see you again." She sounded more respectful and serious than Mzia had ever heard her.

"And who are your friends?"

"This is Aasim," Tariq said. "He keeps Lila . . . focused. And this is Mzia; she is a new friend."

Mzia made a little bow, surprised Tariq had used her real name.

"I am afraid she has a light sensitivity," Tariq explained. Mzia suggested this to him earlier as a way to justify why she was looking down at the floor. "She lost her goggles on the way here. I don't suppose you know where we could buy some new ones?"

"I will send Litith down to the market at once to get some," Admiral Grinth said. "And Lila, why don't you and Aasim take Mzia to a back room away from all this light. It's just through there. Tariq and I have some catching up to do, I think."

CHAPTER 34
TO KEEP SILENT

T ARIQ TUGGED HIS JACKET straight, painfully aware of just how many uniform regulations he was breaking. He missed the weight of his pins and cords, reminding him just who he was each time he caught sight of them. A skycaptain. Or he was before he had committed high treason. But now . . . ?

He didn't like unanswered questions.

The afternoon light came in from the tall windows, and it bathed everything in the study with an orange glow. Walls of books from eras past and objects the admiral had collected over the years gave the room a cluttered but cozy feel. The space felt lived in, and Tariq knew his old mentor must spend many hours a day in the study.

Tariq shifted from one foot to the other. "Sir, I owe you an explanation."

Admiral Grinth turned from where he was making tea and handed Tariq a cup. "And what sort of explanation would that be?"

Tariq accepted the cup and looked down into the reddish-brown liquid steaming up. His options were simple: the truth or the elaborate lie Lila had forged. The truth would get them thrown out at best and lose the admiral's respect. At worst . . .

The admiral went around and sat in his desk chair. He set his tea down, folded his hands on the table, and looked up at Tariq expectantly.

Tariq slowly set down the tea on his side of the desk. He couldn't lie to the man who had given him so much. The truth won out. It always did. "Sir, I have done something recently that I never thought I would. And I must crave your patience with me, to hear my story to the end before you pass judgment. I will accept your reaction to this matter and will not hold it against you if you decide to throw me out of your home."

"Well, that sounds serious." Grinth steepled his fingers. "I don't suppose it has anything to do with this royal decree from the palace? About you?"

Tariq went still. He knew. The man knew. Had this all been a trap? Were the soldiers now on their way? "Sir, I must beg your mercy for my sister as she—"

"Tariq." The admiral chuckled, breaking the tension in the room. "You are rushing to conclusions again without having all the facts. Did I not warn you about that before? Sit down."

Tariq hesitated, trying to run all the outcomes over again to see what he missed.

"Sit," the admiral said again, this time as a command.

Tariq obeyed. He could do that. Obey. He was good at that; following orders was familiar. Easy.

"Good, now before you go on spilling about your tale," Grinth's tone shifted back to conversational, "I am going to read to you what the decree says so we are on the same page. How does that sound?"

"Very good, sir." Tariq attempted to focus and not run through all possible ways of exiting the townhouse. There were four ways that wouldn't result in injury, six that would.

The admiral pulled up his handpad, set it on the desk and, after fiddling with a few controls, made what was on the screen project so they could both see it. He read, "'Mark of the Emperor Tariq of the Alang Kingdom, former Skycaptain of the *South Wind*, has been declared an enemy of the state. Anyone with information of his whereabouts should contact the authorities immediately. It is suspected that Lila of the Alang Kingdom, also a Mark of the Emperor, is connected with his plot. Anyone with information of her whereabouts should contact the authorities immediately . . .' And then you can see it descends into some political pandering." He switched off the projection.

Tariq's mind fanned out in several directions. The words "former skycaptain" flashed in time to his heartbeat.

"I was surprised, to say the least, when I read this. But what I find very interesting here is that your crime is not listed. No mention of why Skycaptain Tariq is now an enemy of the state."

"Sir, I must beg—"

But the older man held up a hand to stop him. "Tariq, I'm not going to turn you in."

"What?"

"Just as I said, I'm not going to turn you in. I will tell nobody you are here. Nobody else in my household knows you are on the run. And I would say it will be at least a week before it is even generally known by the public; people don't pay much attention to royal decrees like this when they don't think it affects them. You are welcome to stay in my home as long as you feel safe."

Tariq struggled to find the words. "But sir, you don't even know what I have done."

"No, I don't," the admiral conceded. "And when I read this, I must say I didn't know what I would do if I ran into you. But then you showed up not an hour after I first read it. You came to me." He placed a hand over his heart. "You trusted me, and I can see you want to tell me the truth." He smiled sadly. "And the truth is such a rare thing in this world." He frowned at his handpad. "You know, I am getting so old and forgetful, I don't check royal decrees as much as I should. Why sometimes . . ." He smiled pleasantly at Tariq. "Sometimes, I forget to look for a week or more. Being retired and all, I have better things to do. Do you understand what I am saying, Tariq?"

Tariq considered his old mentor. They called him the Fox because of his craft and cunning. His strategies and theories on war were required reading in the academy. Slowly he said, "You don't want to know what I did."

The admiral nodded. "I could probably guess it has to do with your new friend downstairs. But why would I ask such nosy questions of a friend who just dropped by for a visit when he was on shore leave?"

Tariq nodded, beginning to fit the pieces together. Admiral Grinth wanted deniability. If he never read the decrees, he wouldn't know Tariq and Lila were on the run. And he had invited Tariq to come and visit him before.

"I am just getting so old." The admiral shrugged complacently. "I guess I just don't pick up on things like I did when I was younger."

Tariq smiled a little, knowing this man's mind was sharper now than it had ever been. He wasn't the Fox for nothing. He had always enjoyed letting people underestimate him—a skill he had tried to teach Tariq before he retired.

Tariq's smile slipped. "I would never want to put you or your family in danger, sir. Say the word and we will leave."

"My offer to my friend to stay for his shore leave still stands," Admiral Grinth rose. "You might be called away quickly at some point, I am sure. Perhaps even in the middle of the night a few days from now. I wouldn't consider that strange."

Tariq stood and saluted his mentor. "I—I cannot express my gratitude, sir."

"Nonsense! I invited you to come see me, didn't I? Now run along and tell your sister and her friends they can sleep easily tonight. And leave your shopping list for Litith on your door when you come to dinner. It was a real tragedy that your boat overturned on your way here and you lost all your luggage. Air travel is the only safe way to go nowadays. You should know that, being a skycaptain."

Tariq gave him a grateful smile. "I guess I am a slow learner."

CHAPTER 35
THE IAOMAI

THE NEXT DAY, MZIA woke to the sound of rain. She couldn't remember where she was and sat up in the dark haze of the morning squinting across the room. Her bed was the circular sort that hung from a single point on the ceiling by four ropes. The half stone floor covered in a layer of patterned yellow and white moss checkered its way to the door. The room was of average size for a bedroom but had only one narrow window on one side.

She bolted out of bed so fast her head spun. Of course. Admiral Grinth had given her this room because of the low light. It all came back. Tariq's relief and easy smile when he told them they would all be safe here. Then the dinner where the admiral entertained them with stories of his life and a few funny tales about Tariq's training.

Mzia still felt wary. Even with Tariq's confidence, it all was too good to be true. She fingered the dress Litith, the Admiral's housekeeper, had bought for her at the market. And on top of everything else, how could she pay for any of this with no money?

The dress was lovely, the sort of casual wear young women

wore in the Alang Kingdom. It was a blue and green skirt of ankle length that fitted around the waist and had a sash that flipped up over one shoulder and hung down nearly to the floor behind her.

Litith had also found her a headscarf, less common in the Alang Kingdom but not unheard of. It was a bit different from the ones Mzia was used to, and after fiddling with it in her bathroom mirror, experimentation led her to put her goggles on first then the scarf. Said scarf didn't hang down her back as the others had but twisted and held up her hair so it looked more like a close-fitting hat.

The rain was still pounding away when Mzia ventured out of her room. Voices drifted from the main hall, and she went to see who it was. She cautiously descended the steps and found nobody she recognized in the main hall. There was a woman with a baby on her hip and three other children of varying ages scampering about. Their laughter echoed. The front doors were open and the cool air from the rain wafted into the space.

Mzia wasn't sure if she should go back up the stairs or into another room in search of Tariq when the woman called, "Oh hello!" She smiled at Mzia. "Father told me he had house guests. I do hope my little wild ones didn't wake you. I'm Krith."

Mzia bowed a little in greeting. "Mzia," she said as the other woman walked over to her. "And no, they didn't."

"Well, don't be shy to tell me if they are a bother; they can be quite a handful. Sive!" She looked at a little boy around the age of two. "Don't touch that!"

To Mzia's surprise, the boy took his hand away from the large decorative pot and toddled over to join his older brother in a game of chase.

"Will you be staying long?" Krith asked, keeping one eye on her brood.

"Probably not. Tariq's shore leaves are not very long."

"That's true. I remember Father was only home for short bits when I was younger. But it is so kind of you to share your time with Tariq with my father. Ever since my mother died a few years back, he has been all alone in this big house."

Mzia nodded, unsure what to say.

"So, have you and Tariq been together long? It is a hard life, being with someone in the army, but I know my mother wouldn't have traded it for anything in the world. She was always so proud of my father."

"Oh, um . . . no, not long." Mzia knew her face was seven shades of embarrassment. She was afraid to contradict Kirth as she might find it odd that Mzia traveled with Tariq and Lila if she was not attached in some way, so she changed the subject. Looking at the chubby baby the woman held, she asked, "And who is this?"

"Alitha." The woman shifted the child to her other hip. "She is the only calm one. The Starbreather knew I needed at least one to not be a handful."

As if her words were marked, the little boy, Sive, started sobbing. They both looked over and saw that he had fallen flat on his face.

"Oh dear! Would you mind holding Alitha?"

Mzia took the baby without hesitation and watched the young mother go over to her next oldest. Alitha looked up at Mzia with an unimpressed expression and shifted her head back to the rain falling outside.

Mzia settled the small child on her hip and tried to remember the last time she held an infant that wasn't crying. Little ones she cared for in the clinic were almost always fussy because they were in pain. But Alitha was content to just watch the rain. Mzia moved closer to the open door. That sparked the first bit of interest in the child, and Alitha put out her hand towards the rain. Mzia leaned her out just enough for a drop to land on the small hand. Alitha looked up at Mzia with a baby tooth grin and Mzia melted.

She was lost in the sound of the rain and Alitha's coos of delight and only looked over her shoulder at the room when the oldest child proclaimed, "But I don't want my medicine!"

The girl frowned and crossed her arms. Krith, the patient mother that she was, knelt and drew something from her bag. "I know, sweetie. I know. But you know you need it."

The girl relented and sat down in front of her mother. Krith pulled out a small, clear vial with milky white liquid inside and attached it to a syringe. Mzia felt the world slow. Even the rain nearly stopped as surprise washed over her. Krith injected her daughter's arm with the liquid and said, "There now, that wasn't so bad?" Neither realized Mzia watched from across the room.

Mzia, absorbed in the horror, whispered out loud, "Iaomai."

"You have a sharp eye there," Admiral Grinth said softly beside her.

Mzia turned sharply to find the admiral standing just out of her line of sight. "Tariq tells me you were trained as a healer. Not many would know the Iaomai drug when they saw it; we do such a good job sometimes, pretending it doesn't exist." The admiral smiled grimly and looked over to his oldest granddaughter. "Ciry was born with a lung condition. The healers couldn't do anything for her. It was Iaomai or only a few weeks of life." He shook his head. "Perhaps I am just a selfish old man, but I wanted my first grandchild to live a life before it was taken from her, even if that was a broken life."

The healer's code was clear on this point. She quoted, "All lives have value and worth." She gave the admiral a sad smile. "Even the broken ones."

He looked sad and yet somehow happy all at once, "Thank you, healer," he said a bit gruffly. "I knew that. I just need to be reminded sometimes." He straightened and turned his attention to Alitha, still mesmerized by the rain. "And how is my littlest one doing?"

Mzia handed the child over and watched how he cooed and

tickled her until she giggled. Mzia hugged herself and a wave of sadness swept over her. Yulia and Anuva . . . the family ripped from her. She would never have this. Not even if they found a place to hide, not even if she was somehow able to get back to her sister. She would always be on the run. Always hiding. She turned and walked quickly from the room.

The house went on for a while, and she was able to find an empty side room that appeared to be a sitting area. Small and cozy, there were a few chairs, a tea table, several windows along one wall and a set of cabinets on the other. Her goggles were completely fogged from her tears and she pushed them off, her scarf falling off with it. They both fell to the ground in a tangled mess. Frustration at everything boiled over and she knelt, face in her hands, and wept.

CHAPTER 36
ORDINARY

TARIQ STUCK HIS HEAD into Lila's room, "Have you seen Mzia?"

"No," she said with a shrug. "She wasn't at breakfast, so I thought she was sleeping in."

"I got her something from the market. I just wanted to make sure she didn't need anything else."

He turned to go when Lila added, "But you might want to act like you have known her more than a week."

Tariq turned back and stepped fully into the room. "Why?"

Lila did not look up from her handpad. "Because I *might* have been asked how I knew her and I *might* have said you two are dating."

"What . . . I . . ." Tariq threw up his hands. "Why would you say that?"

She looked up at him at last "I couldn't think of anything else."

"Oh really. Nothing else?"

Lila shrugged.

Tariq swore under his breath.

"Wow. You kiss our mother with that mouth?"

"You're impossible," he said as he stalked out.

"I love you too!" Lila called after him.

Tariq knew that Lila was just trying to get under his skin. That she could think perfectly well on her feet. But that didn't matter because he had to find Mzia. He had already checked her bedroom, so he went to look downstairs. Tucking the bag he had bought for her into the crook of his arm, he jogged down the main stair. In the front hall, the laughter of small children exuded from one of the side rooms; the admiral's grandchildren must be visiting. He spoke of them often as the joy of his life.

Not wanting to get caught up in pleasantries, he went the other way, through the dining room and into a study of sorts. This led into yet one more room, and he paused at the threshold. Someone was crying. Peering inside, he found Mzia knelt on the floor, her headscarf off. He inspected the rooms to make sure nobody else was around to see her like this before stepping forward and closing the door behind him.

Mzia jerked up in surprise at the sound of the shutting door. Her white-gold eyes were red as if she had been crying for some time.

She touched her hair. "I'm sorry, that was stupid. Someone could have seen." She picked up the headscarf and started fiddling with her goggles to try to separate them, but her hands were shaking. It struck an odd chord, seeing her so helpless like that.

"Let me do that." He sat on an ottoman next to her and pulled the tangle from her hands.

"Thanks." She sniffed.

He pulled out a handkerchief, something the admiral said a person should never be without, from his breast pocket and handed it to her.

She took it without comment.

He frowned as he tried to figure out how she made such a mess with just the goggle strap and her headscarf. "You want to talk about it?" he asked.

She shook her head. "No."

"Well then, why don't you talk to me about something else?"

She eyed him sidelong as he tried and failed to separate her goggles from the fabric. She sniffed. He was pretty sure she would say nothing and they would have to sit in the awkward silence when she blurted out, "Krith thinks we are . . . together."

He paused a second in his work but didn't look at her. "And Krith is . . . oh wait. She is the admiral's daughter? He has so many children I lose track." He smiled a little. "I think we have Lila to thank for that misunderstanding. She hasn't been able to cause me a headache in a while since I've been on assignment, so she's making up for lost time." He pulled the goggles free at last and held them out to Mzia, "I should have warned you sooner about her mischief making. Don't take it personally. It is completely directed at me as she doesn't know you well enough to tease you."

Mzia took the items from him but didn't put them on. "Lila has actually been rather nice to me." She fiddled with the hem of the headscarf, "So are we, like, supposed to be married or . . . ?"

"No. Thankfully, Lila knows such news is much harder to fake, especially with military families. No, we are just dating, according to her."

"Oh." Mzia looked down at the goggles. She looked like she wanted to say something but couldn't get the words to come out. And she still looked sad.

"Still not going to tell me what is going on?"

Mzia pursed her lips. Without looking up, she confessed, "So many people are addicted."

Tariq was surprised she had answered at all. There was clearly something she was omitting, as what she claimed to be bothering her was so obvious. Of course there were so many people addicted.

"Haven't you always known that?" he asked, though not

unkindly.

"Yes, but before . . . before in my village, I thought I was doing something about it. I was keeping some people from being addicted, so that was something. But now . . ." She made a vague gesture and fell silent.

He considered her a moment, what it must be like to have that kind of power and be afraid to use it. He remembered her reaction to the cemetery. But they faced a very harsh reality. He sighed. "You can't save everyone, Mzia."

The firm line set her mouth in showed her defiance at the thought. No doubt he wasn't the first person to tell her that. More than stubbornness in her countenance, a determination to see a task completed. That much, at least, he could relate to. Which reminded him.

"Oh, I got you something." He pulled out the healer's bag he had asked Litith to purchase with his own money even after the admiral said there was no need. "I know it probably isn't as well put together as your last one. But it has all the basics, and I thought you could add to it if you saw gaps. Just write them on the shopping list."

Mzia opened it and started to finger through the items. "You got this for me?"

"Well, yes." He couldn't read her face. Did she approve of it? "I felt at least partly responsible for making you lose the last one, so . . ."

Mzia closed the bag and clutched it to her chest. "Thank you," she whispered. "I didn't even think . . . I mean, I wanted a new one, but you have already given me so much I can't pay for."

Tariq rubbed his neck; the warmth of her appreciation was clear. "You're welcome, and don't worry about that."

She looked about to say more when footsteps sounded in the adjoining room. With impressive speed, Mzia pulled on her goggles and headscarf. Tariq stood, thinking he might have to offer a distraction, but it was Lila who stuck her head in.

"I am sorry. Am I interrupting?" Lila sounded all too pleased with herself.

"If you have to ask, you already know the answer." Tariq crossed his arms. "Now tell me everything you told Krith so we are on the same page."

"I hardly told her anything," Lila said, leaning on the doorframe in mock offense. "I only let slip that you two started dating six months ago when you met her on assignment in the Gao Desert."

"And what else?" It was never simple with Lila.

"Oh, just some minor details about how she saved your life when you wandered off base. Now don't get angry with me, I was inspired by true events."

Tariq took a calming breath. It didn't help. "What else?"

"Nothing! Okay fine. Just that you are madly in love but her parents have forbidden a relationship because she has been betrothed to someone else since birth. So you both plan to—"

"Lila." Tariq felt a headache coming on, "Isn't that the plot to that play you made me go see last summer?"

"Is it?" Lila was the picture of innocence. "What a coincidence!"

"Lila, I swear, if you—"

Mzia interrupted the argument by laughing. The siblings turned to look at her, and she clapped a hand over her mouth to make herself stop. "I'm sorry," she said to Tariq after a moment. "I know it isn't actually that funny, but I needed to laugh today. And I think I have read that play; it's quite good."

"See?" Lila said, as if she was completely justified in her actions, "Mzia can appreciate a good story, so why can't you?" Lila stepped into the room and held out her hands to Mzia, "Come on, let's go think of things to say to make my brother blush at dinner. Particularly about his facial hair which he insists on keeping."

To Tariq's surprise, Mzia took Lila's hands. But Mzia looked back on her way out the door and whispered, "I *am* sorry."

He watched them go with a mixture of apprehension. He scratched his cheek. He had never worn a full beard before as it was against the dress code, but grew it out now to make himself less recognizable. How any man grew them on purpose was a mystery. It was so damn itchy.

Then he smiled a little. It was good to see his sister in such good spirits. And it was nice to be worried about something so trivial as having embarrassing things said at dinner. And Mzia had laughed. That was the first time he heard it. Loud and sudden as a gust of wind. She needed to laugh more.

CHAPTER 37
UNEXPECTED ALLY

MZIA SAT BETWEEN LILA and Tariq at dinner that night. And despite all the blush worthy threats Lila had made, she appeared to have much more fun sitting back with a sweet smile while the admiral told a story about some stray dog that had gotten into the house a few weeks ago. Aasim and the admiral sat opposite them, and after the dog story made small talk about the weather and the addiction levels that year. The admiral was of the opinion that there would not be another drug battle, seeing as the Iaomai crop was predicted to be quite large and there had been only minor illnesses popping up.

Litith, the housekeeper, came in and whispered something in the admiral's ear.

"Oh good." Grinth smiled. "She's here. Show her in."

Lila stopped eating mid-bite and Tariq's voice sounded tight when he asked, "You were expecting someone?"

"I invited someone." The admiral said. "Not to worry. She won't tell anyone about your new friend."

Tariq protested. "Admiral, with all due respect—"

But before Grinth could answer, a middle-aged woman entered whose dark hair was plaited into a crown. She wore a very on trend tan dress with layers of transparent fabric painted to look like moth wings.

Tariq stood up so fast he knocked his chair over. Mzia touched her headscarf with one hand and gripped the edge of the table with the other, feeling his apprehension. Lila kept eating like nothing had happened. Aasim, on the other hand, let out a sigh that sounded like relief.

The woman ignored everyone except Admiral Grinth as he stood to greet her. "Lady Ishtar," he greeted with a smile and they embraced.

"Grinth," the lady said. Her voice had a familiar lilt to it that Mzia couldn't quite place. "It has been far too long."

"I couldn't agree more."

The woman turned to them at last. She had a stoic, commanding face but with deep lines around her eyes that said she smiled often. Only the smile she wore now was forced. "Surprised to see me?" she asked Tariq. "Didn't think your mother would find out what you were up to?"

Mzia felt the blood drain from her face. Lady Ishtar was their *mother*.

"Mother, I . . ." Tariq paled. "You shouldn't be here. You don't know how dangerous—"

"Don't." The fake smile was gone. "I am mother to not one but two of the emperor's children. I live danger. But you! I thought you were dead!" Her voice dropped to a whisper. "I had to learn through secret channels that you were here. You didn't think to tell your own mother that you are alive?"

Mzia looked up and saw Tariq didn't have an answer. The only sound was that of Lila, who still ate and failed to hide a growing smile.

Lady Ishtar turned on her daughter. "And you. Why do you look so smug? You are in just as much trouble, running off without telling me where you were going!"

Lila picked up her tea and shrugged. "I am always in trouble, Mother; that's just a Tuesday for me. But Tariq? I'm not sure I have ever heard you raise your voice to him like that. Go on, tell him what—"

"Enough!" Tariq finally found his voice. "Lila, now is not the time to gloat, and Mother . . ." He sighed. "Would you let me explain?"

"I think I am going to take the rest of my supper in the study," Admiral Grinth said to nobody in particular.

"Mind if I join you?" Aasim asked. Lila shot him a glare, which he ignored, and the two men gathered up their food and left.

When the door closed, calm once again returned to Lady Ishtar. For the first time she turned her gaze on Mzia and said, "Why don't we start with you introducing me to your friend?"

Mzia was sure Lady Ishtar had been speaking to Tariq, but it was Lila who said, "This is Mzia. She is an Iaomai Child."

Lady Ishtar put a hand to her heart and whispered, "A what?"

Mzia felt frozen under the lady's intense gaze. What was this? How many people knew the secret now? How could she keep track of them all? What if they told—

Tariq touched her shoulder. She looked up at him and he said, "What my mother learns here will not leave this room." He forced a smile. "She knows how to keep secrets."

Mzia took a deep breath and stood slowly. As she gave a bow of respect for Lady Ishtar's rank, Tariq gave a more formal introduction. "Mother, this is Mzia, healer of the Utara Kingdom. Mzia, this is Lady Ishtar of the Elaomayn Kingdom, my mother."

Mzia straightened and met Lady Ishtar's eyes. The lady's face, while used to merriment, was deep and serious now, much like

Tariq's. She sized Mzia up, glanced between her two children, then folded her hands and took a seat in one of the empty dining chairs. "Tell me everything."

TARIQ DID MOST OF the talking, although he looked to Mzia often, pausing to see if she wanted to add or correct anything. She merely nodded and let him continue, wanting to hear his side of this story. And Lady Ishtar watched Mzia carefully while listening to her son talk. Her fingers plucked at a string of pearls that must have cost enough to feed Mzia's village for a year.

". . . And then we came here." Tariq ended the story as the evening grew old. "I wanted to tell you, but it didn't seem right, to place you in so much danger."

"You let Lila come along." Lady Ishtar eyed her daughter as Lila drank what must have been her third glass of wine.

"I didn't have a lot of choice in that." Tariq sounded reluctant. Mzia couldn't blame him for wanting to keep his sister safe. Death now followed Mzia wherever she went. Tariq went on. "The prince let Lila come after me, mother. Prince Orinth let her go knowing it was the Separatists who shot down my skyship. Knowing they could be there."

Lady Ishtar took a breath. "I know you have already made up your mind about this, about the Iaomai Child." Her voice was even and calm. "But have you really considered all that this means? This is the hill you . . . choose to die on?"

"I don't intend to die."

"Nobody intends to die when they start such a path. But you know what becomes of Marks that refuse the call. Of those who try to get away before they are recognized officially and those who try to leave after." Her voice hardened. "It doesn't go well for them."

"Princess Ezhno would never let me live after what I have done, so there would be no going back now if I wanted to." He studied Mzia, his eyes so intent she looked away, unable to bear the weight of his words. When he spoke, his voice was soft. "But I don't want to go back." Then louder, "I know the truth now. And if I could go back, I don't think I could do it anymore—knowing so many could be cured and are not."

"I agree," Lila said, her words just a little slurred. "The truth is too important."

"And you." Lady Ishtar looked at Mzia. "you have been rather silent."

Mzia peered at Tariq. "Tariq has said all there is to say."

"I don't know about that. I still don't understand a few points of the story. Perhaps you could clarify?"

"Tariq told you the truth of it all—"

"Oh yes, I know my son told me his side, but I am curious. I am extremely grateful you saved his life, both after the crash and when he was addicted but . . . what I don't understand is why. Why did you help him escape the Separatists?"

Mzia fiddled with the hem of her dress. "Does one need a reason to save another's life?"

Lady Ishtar gave a knowing smile. "Ah, so you have one then?"

"That isn't what I said."

"No. Not with your words."

"I am a healer," Mzia said, very uncomfortable under Lady Ishtar's piercing gaze. "I took an oath to do no harm."

"What are you hiding behind those goggles?"

"Mother!" Tariq interjected. "She saved my life and you're being very rude as if she has done something wrong."

"Perhaps," Lady Ishtar agreed. "But then my children's lives have never been in greater danger than they are now." She frowned. "I suppose the admiral told you what happened to the Separatists who found you?"

Tariq nodded.

"I didn't hear," Lila piped up.

Lady Ishtar began to pluck at her pearls again. "Officially, all the Separatists died fighting. I had to learn through my own means that they killed everyone in the temple, nobody left alive."

Mzia put a hand to her mouth. Kimya, the kind cook, and Lukus. Dead. She might throw up.

Lady Ishtar went on. "I had enough reason to suspect that if you survived the crash, you were there, Tariq. And if the Starbreather wasn't watching, Lila too. I spent nearly a day thinking you were both dead." Her voice cracked on the last word. The heartbreak of a mother.

Nausea rolled over Mzia and she felt hot. All her clothes itched, and she wanted to rip them off, especially her goggles and head scarf. Imbalance. It was out of balance. People died. And she was the cause. Again.

Lady Ishtar looked at her nails, manicured to perfection, as if they had never known dirt beneath them. At last, she spoke. "I don't approve of you, Iaomai Child, or the choices my children have made." Her eyes flicked up to meet Tariq's. "But I didn't come all this way just to tell you I disapproved." She leaned forward and dropped her voice. "I came to tell you that where you should go next is the Gao Desert."

"The desert?" Tariq shook his head. "Mother, there are much easier places to disappear—"

"Oh, to be sure," she replied. "But no other kingdom has distant relatives that will help hide you."

"I had considered them," Tariq admitted. "But I wasn't entirely sure how to get in contact with them."

Lady Ishtar drew a small leaf shaped pendant from the folds of her dress. It was an information drive of some sort. She stood and placed the pedant on the table, "This will help you find them. Now come, give your mother a hug. My lady's maids will notice I am missing in less than an hour, and I mean to be far away from here before then."

Tariq stood and Lila more reluctantly so. Mzia watched Lady Ishtar embrace her children, and pain stabbed her somewhere around her heart. She hugged herself and looked away, remembering what warmth Yulia's arms felt like. How important it had been to Yulia to keep Mzia safe, just as Lady Ishtar was trying to protect her own children.

Now it was all the more important that Mzia kept Anuva safe.

CHAPTER 38
DARKNESS

MZIA WAS WOKEN ROUGHLY in the middle of the night. Lila shook her. "Get dressed. We need to go." Mzia was halfway into her traveling clothes, something Tariq made sure was purchased on their first full day in town, before she asked, "What's happening?"

"The Admiral got word that Ezhno will be in town tomorrow. He isn't sure if she is actually on our trail or not but Tariq doesn't like the odds." Lila danced impatiently from one foot to the next. "I have some of my own things to pack. Just come to my room when you are ready to go. Tariq says five minutes but I think we could spare ten." Then she left.

Ten minutes. Mzia was easily able to gather her few new belongings in just two, including her new medical bag. She fastened on her goggles and head scarf.

An idea came to her as she tugged on her new shoes. Before she could stop herself, she pulled out a syringe and vial from the kit.

THE ADMIRAL'S OFFICE STOOD at the end of the hall. She would leave it on his desk with a note. The directions would be clear enough and he would understand what they implied. She wouldn't have to spell it out for him to connect the dots.

She slipped into the dimly lit room. His big desk sat on the other side, and she walked across to it, scanning for something to leave a note with.

"Shouldn't you be packing?" The admiral held his handpad and stood off in a corner she had neglected to check. She chided herself for allowing this man to sneak up on her twice now.

He came closer and she said, "I finished packing."

"I see. So you have come to see me?" He sounded pleasant enough. His eyes dropped to her clenched hand. "To give me something?"

Mzia was a bit surprised. She was talking to a man with many secrets of his own. Perhaps he would be willing to keep hers. She held out the vial.

He took it and frowned, clearly unsure what it was. "And . . . what should I do with this?"

Mzia swallowed. Tariq had told her of his conversation with the admiral. "How much do you want to know?"

He frowned harder and examined the vial closer. His expression changed suddenly. "Is this . . . blood? Is this your blood?"

Mzia nodded. "It's not actually for you. It's for your granddaughter. The oldest one."

"Ciry?

Mzia nodded again.

"Why would . . ." He looked again between the vial and Mzia. An understanding washed over his features. "Healer." His voice came out in an unsteady wobble. "Will this . . . help her?"

"It will cure her," Mzia said, her own voice catching. "You should give it to her first thing tomorrow. It needs to go into a vein."

He slumped down into the nearest armchair and passed a hand over his brow. "Oh, bless you, child. Starbreather bless you . . ." He dissolved into hiccupping breaths and cried.

Mzia stood awkwardly for a moment before saying, "I should go."

"You should." The man collected himself. "Keep Tariq out of trouble, will you? May the Starbreather guide you on the path you need to take."

Mzia bowed with a hand on her heart. "And may he light your way to the end."

She slipped out of the study and shut the door, knowing she had done the right thing. A foolish and perhaps very dangerous thing, such as when she healed Tariq, but the right thing.

"What were you doing in there?" Tariq's voice close at hand made her jump.

"I was just saying goodbye to our host." Mzia walked past him. He didn't look like he believed her, but he followed her to the end hall and down the spiral staircase.

The four of them met in the front room. "Everything is a go," Aasim said. "We have one hour to get to the next checkpoint."

"Are we going to the Gao Desert?" Mzia asked Lila as Tariq went over the checklist for their gear one final time. Each of them wore a pack, and they planned to purchase even more supplies along the way.

"To the Elaomayn Kingdom, yes!" Lila looked far too awake for so late at night. Or early in the morning, depending on how one looked at it.

"Are we going to walk there?" Mzia asked, remembering with dread her walk with Tariq in the mountains. "Isn't it on the other side of the Central Mountains?"

"We are taking a skyship, silly," Lila said, giving Mzia's shoulder a playful shove. "Walk to the Gao Desert, and Tariq says I am the crazy one. Only pilgrims are insane enough to—"

"Quiet!" Tariq commanded and a hush fell over the group. Outside, someone shouted.

They went to the front windows, which gave a pretty good view of the city and the river.

Across the river, something was happening.

Street lights began to wink out, one by one. The valley city of Lembah that was once glowing with blues and greens of the bioluminescent light was only now a faint flicker on the plains.

"What is going on?" Lila asked.

"I'm not sure," Tariq said. "I have never seen anything like this. It doesn't make sense."

"I have heard rumors," Aasim offered. "That there is a smoke that cuts the lights and confuses people. Perhaps they mean to turn us around."

"I know about that," Tariq said dismissively. "I didn't think it was ready yet, but even if it was, it's a strange tactic to smoke out a whole city and turn it dark. Wouldn't that just throw in more confusion and make it harder for them to find us?"

Mzia considered this. The smoke they spoke of was not unknown to her. Yulia had experimented with something similar in her university days and Mzia, having discussed with her enough chemical compounds, understood the key components. But it wasn't the ratios of each ingredient in her mind during that moment, but the analogy Yulia had used to explain the smoke. *Like subduing bees in a hive, the smoke confuses and calms.*

"They mean to make us sleep," she said. "Yulia said it was used to subdue. If we are caught in it, we will become confused and eventually unconscious."

"They know of my connection to the admiral." Tariq pushed a hand through his hair. "They'll search here first, perhaps before the smoke even reaches here. But our main problem now is that they will have all the city exit points covered if they are already trying such tactics as these."

"I may have a solution," the admiral said from the top of the stairs. "I didn't want to get involved in . . . whatever this is, but I have to now."

"Sir," Tariq said. "I can't ask for your aid. Your family—"

"It is for my family that I do this," the admiral said, looking at Mzia as he descended the stairs. Tariq followed the look and tried to say something. The admiral cut him off. "I thought you would be able to get out fine on your own. I didn't think they would fog a whole city. But if they are willing to do that, then there isn't much they aren't willing to do. The governor of this province lives in this city and has an emergency exit. A tunnel. From his back garden."

"An emergency exit to where?" Tariq asked.

"Through the foothills towards the mountains, I am told."

"Have you been in it?"

"No, but I have seen the entrance at a private dinner party. And they say he can somehow leave his home without being seen. Only a handful of people besides myself know of its existence. So, if they discovered you used it, well, I would clearly be implicated." He smiled sadly at Mzia, "But I think it will all be worth it in the end."

"Where is this house?"

"I am afraid you will have to cross the valley, but it is only a few streets up from there. Here." He brought up his handpad and typed in something. Tariq's wristpad vibrated. "Those are the quickest directions. Starbreather guide you all on the path ahead."

"May he light your way to the end," they all murmured back.

Goodbyes finished, all at once they were filing out the back door into the narrow alley. Tariq went first, followed by Mzia, then Lila and Aasim bringing up the rear. They shifted from shadow to shadow, as the lights were still on in this part of town.

They went up several flights of narrow steps between some

homes, and Tariq brought them all out onto one of the many walkways across the valley. A cool wind wafted up. Mzia was very grateful for the handrails as the walkway was so narrow only two could walk side by side. But stepping out onto the bridge meant stepping out of cover, and they were completely exposed as they marched across the bridge. Mzia would have liked to run, but Tariq kept them at a clipped walk, brisk but not urgent looking.

At nearly the halfway point, three men entered the walkway from the other side. Tariq didn't hesitate but whispered back. "Keep going, keep your heads down when they pass."

Mzia wished to be anywhere but there at that moment and feared the very pounding of her heart would give her away. The men approaching looked ordinary enough, perhaps just some night workers. But as they passed by each other on the walkway, Tariq made an odd gesture with his right hand.

The last man in line lunged at Mzia, and before she could even flinch, Tariq tripped him and tackled him to the ground. Aasim and Lila did the same with the other two. Mzia clutched the bridge rail in shock as she heard bones crack and muffled cries. Seconds later, Lila pulled a bloody knife from the man she had taken down. The night went silent again.

Aasim and Tariq stood, and Tariq surveyed the scene. "Lila!" he admonished in a loud whisper. "I said no killing! That will put us higher on the priority list."

"I didn't kill him," Lila shot back, cleaning her blade on the fallen man's cloak. "I just stabbed him a little in the arm. It was an accident."

"Will he bleed out?"

It took Mzia a second to realize Tariq was talking to her. She knelt and pulled back the fabric on the attacker's arm. The trail of blood was only a trickle and already clotting. "He won't bleed out, no major arteries cut."

"There, you see?" Lila sheathed her knife.

"Good. Then keep moving."

"They don't look like soldiers," Mzia said. "How did you know they were going to attack us?"

"I know a soldier's walk."

Mzia got back up to unsteady feet and had to force herself to keep up with them. They exited the bridge and entered again into the shadows.

At last, they came to a street that was slightly wider than the rest, nearly wide enough for the four of them to walk abreast. A huge mansion with stone pillars and a gated garden took up well over a normal city block in length. The gate to the garden was locked, and vines grew around the ancient hinges. Even if they had a key, it wouldn't open for them. It must always be accessed from the house. The stone wall around the garden stood nearly ten feet high.

The lights at the end of the street started to wink out; they needed to move fast.

"I will go first," Tariq said. "I'll see what the other side holds. Then, Aasim, help Lila up."

Mzia watched with a touch of envy as Tariq scaled the wall with little trouble and swung one leg over to sit astride. He paused a moment before he whispered, "All clear." He reached down with one arm. Aasim knelt, and Lila used his knee to boost herself up and grab Tariq's arm. In two seconds, she was atop the wall with him. The next second, she had disappeared over the edge.

Tariq leaned down again to help Mzia up. "I am not sure I am strong enough to pull myself up," she said.

"No need," Aasim said. "You're light. I'll get you most of the way. Face the wall."

She did so, and he lifted her by the waist. He gave her enough of a boost to grab Tariq's outstretched arm. She managed to scramble up to sit astride the wall, but with not nearly so much ease or grace as the Marked Ones had.

Aasim was last and got up with a little help from Tariq. They dropped down to join Lila. Tariq turned back to Mzia with his arms up for her to jump. She did, and only landed injury free because he caught her.

"Nicely done," he whispered, setting her on her feet.

"I feel like a fish trying to fly around you all," Mzia said, straightening her pack. "Just how long have you practiced scaling walls?"

Lila whispered, "Walls this short? Since we were 7."

An alarm sounded somewhere in the city. Panic pulsed through the air. Apparently, the mist hadn't calmed everyone yet.

"This way." Tariq turned towards the back of the garden set into the valley wall. They wove between hedges and tall grasses. It was a beautiful garden with ornamental plants and fruit trees. The sort of place to spend a lazy afternoon. The lights just outside the garden winked out. The fog had arrived.

They rounded a final twist in the path and found a doorway of sorts carved straight into the mountain. Unlike the doorway into the temple of the Starbreather, this doorway looked unnerving, like the entrance to a tomb. There was no door.

They all stopped several steps before the threshold.

"Mzia, you could see the separatists long before I could. Can you see in there as well?" Tariq asked.

Mzia went right up to the doorway. Inside was just what she feared. "It's a mausoleum. This first room. But there is another doorway, straight across from here. It goes so far back . . . more rooms and it turns so I can't see the end of it." The air wafted out and whispered of ancient depths.

"If we use any lights, they might see us even with turns," Aasim said.

"And worse yet, I feel a pull of air inward," Tariq said. "So I think the smog would follow us and make it impossible to use lights anyway."

"Well," Mzia spoke up. "Good thing I don't need a light."

"Even if there is no light at all? That doesn't seem possible."

"I've never been somewhere I can't see."

Lila looked impressed. "Is this connected to the Iaomia? What other magical powers does it give you?"

"It's not magic, just perfect vision." Mzia categorized it more as a side effect than anything else.

"*Just perfect vision*," Lila mimicked and then she yawned. "Either way, I hope it works."

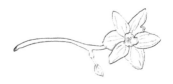

CHAPTER 39
INTO THE DEEP

W E SHOULD PROBABLY HOLD onto each other," Tariq suggested, rolling his shoulders.

Mzia took Tariq's hand. "All together then?"

Tariq nodded and took Lila's hand, and Lila took Aasim's. Mzia felt the sudden weight of it all. If they lived, it would be because of her. If they died . . ." She shook off the thought. "It's three steps down, then across the room, then three steps up."

She took a breath of smoggy air and felt her heart rate drop. Not an ideal way to start. Maybe this was a bad idea.

"Can we pause for a second? I am not feeling well," Lila said slowly.

Tariq shook his head. "I don't feel right either. Maybe we should just consider other options."

"No!" Mzia yanked the chain of people forward. "That is just the smoke. Keep going and we might get ahead of it. Keep your breaths shallow."

They stepped into the passage on the other side of the tomb; it was only wide enough to walk single file. Her feet dragged and

Tariq's hand felt heavy, but she kept going. This couldn't be where they ended.

The hall forked several dozen steps in, and Mzia found one way led to a short hall and another room meant for burial, full of little tombs, piles of stones over where each person had been laid to rest. The other fork led deeper into the mountain. They crossed another fork and another, and Mzia was in shock at how many were buried there. Old and ancient was that place, as tombs below ground had been abandoned long ago in the empire in favor of above ground cemeteries. Was it because tunneling rock was so time consuming? Or because nobody liked visiting graves like these, so far away from the sun or any growing thing? Mzia shivered.

Every little sound echoed down the rock walls, so they all tried their best not to shuffle or step too loudly. Only rock stretching on and on before her. How much further?

At each new split, the doors to the tombs were carved with a loopy script at eye level. Probably denoting the family or people buried. The way forward was unmarked by any carvings or symbols.

As they walked deeper into the ground, Mzia experienced for the first time what it must be like for normal people at night, for even she had her limits, unable to see in complete darkness. And the further and further they walked from the starlight, the harder it became to make out the texture of the rock walls and the distance they still had to walk. The corners of the tunnel faded into nothingness. She pushed the goggles to her forehead and squinted into the darkness.

It came to a point where she had to pause to feel out for the carved signs to know which direction not to take because her eyes failed her.

Everyone's breathing was so loud. Despite the coolness of the tunnel, her hand holding Tariq's began to sweat.

How much further? How much further in this empty place?

Well over an hour passed in the unending darkness. Then . . . it might be wishful thinking, but the passageway around her seemed to take shape. The color came back to the rock. And the air! Oh, the blessed air smelled of something other than damp, dead stone. And at last, the most wonderful sight of all.

"Light!" she dared whisper. The stone hissed it back to her a thousand times but she didn't care. She gave Tariq's hand an encouraging squeeze and picked up the pace. She knew the exact moment the others saw the light because Lila gasped and rushed them on.

A set of stone steps appeared, and Mzia dropped Tariq's hand to grab her skirt and climb. It was several flights up, and her thighs were burning when they all tumbled out into a large chamber lit with early morning light. A round pool filled with algae sat beneath a crumbling hole to the sky. Another ancient temple.

Only one other entrance to this room presented itself, so after a short break to collect themselves, they set off again. Outside, they found themselves in a wooded glade in the foothills. A poorly maintained walking path leading off into the woods suggested the tunnel wasn't used often. This side of the tunnel looked more like a natural cave and could easily be missed if one wasn't looking for it.

Mzia and Lila grinned at each other in relief. "If your eyesight isn't magic I don't know what is," Lila said but Tariq motioned for them to stop talking. Both of them did a quick search of the area. When the siblings disappeared into the trees, Aasim said quietly, "Well done."

Mzia nodded and shook out her hands, cramped from holding on to Tariq's for so long. She got the impression that Aasim didn't pass out compliments often. And it did feel good to be useful to this group of well-trained soldiers. She tugged the googles back into place.

Without meaning to, her thoughts wandered to Anuva.

Nobody had discovered her, she was sure, because nobody was looking. But if Mzia tried to get back to her, she might lead the empire right to Anuva. As hard as it all was to accept at that moment, staying away might be the only thing keeping Anuva safe.

Mzia found tears in her eyes. How long would it be until she could see her sister again? She was grateful for the goggles and headscarf that helped hide her emotions.

Tariq and Lila returned. "Nobody around," Tariq reported. "The path leads to a road. If my map is correct, it will take us to the train. Slower than the skyship but maybe safer if we can get on a cargo car."

TARIQ WAS EASILY ABLE to access the public train schedule and find a small village where it would go southwest before turning full west to take food to the desert. They walked down the old trail and were in the railyard before midmorning. The train stood waiting for them. It was a simple matter of finding an empty cargo car scheduled to be filled with spices once it reached the coast. Or at least, Tariq and Lila made it look easy. After checking the area was clear of people, Lila used her handpad to open the cargo car door. They climbed in and Lila shut the door behind them. The train was made of a similar metal alloy as the skyships, but the inside was coated with very durable and spongy moss that acted like cushions to protect the cargo.

After they snuck aboard, Lila managed to hack into the train's security and delete the footage. Mzia slept and woke up in the early-afternoon. The train was going much faster then, an almost terrifying speed. The light vanished, and they entered the tunnel that ran under the Central Mountains. Lila looked up from her handpad just long enough to explain that the next time they saw the sky, it would be when they came out the other side in the evening.

Tariq kept busy on his own handpad, and Aasim slept, so nobody talked much.

Lila sighed dramatically a few times before Mzia asked, "What are you doing?"

"Trying to break into the files about you."

Mzia looked at Tariq. "What files?" they asked at almost the same time.

Lila shrugged. "Just some information Princess Ezhno recovered from your clinic. Files Yulia apparently tried to erase."

"You stole encrypted files?" Tariq sounded more exhausted than angry.

"You were missing in action, and nobody would help me," Lila said "I needed all the information I could get."

"Guess I am nobody now," Aasim mumbled.

"The princess was able to recover files from the clinic?" Mzia tried to look calm. Those files, in addition to having thousands of tests on Mzia, were also littered with mentions of Anuva. Not by name, but she was referenced. And if Ezhno found out there was another Iaomai Child . . .

"What's wrong?" Tariq asked.

"Oh, nothing. Just I don't want her to know anything about me. More than she already does."

"You don't have to worry about that," Lila said. "I am nowhere close to breaking the encryption, and I wrote the encryption for a lot of stuff in the palace. And I am basically the best."

"So, you are saying . . . nobody else should be able to open them?"

"Well, I suppose after enough time and resources someone could. But I would give it months at best depending on how much of a priority they give this." She eyed Mzia. "I don't suppose you could help me break it sooner? Know any of the original passwords?"

Mzia shook her head. "Yulia handled all the computer stuff," she lied.

Lila shrugged and went back to her handpad. Tariq got up to pace and stretch. Mzia stitched the seam on Tariq's tunic back together using matching threads she found in her kit. She had only months to get back to Anuva. And much sooner than that if she didn't want to tell her new allies about Anuva. They didn't need to know about her. If all of this went horribly wrong and they were captured, at least she would be able to go to her death knowing Anuva was safe.

THE TRAIN SHOT OUT of the dark in the early evening at the edge of the Gao Desert. Mzia, despite all the sleep she had gotten, didn't feel rested. As they prepared to depart, the others in the group donned goggles to protect them from the sandy winds.

"We are coming up on the town," Tariq said. "My contact will ask no questions."

Lila arched an eyebrow in skepticism. "You know someone who doesn't obey rules?"

"Yes, I do." Tariq refused to elaborate further. He whispered to Aasim for a time, and Lila glared at them in offense. But they weren't talking about his contact. Mzia caught a few of the words over the sound of the train. They were discussing what to do if they were spotted. Aasim was to get Lila to their relatives and leave Tariq behind at the first sign of trouble. Something Lila would probably object to so they weren't going to give her time to argue about it.

The moon was rising over the distant dunes when the train slowed to a stop. They leapt from the cargo car on the opposite side of the train platform, and Lila had timed it so the camera's sensors conveniently went black for that time. They slid between the cars and joined the mingling crowd of several dozen people disembarking and embarking onto the train. Nobody seemed to notice them.

Mzia shook the sand from her skirt even as more blew up. Somehow it was still warm, the day's heat radiating back up to her from the ground around her. Besides the train and the merger platform, there was nothing around but dunes and moonlight.

Tariq came up and stood beside her.

"Where is the town?" she asked.

He cocked his head, "You mean you can't see it?" He pointed out in front of them.

Mzia looked again at the closest dune. It looked ordinary except a bit smoother. A distant bell chimed, and cracks of light appeared. The light was pale green, only bright because of the absence of all other light. The cracks in the dune expanded to become irregular shaped openings—a dome several stories high.

She smiled at Tariq, and they went forward. A few of the openings were at ground level, allowing for people to pass in and out. Many streamed out into the night, and laughter drifted over to them.

A single man broke from the crowd and came out to greet them. He wore white and blue striped robes. "There is my old friend!" He made a bow before pulling Tariq into a hug. He was only a bit older than Tariq, perhaps early thirties. But there was something off about his voice that Mzia instantly distrusted.

The man kept talking, "It is so good to see you! I was delighted to hear you were coming. And you have great timing. We just had a sandstorm earlier today and the dome was all shut up. You wouldn't have been able to get in." He waved a hand back at his town. "Now look at everyone, so happy to have the all clear. Come, come. We will eat a late dinner, and you can tell me all about your friends."

As they entered the dome, the light didn't seem so bright as their eyes adjusted. Dozens of giant mushroom-stalk supports reached the ceiling of flat, overlapping caps. The town was an uneven sea of tents. The colors swirled and some were patterned with outlines of fantastic animals like dragons spitting water and turtles with whole islands on their backs. The town sat like a brilliant gem in the dull sand of the desert.

Mzia stuck close to the group as they followed the man through the maze of tents. The roads were long and none were straight. Some curved around and reconnected with the one they were on and others went at a diagonal and ended in a group of tents. It was down one such short path that he took them near the middle of the city. They entered a tent to the left of the dead end, a purple and blue striped one that was larger and grander than most.

"Sit, sit!" The man directed them around a circle of cushions. He wouldn't stop smiling at them. "Eni! We have guests!"

They all took off their shoes just inside the door and sat. Layers of rugs covered the sand. Mzia sat next to one of the huge baskets that pulsed green light from some odd, moss-like substance that didn't seem to need any soil to grow and glow. She brushed her hand against some that crumbled into the rug, and the glow stuck to her fingertips.

A woman came through a flap to their right, pregnant but nowhere near her due date. She looked surprised when she saw Tariq, who jumped up quickly to bow.

"There is the skycaptain!" She said coming over to them. "I was sure you had enough sense never to come back here again." She sounded tired, but she smiled.

Tariq bowed again. "I am afraid need drives us."

"Well, you must be desperate indeed to come back here again. I am pleased to see you, of course, because of what you did for my Quitz." She turned to the man who had brought them there. "But I would like some more warning when we are hosting guests."

"Don't be mad like that, my star," Quitz said, taking her hand. "I didn't believe he would actually come until he showed up. He only sent me a message yesterday. I didn't want to make you fuss for nothing."

"Take the risk next time," she said dryly. She sighed and turned back to the group. "I will have your rooms made up." She shot Quitz a we-will-talk-about-this-later look and left the tent.

Quitz served them tea that Mzia had never had before, and she eyed it with as much suspicion as her host. She didn't like the way his eyes shifted. And when he asked about who they were, Tariq merely said, "They are friends of mine, Quitz. I don't ask questions about your friends."

"No, indeed. Indeed. And I don't mean to sound nosy, but might I know how long your charming visit will last?"

"Too long, I am sure," Tariq said without blinking.

Quitz just laughed and moved on to a story about a horse he was betting on in that week's race. He was sure he would win.

Mzia was extremely tired and wanted nothing more than to go to bed. She supposed she would be sharing the space with all of them, and it made her feel just a bit safer to know she wouldn't be alone.

When Eni finally came back to say their rooms were ready, Lila jumped up so fast she nearly spilled her tea. She and Aasim were right on Eni's heels through the tent flap. Mzia and Tariq were a bit slower, following everyone across the courtyard area and into another tent. There was a good opening to the sky directly above. It was so clear that Mzia stopped dead between the tents in wonder. Tariq ran into her from behind.

"Sorry!" they both said at the same time, then laughed a little.

Tariq glanced up. "It is nice out tonight, isn't it?"

Mzia nodded, and her eyes traced the constellations she knew.

"Look at that," Tariq said with a smile in his voice and pointed. "Isn't that The Aster?"

"Yes." Her heart whispered, *you remembered?*

"The River is harder to see with the dome as it is, but I

er three, just at the edge of the opening, see?" He pointed and Mzia stood on tiptoes.

"Yes, I think you're right." She hugged herself, cold in the night air. But it was so beautiful she would brave the cold for a little while longer.

"The River is my favorite," Tariq said. "Because it was the first one I learned to recognize. I sort of built my knowledge of the star patterns around it." When Mzia was silent, trying not to think about how cold she was, he asked, "Why is the Aster your favorite?"

"Oh, probably because of the r-r-rhyme." Her last word caught in her chattering teeth.

Tariq shrugged off his coat and wrapped it around her shoulders. Its warmth enveloped her like a hug. "Just keeping you alive," he joked lightly. "What rhyme?"

"Oh, you know, the nursery rhyme? About asters?"

He shook his head, so she quoted, "Do asters grow beneath her tower? Does sunlight reach them there? Do asters grow beneath her tower all tangled in her hair?"

Tariq smiled and shrugged. "I never heard that one."

"The girls all skip rope to it. It is very popular, but maybe just in the Utara Kingdom. It's about a princess trapped in a tower."

"What happened to the princess?"

"Obviously a prince rescues her; that's how all the stories go." She shook her head and pulled Tariq's coat closer. "If only real life were so simple." No fairy-tale ending for her; she always understood that.

"Well, it might be easier," Tariq said. "But real life has a beautiful sort of complexity. Like a puzzle you have to solve."

Mzia only nodded. It wasn't that she didn't disagree, but she had lived in the complex all her life, and she could stand to take a little simplicity.

 15

She hugged herself and pretended that she wasn't running for her life. She wanted to hang on to this feeling, this moment, if just for a second longer. Standing under the stars with Tariq, it reminded her of the nights she and Anuva would sneak out to look at the stars long after it was bedtime.

She stayed out there with Tariq long enough that Eni came back out.

"They are beautiful." Eni followed their gaze upward. "Your beds are made. Sweet dreams."

Maybe it was just the beauty of the night, but the two of them stayed out much longer than they probably should have.

CHAPTER 40
THE PAST

THE NEXT MORNING AFTER breakfast, Mzia went back to the sleeping tent. She needed to grab her lighter headscarf to go to the market as well as a pack to hold a few things.

Tariq ducked inside the tent a moment later.

"Hey." She smiled easily at him.

"Hey," he stood glancing around the tent.

Mzia rifled through her stuff. "I don't really trust your friend. He seems . . . off."

"I don't trust him either. He is a horse thief and a swindler."

Mzia paused. "Then why are we here?"

"Because I saved his life back when I was on assignment here, so he owes me. And no one else will give me horses so we can travel covertly."

"Ah."

The tent was low and didn't allow for Tariq to stand without stooping, so he sank down on his knees on the carpet.

"What's wrong?" Mzia asked.

"I just, I just need to know what you were doing in Admiral Grinth's study the night we left."

Mzia blinked. "As I said, saying goodbye to our host."

"Don't lie to me."

"I am not lying!" Mzia shoved her things aside. "I did say goodbye."

"And what else?"

Mzia ran the fabric of the headscarf between her fingers. "I don't see how it matters now," she said stiffly. "We are here now, not there."

"Why are you getting mad at me? I am just trying to keep us alive. And I can't do that if you won't tell me the truth."

"Why do you want to know all of the sudden? You could have asked me last night when we were alone."

He worked his jaw, frustration oozing out of him. "You evading the question just makes me think it is worse than it really is. So just tell me."

"Fine." Mzia crawled over to him and sat so their knees nearly touched. She whispered as loud as she dared, "I left him a vial of my blood."

Tariq frowned. "Why would you do that?"

Mzia blinked. "He never told you? His oldest granddaughter, Ciry, is addicted. Or rather was, by now she should be cured. I didn't tell you because I knew you would say I was being rash and stupid—"

"Because you were! Mzia, you can't cure everyone you come across."

Mzia frowned and looked away. She tied on the lighter headscarf. "You sound like Yulia."

"Well, she was right, wasn't she? I mean, wasn't you curing people why you are in this mess?"

"What? How could you—"

"I overheard some things at the temple. During the war council and after. Things that didn't make a lot of sense at the time. But now I understand. That is how Princess Ezhno found you—the low illness and addiction rates in your town. She will work twice as hard to find us now if she thinks you are curing people who might tell the truth."

"So, you would have let Ciry die?" Mzia hissed, bringing the conversation back to more stable ground.

"It isn't that simple! You have put them all in danger with—"

"No, Tariq, that's the problem with you." She leaned back, snatching up her pack. "There are so few things in my life that are simple. I get that life isn't a fairy tale where the warrior just shows up and beats the dragon. But Tariq, there *are* dragons in our world."

Tariq huffed. "What are you talking about?"

"The sick, the injured, the addicted—they fight dragons much worse than in the stories. And it's not right. It's not . . ." She searched wildly for the right word. "It's not balanced. There are dragons but no brave warriors."

"What does this have to do with—"

"Because it *is* that simple." She slung her pack over her back. "In a world of brokenness and imbalance, this is the one, small, simple thing I can do. I can heal people."

"I am not saying you shouldn't heal."

"That's exactly what you are saying!"

"No." He ran a frustrated hand through his hair. "What I am trying to say is there is a time and a place for that, but you have to weigh your—"

"You don't get it. This isn't a puzzle to be solved, Tariq, because it isn't complicated."

She expected him to bite back but when he didn't, she stood and walked past him out of the tent.

THE MARKET HELD MANY strange and wonderful distractions. Distractions that kept her from dwelling on her spat with Tariq. Wandering after her companions through the stalls, there were things for sale that Mzia had never seen before, from animals to objects. Small rodents and lizards captured from the rocky north country squawked at each passerby, and one peddler boasted he had the best knitting machines. Everything was framed in bright and festive reds, blues, and yellows. Even the skies showed dozens of kites, dancing in the wind above the sand dunes just outside of town. All but the bottommost caps of the dome were spread open, so they had shading from the hot sun but exposed sides to let in any stray wind.

As they went into and out of shops, Mzia found herself waiting outside one tent while Lila and Tariq tried to bargain for some travel gear. They planned to go out further into the desert in a day or so and travel to the coast. Mzia had a hard time believing there was a more secluded spot than this one.

Aasim came out to join her, shaking his head. "They will never talk the man down, but Lila refuses to give up."

Mzia nodded. "She doesn't like to lose."

"Nope."

A silence stretched between them.

Mzia looked back into the tent and saw Lila put her hands on her hips, determination in her eyes. Mzia smiled a little at the sight and turned back to Aasim, who was frowning at her.

"What?" she asked, touching her headscarf self-consciously.

Aasim squinted out into the bright sunlight, ignoring the goggles on his forehead. "Can I ask you a question, healer?"

Mzia nodded slowly. He could ask anything. That didn't mean she could or would give an answer.

"You know Tariq is just trying to protect you, right?"

Mzia glanced about to be sure nobody was listening, but those on the street were all preoccupied with their own affairs. It was shamelessly hot even with the shade of the dome.

She wiped her brow. It irked her that Tariq already filled Aasim in on the disagreement they had had a mere half hour ago. She straightened her goggles. "Of course I know that."

"Then stop keeping secrets from him, from all of us. Lila does that. Now you."

Mzia felt suddenly exposed by his words. This rather stoic man had an air of knowing about him, like he saw things others didn't.

"Stop being selfish," he went on. "You are still hiding things. I know it and so does Tariq."

"You know nothing," Mzia said, her throat tight. This damn heat.

"He is trying to protect you. And you're acting like . . . like . . ." He wiped sweat from his face. "Like, I don't know, you are the one doing the protecting?"

Mzia tried to deny it, but words refused to come out.

Aasim's posture changed. He uncrossed his arms and cocked his head. "Am I right?"

"No," she answered, but she couldn't make it sound convincing.

"There is someone else? Someone *you* are protecting?"

She wished the ground would swallow her up. Stupid. How could she be so stupid? It was this Starbreather cursed heat. "Please don't say anything. I would die if . . . if . . ."

At that moment, Lila stepped out of the tent. But she didn't hear Mzia's words because she was saying something to her brother. She held up her purchase to Mzia and beamed proudly. "Look what I got for half his asking price!"

Mzia nodded and forced a smile. She looked nervously at Aasim, whose only comment to Lila was that it would do fine for the journey. Ever practical. Mzia caught Aasim's eye, and he frowned. He looked at Lila, who was prattling on and on about what she would be able to fit in the new bag and how much better it would be than her older one. An odd look passed over his face then he said, "I won't."

Lila paused. "What?"

Tariq came out of the tent and Aasim asked, "Where to next?"

Mzia could have melted with relief. Or just melted. She was dehydrated. She took a long swig of water and followed after the others to the next stall. She kept one eye on Aasim as he bought and bargained for goods with the others. Nothing about him changed. He was his normal, unreadable self. That was a big difference between him and Tairq. Tariq always appeared to be driven to a certain appearance, carefully and proudly built over the years while Aasim was just at default mode all the time—what you saw was what you got. Few things would give him pause. He was the opposite of Lila in many ways and that must have been why Tariq had hired Aasim.

CHAPTER 41
BLOOD ON THE SAND

LILA KNEW SOMETHING WAS up with Mzia, as she was more silent than usual. Aasim had said something to the healer, and he was not giving any hints as to what it was. He had the annoying knack for moving on from things once they were said instead of dwelling on them for days like a normal person.

She, however, had other concerns as Tariq was being his vexingly efficient self and insisted that they split up to buy the rest of the supplies.

"Tell nobody who you are," he instructed as if she didn't know.

Lila rolled her eyes and grabbed Aasim's arm to drag him over to a stall with some sweet-smelling jelly.

"That's not on the list," Aasim said, as Lila bought them each one.

She handed him a jelly and plastered on a smile, "Neither is you being all secretive with the healer, yet here we are."

"Secretive?"

"Don't pretend you don't know. I saw you two talking."

Aasim pulled out his pad, "What's next on the shopping list?"

"Are you ignoring me?"

"Looks like we need one more tent." He squinted up at the market. "This way."

Lila gave his retreating back a rude gesture before following him over to the tent maker's shop. She watched him bargain and let him pay more than she would have for the tent out of spite. He didn't seem to notice his failure and bagged the tent before returning to the list.

Lila scanned the market. There was something off about today. Maybe it was just the heat. Her eyes found Mzia and Tariq a street over between two large tents. Their heads were bent close, both frowning at something on Tariq's pad. They were probably just discussing what to do next, but they were standing awfully close. Especially in this heat.

Her brother would never hear the end of that.

She turned to Aasim. "Look at them! You would think—"

He grabbed her shoulder and violently jerked her back a step. A popping sound echoed across the street.

"What are you—"

Aasim grunted and dropped to his knees.

"Aasim?" Lila knelt beside him as his face drained of color. She searched the market but saw nothing out of place, nothing that would cause this distress.

Aasim placed a hand on his chest where a dark stain was forming. He slumped to the ground.

Lila was frozen, unable to move as the man who had protected her for years reached a bloody hand for her. He had been shot. He had pulled her out of the way. And he had been shot instead. Instead of her. She tried to say something. *Instead of me.* Her throat closed. *Instead of me.* Panic gripped her insides.

One raspy word came from Aasim's lips. "Run."

A SCREAM PIERCED THE afternoon. Tariq and Mzia both turned to look towards the market erupting into chaos.

Tariq knew it was Lila's scream. He just knew. His body was moving before his mind could form a plan. He surged forward, struggled to keep his footing on the loose sand.

Entering the next street, his mind registered several things. First, the panic of people shouting and crying provided a good distraction. Second, military men flooded this street. Third, there was a body, Aasim's body, lying still on the ground before them. A dark stain around him on the sand. Fourth, Lila was being held at gunpoint near the middle of the street, a few stalls away. And finally, Mzia arrived panting beside him just seconds after he came to a stop—she hadn't hesitated to run towards the chaos after him.

It took just three heartbeats for him to assess what was going on and make a decision. There was no reason to kill Aasim, he was just a bodyguard. They hadn't been aiming for him . . . they had been aiming for Lila. And they missed.

Mzia moved, shifting her body to run again, to go out there and expose herself to the soldiers. She was willing to risk it all to save Aasim, a man who, at best, tolerated her.

It is that simple.

To save people. To reach out and help someone in need. Because that was how she saw the world—full of people who needed her.

But Aasim was beyond any help she could give.

Before they could be noticed, Tariq grabbed Mzia's arm and using her forward momentum, pulled her around after him so they tumbled back to the ground between the tents. He landed half on top of her.

"What are you doing?" Mzia hissed, trying to push him off. "Aasim is—"

"Dead," Tariq said with a sick kind of confidence. As he got to his feet, he pulled her up with him. They had to keep moving.

"You there!"

Tariq acted, pulling the small gun he had from its hidden holster against his side. He turned. Instinct and thousands of hours of practice made his aim true. The man was falling to the sand prior to Tariq registering him to be a soldier. Tariq pulled Mzia back across the next street and into a tent.

He dropped Mzia's arm and assessed their surroundings searching around the tent for anything that might help them. It appeared to be a storage area for one of the market stalls.

Mzia pulled her goggles down around her neck, her eyes glazed with shock. She struggled to speak. "Are you sure he is dead?"

"Yes."

"Tariq, I might still—"

"No." Tariq cut her off. "Aasim did his duty; he protected my sister. They won't hurt her, not in public like this, anyway. She is safe for now."

Mzia blinked, stunned at his blunt words.

"Aasim did his duty, now we must do ours. We have to get out of town before they find us. Do you understand?"

Mzia gave a sharp nod then took a gathering breath. Her eyes refocused. Good. She wouldn't fall into hysterics.

She squared her shoulders. "What do you need me to do?"

Tariq began to search the tent. "Keep watch at the door," he told her.

She obeyed, pulling back up her goggles and going to the tent flap.

There were boxes and crates of different things, and he went to the nearest and found some fireworks. He moved on to the next.

"Tell me what you see."

"The soldiers are regrouping. Most of the people have calmed down or left the market."

"They will start searching the tents soon," he said, sifting through a box of wicks. "We won't get out of here during the daylight, but they might find us if we stay until dark." His mind flicked through worst case scenarios.

"Should we try to get back to your, um, friends?"

Tariq laughed bitterly under his breath. "It's likely those friends were the ones who ratted us out. I should have known better than to trust a horse thief." He started shoving some of the random food items he found into his travel bag. They would need everything they could get.

"What are you doing?" she asked.

"Trying to decide if I need anything else before we leave for the ruins at Tashni. That's the only safe place for us now to lie low for a while." He turned to her. "Toss me your bag. And keep an eye on the road!"

She threw over her bag and looked back through the tent flap. "They have restored order. They are putting Aasim on a stretcher. Oh, I see Lila. They are taking her—"

Tariq was at her side in an instant. They watched together through the narrow opening as the soldiers cuffed Lila and forced her to stand and walk away with them. All the soldiers, everyone visible at least, left the market street, marching back toward the direction of the train station.

"They are going?" Mzia asked, just as confused as he was.

"No. They shouldn't. Protocol dictates . . ." When searching for fugitives, one conducted a thorough search of the surrounding area, even if there were no known accomplices. And surely they knew where Lila was, Tariq would be. This didn't make sense. Yet he couldn't deny that the soldiers looked and acted like they had gotten what they had come for. Perhaps because they had failed to kill her, they needed to regroup and consider how else to draw him out? If that was the case, they needed to get out of town as soon as possible.

"Something's wrong," he pronounced. "We need to move."

They walked down the street as if they were not fugitives on the run. As if Aasim wasn't dead and Lila wasn't captured. Tariq saw the hundred ways they could hurt her and pushed it out of his mind. Not now. They had to get out of here. The government might use Lila as leverage to get him to turn in Mzia, but they couldn't do that if they couldn't contact him. If he could get away soon enough, the soldiers couldn't even be sure that Tariq knew about his sister. So that was step one—leave the city.

CHAPTER 42
NIGHTMARES

SAND. THAT WAS ALL there was in the world. Sand. Dune after endless dune. Only the stars kept them company on their march. At first, Mzia had been relieved they made it past the first dune. Only sand meant nobody was following them. The wind that lifted the kites had picked up a bit and their tracks disappeared before the daylight did. But when the sights refused to change and each hill looked just like the last, she started to feel lost.

Once the sun disappeared, things got a little easier. It was so quiet after the bustle of the city and was not like any stillness that she had ever encountered. It was the emptiness that pressed itself upon her the most. The sheer nothingness around them. No animals, no plants, no people. Nothing. At least back in the tent city, there had been people. And back in the mountains, there had been plants and wildlife. The stars told her enough to know they were not walking in circles, but north. They spoke very little and only paused long enough to drink water before moving on.

"Please," Mzia panted, "we've been walking most of the night. Couldn't we stop?"

Tariq paused to check his wrist positioning device. "We are still a ways out. I don't want to be in the open when daylight comes again. They could just fly overhead and see us."

"How much further to these ruins?"

"Another hour." He looked at her, his own weariness showing through the mask of darkness. He was just as tired as she was, maybe more so. And his silence had worried her. He hadn't been afraid to speak these past few days. Maybe because he had a plan. He had known what the next step was. But now? Now Lila was captured and Aasim was dead. And he hadn't spoken a single word about them since fleeing the city.

So she said the only thing she could think of. "Are you all right?"

"No, I'm not," Tariq said tightly. "In case you didn't notice, they just tried to kill my sister. So no, I'm not all right. I haven't been all right for a while now."

"Is she . . . Tariq, will they hurt her?"'

"I don't know!" He rounded on her, his anger flaring across the sand. "I don't know, and that terrifies me, Mzia. She's my sister and I'm supposed to keep her safe and I failed. I failed." He sat down abruptly. Breathing hard, he dug both hands into his hair.

She didn't know what to say. He had every right to be angry. The pain and responsibility of protecting a sibling was one she understood well. Mzia was helpless, so powerless to do anything to protect Anuva when she was so far away. She sank into the sand beside him knowing there was nothing she could say to make it better. Her eyes landed on his hands, the only part he hadn't covered up. They were starting to turn red from the day's sun.

Mzia searched her bag and brought out the medical kit. She found the lotion for burns and opened the container. Without speaking, she reached out and gently tugged one of his hands from his hair. He said nothing as she spread the cooling gel over the back of one hand and then the other. She used her fingertips to massage it in with light strokes, wishing the mind could be so easily cared for as the body. Tariq's hands were those of a soldier—his nails blunt and short, fingertips calloused from years of repeating certain drills. And his hands were strong, like the rest of him. That extended to his mind as well.

She could feel him watching her, and his posture relaxed a bit. She glanced up. In the darkness she could read his face. Just as his hands would heal, so would his mind. But she didn't have a salve to help it along. He would have to do that on his own.

"Thank you," Tariq murmured.

"You're welcome." She closed up the container and put it away.

They sat in silence for a time listening to the wind.

WITH DAYBREAK, TARIQ AND Mzia found themselves on more rocky ground. Here and there, a few palm trees grew between the uneven mounds of sand and hard dirt. A castle from ages past rose up in that place, crumbling down as much as it stood. Walls were only half there in places, and many of the once grand towers had fallen. Tariq only allowed himself a moment to take it all in. The spirits of his ancestors whispered down to him from the stars. This was where he came from and he had never expected to see it in person.

As they entered the main gates, it became clear the damage was not just from age. The front gates had been broken inward from the outside. Parts of the walls were not crumbling but smashed, also from the outside. Statues in the courtyard of long-ago dead queens were purposely defaced and almost no door left on its hinges. The fight the people of this kingdom had put up before joining the empire colored the culture to this day.

Tariq checked an old map before he led Mzia up a set of broken steps, along the top of a wall, and through a few archways. They came to a room with four knee deep square pools, each pouring into the next. An old Pokok tree grew out of the first pool, its roots responsible for drawing the water up from deep in the earth and into the pools. Gnarled branches reached towards the cracks in the ceiling. At the far side of the pool sat a crumbling throne for a dead king. This had been the seat of the kingdom once upon a time.

The room itself was surrounded by archways that led off in every direction. The far side of the room opened out onto the ramparts to the east, and they could see a good section of sky. This was a strategic location to stay the night.

"Can you test the water in pool with the tree?" Tariq asked Mzia.

She nodded, weary. She knelt on the blue and green hexagon tiles and pulled out a testing kit. The four pools had different uses, if his history teacher had told him correctly. The first was probably used for drinking, and perhaps the others for bathing and washing.

The water tested clean, so they set up camp. As the sun rose over the plains to the east, they eventually fell asleep.

"MZIA, WAKE UP!"

Mzia shot up, panting and dripping in sweat. The hot air scorched her lungs as she gasped for clarity, for an anchor to pull herself out of the fog in her mind.

"You were dreaming," Tariq said. "It was just a dream."

Mzia pushed herself to stand and stumbled over to the closest pool. She knelt by the edge and plunged her hands and face into the cool water. It took every ounce of self-control not to pull herself over the lip and immerse herself. As if the water could wash away the emotions and fear as easily as it could the sand and sweat.

She coughed and swallowed wrong, then coughed and swallowed more. At last she turned, trembling, and pulled herself up to sit by the pool and catch her breath. It was a dream. It was just a dream.

Tariq stood pensively a few steps away, hands balled into fists and knuckles white.

"Did I cry out?" her voice croaked.

He nodded then took a few hesitant steps forward to sit slowly down beside her. "I—I was asleep myself or I would have woken you sooner . . . I didn't really understand what I was hearing . . ." He shook his head and rubbed his face. Only then she noticed how pale he looked. He took a deep breath. "Who is Anuva?"

The hot day turned suddenly cold at his question. Had she said her sister's name? Had her weak body given away her own deepest secret? Betrayed her? She licked her lips, "What, exactly did I say?"

Tariq looked down at his hands and frowned, "Why? So you can lie to me again?"

Mzia opened her mouth in protest, but Tariq went on. "Look, I get it. Your whole life has been a secret. The only reason you are alive is because you're good at lying. But I am not stupid, Mzia. I know you are not telling me everything."

Mzia refused to lift her eyes from her lap.

Tariq sighed. "I know you are just trying to protect yourself. But has it ever occurred to you that I am trying to do that as well?"

"That's what Aasim said," Mzia whispered. She finally lifted her head, but she didn't look at him. She looked at the crumbling archways, the dusty afternoon sunlight slanted across the room through cracks in the ceiling, and the meager pile of their belongings against the far wall. She looked at anything but him.

First Yulia, then the Separatists' cook and guard, now

Aasim . . . People who knew the secret died. Who would be next? Lila? Tariq? Anuva? Was Tariq right and she had put the retired admiral Grinth in danger as well?

"Maybe . . ." she said after a pause. "Maybe I am trying to protect you." It was a bit of a stretch. Anuva came first, always. But she didn't want Tariq to die. He had been . . . well, so much more than she could have asked for. "People die around me," she finally got out. "People die and I can't stop it. I can't even . . . Tariq, I don't even get to bury them." She was rambling now and didn't care. "They just die and I have to go . . . on." The ache of everything felt fresh again, like the day she had left her sister alone on the mountain.

She sniffed and wiped her nose with the back of her hand. Tariq stirred and pulled out a handkerchief. How on earth had he managed to keep that clean after all the sand they had trudged through? She blew her nose and smelled the hot air for the first time. It was stifling.

"I need to walk a bit, I think." She rose on shaky legs, and he stood as well.

"Just stay within the castle walls," he cautioned.

CHAPTER 43
GRAVES

TARIQ KICKED A ROCK off the top of the wall and watched the sun, now sinking to the west, lengthen the shadows. He was exhausted and yet sleep was the last thing on his mind. He left the pool room soon after Mzia had with the excuse that he needed to check the perimeter again. He was determined to give the healer space, even if it was infuriating, so he kept out of her way as she wandered down to the main courtyards of what once were grand gardens.

Tariq frowned, thinking back briefly on nearly every interaction he had with the healer. What was it about her that made him lose his sense of . . . control? Was that the right word? Focus? No, that didn't seem right either. He felt compelled to help her, to aid her beyond his sense of duty, his promises. Well, whatever it was, he would need to be careful. This was new territory they were entering now. Having worked for the empire all his life, he understood how thorough they could be at tracking down criminals. And that is what he was now. A criminal. Worse, he was a Marked One who had broken his oaths to serve the emperor and empire with his life. He knew the punishment for such treason.

He let himself think of Lila. They wouldn't hurt her; she was too valuable to kill or send to prison. But they could hurt her in other ways. They could take away what freedom she had earned, force her to work and not see others, not let her go to the parties and plays she loved so much. That might be worse than killing her. He saw her now as he had last seen her, kneeling in Aasim's blood on the city street.

Aasim. The sight of his lifeless body had flashed in and out of his mind the night before as he and Mzia trudged the sand dunes. Another death on his hands. Like that soldier in the market who had spotted them. He didn't regret killing him. Maybe he should have— a quandary for another time. The body count for this rebellion was likely to only rise further.

But for some reason, none of that altered his conviction to help Mzia. Even in the marketplace, when Lila was captured, his first thought had been to keep the healer safe. Was it foolishness or faith to trust he was supposed to do this? The best thing that could become of them was fugitives, forever on the run.

Or was it?

Could they be something more? There were other Marks who had disappeared, others unhappy with the government. This addiction was bad enough, and if the people learned there was a cure. If Mzia could maybe cure someone powerful enough that even the government couldn't hush it up, then just maybe they could gain a foothold.

Tariq remembered things his mother had whispered to him. Old family connections that nobody spoke about. Part of the reason they came here in the first place was because he knew it so well. The rebellion still stirred in the minds of the people who lived in this kingdom. The scenarios and possible outcomes flicked through his mind. The best case, the worst case, the most likely. Like a million threads connected to the same knot, Tariq couldn't sort them out. He would pull at one idea only to find himself chasing another. And at the center of it all—Mzia. Mzia and her world-changing blood.

Starbreather, what was he doing? He was tired, that's all.

He found he had walked all the way to the northwest corner of the wall where it crumbled down to the stony earth. The last of the sun vanished and he sat down, looking across the empty land.

A scraping sound caught his attention in the twilight. Turning back to the courtyard, he saw Mzia moving among the rubble across from a long dry fountain. She pushed a rock the size of her head along the ground to another rock about the same size. He got up and walked back along the wall to get a better look.

Oblivious to his presence, Mzia went to collect a third rock from the crumbling part of the wall and then another. The pile she was making was in an empty space of the courtyard.

Tariq climbed down from the wall with the aid of a broken statue, and walked over closer, still at a loss as to what she was doing. Mzia turned from the wall and gasped, dropping several smaller stones at the sight of him.

"Tariq! You startled me!" She picked up the stones. "I was just . . . I was . . ."

In the dim light, he could see that she had drawn in the packed earth a wide circle around her growing pile of stones. A common practice for . . . "You are making a grave site?"

She nodded, coming forward to set her stones on the pile. At this rate it would take her all night. *I don't even get to bury them.*

"Who's it for?"

She sniffed, "For Yulia and I thought, maybe, for Aasim?" She looked up at him and he realized she wanted his consent.

"Let me help you with that," he said, going to the wall.

237

THEY SPOKE VERY LITTLE and only when necessary. Tariq made it look easy to pick up some stones much too heavy for Mzia, and she contented herself with filling in all the gaps with smaller ones. She was glad for the work. Keeping her hands busy kept her mind from spiraling. From thinking about what they were doing or who they were doing it for.

Even with Tariq's help, the task took most of the night. Without speaking, they mutually decided to fill out the whole circle around the two mounds with smaller stones. It was something done at more elaborate old mounds. And maybe she didn't want the task to end because she didn't know what to do next. They briefly paused only a few times to drink and once to eat, even though Mzia wasn't hungry.

But the task did end somewhere in the early hours before dawn, and they stood, side by side as the graves lay side by side. She should say something, honor Yulia and the life she had lived. She should thank the Starbreather for Yulia and mention her many accomplishments. Her throat closed. She could hardly breathe, let alone speak.

She peered up at Tariq, who wiped a dirty arm across his already dirty forehead. He had ditched his shirt and jacket long ago, for the night was still warm. Somehow, he sensed her distress because he said, "My mother is from this kingdom. I know the rites for here . . . if you would like?"

She managed a nod and Tariq whispered the chant, the prayers to carry the spirit to the stars where it would rejoin the Starbreather. His voice was low and dry. Mzia listened in silence, not knowing the dialect but hearing the sad tone of the words. She hugged herself as her body shook with silent sobs. Covered in sweat and dirt, she forced herself to stand, to stay and listen to the rites when she wanted to run away into the night and never be seen again.

When Tariq fell silent, Mzia made herself do the next thing.

Almost as if she was watching someone else perform the movements, she pulled off her shoes and walked barefoot across the rocky circle to the first grave. She knelt and pressed her forehead to the mound of rocks that was for Yulia. After several failed attempts she rasped out, "The Starbreather has guided you on the paths you needed to take." Her tears splashed down. "And he has lit your way to the end." She kissed the stones and after a few gasping breaths, she forced herself to her feet.

She knelt again and said the words at Aasim's grave but felt even less like herself. By the time she stood again and faced Tariq, her face was dry and she hobbled over the stones back to him. She was empty now. There was nothing left in her to come out.

They stood a long while before Tariq said, "We should go."

Mzia shook her head.

"You need rest."

"Just a little while longer?" she begged. She couldn't go, not yet. To walk away would be to make it final. "Tell me more about how you know the rites of this kingdom."

Tariq cleared his throat. "Only if you sit down here with me."

Mzia hesitated only a moment before agreeing. Her knees were about to give out anyway. Once they were settled, sitting cross-legged before the circle, he spoke. "My mother is related to the kings that used to rule this kingdom, before the continent united. But, as you probably know, all direct lines were cut off when this was the one kingdom that refused to join the others to form the empire. Thankfully, my mother's grandmother was only a female cousin and the heir must pass through a male line. But my great grandmother grew up here." He gestured at the crumbling palace walls. "She used to tell my mother stories about this place, and my mother told them to me. If the other kingdoms hadn't united and this one overrun, I might have grown up here as well."

Mzia studied his face if only not to look at the stones. There was a touch of sadness there. For the life that could have been. Mzia could see a young Tariq brought up like a prince and not a soldier. One who never had to kill.

He leaned forward, stretching his neck and rounding his shoulders. Her eyes drifted to the tattoos and scars on his back. He could have been someone who was never hurt like that.

Tariq caught her eye. "I promised to tell you how I got those scars, didn't I?"

Mzia nodded. If he kept talking, she didn't have to.

"Lila and I went through training together to become Marked Ones. Combat training is probably the best term for what we did, but it is intense and very difficult, physically and emotionally." He sighed. "I don't mean to sound conceited, but I worked hard and eventually excelled in nearly every skill we were tested in. Lila would tell you I was good at everything, but nobody is good at everything." The lightness in his voice when he spoke of his sister vanished when he said, "But Lila . . . struggled. She was good at computers and not much else. It became a sort of hobby, late at night, to see what she could hack into."

A hardness entered his eyes as he went on. "She decided to push boundaries, like she still does, and she hacked into the security mainframe of the palace. Just to set a silly prank with the lights, but it set the empire on high alert. She wasn't as good at covering her tracks back then, so they traced it to our training camp. I knew it was only a matter of time before they figured out who it was, and there was talk of . . . expulsion. Do you know what that means for a Mark?"

Mzia shook her head.

"That means you disappear and are never seen again. They take our loyalty very seriously because if we are not useful to our emperor, we are nothing."

"How old were you?" Mzia dared interrupt.

"We were thirteen," he said bitterly. "She was *thirteen*, and she was about to die. So I spent all night making a plan. I was at a loss at first, but then the next day I went to our instructors and told them I had done it. That I had encouraged Lila to teach me some things and that I had broken in using her algorithms. I could tell my instructors didn't quite believe me seeing as I hadn't really done anything like that before. But the higher ups were looking for someone to blame. My instructors negotiated on my behalf. They said it was my one little rebellion, my one little dark spot in an otherwise bright future. So instead of an expulsion, they agreed to 30 lashes. They wouldn't have been so kind to Lila because her record was far from spotless."

Mzia's stomach dropped. She didn't know what to say. All at once the night felt cold, and even the stars above them, which she had always found comforting, were frozen and distant.

The only thing not distant in that moment, the only thing real, was Tariq. Tariq who would do anything for his sister. Tariq who might just understand her need to get back to Anuva, *her* sister.

Yulia, who would always advise caution, would tell her to say nothing. People couldn't hurt you if they didn't know your secrets. That was how they had survived—secrets.

But it was also how Yulia had died.

"Hey," Tariq said, startling her from her reverie. "Should we go back now?"

Mzia shook her head. There was one last thing she had to leave here. She took a steadying breath.

"She's my sister."

"What?"

Mzia looked at him, determined. "Anuva. The name I called out in my sleep. She's my adopted sister. She's an Iaomai Child like me. Yulia found her as an infant, eleven winters ago. We have a safe house in the woods. That's where I was taking her, the night you kidnapped me." She dusted her hands. "I didn't tell you because my sister is my life. I do this for her, all of it. She hasn't come out yet, into society. We were waiting, until she was old enough to keep our secret, like Yulia did with me. I was hoping I would fix things before then. So that she would never have to face the world as I have . . . until this moment I was the only living soul that knew she existed."

Tariq shook his head. "All this time . . . there is another?"

"I need your help. I need you to help me get back to her."

"Of course," he said, looking more awake. "She shouldn't be left alone. The empire may find her." He stood, clearly trying to think through all the new possibilities. "We can't go right away. We don't have enough supplies to make it. But if we get in touch with my family's contacts . . ." He looked down at her. "I can't make any promises at this point, but as soon as we are able, we will go after her."

Mzia could have melted in relief. "Really?"

"Of course. She is your sister. Did you expect me to say *no*?"

"I don't know what to expect anymore." She was finally able to stand. That empty place inside her, an ache that wouldn't soon go away, still existed. Yet she felt lighter. And she was ready at last to walk away from the graveside.

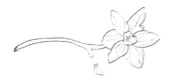

CHAPTER 44
A DANCE

THEY RETURNED TO THE pool room and began to wash the dirt and sand from their arms and legs. The night was already cold, and so was the water, or they would have bathed fully. The night slipped lazily into day, the eastern sky brightening as they finished cleaning up.

"I'll take the first watch." Tariq sat down to organize his pack.

"You need rest," Mzia protested. "You've been working all night."

He laughed a little.

"What?" she asked.

"Don't you remember? I said something like that to you, right after the crash."

"That feels so long ago."

He looked up at her, a searching look she hadn't seen him use before. "At least you talk back to me now, most of the time."

She ducked her head and spread out her blanket.

"Oh sure, prove me wrong," he teased, his mood shifted, possibly from the exhaustion. "I will learn all your secrets one day, healer. Mark my words."

She should have said nothing. She should have just nodded and gone to sleep. But her exhaustion told her to say, "I don't know about that."

"Don't you?" He stretched. "Somehow, I got you to tell me deep dark secrets, didn't I? How many more could you possibly have?"

She shook her head and looked up at him. "No more sad, dark secrets. You know all of those."

"Do I?" His tone turned soft. He leaned back on his elbows, the picture of ease. "So, tell me a happy secret then. I haven't heard enough of those."

Mzia squinted at the brightening sky. "Maybe later."

"Oh no, you are not getting off that easy. Come on. We've talked and done so many sad things, I want to hear something good."

Mzia considered him for a moment. "I can dance."

"What?" He sat up.

"I can dance," she repeated, smoothing out her blanket.

"What kind of dancing?"

"Oh, the kind they always do at the parties for the Solstice. And I am not talking about the easy group dancing, either. The difficult dances that they do in pairs? That kind."

"Where did you learn?"

"There isn't a lot to do in a mountain village," she said. "We had a retired dance instructor settle down there because that is where his family was from. But after the first solstice, when he saw that very few knew the dances, he set up a school to teach us. He taught us all the ones from our kingdom and the ones they always do in the capital." Mzia smiled at the adolescent memory. "I danced all night on the shortest night of the year. Our instructor told us that in the Alang Kingdom, people believe that dancing through the solstice night would please the Starbreather and bring good fortune. Is that true?"

"That's what my mother always told me."

"Yulia used to say I was the best dancer, but—" Mzia's smile slipped. "I think she was a little biased."

Tariq got to his feet and walked several steps towards the fountain. He turned back to her and held out a hand. "Prove it."

"What?"

"Prove you can dance."

"Tariq." She rubbed her face. "We have been building graves all night."

"What? Are you afraid I'll find out you're not that good of a dancer?"

She crossed her arms. "Oh, and you are, I suppose?"

He gave a modest bow. "I guess there is only one way for you to find out." He kept his hand held out to her, a twinkle in his eye.

She should say no, but . . .

She got up and walked over to him, both of them barefoot from washing. The sun was coming in through the open archways to the east, casting long shadows across the floor. Mzia took his hand and they bowed to each other.

"Shall we start with the Sun Greeting?" Tariq asked, naming one of the more popular solstice dances.

"Well, then you had better start," she said, for those of higher rank always led the dance.

The smile he gave her should have been her first clue that she had met her match. For the next few minutes, she was caught up in the pattern. First spinning, then stepping, then swaying to music they only heard in their heads. The Sun Greeting was a dance to mimic the rising sun. It started with small movements. The pair held hands and did small sways and steps that mirrored one's partner. As the dance progressed, the motions became larger. Elegant spins and sweeps of the arms to skips and jumps across the room.

Mzia blocked out everything else. She blocked out the death, the secrets she had spilled, the secrets she had learned. The past few weeks vanished in the movements. Tariq was an excellent dancer. He kept the rhythm with her, never missing his cue. His steps were sure and his movements confident, much like everything else he did in life. And for a few minutes they were not a skycaptain-prince and an Iaomai Child-healer; they were just two people dancing with the rising sun.

When the dance ended, they collapsed down at the edge of the pools, completely out of breath.

"So, you can dance," he said.

"You thought I would lie?" Mzia said in mock offense.

"No, not about this." He gave her that quizzical look again. "You never cease to amaze me, healer."

Mzia reached up to adjust her goggles and headscarf only to remember she wasn't wearing them. She felt oddly exposed without them. Especially around Tariq.

Tariq stood with a groan. He rolled his shoulders and winced. "Okay, I have learned my lesson—don't challenge you. I will be paying for this dance later I think." He walked over and offered her a hand up.

She took it, but as she stood, she tripped and stumbled a bit.

"Oh, so now you misstep," he teased, righting her on her feet, hands on her waist. "Maybe you are not such a great dancer."

She looked up to throw a retort but found him so close. Her throat closed and she couldn't speak. What was she doing? She wanted to look into his dark eyes until she was lost in their depths. But she had no right. No right to ask any more of him.

"Mzia?" His voice was soft. "Why did you tell me about your sister?"

Mzia tore her eyes away. "I don't really know . . . I guess when you told me what you did for your sister, I thought, if you could do something like that, then maybe." She swallowed. "Maybe if you kept secrets that dark you could be trusted with mine."

"Oh, Mzia."

The way he said her name made her heart leap. She wanted to look at him. But they were running for their lives, basically lost in a desert. And she had Anuva to think about. She didn't want to add another complication to the pile that was already swallowing them whole. She couldn't deal with the reason her heart was tripping over itself worse than her feet had.

So, she didn't listen to her exhausted brain. She gently pushed his hands away and stepped back. "I am tired," she declared like this was new information. "We should go to sleep."

"Yes," he agreed, looking away from her to the west. "I'll just, um, walk the perimeter once. You get some rest." He turned and left the room.

CHAPTER 45
A CHANGE IN THE WIND

NEITHER OF THEM SPOKE much the next day. Especially not about their dance or the secrets they had told each other. Maybe Tariq came to the same conclusion that she had—that now was no time to bring up new feelings.

Not that Tariq had any feelings for her beyond friendship. She had most definitely imagined or projected onto him the emotions she felt. The very idea was so absurd. She had only known him for a span of days. And he had lived a whole life she knew next to nothing about. He had been willing to send her to her death less than a moon cycle ago. She was lucky to be able to call him a friend.

Tariq spent his time pouring over maps and making plans that Mzia only half understood. There were so many pieces and so much to decide, such as who they might contact next. He seemed confident that some of his mother's distant relatives would take them in without question. Mzia sensed his hesitancy to involve more people, however. She understood that perhaps better than most. Anyone they brought into this was in danger of losing their lives or much worse.

On the day after the morning of their dance, Tariq told her they would move out soon. Their food was getting low and someone might chance upon them, accidentally or not.

Mzia sat on the lip of the fourth pool with her feet in the water washing all their clothes, bags, and blankets in preparation for the move. She wanted to take as little of the desert with her as possible. Barefoot and in only a single layer of dress, she scrubbed a dark stain from Tariq's jacket with a powdered soap. The memory of doing just this thing right after the skyship crash hit her so hard she dropped his jacket back into the pool with a splash.

"You okay?" Tariq asked, looking up from his handpad.

Mzia shook her head and retrieved the jacket. "I'm fine. I just . . . remembered the last time I washed your jacket."

"Oh. Well, I can do that if you don't—"

"That isn't what I meant," she said standing up inside the pool and shaking the extra water from his jacket. "I was just thinking . . ." She frowned.

"Tell me," Tariq prompted gently.

"Just thinking about how I didn't even know your name then."

"Well," Tariq said a little ruefully, "you may come to regret knowing it. If Lila is to be believed, I complicate other's lives, especially hers."

Mzia wanted to laugh. Before she could, Tariq's entire posture changed. He cocked his head to one side and his eyes darted to the far side of the room.

"What is—"

Tariq raised his pistol and shot at a space between the doorways. With a grunt, a soldier fell forward into the light. A soldier in black.

"Get down!" Tariq shouted, sending off three more shots. Rocks splintered and shouts echoed as soldiers materialized out of the shadows.

Mzia plunged most of the way into the pool and Tariq ducked into a doorway for cover. She couldn't see much over the rim of the pool and wished she had a weapon, any weapon that she might at least defend herself.

To her right a soldier ran at the pool. Mzia froze as he pointed his weapon at her—only to be shot himself and fall face first, dead before his body hit the water. Crimson blood seeped out from his body.

Another soldier ran at the pool. And Tariq must have been otherwise engaged for he was able to leap over the side and land beside her, unharmed. Mzia seized the powdered soap and flung it in his eyes. He cried out and Mzia stood up only long enough to bring his head down onto her knee. More blood. He wasn't dead but floundered in the water, unable to stop Mzia from taking his weapon.

Her hands shook, and she fired at the next blur that appeared above the lip. It took three shots to hit the soldier, who crashed to the floor with a sickening thud. She had done that. She couldn't know for sure she had killed him, but . . . not knowing was almost worse. The gun jammed. She tossed it away in a panic.

Tariq's voice rose above the fray. "Call them off, princess! How many more of your men must die? Call them off and we can talk."

The firing ceased. "What is there to talk about?" Ezhno's voice echoed off the stone. "It's only a matter of time."

"We both know explaining my death to the grand prince is not a conversation you want to have. I am worth more alive to you than dead."

She scoffed. "You are considered a traitor now. Your life is worth nothing."

"I have something you want."

"And what is that?"

"Call off your men and I will tell you."

Several moments of silence passed and then a scuffling of

retreating feet. The man whose nose she had broken even shuffled out of the pool and out of the room. When it was once again quiet, Mzia dared lift her head above the lip of the pool. She could see Tariq, crouching in a dark archway that led to nowhere. He was trapped. She could also see Ezhno, several arches away, alone. Only the dead would be privy to the next conversation.

"Go on now, Skycaptain," Ezhno said. "Tell me what it is you have that I want."

"You want power, and I can give it to you. I have the ear of the prince; he will listen to me. I will align myself with you and feed you all his secrets. But you have to let Mzia go."

Ezhno laughed, "How simple you must think me. As if I would ever let my wonderful prize go."

"Then why did you bother to speak to me if you have no intention of bargaining?"

"Because." A sinister smile colored her voice. "I'm here to tell you what happened to your sister."

Tariq's breath hitched. "Nothing happened to her. She was taken in broad daylight in front of dozens of witnesses."

"You so sure about that, Marked One? I mean, that was before you all became so infamous. Could anyone there really have known or bothered to learn who she was? Why I might even say—"

"Enough mind games," Tariq cut her off. "What do you want?"

"Oh, so there is a brain up there under all that raging testosterone. Maybe you will listen because this is how the next few minutes are going to go down. You will put down your weapon or my men will *persuade* you to do so, then you two will come with me. The Iaomai Child will return to the lab Yulia stole her from all those years ago and you, Tariq, will get a front row seat to watch me end what's left of your sister."

Mzia wanted to say something, to offer him comfort. Yet there was none to be found.

Ezhno went on, "Then you will live what is left of your short life in the mines of the south and Lady Ishtar will learn nothing except that her children died in disgrace. What a terrible disappointment you both turned out to be. I doubt the emperor will show her favor ever again."

Tariq glanced over at Mzia then away again. He opened his mouth and then shut it.

"What's this? No clever retort? Have I finally broken the proud skycaptain?"

"Leave him." Mzia surprised herself. She stood slowly up out of the pool. "I am the one you really want." She looked at Tariq. She had lied when she said he knew all her dark secrets. "I am the reason your son is dead, so leave Tariq be. I will go with you without a fight if you let him go. Nobody else needs to die."

"Stupid girl!" Ezhno raged. She nearly stepped out from her cover and only checked herself at the last possible second. "You think this is just about revenge on you? This is so much bigger than both of you. And if you are unlucky enough, you might live long enough to learn why."

Tariq looked at Mzia. He understood too. There was no happy ending, not to this story. Not even the bards of old could twist this tale into something good. His eyes took on a determined set. A shift—as some realization snapped into place. Before she could ask what his plan was, he looked back towards where Ezhno hid and said, "What if I told you there is another Iaomai Child?"

Mzia felt her world drop away. He wouldn't.

Ezhno cocked her head. "I'm listening."

"There is another, and I know where she is."

"Tariq . . ." Mzia could barely hear her own voice.

But he ignored her and went on. "And she isn't an infant, she's old enough to cause all this trouble for you and your emperor all over again."

"Tariq—"

Ezhno cocked her head. "Tell me where she is and I might let your sister live."

"I'm not stupid." Tariq refused to look at Mzia. "I know this information is the only thing keeping us alive. So this is what's gonna happen: you will take me to town where I will contact Prince Orinth and my mother. I will feed each of them any story you want, probably about how Mzia died here in the desert. How I was coerced, threatened, into coming with her, helping her. I don't know, you make up the details how you want. Once they all know that Lila and I are alive and well, then I will reveal the location of the Iaomai Child."

Ezhno turned to Mzia, "Maybe I will just go looking on my own." Mzia knew with horrifying certainty that if Princess Ezhno went looking, she would find Anuva. How could Tariq do this to her?

"You could do that," Tariq said. "But that's a pretty big risk to take to have to do this all over again in a few years. Only then, you may not be able to stop the story from spreading. I don't think the emperor would look kindly on you for ignoring that. Who knows who the Iaomai Child will tell before you find her? Plus, you won't have me to cover for you. And as you know, the prince trusts me."

Princess Ezhno smiled again. "I underestimated you, Skycaptain. You have offered me something I didn't even know I wanted. Perhaps keeping you alive will be more beneficial to me than ending you."

"Perhaps we are better matched than you thought," Tariq said tightly.

"Perhaps. You have a deal."

Tariq stood and threw his gun down onto the floor. He refused to look at Mzia as he came out into the room. Mzia couldn't think, couldn't force any words out as the soldiers swarmed the room again.

And just like that, it was over.

CHAPTER 46
SACRIFICE

MZIA COULDN'T DECIDE WHAT was worse. The fact that Tariq wouldn't speak or look at her, or that they didn't even bother to tie her up. They didn't bind her hands or lock her in a room. They knew she wasn't going anywhere—that Tariq had broken her with his words. The men on the small skyship had her sit in the general seating area along one wall. The craft, which had landed just out of sight from the ruin, was light and swift. They were out of the desert and into the sky before Mzia could adjust her mind to the deal that was struck.

How had things gone so terribly wrong? How had the world shifted so quickly? The one and only thing she had been living for in this world was given up. It was only a matter of time. Only a matter of time before her sister ended up in the same place she was.

Something splashed onto her hands—tears. She quickly ducked her head and wiped them with her sleeve.

Princess Ezhno came up to her, pad in hand. Mzia didn't meet her eye.

"I need you to see that I am a woman of my word," the princess said and placed the pad in her lap. On the screen was a live broadcast. It proclaimed that Tariq and Lila had been found, kidnapped by the Separatists. They were alive and well, clear of any wrongdoing. No word about an Iaomai Child. As if Mzia never existed.

"I wanted you to see that." The princess took the pad back. "Because that was a decision I made a mere hour ago. My decision to repay Yulia for what she did to me was made twenty years ago. I will leave you to consider how well I will keep that."

So that was it then. In the space of an hour, she had been wiped from the empire. All that she had done, could have done, would fade into history. And sooner rather than later, if the empire had anything to do with it, history would become myth. And she would disappear altogether. Maybe even Tariq would forget these brief few weeks of his life.

Mzia, on the other hand, would be cursed to remember every detail.

Starbreather, save me. What do I do now? She fought back angry tears. *I followed what I thought you wanted. I saved him and this is what it got me. Is this really what you intended for me all along?* She had to keep it together. Yulia wouldn't want her to despair.

That's what she kept telling herself when the skyship landed. When they ushered her out onto the landing pad of a hospital building in the capital city. When they brought her up to the highest room in the tower. But when the door shut behind them, and she knew she would never again leave that floor, she quit telling herself anything. Because nothing mattered anymore.

LILA WAS MORE THAN a little surprised when Tariq showed up

at the detention facility to bail her out. She had expected to stay there much longer, or to have their mother come with some sob story about how Tariq was missing or dead.

Aasim's death had made Lila lose her mind for a few days. When Tariq met her at the front desk and gave her a hug, she didn't even know what day it was.

"How long was I here?" she asked as they got into a train headed towards the capital city.

"Three days," Tariq said without looking at her. The train took off, their cabin empty of other passengers. He did not appear to want to talk any more for the ride when he suddenly shook himself a little and asked, "How are you doing?"

"Just dandy," she said flatly.

"They treated you okay?"

Lila crossed her arms. "Yes, no need to worry about me, brother dearest. I'm sure I will have a new bodyguard the moment we get back. You'll probably get one now, too."

He made a noncommittal sound.

She adjusted herself in the seat. "What does Mother know?"

"Only what they want her to." He leveled a look at Lila. "And it stays that way."

"I see." She could feel the walls closing in, despite being set free. "And just what is that?"

Tariq sighed. "That Mzia double crossed us in the desert. More Separatists came to her aid. We were held hostage until Princess Ezhno came to rescue us. Mzia was killed in the chaos."

"Is she really—"

"Not when I last saw her." He rubbed the side of his leg.

"So, what actually happened?"

He frowned and looked back out the window.

She crossed her arms. "Fine, I will guess."

"Lila—"

"There was an epic battle where the two of you fought them off with only sand and—"

"No. Now would you—"

"You just woke up one day and decided it would be better if she just ended all this with—"

"Lila—"

"She fell madly in love with you and couldn't stand what she was doing to you so she decided—"

"Enough!" He stood up, startling her. "Enough of your games! Lila, do you have any idea how much trouble we should be in right now? I should be slated for hard labor in the mines of the south and you should be dead."

Lila tipped her head to one side. "And yet . . . we're not?"

Tariq slumped down in his chair again. "No, we're not." He leaned his head back and closed his eyes. "But right now I . . . almost wish I was."

PART THREE

LIGHT

CHAPTER 47
NUMBER EIGHT

THEY STRIPPED MZIA of everything. First, her clothing. She was given a shapeless hospital gown that was easy to take on and off. Second, her hair. It was cut just above the shoulder. Apparently, it would get in the way of some of the procedures. Third, her name. They didn't even call her *healer* or *Iaomai Child*. She was assigned a number. Eight. She was number eight. A number Mzia would come to learn coordinated with the number of times they thought they had found her but it turned out to be a false rumor.

She was also assigned not a room, but an entire floor. The highest floor in the tallest hospital tower. But there would be no daring escapes from this tower. No act of bravery, heroism, or stupidity would see her leaving there alive. It might be years, but eventually they would find another and she would lose her usefulness. And so, from the first hour there, it became a countdown.

Mzia noticed things passively as the hours slipped into days. There were twelve rooms on this floor spiraling out from a center station. Three doctors that worked in shifts with Ezhno. One man and two women and never more than two on the floor at a time. There was only one exit, a door with a fingerprint lock. They didn't mind running tests at any time of the day or night. They didn't really care which of the twelve rooms she slept in. But sleep was not offered here and most of the time she merely snatched an hour here or there between tests. More often than not she was glad the pain would cause her to faint for it gave her longer periods of rest. If they wanted her to move, she always knew.

There were other things she noticed too, things they didn't want her to notice. They never spoke to her except to give her orders. Sit here. Lift that arm. They didn't look her in the eye. Not even when she stared them down as they took blood. When they poked and prodded and pierced. They wouldn't look at her because she wasn't human any more. She had never been human to them, just a test subject, an animal to be experimented on. Or worse still she wasn't even that, she was just a number. Number eight.

Sometimes she wondered how old the other Iaomai Children were when they were brought to the lab. Yulia had told her none had survived more than a few years. But Mzia had spent time with small children in the clinic. They felt pain and had emotions. They knew when a person didn't like them and when something bad might happen. Did they live long enough to understand what they were? What they could be? Did they ever know someone had loved them, or had they been given up the moment they were born, lambs to the slaughter?

Had someone ever held them and soothed them back to sleep the way Yulia had done for Mzia and Anuva? Were they given names before they were turned into numbers? Were their bodies given back to their mothers or just buried in an unmarked grave? Did their fathers still weep for them?

Mzia wondered about these things because it was easier than thinking about the *now*. It was easier than wondering how many times they might draw blood from her. How many more days she had left. How much longer it would be until whatever painful experiment they were doing on her back was over. Easier than counting how many times she lost consciousness.

Wondering about the ones that came before her was painful, yes. But not as painful as the *now*.

The only thing that disrupted the routine was when Ezhno came to visit one afternoon. Mzia was strapped to an examination table as they ran tests on a variety of poisons. Some had made her violently ill while others had no effect. Currently her skin burned with a rash.

Ezhno watched with a slight smile as Mzia fought the latest round of poison. She said nothing at first, studying Mzia's face. Then she pulled something out of her pocket. A white stone star dangled from a woven chain.

"Recognize this?" Ezhno let it swing and catch the light.

Mzia failed to let the sight of her sister's necklace not touch her dying heart. She closed her eyes and turned her head away.

Ezhno laughed. "It was so easy to find her once the skycaptain told me where to look. She came with us willingly, thinking we were there to help her."

Mzia forced herself to look back at the pendant. The cord that it hung by she had braided for Anuva.

"Take a good long look, Iaomai Child. This is all you will ever see of your sister."

Ezhno set the pendant down casually on a counter, a reminder to torture Mzia each time she saw it. The princess looked at the screens that held all the data from the latest poison tests. "I must admit," Ezhno said. "I was upset that I had to bargain with the skycaptain, but to have not one but two of you now at my disposal? Well . . . do thank him for me when you see him in the next life."

And she left. As Mzia watched her disappear around the

doorway, something broke. A crack formed in her soul and ripped her open wide. A flood of emotions she had refused to feel spilled forth. Her mind sharpened to a focus she hadn't allowed in weeks. The pain, the anger, the betrayal all fueled the fire until it threatened to consume her whole.

And as she gazed inward at the flame she had created, she knew that she had to get out of here, dead or alive. And for Anuva's sake, she would try to make it out alive.

CHAPTER 48
ONE MORE LIE

TARIQ CALMED HIS NERVES by tugging down the front of his uniform. A mixture of emotions had washed over him when he had donned it that morning, summoned to go before the grand prince. Tariq rather liked his older half-brother. At least he had. Before.

Before the lie.

His uniforms had been waiting for him back in his apartment, as if the last few weeks hadn't even happened. His mother knew there was more to the story, more details of what happened in the desert that he wouldn't tell anyone, but she also knew better than to ask. He was officially on leave after the trauma of the skyship crash and all that came after, but he would be called up again for duty soon enough.

Apparently soon enough had come.

The uniform felt ill fitting, somehow too tight and too loose at the same time. He tugged at the hem of the jacket again and waited.

The doors to the prince's chambers opened and his personal guard said, "You can go in now, skycaptain."

He saluted and entered the vast chambers. In the back right side of the round room sat a bed with so many blankets draping far over the edge that a whole world might have been hiding underneath. To the left was a seating area with several sofas and large armchairs and tea tables.

Prince Orinth sat in one of these chairs, clothed in a red velvet robe. He motioned for Tariq to come forward. Tariq moved to a respectable distance and saluted, hand to fist, then bowed.

"Why so formal?" the prince asked easily. "Have we been apart so long you must greet me like the other soldiers do?"

"I only wish to show my respect." A respect he no longer felt.

"And your gratitude, I presume. Sit." He waved at the sofa to his left.

Tariq didn't hesitate to obey. He could follow orders. He knew how to do that.

"No doubt you are wondering why I summoned you here while you are still on leave. I do hope I am not asking something of you too soon."

"I am fit to return to duty when you ask, My Prince," Tariq said with an incline of his head.

"Yes, I am sure you are eager for things to return to normal." When Tariq didn't respond the prince went on. "But I didn't call you here to give you a new assignment." He waved at his guards. "Leave us."

The prince did not speak until they were alone. "I have a feeling my dear sister, the princess, was rather, shall we say, stingy with her details regarding your recent adventures in the desert. You know how I like to have all the facts. I think we both inherited that from the emperor."

"As you say, Prince." Tariq inclined his head.

"Good, then we are in agreement." Prince Orinth reached for his tea. "So, tell me everything that was not on the official report."

Tariq shifted, watching the movements the prince made. Maybe he could somehow tell Orinth the truth about Mzia. That Princess Ezhno was keeping her tucked away in some lab, secret for her own reasons. Saying he was going to lie to this man and actually lying to him were two different things. If he told the truth, surely Ezhno would find out. She would kill him or worse—she would kill Lila.

He was so engrossed in this line of thought that he almost didn't notice the subtle rattle of the prince's tea cup as he set it back down on the table. The small tug the prince gave to the collar of his robe. A collar that wasn't quite high enough to cover a spreading rash. The world shifted. Tariq wanted to deny it, to refuse to believe his own eyes. But the prince's once rock-steady hands were trembling, and the color of the rash on his neck was unmistakable. That could only mean Princess Ezhno's treachery went so much deeper than he had originally thought. She wasn't just keeping the cure from someone the prince knew—she was keeping the cure from her own brother and heir to the throne.

He needed time to sort this out. Time to think. And the only way to buy that time was to continue to lie.

So, Tariq lied. It was a lie Mzia would be proud of. He wove in just enough truth, ties to the official report that he also read, to sound believable. He told the prince how Mzia had saved his life but only to get him to promise her a chance. He said that he was beguiled and enchanted by her. That she threatened and promised him things, and he felt he couldn't refuse. That, in the end, she had died trying to escape him after double crossing him in the desert.

When he was finished, the prince sighed. "That was quite an ordeal for you, Skycaptain."

Tariq nodded in agreement, uncomfortable with just how easily the lies came to him and how he felt no regret in telling them.

"Well, it is over now. And I thank you for telling me

everything." He called for his guards. "You may go now. And rest assured in a few weeks' time, you will be given a new commission."

Tariq stood and saluted. "Thank you, Your Majesty."

As Tariq turned to go, the prince added, "And don't feel bad. You are not, after all, the first man to be swayed by the words of a woman."

Tariq could only salute and hurry from the room. He had to fight to keep his breathing under control. Only once he got back to his apartment did he let himself consider all that had happened.

"There you are!" Lila said cheerfully as she walked into his front room. "I came to see you because—"

"Not now." Tariq brushed past her, unbuttoning his jacket. "I don't feel like talking. Please leave."

"Oh, but you'll want to hear this."

"Lila!" He turned on her. "I don't have time for your foolishness! I've just been to see the prince and I . . . No, it is too much. I can't tell you yet. I need time to think."

"Yes, blah blah, I know. But just because you don't have time to unravel a secret code, doesn't mean my computers didn't!"

"What are you going on about?"

"All that encrypted information that Ezhno copied? Well, I finally got in! I would have gotten in sooner, but I had to really be careful because they were watching me worse than that time I broke into—"

"Lila, unless this is leading up to something—"

"It is. But you tell me your news first."

"No. I can't involve you again. This is too—"

"Does it have anything to do with our dearest prince being addicted?"

"What. How could you—"

"Figure that out? Well, to be fair, I didn't. Doctor Yulia did. Several years ago, actually."

"Well, it's worse than him just being addicted. His hands were trembling and I saw a rash. He has weeks at best."

"So he will be dead in a month and his sister still won't tell him she has the cure? I never again want to hear mother say our rivalry is bad."

"We never really had a—wait. How did Doctor Yulia know about the prince's addiction?"

Lila shrugged. "She apparently had contacts she kept at the palace before she left. I am rather envious of her network. But you want to know the best part? I can use this information to contact them. And I will bet you they know—"

"Where Mzia is?" Tariq's mind began to race through the possibilities. "And perhaps they can help with . . . Tell me everything."

"Now there is the brother I know and tolerate. Where has he been these past few weeks?"

CHAPTER 49
A NEW HOPE

U PON REFLECTION, IT WAS the army that gave Mzia the idea. She would need a distraction of epic proportions to reach the elevator. But the distraction couldn't be limited to just this floor. It would need to consume the hospital whole. That's when she remembered the night they left the admiral's house and the mist that fogged the streets.

Being the only clinic in her province meant that Mzia learned a little bit of everything. This included what chemicals and medicines should never be mixed and the byproducts of that mixture. And one of the mixtures? The fog that caused the glow lamps to lose their light temporarily.

And this lab had everything she needed. She had casually noted the ingredients during different procedures over the last few days. And while their fog made people docile and sleepy, the addition of just a few things could produce the opposite effect. All she needed was a method of dispersion.

It was just past midnight when all the pieces came together and she attacked. There was only one doctor on the floor that time of night, Sekcio. The man Ezhno had brought with her to capture Mzia. How fitting.

Mzia pretended to faint from exhaustion from the last test he ran, something she commonly did. Sekcio unstrapped her from the table to move her onto another. But he turned his back, and that was a mistake.

Mzia grabbed the syringe of sedative meant for herself and stabbed it into Sekcio's neck. The man gave a strangled cry before collapsing to the floor. Mzia ripped out her IV and sprang from the table to unsteady feet. She staggered over to the counter on the other side of the room with blood dripping from her arm.

She snatched Anuva's pendant and held it to her chest. With a shuddering breath, she vowed to give this back to her sister. No matter the cost, no matter who she hurt, Anuva would wear this necklace again. Pulling it on over her neck, Mzia got to work.

She ignored the itching pain all over her back and gathered the ingredients she needed, breaking jars and turning over test papers in her haste. The altering of a few ingredients made it more of a stimulant than a sedative. She mixed the powders then added the final liquid, her hands burning in the process.

The black fog rose up and spilled over the edge of the counter. Only when the fog brushed her toes did she remember that she needed a mask. One of the lower cabinets had several extra masks in case of chemical spills. They weren't perfect, but they would keep her level headed enough to complete the task. Mzia grabbed what she needed for her next few batches and a pair of scissors before leaving the room. Fast as she could, she found the vent in the hall. She knelt and deposited her ingredients on the floor, then used the scissor blades to pry open the vent.

At this point the fog had filled the room and half the hall. Lights winked out all around her, and Mzia used the small handpad in the wall to alter the ventilation settings. On a normal floor they would have been password protected but not here, not where they thought nobody could mess with them. Buildings this large needed the air flow to distribute the carbon dioxide people breathed out as well as regulate the internal growth temperature. It was mostly self-regulating with grown-in air fans and temperature sensitive leaves. But hospitals sometimes needed to have certain rooms secluded for infectious reasons and had ways of opening all the vents to scoot the air around where they needed it. She set the flow to direct air from her floor down to the floors below. By the time she created a second batch right in front of the vent, all the lights on her floor were out.

She repeated the process at the second vent at the other end of the hall. She had just risen when an alarm sounded below. She gathered the remainder of her ingredients and returned to the lab room where the unconscious doctor lay.

Mzia created her final batch but withheld the last ingredient. She stripped the doctor of his lab coat, put it on herself, and filled the pockets with the dry ingredients. She heaved Sekcio up onto the gurney; thankfully, he was not a heavy man, and she wheeled him to the far end of the hall. At the handpad, Mzia took his hand and used it to unlock the elevator. She dashed inside and pushed the only button. Nothing happened.

Panic threatened to consume her before she noticed a card reader. From Sekcio, she took a lanyard and swiped before pushing the button again. As the doors closed, Mzia added the final ingredient to each of her pockets.

By the time the doors opened again, the fog had filled the lift and poured out into an already chaotic scene.

Patients and doctors were screaming, scrambling to find out why none of the lights were working. Alarms blared and several nurses ran about blindly, fumbling to find their location. Because the hospital tower sat alone on this block, none of the lights from the other buildings were of much help. The halls with no windows were as black as the space between stars.

Mzia wasn't sure what level she was on, but she walked out, past the nurses and doctors. Past the crying patients. And for once she didn't care what sort of chaos she caused. What harm she did. The sounds blended into a beautiful, reckless symphony—her freedom song.

She found a stairway and the lights winked out as she descended. She shed the coat at the last door. There was still panic on that floor, though the smoke had only just started to reach. She slipped out and walked down the mostly dark hall, where the nurses had better things to do than stop a wandering patient. A glance out a window told her she was still many floors up. The thrill of her plan working surged her onward when someone grabbed her from behind.

Jerked into an empty room, her back was pressed to a wall. A young male doctor, masked as she was, squinted at her in the near darkness.

"What are you doing down here?" he hissed. "The rescue isn't supposed to take place until tomorrow night! Tariq was very specific about—"

Mzia pried his hands off her shoulder. "Who are you?"

"I am Doctor Tivit. And I was supposed to be the one who got you out while Tariq and Lila established alibis at a party." He stepped back and looked her up and down. "How did you get out, anyway?"

Mia shrugged. "I made the smoke." She frowned. "How do you know Tariq?"

"I don't know him. I have never met him in person, but I do know of him. He arranged for me to get you out of here. He has a connection to Doctor Yulia, as do I."

Mzia blinked. "You are one of her contacts?" The memories of the late-night discussions with Yulia flashed across her inner eye.

"Yes, and that's why I am here, gladly risking my life to get you out. You're our only hope."

Mzia slowly shook her head. None of this felt real.

A new alarm began to sound and startled them both. Doctor Tivit shook himself. "You know what, maybe this will still work out. They are at another party tonight so that will place them across town. Maybe we can just move up the schedule." He rubbed his face, considering. "I do already have the supplies. I just won't contact him until my shift is over. Yes, this could work." He held out a hand. "You wait here."

"Why should I believe you?" Mzia said, her clarity slowly returning.

"Because I am your only chance at walking out of here alive."

THE SKY BRIDGE WAS crowded with hospital visitors, all who had been asked to leave in the wake of the strange fog filling the building's top floors. Many were pilgrims, robed in red and visiting loved ones on the days leading up to the solstice. The nights were short, and each one had a celebration, keeping half the capital city awake until dawn. Nobody noticed another hooded pilgrim slip among them.

Mzia could have gotten out of the hospital herself, there being so much else going on. However, when she emerged into the open air and away from the noise of the hospital, she conceded that she didn't have a plan for what came next. Getting out was her objective, and she was only half sure before she started that she was going to survive the process. So, what to do after getting out was sort of low on the list of priorities.

By the time she came to the sky bridge, doctors were rounding up patients and hospital security was checking anyone who looked out of place. She was grateful for the hood and simple party mask to hide who she was, as certainly she would have stood out among the party goers in her hospital gown.

Amidst this chaos of the evacuation, Mzia walked away over the sky bridge. The rivers ran below and the canopy of branches framed the stars above. Never had she witnessed such an expanse of city. She followed the directions the small handpad gave her. Doctor Tivit had been very specific about where she was to go. Nobody could go with her, all people involved in her rescue would be seen elsewhere establishing alibis.

Night wore into the early pre-dawn hours and instead of the parties fading out they appeared to ramp up. The parties in the main rooms of just about every tower she passed through were packed with people who only got rowdier and more inebriated as the night went on. Dances, which were a fine art form in most places, disintegrated into spiraling bodies. The bright reds of hoods along with other colorful costumes of heroes and animals smeared into a kaleidoscope of chaos. The common masks that matched the traditional costumes started the evening as a fun flare and became sinister by the end. Who was behind that foxy mask? Why did that bear seem to follow her across the room?

People kept bumping into her, mostly by accident. They were not watching where they were going in a room crowded with people all trying to do a complex dance. Although some grabbed her arm on purpose, demanding she join in. She dared not look anyone in the eye, even with her mask she was afraid they might see her white hair in the depths of her hood. And the people this deep into the solstice parties were loud about what they saw, just like overconfident toddlers. So, when asked to join she pulled away quickly, wrenching her arm free and making for the nearest exit.

As she walked on the bridges where fireworks exploded uncomfortably close, she hugged herself to stop herself from shaking.

The sudden cracks of sound and light made her second guess herself. She checked her handpad, only to look at it again a second later, forgetting what was there. Music from dances competed for dominance. In her right ear, she might hear a playful ballad and in her left a more upbeat rave.

And people. People everywhere. Nothing like the empty dirt streets of the hamlet she grew up in. Thousands of strangers whose names and lives she would never know brushed past her in unending waves.

The only thing that kept her from breaking down in tears was the reminder that she had a destination. Doctor Tivit had called it a safe house. Her handpad told her to enter one of the few buildings that didn't have some sort of gathering—she had arrived at last.

The lobby was silent in the early hour before dawn. No people, just a row of lifts. She went to the third on the right as instructed. She passed the key card the doctor had given her across the screen and the doors slid silently open. Inside had only one button just like the hospital elevator. She swiped her card across a second screen and pressed the button.

A clean automated voice asked, "Your card is for the 23 floor. Is that the floor you would like to visit?"

Mzia froze. Was she supposed to answer?

The automated voice repeated the question.

Mzia fought the urge to look up. "Yes?"

"Thank you and welcome."

The doors slid shut and the lift moved up. Mzia fiddled with the key card, turning it over and over, until the door opened again.

She stepped out into an entrance hall with high ceilings. Blue moss manicured into ornate patterns carpeted the floor. Delicate glow flowers in soft yellows hung in bunches from the ceiling. Three archways opened from the hall into spacious rooms. The one on her right appeared to be a dining room, her left a sitting room, but the one in front was mostly empty. She could see all the way to the wall that was nearly all window, showing the graying sky of morning.

Mzia felt lost, realizing that she hadn't been given directions about what to do once she got here. She remembered now the doctor saying someone would contact her. Exhaustion came over her all at once, and she shuffled forward, shedding her robe in the archway. This space held a table with flowers but not much else. To her right, a staircase wound up to another floor. So apparently this apartment spanned several floors.

She wanted to lay down. Surely in a home this size there would be several bedrooms. She winced her way up the steps and into a long, dim hall lit from below with glowing lights along the floor. The first door she tried was locked, but the second opened easily. It was not a bedroom, but a study, set with a desk and several comfy chairs. Something in the orderliness of it all felt oddly reassuring.

The next two doors were locked, but the final door at the end of the hall opened for her. It was a bedroom, and she was so happy to see a real bed she nearly cried. The space was clean but felt lived in with a wall of windows with the curtain pulled back to show the city, sliding doors across a closet, and a door on the far side that she assumed led to a bathing chamber. More manicured blue moss on the floor and soft golden flower lights, like those in the front hall. The bed was round and suspended, as was common in the Alang Kingdom. The blankets were neatly tucked and folded smooth.

Mzia stopped in the middle of the room, pausing as an odd sensation came over her. Like she had been here before. No. She would remember a home as nice as this. And she had only been to the capital once, when she had first been stolen from her parents, so she couldn't have ever been here. Yet something felt . . . familiar. A scent in the air. Mint.

Despite all the pain and exhaustion, she hobbled over to the closet and slid back the silent doors. There hung three uniforms.

Skycaptain uniforms.

This was Tariq's apartment.

CHAPTER 50
TOO LATE

*M*ZIA, A SOFT VOICE called to her in her dreams. It reminded her of the pink laughter she had heard once. *Mzia.*

"Mzia?" The voice was louder now, more urgent. A voice she knew. But it couldn't be . . .

She cracked an eye open, for that was all she had the energy to do, and found Tariq staring down at her.

It all flooded back. The escape, the painful walk there. Falling asleep in Tariq's bed, even as she had been determined to wait for someone to come. This. Was. Real.

She sat up so fast her head spun. "No," she breathed.

"Not so fast!" Tariq grasped her shoulders. "You're not well."

"Tariq . . ."

"How are you here already? The plan was tomorrow night. Doctor Tivit hasn't contacted me."

She pushed his hands away. "I broke myself out of that hell. Sorry to disrupt your perfect plans."

"Don't be ridiculous," he said. "I am pleased to see you. Only we will need to move up the timelines for—"

"No." The firmness in her voice stopped him. Tears she had long since stanched welled up. "*You* told her about Anuva."

"Mzia, I—"

"No!" She pushed him away again. "You told her about my sister! I trusted you and you told her!"

"She was going to kill Lila." He looked distressed.

"I don't care!" She didn't care about his distress either. "Ezhno has my sister!" Her hand moved to the collar of the hospital gown, to the one thing she had taken from the lab. She pulled out the necklace, the stone star warm from sitting against her chest. "This belonged to Anuva. Ezhno gave it to me to taunt me. This is all I will ever see of her and it's your fault!"

"Mzia, please you have to understand—"

"I understand all right," Mzia bit out. "I understand that your life and sister is more important than mine. That you don't care about me and you never did."

"That's not true—"

"What have you done?" She was shrieking now. "She has my sister!" Her entire body shook as the rage she'd built up over weeks spewed out. She threw aside the covers and swung to her feet. She had to get away from him.

Tariq tried to stop her, but she shoved him aside, getting her feet underneath herself just long enough to topple onto the floor. Pain slammed into her knees and elbows, sharpening her resolve. Tariq scooped her up, but she fought against him, slamming her fists into his chest with all the fragile force she could muster. Tears and outrage blinded her.

He kept saying, "I'm sorry. I'm sorry." But it was too little, too late.

She was back on the bed, Tariq holding her down as she thrashed.

"No!" She struggled in vain. "Get away from me. I never want to see you again. Let go of me!"

"Fine." He let go of her and stood, both of them panting heavily. "I will go. But please, just—stay here."

With that he left the room.

"SHE WON'T SEE ME," Tariq told Lila. He tried to sound nonchalant about it. Lila had watched him plan and scheme and fight sleep for nearly a fortnight just to get Mzia free. And now she wouldn't talk to him. Wouldn't look at him.

He had messaged Lila as soon as he found Mzia asleep in his bed. He didn't say what for, but when she arrived, she found him quite distressed, pacing the sitting room. She thought something had gone wrong with the plan, but then he explained that Mzia was already there. A day early.

"I did what had to be done," Tariq said. Lila nodded, fighting the urge to yell at him. He was foolish, not anticipating the backlash Mzia would give him over endangering her sister. The irony was that Tariq had refused to let Lila set a finger on Mzia's rescue operation. To protect Lila. His sister. Because he didn't want to put *her* in danger. Lila scoffed. *Men.* But she didn't yell or even lecture like she wanted to because Mzia had already taken him down a few notches. More than a few.

"They cut her hair," he said suddenly.

"What?"

"Her hair, they cut it short." He sounded . . . sad.

This ordeal had humbled him more than she anticipated.

Lila rose from her seat. "I am going to go check on her."

He paused in his pacing. "Thank you."

"Where did you put the clothes I sent over?"

"They're in my closet. Top shelf."

Lila left him and climbed the steps. Neither of them had gotten any sleep the night before, being at a solstice party their mother was throwing. Lila shook her head. She would need to make herself some strong tea after this.

Standing outside Tariq's room, she paused, her hand on the door. What if Mzia didn't want to see her either? That was a chance she would have to take, so she pushed open the door.

Mzia lay on her back, blinking slowly at the ceiling. Lila came into the room and sat on the edge of the bed.

Mzia opened her cracked lips and then closed them. She blinked, and a tear slid down the side of her face.

"None of that now. You need sleep." Lila chided. After a pause, she went on, "Tariq told me about how you wanted to go to Aasim, after he was . . ." She picked at her shirt sleeve. "I just wanted you to know I am grateful for that."

"How can I ever sleep again?" She looked over at Lila with glassy eyes "*She* has Anuva."

"I know, and maybe it doesn't seem good, but—"

"Did you know? Did you know that he told the princess?"

"He told me." She tried to decide what to say. "Believe what you like about all this, but you have to know he didn't want to hurt you."

Mzia scoffed. "He isn't stupid. Tariq is many things, but not stupid. But he is cruel. Because he knew, Lila. He knew what Anuva meant to me, and he still told Ezhno about her. I don't want to talk to him now or ever again."

"That's understandable." Lila stood up. "But you should know my brother only did what he thought he had to do." Tariq hadn't been himself since the desert.

When Mzia said nothing, Lila turned and went to the closet. Between the annoyingly well-organized stacks of clothes, Lila found the box of things she had picked out for Mzia to wear. She plastered on a smile and turned back to the healer. "Now, let's get you out of that ugly hospital rag and into something comfortable."

It was easy to persuade Mzia to shower. While she was in there, Lila checked into the security of the building. She had hacked the system over a week ago to send her all the footage first before it went anywhere else. She quickly cut and spliced the footage of Mzia entering the building that morning. Then she deleted the lift records so it looked like Tariq was the first to arrive.

Mzia emerged, wrapped in the soft new clothes.

"What's that on your shoulder?" Lila said, coming closer.

Mzia tugged up the wide shirt collar and whispered, "I don't want to talk about it."

Lila shook her head. She couldn't deal with this now.

Mzia sat on the edge of the bed, her eyes empty. Her body was frail and thin. So different from the healthy person she had been a few weeks before. Her skin was sallow and much paler than it should be.

Without anything else to do, she tucked Mzia into her brother's bed and turned to go.

"Thank you," Mzia whispered.

CHAPTER 51
GRATITUDE

MZIA LAY AWAKE, WATCHING the light leak from behind the curtains, grow and shift to afternoon. After several restless hours, she gave up on the idea that sleep would find her again. She sat up and rubbed her face. A different sort of quiet occupied Tariq's room than in the hospital lab. The hum of equipment and hushed tones of the doctors had followed her everywhere. And everything was so clean and sterile. Here only the rumble of the city could be heard, and while immaculately clean— as she had always supposed Tariq's home to be—it felt lived in. It smelled of him too. She didn't hate that, but she probably should.

Pushing off the bed and leaving it to sway slightly behind her, Mzia crossed to the window and gazed out at the city through a slit in the woven blue curtains. She fingered Anuva's necklace, her eyes unfocused. At midday, the towers' highest branches provided decent shade and a slight breeze kept all in a dappled, swaying light. The water far below at the buildings' roots reflected back shimmering, sharp sparks.

The door opened behind her.

"You don't want to be here," she warned. "I have rested now and remembered all the things I planned to say to you."

Tariq cleared his throat. "Mzia, please I—"

"There is nothing you could possibly—"

"I know where your sister is."

Mzia spun to him. "What?"

Seemingly encouraged by her tone, he came around the end of the floating bed. "I know where Princess Ezhno has her or a pretty good guess and I plan—" He paused, mid-step and mid-thought. He was looking at her shoulder, where the wide collar of her shirt had slipped slightly down one arm while she played with her necklace. She tugged the collar back into place but it was too late. He had seen.

He came closer, his brows drawn tightly together. "What is . . . ?"

"Tariq, it's not—"

But he ignored her, drawing back the curtain slightly to let in more light. Realizing there was no point in fighting him, she turned so the light fell where the wide collar exposed her shoulder and back. Etched across her shoulder and down her back were the spindly white lines of hundreds of scars.

"How old are these?" His voice wavered.

Mzia had to think. "Some of them are weeks old."

"But I thought you couldn't scar?"

"I thought so too." Mzia knew she should be more upset about it and should be more horrified by this violation of herself, and yet she couldn't bring herself to care.

"How long did they take to do this?"

"Tariq, please, it doesn't matter—"

"How. Long."

"I am not exactly sure," she conceded, turning back to face him. "I wasn't . . . conscious for a lot of it. But every day, many times a day, they cut the same place over and over for . . . nearly the whole time I was there?"

Tariq swore more violently than she had ever heard from him, and his eyes flashed with rage. "I am going to kill her," he whispered. Then it was like he suddenly remembered who it was he was talking to. But there was no regret in his features. He meant his words. Mzia knew him more than capable. He probably already had three plans and six backup strategies. The bitterness in her heart softened a fraction.

"How could anyone be so cruel?" he asked.

"She must be suffering herself, I think. In ways I don't understand."

"That's no excuse to be sadistic."

"I suppose not."

"And . . . your hair?" he gestured to her shoulder length shorn ends.

"Apparently it got in the way of torturing me." Mzia couldn't look at him. If she looked at him again, she would see the pain he felt and she didn't want any of that. She couldn't let herself share his emotions now—she had too many of her own and couldn't spare any space in her heart. Even if he was just concerned about her.

He betrayed you! Bitterness hissed as if Mzia needed a reminder. *He told her about your sister!*

"Mzia, I . . . There's no excuse for what I've done, what I put you through. No excuse for endangering the only family you have. But I'm not here to ask for your forgiveness."

Good because she wasn't about to give it.

"I can't go back and change what I've done. I can only start now and attempt amends."

"And how," she fought to keep her voice even, "do you plan to do that, Skycaptain?"

"Freeing your sister and keeping you both away from the royal family, to start. But if you wanted to walk away from it all, including me, I would understand. You don't have to stay here if you don't want to. I just thought here would be safest."

Mzia hugged herself and looked out at the city. "I should like . . . some time to think."

"Of course, whatever you need. Maybe I could explain my findings to you? See, I tracked—"

The door opened. "Tariq!" Lila leaned into the room. "You were supposed to ask her if she wanted tea! And food. I'm sure she is starving."

Mzia smiled a little despite herself. "Tea sounds nice."

TARIQ WAS ENVIOUS OF the easy way Lila threaded her arm through Mzia's and led her from the room. Mzia had always been a little untouchable to him. She kept so many secrets that until the night they built the graves and danced in the desert, he never really felt he knew her. And now that was all gone—burned with his betrayal.

At the stairs, he watched her hobble her way down, frailty coloring every movement. He wanted to offer her help. Such an offer by him would be rejected, however, so he didn't make it.

Lila set out the tea and various finger foods on trays in the sitting room. Tranquil green lights of the bioluminescent mushrooms cast a calm over them all. Lila sat next to Mzia on a sofa and chatted about the party they had been to all night. Tariq drank tea but couldn't bring himself to eat anything. He had managed only a short nap in a guest room after finding Mzia in his bed and was regretting staying until past dawn at the party.

Doctor Tivit should contact him as soon as it was safe. Yulia's contacts agreed to help smuggle Mzia out of the city with the exodus of pilgrims after the solstice. He would, of course, honor her wishes to stay with whomever she wanted once she left, but he selfishly hoped he would get to see her often as they worked out a strategy to rescue her sister.

Almost as if she could read his mind, Mzia said, "Tell me about Anuva."

He pulled out his handpad and set it on the tea table. A few taps and swipes sent up a projection as wide and tall as his arm span. It showed a map of the continent with several locations marked and lists of names, dates, and paragraphs of notes.

"This is everything I have been able to find out about your sister," he said. "She is somewhere in the Selatan Kingdom, according to my contacts in the military. Ezhno has been particularly good about covering her tracks, but I have managed to narrow it down to a few possible locations." He scratched his face. "I have several informants who update me every day and in turn, I update this master list. They don't know exactly what they are tracking, only that it is a prisoner of the princess."

Mzia studied the projection. Her face gave away none of what she was thinking as her eyes flickered and absorbed the information.

At last, she asked, "How long have you been working on this?"

He cleared his throat and admitted, "Since the day I left you." He wouldn't say it was the only thing that let him sleep at night, keeping track of her sister—the knowledge that he could somehow fix what he did.

"What?" Lila asked indignantly. "And you never asked for my help?"

"I told you." Tariq's mind snapped back to the present. "You can't be a part of this next phase, at least not like before. Maybe minor support that is untraceable. But not like before. Not again."

Lila cocked an eyebrow. "Shouldn't Mzia get to decide who—"

"No." On this one point, he wouldn't yield. Not now, not ever.

Lila huffed and sat back, crossing her arms. Had she been more awake, he was sure she would have argued better. And she was sure to bring it up again. But he was decided.

"How long will it take to get to her?" Mzia asked, ignoring the staring contest the twins were having.

Tariq turned to his gathered information. "If all my sources are correct and everything goes perfectly, two weeks maybe three after the solstice?"

Mzia touched her necklace. "So soon?"

"If everything goes well," he repeated, trying not to give her false hope. "But I plan on making it go well."

A ghost of a smile crossed her face as hope filled her eyes. She turned that hope on him for just an instant to whisper, "Thank you."

He was undone.

The lift chimed, announcing a visitor.

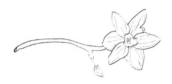

CHAPTER 52
A CHOICE TO HEAL

TARIQ WAS ON HIS feet in an instant.

"Were you expecting anyone?" Lila asked, rising.

"No." He checked his handpad. "They have a full clearance card." He turned to Lila. "Did you tell her?"

"Please, I am no tattletale," Lila said, slightly offended. "But it will be interesting to see you explain your way out of this one."

"What if she brought someone?" Tariq bit back, gesturing to Mzia, who was without a headscarf or goggles. It wouldn't be the first time his mother turned up unannounced with guests.

"Oh." The color drained from Lila's face, and she dashed around the couch to the entry hall. There was no time or place to hide Mzia in the sitting room. The lift chimed again to announce its arrival. Tariq had just enough time to pull Mzia up and forward so he could step between her and the archway to the front room.

The elevator doors opened and his mother walked out. The doors closed. She was alone, thankfully.

She addressed Lila first, who was in the doorway between the sitting room and the entry hall. "I knew you must be up to something;

you never respond to my messages as fast as you have today." Her eyes passed her daughter and landed on Tariq. "And you? Hiding something from your mother?" She walked forward, "Or should I say, someone?"

"Mother, please." Tariq fought to sound reasonable. "You don't want to be messed up in this. Please just trust me on this."

"For once, I agree with Tariq." Lila shrugged. "I know, I am shocked too."

Lady Ishtar merely crossed her arms and leveled a stare at Tariq. Starbreather save him from the stubborn women in his family. He stepped aside so she had a clear line of sight to Mzia.

"Tariq." She came forward, concerned. "What have you done?"

"There is so much you don't understand—"

"I know enough. I just thought you knew better than to cross the princess like this."

"She doesn't know it was me. I am already lying for her. She thinks I am on her side because of . . . promises I made." He glanced at Lila. He had told his sister most of it but they agreed to keep it from Lady Ishtar. "There is a lot going on here you can't know about."

"Fine." She walked slowly around them and sat in his chair. "If my own children won't tell me things, then I will have the truth from the Iaomai Child."

"Mzia doesn't want to talk with you."

"I should like to speak for myself," Mzia said softly.

Tairq turned to her and had to stop himself from arguing. He had lost that privilege, to give advice she might listen to. He had thrown it away with her trust.

Mzia sat back down on the sofa. "I will speak with Lady Ishtar."

"Good." His mother folded her hands.

"Mother, don't—"

She silenced him with another look. She would not be moved. Tariq cursed under his breath and claimed the seat across from Mzia. Because it didn't matter how high of a rank he gained or how many men were under his command, his mother held an authority he never dared cross.

MZIA SIPPED HER TEA and looked up at Lady Ishtar. The lady was plucking her pearls and studying Mzia. At last, Lady Ishtar said, "You don't trust me."

Mzia set down her tea. "How can I trust you? You let your own children be used—abused—by the emperor."

"I didn't have much choice in that."

"Lies. We always have a choice."

Lady Ishtar's pearl-clutching hand stilled. She nodded once, as if Mzia had confirmed something. "There it is."

"Where is what?"

"The fire I was looking for. You were just held prisoner by the most powerful woman in the world for what? Six weeks? And yet you have the audacity to question someone who might give you aid? I was hoping you hadn't lost that fire."

Mzia shifted and wished she wasn't so angry with Tariq that she might ask him for help. She didn't care for the piercing look his mother was giving her.

"Now," Lady Ishtar went on. "You have suffered greatly, and I suspect my son is in some way responsible because you haven't looked at him once since I walked in here. That and he has been more withdrawn than usual since he came back from the desert."

"Mother, please . . ." Tariq started to say.

"You think you hid it well, but a mother notices everything. For instance, the cold way the princess and prince have been treating each other at the parties, and how they go out of their way to avoid speaking of the other. I am also well informed on matters you think I am ignorant of. Let's see how well you are informed. What does this have to do with Mzia?"

This sudden turn seemed to catch Tariq off guard but he collected himself enough to say, "Mother, as I said, I don't really want to involve you—"

"Prince Orinth clearly wants Mzia and Princess Ezhno won't give her up. He thinks she's dead like the rest of the empire, doesn't he?"

Tariq frowned. "I am not going to give up information."

"You don't need to. I saw his rash."

Mzia started. "The grand prince is addicted?" She searched all three of their faces. "Are you certain?"

Tariq sighed. "I am afraid so. I saw his rash too. Several weeks ago."

"Then he has days at best." Mzia put her face in her hands, taking it all in. The grand prince was dying.

"Think, Tariq," his mother went on. "The princess is making a play for the throne. She lets the prince die in his addiction. His only children are illegitimate or too young, so—"

"So, she takes the crown." Mzia hugged herself, the room suddenly cold. Ezhno as empress. The kind of empress who would make sure nobody knew of a cure.

Tariq stood and began to pace. "This may work to our advantage. With so much going on, Ezhno has to drop something. If we assume her play for the throne is her top priority, then she will be less likely to be focused on Anu—our target."

"Oh good, more secrets," Lady Ishtar said without humor. "Well, while you spin your webs without me, may I remind you that your loyalty will be to our new empress, and she won't hesitate to end anyone who got in her way before she took the throne."

Lila perked up. "Does this mean we get to go into hiding?"

"Lila, this isn't a game," Tariq bit out. "This isn't some play or fairy story where everything always turns out well in the end."

"Life is a game," Lila argued. "And stranger things are sitting here in this room with us than I ever heard tell in a fairy story."

Mzia tried to say something but Tariq said, "This is why I didn't want to involve you. You never take anything seriously. We are talking about the fate of the empire here!"

"I know that! That is why you need my help with—"

"I can't have you getting involved with this."

"You don't have a choice if we are going to—"

Mzia felt an overwhelming surge of weariness wash over her as the argument faded into the background. Just when things might get better, they were getting worse. So, so much worse. What if she retrieved her sister only to forever live in the shadows, even deeper than before? To sit back the rest of their lives and watch everyone suffer was a fate worse than death. But nobody would listen to them, to her. She was a myth, and the people didn't need another myth. They needed proof.

They needed a demonstration of her ability that nobody could ignore. What was it Tariq had said, when they were first making plans? Before the desert felt like a lifetime ago. He had said she would have to cure someone. Someone powerful and influential who would be grateful and who might just listen.

The twins were still arguing when she blurted out, "What if I healed the prince?"

Lila and Tariq both stopped mid-word.

Tariq turned to her. "What?"

"What if I healed the grand prince? Tariq, you know him best. Would he listen to us?"

Tariq frowned, eyes unfocused as he considered her words. When he spoke, it was with slow deliverance. "The prince will do what appears best. The people don't know that he is addicted, but if they did . . ." He began to pace again. "Yes, and then we find a way to cure him, publicly, where there would be witnesses. We couldn't warn him, of course, because then he would find a way to spin this to his own purposes, but if we surprised him, it would surprise everyone . . . then maybe." He stopped pacing to grip the back of the chair and look at them all. "Yes, it could work except—Mzia, could I speak with you alone?"

Mzia nodded, somehow knowing she would want to hear him out. She got up to follow Tariq out while Lila muttered under her breath about always being left out of things.

Tariq led her across the entry hall and into a dining room with a circular low table and growing paintings of lilacs on open fields. They passed through that room into the kitchen.

He paused, his back to her, and said, "I know I have lost your trust in this and everything else, but I need you to know that healing the prince comes with a lot of risks." He turned. "And one of those risks is your sister."

Mzia's breath caught. "Why?"

"Because even if this crazy scheme worked, if you can cure him in some public way that would leave no doubt, well then, we could lose track of your sister. If the princess sees her play for the throne fail, she will clutch tighter any assets she has, and that includes your sister. Not to mention if everything went perfectly we would both be in the public eye and certainly given duties that would keep us away from finding her."

"I see." Mzia crossed and uncrossed her arms.

"You deserve to know the truth. I won't keep things from you."

Starbreather, she hated the tight feeling in her gut, like she was somehow in the wrong for hating him.

She squeezed her eyes shut, hoping to block out the threatening tears. It wasn't fair. He was only trying to be clear about all the outcomes but it wasn't fair. It wasn't fair that such a choice should come down to her. Her blood was the only thing that set her apart from an ordinary healer from a poor mountain village. And now the fate of the empire was somehow her decision.

"Mzia?"

Mzia fiddled with Anuva's pendant.

"Mzia?"

She shook her head and opened her eyes.

Tariq started to say something then stopped. He blew out a breath and glanced around the room like he was searching for answers. After a time he said, "This is a lot. We are talking about world changing stuff and such a decision shouldn't be yours. But it is. I don't imagine anyone wants such a choice. I certainly don't."

"I don't . . . know what the right choice is."

"I am the wrong person to ask."

"Why?"

"Because I chose my sister over yours." He rubbed the back of his neck. "This decision has to be yours because you are the one most affected by it."

That wasn't true. Millions could be affected by her choice.

It was that simple.

Anuva was alone and imprisoned. Mzia could save her sister and damn the world. Or save the world and damn her sister. She clutched Anuva's pendant tighter. If Mzia chose her sister, she chose to condemn those like her to the same fate she had. To a world that would keep doing this to Iaomai Children. To the next one that was born. And the one after that.

Unless she did something about it.

Unless *they* did something about it.

It was that simple.

Before this moment, before Tariq, she hadn't really considered it possible. She had dreamed about it, of course, of a better world.

But she never really thought, deep down, that it could be. That was why she healed where she could because that was all she would ever be able to do. Save those in front of her. To balance her own world even as the world around her fell out of balance.

If Tariq, of all people, thought this was possible, then just maybe it was.

She didn't forgive him fully for giving up her sister. But she didn't have to forgive to do the right thing.

And in that thought lay the very worst possible part of this decision—it wasn't really a decision. She had already made up her mind because this path was chosen both for her and by her long ago. She walked the high road since birth—others came first—and that's why it didn't grieve her as much as it should. It should hurt more, shouldn't it? To know that if she never saw her sister again, it would be her own doing?

Starbreather, she prayed. *Give me strength. And help Anuva understand what I have to do next.*

Mzia shook off the shuddering breath that escaped her and squared her shoulders. "The decision isn't really mine, Tariq. I was graced with this ability, and I need to use it to help others. I have always known this. I am the only one who can end the suffering, so it is my duty to do so. If . . ." She faltered. "If you will help me."

"Mzia . . ." Sorrow touched his features. "You are . . . more brave and selfless than anyone I know."

She waved him off. She didn't feel brave at that moment.

"If that is your decision, then I will help you in any way I can."

CHAPTER 53
SUMMER SOLSTICE

OVER THE NEXT TWO days, the plan took shape. Mzia had to do very little. Lila got right to work spreading the rumor about the grand prince being addicted, via both Yulia's and her own contacts. She split the rest of the time between having fittings for her Solstice dress and deciding how to best hack the palace cameras. Occasionally, she did both at the same time.

The only truly public event that they could be sure over half of the empire would be watching was the Summer Solstice party at the palace. Curing the prince at such a public event would mean that it would be nearly impossible for him to deny what went on and how.

That taken care of, the next phase was how to get him the cure.

"I don't want you anywhere near the palace if we can help it," Tariq told them over late night tea.

"I would rather not go either," Mzia said, "if I could even get in, but—"

"Oh, I can get you an invitation." Lila said, not looking up from her pad.

"How?" Tariq asked. "The guest list was decided months ago."

"Do you really want to know? It's slightly illegal."

"Only slightly?"

"Yes." Lila refused to elaborate further.

"As I was saying," Mzia went on. "I might have to because neither of you can find a vein, can you?"

The siblings looked at each other and shook their heads.

"Maybe you could teach us?" Tariq suggested.

So, she tried to teach them to find one of her own veins. Tariq managed to do it successfully, but it took him a full twenty seconds. She couldn't tell if it was somehow part of his hesitation to hurt her in any way but, it didn't matter because those were seconds they didn't have. While Lila was better at it than Tariq, she blanched at the sight of blood and would panic and either stick the needle in too far or not far enough. Mzia didn't plan to give the prince time to argue about taking her blood.

"What about Doctor Tivit?" Mzia suggested. "He was willing to help us before. Lila could get him an invitation?"

Tariq shook her head. "Helping you get out of the hospital came with risks but not like this. The likelihood of us failing is much higher and I don't know how he would perform outside of his element. With something this complex, I would rather not add another wild card."

Eventually it was decided that Mzia had to be the one to inject the prince, therefore, she had to be at the party for that to happen. So, Lila procured her an invitation.

On the evening of the Solstice, Mzia, Lila, and Tariq emerged from their private tram at the front gate of the palace. Mzia fidget in the dress Lila had put her in. The blue and silver gown swept down to hover just off the ground around her feet in several leaf-shaped layers. It had belonged to Lila when she was younger, and just a few alterations had it fitting Mzia perfectly.

Lila's flaming orange gown trailed behind her as she marched ahead to show her invitation to the guard. Her mask matched her dress and hid half of her face, including her eyes, behind orange lensed goggles. Large maroon and black feathers plumed the top of the mask and her hair.

Tariq wore a gray tunic with a tulip collar and black trim over his dark trousers. Sensible and yet formal. The back of the tunic had a vine and leaf pattern where some of the leaves were cut outs, revealing his tattoos. He might have worn his skycaptain's uniform except that all those Marked by the emperor were required to wear something exposing their marks while in his company, at least at public events. The emperor was unlikely to make an appearance here, being so old and rumored to be ill, but the tradition was demanded anyway. In the few seconds after stepping out of the tram, Mzia saw looks of admiration, intrigue, and disgust tossed their way. Apparently, everyone had slightly differing opinions on those Marked by the emperor.

She nervously adjusted her own mask and wig. Her invitation clutched in her gloved hand, Mzia looked up at the palace, lit with lights that shifted from one tone to the next. She was actually there. At a ball. And not just any ball, but the Summer Solstice ball. She held her invitation harder. How wonderful. How wonderful and yet, how terrifying. The weight of what she had to do kept her rooted in place. Part of her, the part that was always trying to stay alive, told her she should have disappeared with Tariq when she had the chance, to spare the heartache that now crept in around her and held her tight like a vice. Save what little she could and be content with that. It was a good thing, to stay alive, to save her sister. So Mzia stood frozen in that moment, teetering on the threshold of what was and what could be.

She glanced over and Tariq was at her side, arm offered. She couldn't read his expression well, half his face covered with a dark mask of an animal that was somewhere between a tiger and a fox, but his smile was soft and encouraging. She took his arm, and entered the palace like a princess in a fairy tale. Only she wasn't there to dance; she was there to change the fate of the empire.

THE THRONE ROOM WAS decorated in all the splendor of the kingdoms. Marvelous swirling banners from each of the countries dangled from different points on the clear, glass-like ceiling. With their bright colors and symbols, Mzia recognized several, including the banner from the Utara Kingdom. They spun on phantom winds around a huge eight-pointed star that hung in the center above the throne. A circular dais raised several steps off the floor, the throne looked more like a huge bed because it had no back so the emperor could face any direction he liked. Of course, he was not there now, absent as he had been for the past few years due to health reasons.

The rest of the throne room was separated into sections. One part had been set up with tables of foods, fruits, and delicacies from all over the continent that spilled over their platters. Goblets upon goblets of bubbling wine took up an entire table alone. The smells of the spices and roasting meats that wafted over were irresistible. So much extravagance. How could so much food be consumed in a single night?

Another section was clearly set up as a dance floor, the musicians playing in groups in several corners of the room. Calm background music floated over to the crowd as they entered, strings and pipes creating a soothing melody. The orchestra was composed of, no surprise, traditional instruments from every corner of the empire. Most of them were familiar to her, made popular in most of modern music.

The final section of the room was set up, as Lila had described it, for gossiping and backstabbing. A place to judge everyone's choice of clothing. To form alliances and learn secrets. To mingle with those who knew or pretended to know more than everyone else. A pit of vipers.

The grand prince was nowhere in sight.

"Why isn't he here yet?" Mzia asked.

Tariq whispered, "If the prince is well enough, he will make his entrance later during the toast." This ceremony was given in honor of the Starbreather, to thank him for his gift of the world and of the stars. Conversations about how the Starbreather would be pleased by the dances this year and grant good fortune brushed past them as Mzia and Tariq walked through the room.

A livelier tune began, and people started to drift towards the dance floor. Mzia stayed at Tariq's side, afraid she might have to engage in conversation with someone otherwise. She caught sight of Admiral Grinth chatting with several people and was pleased to see him looking happy. Perhaps his own wealth and power had kept him safe. Or maybe he was just as good of a secret keeper as herself.

"Skycaptain Tariq? Is that you?" A middle-aged woman in emerald green called.

"Lady Wint." Tariq sketched a bow. "A pleasure as always."

The lady came closer and lowered her mask, which was set with green feathers. "Is your mother here tonight? I haven't seen her."

"She is about somewhere," Tariq said, scanning the crowd.

"And who is your beautiful companion?" she asked, gesturing with her feathery fan at Mzia. It was an odd comment seeing as nobody could see half her face or head with the mask and wig.

"A friend," Tariq said evasively. "This is her first ball."

"Is that so?" She turned to Mzia. "Well, perhaps you didn't hear the latest news then?"

"And what news would that be?" Mzia tried to make her voice deeper than normal. Not that anyone here would recognize her, but it didn't hurt.

Lady Wint glanced over her shoulder. "Well, you didn't hear it from me—rumor has it that our grand prince is ill."

"Ill?" Mzia kept her voice steady.

"Yes. He hasn't been at events like he normally does, and some even whisper that it might be that he is *addicted*."

"Really?" Mzia wanted to smile but kept her face blank. Lila was brilliant. If random people were bold enough to whisper it in the emperor's own ballroom, it must have gotten around.

"But listen," Lady Wint went on. "You simply mustn't stay with Tariq all night. He is often away because of his position, so he has only been here four times and you don't really know what is going on until your eighth. Ah! There is Madame Virtie. I must go and see how her children are coming along." She glided away into the crowd.

A flare of trumpets had everyone turning, looking towards the entrance doors. The fanfare announced the arrival of royalty. So, the grand prince had come at last. This was the next step in the plan.

But as Mzia craned her neck to see over the crowd, it wasn't Prince Orinth that stood, surrounded by guards, but the mighty Emperor Kaisar.

CHAPTER 54
THE COMPASS SPINS

SOMETHING WAS WRONG. Tariq gripped Mzia's arm and his eyes darted about the room. The emperor was not due to come tonight. He hadn't made a public appearance in many months. Prince Orinth was already approaching middle age, so the emperor had reigned a long, long time. He was old.

But he stood tall now, tall and proud despite the white beard that reached to his midsection. The room hushed, and then, like a ripple, people began to bow. Those nearest him dropped to their knees and soon the rest of the room followed suit. And despite his age, the emperor walked to his throne, holding his head high. There was no catch or shuffle in his step, his strides long and even. And Mzia felt her stomach drop.

This is where her blood had been going. To the emperor. To keep him alive when old age should claim him. To sustain and prolong his life. She wanted to throw up. Instead of healing the young, her blood had gone to saving the man who was responsible for Yulia's death, for the deaths of thousands, if not millions of others. Mzia was a little surprised that Ezhno hadn't bragged about it to her.

But perhaps she was saving that for the end, when they broke her at last.

Mzia pressed a hand to her midsection, willing the nausea to go away. Did he know, somehow? Did the emperor catch wind of their plan? Despite Tariq's careful strategizing and Lila's skilled hacking, did they fail before they had really begun? If the emperor was here, where was Prince Orinth? She peered at Tariq, but he didn't have any answers. She looked around for Lila, but she had already slipped away to the control room long ago.

Emperor Kaisar made it to the dais, took up his seat, and waved a releasing hand over the silent crowd. As if freed from a spell, the room came alive. People rose to their feet and all started talking at once about this unexpected surprise.

"The emperor!"

"But where is the grand prince?"

"Where is the princess?"

"The emperor is looking so well!"

Tariq took Mzia's hand, and they were moving towards the dancing part of the room before she had time to process. The musicians struck up a chord and an easy group dance started.

With forced lightness she asked, "Where are we off to?"

Tariq said nothing until they were among the dancers. They joined the dance as a pair and started the elegant, slow steps of the ballad.

"The emperor is very healthy," Tariq said, softly.

"Yes," Mzia agreed. They stepped apart and then back together.

"Will that change?" Tariq understood it was Mzia's blood at work.

Mzia nodded. Her blood could keep the emperor healthy but it couldn't stop death. When his time came, the Starbreather would claim him for the stars.

They progressed through the dance. Mzia fought to keep her face neutral. When the steps brought them close for a slow spin, Tariq whispered to her, "Side door. We go to him."

They allowed the dance to bring them round to the edge of the room as casually as possible, then they slipped through one of the many side exits into the long hall that wrapped around the throne room. Tariq took the lead, knowing the palace layout. He sent a quick message on his wrist pad to Lila. Now that their plan had shifted, they needed to put some time and space between them for the distraction to be set up.

They took a narrow back stair that could only be used for servants. Down they went in spirals until Mzia's knees trembled. The walls around them turned from the growth of the towers to old, fitted stones. A cool dampness pressed in from all sides along with the scent of mildew. The bottom of the flight led out to a small door into the main courtyard. The garden, lit by plants and the lights from the glass floor of the throne room high above, danced with fireflies. The eight mighty spires that held up the throne room broke the night sky into even sections all around them.

They crossed the garden much quicker than Mzia would have liked. Her heart pounded out of her chest with worry and the beauty of the gardens was lost to her. They crossed an artificial river on a moon bridge made of stones as old as the palace. The water reflected the light from the party above them.

Tariq paused abruptly there in the middle of the bridge. He checked his wrist pad. "We still have several minutes before we need to be at the next door."

Mzia took the moment to catch her breath. She expected him to say something, yet he remained silent, pulling off his party mask and just looking about the garden.

"We should go," she said even though she hadn't fully recovered. She looked to Tariq, but he remained still, staring at her.

"Mzia?" He stepped forward and his fingers brushed her cheek. He pushed her party goggles off her face. "Are you sure about this?" He searched her face like he expected to find something important there. "It smells of a trap. I don't know where the princess is, and I don't like having no safety net."

"I have never seen you like this." He looked a little wild, honestly, "What's wrong?"

He made a vague gesture with the hand that held their goggles.

She sighed and tried to calm her voice like she was talking to a frightened patient. "Use your words." *Where does it hurt?*

But he just continued to look at her in that searching way, and she found she couldn't bear it.

"Tariq, you need to tell me what's wrong. I am not a mind reader." *Where does it hurt?*

"I just . . . before we go, in case we don't make it out, I need you to know that what I did to you in the desert is the biggest regret of my life, a stain I will carry with me always." He put a hand to his heart.

Where does it hurt?

"Tariq this isn't really the time for—"

"No, this has to be the time. Because there's no time for me to make this up to you. If Lila's life hadn't been on the line, I would have gladly died in the desert for you, no regrets. So because we might be walking to our deaths, and I need you to know that if we somehow survive, I'll wait. I won't rush you. I'll wait for you to forgive me. I'll wait until—" he looked around, "the stars burn out. I get that it might not be in this lifetime. I just need you to know that before we go on."

Mzia squeezed her eyes shut to keep the tears at bay. Curse the lack of goggles to hide behind. She *wanted* to forgive him. She *wanted* to fall back into the friendship and trust and the maybe something deeper she had found between the crash and their dance in the desert. But wanting wasn't enough.

She put her hands on her head.

Where does it hurt? Use your words.

She took a steadying breath and lowered her hands. "I don't have an answer for you right now."

He nodded. "That's fair." No insisting. No demand for an answer. Nothing like when they first met. He passed her back her party goggles. "I just needed you to know. I'll wait for you."

CHAPTER 55
JUST ONE KISS

THEY REACHED THE OTHER side of the garden and found another small door. The stairs only spiraled up a few flights before Tariq paused at a door with a curved top. "Lila?" He said into his wrist pad. "We're at door three."

Only a moment later something clicked, and Tariq pushed open the door. He looked out into the hall before gesturing for Mzia to follow. They went along and turned left to find a set of lifts. "Door four, lift two." He told Lila.

The lift doors slid open and they went inside. "Remember," Tariq said to Mzia. "We are lost and slightly intoxicated party guests." He pulled out a small flask and rubbed some of the alcohol under his jaw line so he would smell of it. He passed it to Mzia so she could do the same. The scent made her eyes water.

"I distract the guard," Tariq said, "you go inside."

Mzia placed a hand on her pocket and nodded. Her mind fluttered then snapped into razor focus as it had back on the mountain when she was fleeing Ezhno's men. Only this time, she needed the plan to work to save more than herself or her sister.

Tariq sent a quick message on his wrist pad, and within seconds, screams echoed all the way from the ballroom. Nobody at the party was to be harmed. Mzia had been very firm on that, but the palace contacts Yulia had made long ago agreed to create a distraction when called upon, and now they were delivering. That mist that caused lights to wink out now filled the ballroom. Chaos would soon reign as Mzia had explained the change of ingredients. The perfect distraction.

The world slowed to the moments between her heartbeats as Tariq looked down at her and gave her a tight smile. She forced a smile back. This would work. It had to work. She took a deep breath. Balance.

The doors opened, and Tariq put an arm around her shoulders. They stumbled out, laughing like they had just heard the world's funniest joke.

"What are you doing on this floor?" A patrolling guard demanded.

"Just looking for a washroom," Tariq said much too loudly while slurring his words. He let go of Mzia and took a few stumbling steps forward. Acting so fast his movements were a blur, Tariq took the guard by the head and slammed it down onto his knee. The guard grunted and slumped to the floor.

Mzia had to fight the urge to check on him as Tariq grabbed her hand and they rushed on. They had minutes at best until they were discovered. They rounded a curve and found two men standing outside a door. Tariq didn't hesitate to stumble ahead of her, calling, "I think I found it! This way!" with more slurred speech.

"You there! You shouldn't be on this floor. Guests are—"

Tariq tripped the first guard, and as he pulled the second guard into a headlock, he called to Mzia "Go!"

She ran past him and pried open the door, which Lila had disabled. The room was large and dark, lit only by a single blue light near the huge bed hanging off in the right corner. There she could see the silhouette of the sleeping prince. On the far side of the bed stood his IV pole; maybe they were sedating him or giving him something to ease his passing.

Three steps into the room, a shadow moved to her left. In that darkness, a normal person wouldn't have seen it. Mzia saw it a moment too late. A familiar sound buzzed before something stuck to her upper arm. She was mid-scream when she fell hard on her knees, trying and failing to catch her breath. The moment the pain stopped she yelled, "It's a trap!" Another zap of pain and she crumpled completely to the floor.

The sound of feet. Rough hands grabbed her and drew her up to her knees.

"Search her," said a sickly familiar voice. The men snatched off her mask and wig and touched her none too kindly. Her protests were lost in the fray when they found the vial of blood in her hip pocket.

"No!" Mzia fought back, weak as the pain had made her. But it was useless.

"None of that now," Ezhno admonished, accepting the vial from one of her men. "I can't have you too injured. I need you after all." She examined the vial in her hand. "And just what were you going to do with this?" She laughed a little and turned to her soldiers. "That was the only one?"

"Only one on her," the man confirmed. And he was right. Tariq only let her carry one. He said drawing more blood was dangerous and pointless. Dangerous because she was already so weak. And pointless because what could possibly happen to one vial that wouldn't happen to two? And he had been right, of course. They would have found a second one.

"Good then. We can get this cleaned up. Bring him in."

To Mzia's horror, they led Tariq into the room and forced him to his knees beside her. He had a cut across one arm, and his left eye was red and swollen, likely to bruise. "Sorry," he breathed. "I guess they knew we were coming."

There were eight or so men in the room now, all the princess's personal guard.

Ezhno tapped the vial on her palm and shook her head. "Tariq, Tariq, whatever shall I do with you now? I'm sure your sister is involved in this somehow, too. Don't worry, I have men looking for her. But what to do about you?" She tipped her head and clicked her tongue like she was admonishing children caught stealing. "I guess freedom and your sister's life didn't mean so much to you as your girlfriend here. So, what kind of story could I feed the people about why you died?" She motioned to a soldier, and he pointed a gun at Tariq's head.

Mzia went cold. Ezhno was going to kill him. Right there, right now.

"Let me think, what could make the otherwise loyal and patriotic skycaptain turn against his country?"

Mzia watched Tariq's jaw tighten and his fists clench; he was about to do something stupid and heroic.

"Please," Mzia begged. "I will go with you. I won't make any fuss and I'll do whatever you want. Don't kill him. Please."

Ezhno scoffed. "We have had this conversation before—you already have to go with me, girl. You don't have a choice. But your begging has given me an idea for the perfect cover story. What do you think of this?" She turned to the soldier on her left. "The noble skycaptain was brought low, blinded by his love and the seduction of the Iaomai Child."

The man nodded. "A believable tale, Your Highness."

Mzia almost wanted to laugh at the idea that she could seduce anyone, but the next moment a guard took better aim at Tariq's head, and Mzia screamed, "No! Please! NO!"

"Your lover makes a passionate plea," Ezhno said. "What have you to say, Skycaptain?"

Tariq, cool as an autumn day, lifted his eyes to meet the princess. "If I am to die, then as a member of the military, I would like my right to a final request."

"No last requests," Ezhno snapped. They were treading on thin ice.

"Not even to kiss my beloved goodbye?" Ezhno opened her mouth but Tariq went on. He nodded at the security cameras. "Don't you want video evidence of our affair? Could anyone, even my closest friends, argue against proof like that?"

Ezhno's eyes narrowed like she knew he was up to something but couldn't decide what it was.

One of the soldiers coughed.

"What is it?" She turned on the man.

"Not to question you, Your Highness," the soldier stuttered. "But as skycaptain, he is entitled to a last request."

Ezhno glared at him until the man dipped his head. But then she shrugged. "On closer consideration." She crossed her arms. "Nobody can say I wasn't a merciful ruler before I became empress. Let them up."

The men let go of Mzia's shoulders, and she got slowly to her feet. Her legs shook as she turned to face Tariq, and she fought to keep her breathing under control. Was this the last time she would see him? How long would the princess wait to kill him? There was so much she wanted to say. So much she wished she had told him.

But he didn't look frightened or regretful at all. He just smiled down at her like he was proud of her. Like he was happy to be on this crazy mission, even if he died.

With his life now measured in mere seconds, Tariq reached up with one hand to brush the hair from her face and tucked it behind one ear.

Mzia only had a moment to consider how this would be her first kiss and probably her last one. Tariq's other hand clasped her own and he pressed into her palm a vial of blood. The vial he had insisted on carrying. The one they evidently hadn't bothered to search him for.

CHAPTER 56
FEAR

MZIA TREMBLED WHEN SHE pulled her hand away from Tariq's, hiding it in the skirt of her dress. The dress she looked so lovely in when he first saw her that afternoon. Tariq had somehow known that this would be the last thing he would see her wear. Blue. The color she had been wearing the night they met. Yet even as the memory washed over him, he couldn't bring himself to regret any of the choices that had led him to this very moment.

"Get on with it," Ezhno said, annoyed at the delay.

He wanted to linger, to gaze into her wide, white-gold eyes forever. To kiss her. But it was time. It was time to risk it all. Even her. And so he flicked his eyes over to the sleeping prince and back to her. She nodded ever so slightly. She understood.

He allowed himself a single steadying breath, one last moment to take in her face and the soft blue of her dress. Then he turned and grabbed the man who had a gun on them. He used the man for cover even as he yanked the gun away from him. One shot to the main glowlight caused it to crash to the floor and shatter. Everywhere became either too dark or too bright. In the close quarters, shots were fired in panic, causing the kind of chaos and noise he had been planning for. He shot two soldiers, and dodged a pain disk. Someone tried to trip him, but Tariq managed to evade the kick. His elbow slammed into his attacker before he shot a third man.

While the fight tumbled on, he caught sight of Mzia. She reached the prince, flipped and rolled over the bed, falling to the ground on the other side. Out of sight by the IV pole.

Someone punched him hard in the stomach, and he became overwhelmed by the remaining men, the whole thing over in a matter of seconds. But several palace guards stormed in and started shooting the princess's men. Prince Orinth's personal guards. Had Lila tipped them off? Was it the noise? He didn't have time to consider when someone knocked the gun from hand, so he dived behind a sofa for better cover. The prince's men meant a distraction. But they might not know he was a friend here and not an enemy.

One of Ezhno's men made a run for the other side of the prince's bed. He'd spotted Mzia. Tariq didn't hesitate to tackle the man so they both splayed out on the floor near the far wall. Tariq knocked the man's gun from his hands when they collided. He tried to pin the man down but struggled, his opponent well-trained and strong. The soldier yanked an arm free. A flash of the blade was all the warning Tariq got before the knife plunged into the left side of his chest.

THE FIRST THING MZIA did when she landed on the far side of the prince's bed was disconnect the line that ran to his IV. Some sort of sedative, she guessed, the real reason he was kept away from the party. She screwed in the vial and pushed her blood into his IV as gunshots and shouts erupted. There was stomping and so many yells.

Princess Ezhno swore and shouted.

When the last of her blood slid into the prince's arm, she glanced up to watch Tariq tackle a man running her way. They tumbled to the ground, fighting to get the upper hand. Before she could decide what to do, the soldier stabbed Tariq in the chest.

The world blurred and slowed as Tariq slumped to his side.

His attacker didn't even get to his feet before someone shot that man from behind. Then Mzia was moving, half-crawling, half-running to get to Tariq. He lay still in shock, gasping and yet unable to breath. Commotion and confusion still swirled around her, but she ignored it.

"You're gonna be all right. You're gonna be all right!" she repeated more to herself than to him as she used the syringe she had just given to the prince to draw blood from her inner arm. She yanked the needle from her arm and stabbed it into his. Never had she worked so quickly. Never had she found a vein so fast. But it might not be enough. Injuries were trickier.

There was no time. So, she tore off a fabric petal of her dress with one hand and pulled out the knife with the other. It wasn't a clean wound, but jagged and long. It bled profusely even before she could press the fabric to cover it. "No!" She tore off another petal and wiped the slick blood off her hands on the bodice of her dress. He could bleed out before her blood could save him. She couldn't lose him too. Not Tariq.

The room fell into sticky silence and a soldier grabbed her by the arm.

"Let go of me!" she screamed, trying and failing to pry herself away. "He's going to die if I don't—"

"He is going to die anyway," said the soldier who was clearly in charge. "Now tell me—what you did to the prince?"

These new soldiers had princess Ezhno and her men on their knees at gunpoint.

"She poisoned him!" Ezhno said, trying to stand. The soldier closest to her slammed a hand down on her shoulder and forced her back down to her knees.

"I didn't ask you," the man in charge snapped. He turned back to Mzia, "Answer me, Iaomai Child. What did you do to our prince?"

"I will tell you if you just let me help Tariq," Mzia said. "Please. He will die if—"

"You will answer me now," the man said. "I saw you at the prince's bedside. Now what did you do?"

"It was the cure! I gave him the cure to his addiction. Now please!" Mzia watched as Tariq's breaths became more shallow, "He will die! I will do anything! Tell you anything! Just please! Please—"

"Was it your blood?" said a gruff voice.

All eyes turned to see Grand Prince Orinth pushing himself to sit up. "The amount you gave me, it will cure me of my addiction?"

"Yes, Your Majesty. I cured you. Now please—"

"Take her way." He waved a dismissive hand.

"No! Please!" They dragged her out. She fought every step. "No! Tariq!"

CHAPTER 57
ANGER

ANGER WAS THE ONLY emotion Lila emoted as she was marched through the palace, hands tied behind her back. Fear had kept her in the communication tower long after she should have left. Even after she rigged the feed to show what happened to the entire empire, she had stayed. Her eyes glued to the screen as she watched Mzia yank the knife from Tariq's chest, labor over him to try and save him, then to be dragged away by the prince's guards. There was no sound on her end, but she could read her brother's name on the healer's lips.

Lila should have left then, should have gotten to the safe house, but she couldn't make herself move before the palace guards entered the communication tower. She could have fought harder to stay, to see more, but there were a lot of innocent techs in there who had no idea she had infiltrated them, swapping schedules with the man who was supposed to be in her seat the night of the celebration.

Now the fear for what would become of Tariq and even Mzia was replaced with anger. Each step became a drumbeat of spite that threatened to boil over. This government had stolen so much from her and they were not about to get any more. No matter what happened next, she wasn't going down without a fight.

She recognized the prince's chamber doors when they were opened and she was brought inside. A quick glance around showed that the room had been cleared of Princess Ezhno and her lackeys. The bodies of the soldiers she had watched fall on screen were also gone. And though she was afraid to look at the spot Tariq had fallen, she did. Her stomach turned at the dark stain there on the rug.

Anger snapped her body back into focus, kept it standing when despair threatened to make her knees give out. She was forced to stop near the middle of the room before the grand prince. He sat on the edge of his massive bed, now wearing more formal robes. It took all of Lila's training not to shout out the words that would probably get her executed. This man's actions had killed millions, including Aasim.

The prince took in Lila's disguise—a tech uniform she had stolen from the laundry. It had been laughably easy to take because she hadn't been asked to help design security there. What would the prince say to her? What information would he try to gain? Whatever it was, she wasn't about to give it to him.

At last, the prince spoke to his guards. "Everyone out. I wish to speak with the Marked One alone."

"Your Majesty, is that really wise considering—"

"Wise? No. But we are past conventional wisdom in these strange waters. You may wait outside."

His captain of the guard, whose name Lila couldn't quite place, saluted and ushered the other guards out of the room.

Now alone with her half-brother, Lila fought even harder to keep her words inside her mouth. Orinth rolled his shoulders and shook his head. "I have only one question for you, Marked One. Why did you cure me?"

Lila remembered her training and looked down, refusing to

speak or make eye contact.

The prince sighed. "I could have these answers tortured from you, but as time is short and you are a Mark. I thought I would honor your rank and ask you first." He paused but she said nothing. "I should have known you would choose the hard way. Once your bodyguard died, there was nobody to check your—"

"His name was Aasim!" she spat, all self-control gone. "And you killed him."

"My sister was responsible for that, actually."

"But your actions still caused it to happen."

"If you really believe that, then why did you help cure me?"

The logical reason was close enough to the truth. "Because you should be emperor." Because as much as she hated this prince who cared not that he killed the people she loved, he was still a better choice than Ezhno.

"My own family, the most powerful family in the empire, wants me dead and you dare to contradict them? You are a Mark. How could you possibly think that was your decision to make?"

Lila tossed her hair. "It wasn't my decision."

"Tariq's idea, then?"

Loyal to the end, she forced a smile Prince Orinth would hate and said, "Actually, it was the Starbreather's. You were born first, so it is your birthright. If you're unhappy with this, maybe you should take it up with him—"

"Enough of your games," the prince cut in. "You cured me to expose the Iaomai Child's abilities. Do you have any idea of the disaster you have created for the empire?"

"I can't be blamed. My mother named me after the revolutionary who was known for—"

"Don't recite history to me like I didn't help create it!" He was angry now. Good. "You have been nothing but a troublemaker since training. If Tariq hadn't taken the fall for you back then, you wouldn't still be here. Don't act surprised; it had your fingerprints all over it just as this does. Well, Tariq isn't here to take the blame for you this time."

The anger in Lila vanished and she hardly managed to whisper, "Is he dead?"

CHAPTER 58
ALONE

THEY PUT MZIA IN a small, windowless inner room. It was in the old part of the palace, the walls, ceiling, and floor made of cold, gray stone. Her only light came from a crack under the door. It was enough for her to see that the room contained a toilet and sleeping mat. High in the corner a camera watched her. Before shoving her in there, they had taken her shoes and even the jewelry Lila had lent her for the ball—everything except her dress. Thankfully, she had left Anuva's necklace behind. Knowing it was hidden well in Tariq's apartment was her only comforting thought.

After a few moments to catch her breath, Mzia slowly looked down at herself. Her hands and arms were covered with cracked and drying blood. Large brown stains blotched the front of the once gorgeous gown. Her stomach turned, and she barely made it to the toilet before vomiting. So little was inside of her, but her body didn't seem to know that. Her gut twisted and wrung until she couldn't breathe.

At last, the bout ended and she lay down on the floor, pressing her forehead to the cool stone. Blood had never bothered her before.

As a healer, she had seen more than her fair share of it. But this was *his* blood. Repulsed by the itching feeling of the drying blood on her hands, she almost vomited again. She would give anything to wash and change her clothes. Starbreather save her, how was she supposed to go on after this? She closed her eyes and pretended the coolness around her was that of the night. The stars were still there watching her even if she couldn't see them. The Starbreather could guide her path here, as he always did. Surly, he wouldn't let this be her end.

Several hours later, a shuffling sounded outside her door. She forced herself to her feet, trying to anticipate what would come next. A slot opened in the bottom of the door and a tray of food pushed in. The slot closed.

Mzia knelt down and examined the food. Simple enough bread and hard cheese. They probably wanted her alive to torture later, so she ate and drank what was given to her even though she wasn't hungry.

That was a mistake. She threw that all up too.

Eventually she was able to sleep, curled up in her skirts as best as she could. But she kept waking mere moments after she dropped off, thinking she heard something. Eventually, many hours later, more food was shoved under the door.

Using the meals and her sleep schedule, she tried to count the days. When the scuffling that indicated incoming food sounded, she knelt by the door and asked after Tariq, but whoever it was didn't talk back.

By the second day, Mzia stared up at the camera in the corner, trying to look as desperate as she felt. "Tariq! Is he alive? Please! I just need to know . . . is he alive? Why won't anyone answer me? It's not a hard question! Is he alive? Just answer!"

Tears trickled down her quivering lips, and her throat closed up. The image of his dying body, coated in blood, on the floor, taunted her—seared her mind and wouldn't let her go. Her voice grew hoarse the more she screamed. "Tell me!" She slammed her hand against the wall, instantly regretting it. Her hand stung from the blow; her heart ached endlessly.

Then she tried to protect him.

"Please, it was my idea. He wouldn't have done it if I hadn't asked him." Her mind raced to come up with more ideas. "It isn't his fault. He shouldn't be punished. I will take all the blame. I will do anything—" Tears choked out her words. She cried herself to sleep more times than she cared to count.

In that terrifying space between waking and sleeping, she also worried about Anuva. What had the princess done to her sister? But it was best to keep that to herself. Ezhno probably wouldn't give up her location anyway and Mzia certainly didn't trust her sister's life to the grand prince. So the less people knew, the better. But logic failed Mzia as the fourth or fifth day rolled around. She sounded crazy and desperate. She practically handed them fuel to use against her. But with Anuva out of her reach, Tariq was really all she had left. *Starbreather, give me another chance. Give Tariq another chance.* She wasn't ready to give him up yet because, somewhere in the mess of trying to cure the prince, she had forgiven him.

MZIA WAS OUT OF tears. Out of words. Empty. She lost all sense of time and knew her mental health would only continue to decline. The customary scuffle sounded and she was on her knees by the door before the slot could open for her food.

"Please!" she begged. "Please just tell me if Skycaptain Tariq is alive! I will do anything if you just—"

The door slid open, and Mzia squinted, blinded by the sudden rush of daylight. She blinked up at the man standing there.

Tariq.

He was dressed simply and breathing heavily. Almost like he had been running.

Before she could get a word out, he dropped to his knees over the threshold. "I'm sorry." He was upset and . . . ashamed. His voice shook. "Mzia, forgive me. I didn't know they were keeping you like this. They had me sedated, and I only just woke and they wouldn't let me come down until I had been briefed and—"

Mzia threw her arms about his neck. "You're alive!" She couldn't believe the words even as she spoke them.

He froze for a moment, then wrapped her in a hug.

Her voice trembled. "I thought . . . I thought you were . . . They wouldn't tell me . . . I begged and begged."

"I know, I know." His voice steadied. "That's over. It's going to be all right now. I've got you."

She buried her face in his shoulder and wept. She didn't care that whoever was watching saw how happy this made her. She didn't care that it meant more things they could threaten her with. Here, in this moment, Tariq was alive and well and that was all that mattered. Her arms slid down and she clutched the fabric on the front of his tunic, deciding never to let go. He stroked her hair, saying soothing things she didn't catch.

"Please," she said, fighting to catch her breath. "Please don't scare me like that again. I thought I . . . I thought I lost you."

"I will try not to." A slight smile colored his voice.

She pulled back just a little to look at him, still clutching the front of his shirt. "What happened?"

"I have a lot to tell you, but not here."

"Lila?"

"Lila's fine."

"And the princess?"

"Being dealt with, I hear."

"The plan worked? People . . . know?"

"Yes, everyone knows about you." Tariq pushed back the wet hair clinging to her face. She sniffed and blinked up at him with bleary eyes. He kissed her forehead. "I have a lot to say to you. But first, let's get you out of here." Tariq pried her hands from his shirt.

"Where are we going?"

"Somewhere safe." Without letting go of her hands, he stood and pulled her up after him.

As they stepped into the hall, a door at the other end opened. Prince Orinth, flanked by six guards, entered the corridor and started down towards them. Mzia clutched Tariq's arm.

"Don't be afraid," he told her softly, giving her hand a reassuring squeeze. His tight smile told her he was nervous but not scared.

The prince approached with a disapproving frown. When he stopped several steps away, he said, "How interesting to find you here. I don't recall you mentioning you would come here next during our meeting."

"Forgive me, my prince," Tariq said with a slight bow. "I didn't think you wanted the empire's greatest asset left imprisoned down here. An oversight, I am sure."

The prince's eyes narrowed slightly, flicking down to where Mzia clung to Tariq then to the guards beside him. He waved his hand. "Leave us."

Mzia felt her panic rise further as the guards marched back down the hall. The prince crossed his arms. "I used to think we were so alike, Tariq, you and I. But it seems we have different ideas about a few key areas."

"Forgive me, Your Majesty, I never meant to slight you. I've only just woken up from several days of sedation. I may not be thinking right."

The prince tilted his head to one side. As the silent seconds stretched on, Mzia sensed the unseen battle raging between the two men. The prince who would be emperor and the Marked bastard. Something had happened while she was locked away that she didn't yet understand.

For the prince himself to come down, he must have wanted to be the one to release Mzia. To speak to her first. The idea sent a shiver down her spine. She did not wish to be alone with this man any more than she did Ezhno.

As little as she cared for Prince Orinth, they needed him as an ally for the years ahead. They couldn't afford to start off against each other. What had Tariq said when they formed this plan? The prince would always do what *appears* right? Soothing physical ailments were more her forte, but egos were not so different.

Mzia let go of Tariq and bowed. "I wanted to thank you, Your Majesty, for this opportunity."

The staring contest was over, and the prince seemed surprised she had spoken to him. She had only moments to gain any kind of trust. Her knees shook but her voice was steady. "I wish only to serve the empire under your and your father's guidance."

"Is that so?" He lifted an eyebrow.

"Of course. I look forward to your leadership in the tough times ahead. I wish only—"

"Enough." The prince waved his hand. "I see you are eager to prove your loyalty, Iaomai Child. But I watched you beg for Tariq's life for five days. I know where your true loyalties lie."

She felt Tariq stiffen beside her. What did he know of this?

The prince went on, addressing Tariq. "I never would have questioned your loyalty before these past few weeks. You never defied me before you met the Iaomai Child. She is dangerous."

"Your Majesty, I—"

"Not to worry, I still intend to honor our deal even after this little fiasco. If only because I am sure Ezhno's threats are just as much to blame for your failures. And I can't argue that you are best suited for the task ahead, even if you do seem a little too . . . attached."

There were so many implications to his last words that Mzia didn't have time to unpack them before the prince continued. "You swore to me, Marked One, that you would keep the Iaomai Child in line."

Mzia bristled; he spoke as if she wasn't standing before them.

"And I will, Your Majesty," Tariq said.

"That includes reminding her that her duty is to myself and the empire alone and before all else." At last, he turned to Mzia. "You are kept alive because you are useful to me—you are a means to an end. And the moment you stop becoming useful to me will be your last moment. It will be advantageous for you to never forget this conversation."

Mzia nodded, her head down. A cold feeling circled her stomach. He sounded so much like Princess Ezhno. They were not so different after all. Had she done wrong in saving this man?

Prince Orinth turned on his heel and left them alone in the stone hall. Mzia felt light-headed, as if the prince had taken all the oxygen with him.

Tariq cleared his throat. "Mzia?"

His voice brought her back to the moment. She was free of that horrible dark room and he was alive. She turned and pulled him into a hug, breathing in his cool, mint scent.

"Tell me everything is going to be okay," she said, her voice muffled in his shirt.

"Everything is going to be okay."

"Tell me what happened the last few days."

"I will. Let's go somewhere more comfortable."

CHAPTER 59
MY STAR

MZIA HELD TIGHT TO Tariq as he led her to the end of the corridor where four palace guards awaited them. The men escorted them down another hall and into a lift. On the way, they passed a window where mid-morning light bathed the old stone floor in a warm glow. What was going on? Tariq seemed calm, though not relaxed. What had happened in those days in her cell? She looked up at Tariq, and he gave her a smile and her hand another reassuring squeeze.

The lift opened and they were led out into a hall. They passed no one except a patrolling guard. It felt so normal, walking down a hall between beams of sunlight from the tall windows. So ordinary when the last few weeks had been anything but.

The guards stopped at a door. The four of them took up posts on either side as the door slid open. Mzia and Tariq walked in.

Mzia wasn't sure what this room would contain and paused a few steps in. It appeared to be just a regular sitting room with sofas and chairs and a tea table off to one side. There was nobody else there. The door slid shut behind them and Tariq turned to see why

Mzia had stopped walking.

"What is it?" he asked.

"I just . . . why are we here?"

"So we can talk."

Mzia blinked. "What happened?"

"It's complicated." He dropped her hand, which she didn't care for, and picked up a basket that sat on one of the nearby chairs. "Here, this is for you. Change of clothes. There is a bathroom just—"

"Tariq." Mzia clutched the skirt of her ruined dress. "What does this mean for . . . me?"

"Don't take this the wrong way, but I thought you would want to clean up first." He glanced down at her stained gown. Stained with his blood. What an ordinary thing to assume. Like she had just fallen outside in the mud and needed to clean up. Like she hadn't been sitting in the dark in a dress stained with his blood for the past five days wondering if he was even alive.

"I will tell you everything," he said, pushing the basket into her hands. "And there are many good things to tell."

Mzia looked down at clothes then at the door to the bathroom. "And you, you will still be here when I get out?"

Tariq smiled a real smile and nodded. "I promise."

She believed him.

WHILE MZIA HAD LITERALLY dreamed of showers in that dark room, she spent as little time as possible under the hot water. She scrubbed herself raw in seconds and wasn't even fully dry before pulling on the clothes. The clothing Tariq had given her were simple and elegant: a light green dress that fell to the floor in many generous layers like leaves. Thankfully it wasn't blue. She wasn't sure she could ever wear blue again. The new dress also had a belt with intricate designs of aster flowers in silver thread. A pair of soft gray shoes and makeup were the last things in the basket; no headscarf or goggles.

Mzia dawdled in front of the mirror only long enough to be assured she had gotten all the blood from skin and hair before she darted back into the main room, slightly out of breath. Tariq was still there, as he promised, but he had changed his tunic. This one was of the same cut as the one he had worn to the ball. And the colors nearly matched hers.

"You changed," she said, only realizing after the words came out how accusatory they sounded. As if he had done something wrong.

"I didn't have time before I came to see you." He held out his hand and she took it. He led her to the sofa, and they sat together. A cup of tea sat before her on the low table but Mzia ignored it.

"We don't have a lot of time," Tariq said, "but I will tell you everything I think is relevant and you can ask follow-up questions later. Deal?"

Mzia nodded.

"Good. So, I only woke this morning, a few hours ago. They had me on a lot of drugs since my injury. I don't think they knew just how well your blood would work. Our end of the plan went off perfectly except that Princess Ezhno was there and I got stabbed. But everything else, the prince being cured, the security footage being sent out, the relevant parts anyway, went just as planned. The empire saw what you can do, Mzia. They know now and there is no hiding it."

Mzia smiled. That was good, better than good—world altering.

"The official story that everyone is being told is that Ezhno acted alone, out of spite and revenge to try to kill both you and her brother for the death of her child all those years ago. The emperor and grand prince knew nothing about your abilities and were horrified that the princess would keep such a secret all to herself."

Mzia frowned. "I see. So, officially, I am a new discovery?"

"Precisely. Because naturally our emperor, being the kind and benevolent ruler that he is, would never withhold such information about a cure from his people." Tariq failed to keep a touch of sarcasm from his voice. "While I was healing over the past few days, it seems the royal council was debating just what to do with you. I will skip the political maneuvering and get straight to the point. We are being hailed as patriots, you and I. Ones who were brave enough to stand up to the rogue princess, put country first, and risk our lives to save the life of the grand prince."

"How very . . . noble of us," Mzia said.

"Some of us are just born to be heroes, I guess." They shared a knowing smile and he went on. "And that brings us to today, when I finally woke up this morning and learned about everything that had gone on while I slept." He became serious. "I wouldn't have let them keep you in that place, Mzia. If I had been awake, I swear I wouldn't have allowed—"

"I know," Mzia said, remembering his face when he had opened the door to the dark room. "That's why I was so worried, so worried that you were . . . Tariq, they wouldn't tell me . . ." She looked down at their joined hands.

"I know," he said, rubbing his thumb across the back of her hand. "What Prince Orinth said down there, about how you were trying to make deals for my safety, even when your future was so uncertain, is that true?"

Mzia nodded, unable to meet his eyes.

"I'll never forget that. Ever. Not that I needed another reason to be in your debt," he added with some forced lightness. "How many times have you saved my life now?"

"I've lost track," Mzia said, glad for the lighter tone. "How ever did you survive before you met me?"

Tariq laughed a little. He brought her hand up and kissed it. "I am not sure how I survived without my guiding star."

Mzia found it hard to breathe when a voice from the door said, "You should kiss her face, not her hand, moron."

Mzia turned in delighted surprise. "Lila?"

Lila bounded into the room in a red and orange dress only she could pull off. "Who else were you expecting? It's only a few minutes until the ceremony."

"The ceremony?" Mzia looked at Tariq in question.

"You didn't tell her?" Lila crossed her arms. "Seriously, Tariq, you had one job."

"There was a lot to go over. I was getting around to it."

"Such a man thing to say. Welp, now that you have failed, I'll have to step in and help out. At least this way I get to make sure it turns out fine and—" She stopped and looked at Mzia. "You were going to let her go out looking like that?"

"These are the clothes you picked out!" Tariq protested.

"Without her hair and makeup done. Where is that basket?"

"She looks fine."

"That is where you set the bar? *Fine*? You are about to go out to the royal court and then on screen in front of millions and you are okay with her just looking *fine*?"

"What?" Mzia asked.

"The emperor has an announcement," Tariq explained as Lila retrieved the basket from the bathroom and pulled up a chair to sit in front of Mzia. While Lila applied some eyeliner to Mzia's face, Tariq explained. "We just have to go and be formally introduced to the royal court and then to the empire. In light of your abilities, you will be going on what they are calling a Healing Tour of the empire. You will be giving out your blood to those addicted and each kingdom will get a chance to thank the emperor for his kind and benevolent ways."

"Oh, that's . . ." She should be pleased. It was the kind of thing she had always dreamed about happening, and yet she couldn't bring herself to be happy about it. There was just too much she didn't know, too many unanswered questions.

Tariq must have sensed Mzia becoming a bit overwhelmed as Lila braided back the top half of her hair. "We will talk more about it tonight, all right?"

Mzia nodded.

Lila stepped back to admire her work and nodded. "That will do. Well, if I don't get to be in front of millions, at least my hard work does."

"You're not coming?" Mzia asked.

Lila shot a glare at Tariq. "No. Marks aren't part of the court so the only way I could get an invite is if I was actually credited as helping you, but my name doesn't appear anywhere. As far as the empire knows, the footage just got *accidentally* leaked."

"Lila." Tariq stood. "We talked about this."

"Yeah, for like three seconds on your way down to get Mzia out of her cell. What is the point of helping save the world if nobody knows?"

"The point," Tariq said, "is that you know you did something good and you don't need praise for it."

Lila rolled her eyes. Mzia knew she had more to say. Tariq was doing what he always did—protecting his sister. And Mzia suspected the emperor didn't want it public knowledge that the palace could be hacked, even by the one who designed the system.

A guard stuck his head in the door and said, "It's time."

Mzia stood and followed Tariq to the door.

"I'll just be here." Lila flopped onto the couch they had vacated. "Watching you both on the screen like some commoner."

Mzia felt butterflies chasing her breakfast around as they were escorted by eight guards to the lift. They went up again and stepped out into a beautiful room with several low tables set with food. A well-dressed woman with a handpad stood alone near the middle of the space.

"Here you are," the woman said and bustled over to them. She looked them both up and down and walked around them in a circle like she was admiring some furniture she wanted to buy. "Good, yes, the colors match well. Now you are about to be presented to the royal court. Skycaptain, you have done this before, so take the lead. You will both walk up to the dais and kneel until the emperor bids you stand. You will only speak if directly addressed, and if that happens, keep your responses short. You will probably only be asked to agree with something His Imperial Majesty says. Once your formal introduction to the court is finished, they will bring in the cameras to address the empire. Any questions?"

Mzia had millions swirling about in her head but none she could put voice to, so she just shook her head.

A young lady opened a door at the far end of the room. "Are they ready?" she asked.

"Yes, as ready as they can be." She stepped back and waved them on. "Get out there and don't forget to smile when the cameras pan on you!"

As they left the room to step into a hall that looked familiar, Tariq whispered, "Just follow my lead. It will be over soon."

CHAPTER 60
A GIFT

THE THRONE ROOM FILLED with whispers that fell into silence as Tariq and Mzia stepped through the doors. The space was decorated much as it had been for the Solstice Ball but with the banners now hung in a wide wedge that confined everyone to about one-quarter of the room with the throne now set in the temporary corner. Daylight cast little rainbows across the guests and walls. The royal council and most of the kingdoms' governors, many of which Tariq recognized, stood by the banners, in a more forced intimacy because of the reduced space.

A carpet of golden moss framed with red flowers led straight to the dais, the throne, and the emperor. Tariq had faced battles that felt less intimidating than this room full of the most powerful people on the continent.

He summoned the confidence that had brought him this far in life to keep moving forward. He glanced at Mzia, her face blank as a cloudless sky, but she had a stiffness in her posture. This was the first time she had ever been exposed to so many people. The first time she walked openly among anyone without fear of being discovered.

And indeed, many looks of curiosity and question were thrown her way. The people knew so little about her. And the looks were not friendly. Some were already calculating how they could profit from this, how they could exploit this new discovery.

They approached the throne. Prince Orinth's wife and their two legitimate children, boys in their early teens, sat closest to the steps and off to the right on cushions. There were no Mark Ones there. They were assets to the emperor before they were anything else. Tariq used to take pride in that idea, that his very birth singled him out for a purpose. He glanced again at Mzia. Now a new purpose had found him, and he saw this facade for what it was— exploitation. He would continue to serve for Mzia and nobody else.

Prince Orinth sat to his father's right, arms crossed and expressionless. Their eyes met for the briefest of moments. As Tariq had told Mzia, he didn't trust the prince to do what was right, not after he had been lied to. But he did trust him to do what appeared good. And right now, nothing appeared better than sending the Iaomai Child out to cure the empire.

Tariq turned his attention to his father and as always, felt no connection. Emperor Kaisar had not participated in his upbringing, so others had taken his place.

Beside the emperor, two spots sat empty. One was for the former empress, who had died over a decade ago, and the second would be where Princess Ezhno should sit, were she not imprisoned for high treason.

Together, Tariq and Mzia knelt on the first step on the dais. The same nervous energy swirled inside him as at his presentation ceremony when he turned twenty-one. At that time in his life, he considered it the highest honor he would ever receive. He would have despaired to know how little that title and honor all meant to him now.

The emperor spoke. "My council, governors, what a strange

week this has been." His voice cracked with age but held the easy authority of generations. "Not what we expected, is it? The most exciting Solstice I have ever been to, and I have seen many." He chuckled a little, inviting the tension in the room to break. He raised his voice to better address the crowd. "Many odd events have occurred of late. It would be easy to question, to wonder how the Starbreather could give us what we see before us in this newest discovery. It would be easy to think there might be something wrong, but that would be a mistake. I for one will not question the unknown mistakes we may have made in the past, for we were ignorant."

The emperor had clearly not lost his cunning in his old age. How many of the governors or council were actually in on the secret? Who had known all along that keeping the Iaomai Children from the public reeked of a power play? Were they all willing to go along with it because they suspected their silence would eventually be rewarded?

The emperor went on. "And what a gift it is. So humbled are we that the Starbreather should grace us with it. The empire will be blessed indeed. Think of all your loved ones being restored, addictions no longer a worry."

Yes, those related to the people in this room would certainly be given healing before the common man. Yet another way to pacify them. Who would question this when they were the ones to benefit?

"Let us set aside our petty differences and thank the Starbreather for this miracle. He has guided us on the paths we needed to take to get here."

Murmuring prayers went up in a façade of unity. Nobody dared speak out now, nobody would dare to question the royal family in this.

The cameras were brought in for the empire to watch what unfolded next.

Prince Orinth welcomed everyone. He rehashed the story everyone had been told of his sister's unfortunate betrayal to her emperor and empire. Then he got to the interesting part: the discovery of the cure. He told of the bravery of Mzia and Tariq, loyal subjects who were willing to risk it all. They were both called to stand. Tariq got stiffly to his feet beside Mzia as the people in the room applauded. They turned around slowly to face the people and cameras. The prince became silent, and all eyes turned to the emperor again. The room hushed.

"In a world full of so much uncertainty, it is good to know that the old ways hold true. While many question the need or sustainability of Marking out certain people for service to the emperor, this week has proven there is a very great need.

"I have not known such a great hope as when I first heard, with you all, of the Iaomai Child's abilities. It is my great pleasure now to gift her to my kingdoms." He held out his hand to Mzia. "My people, I present to you the Emperor's Healer."

Applause shook the room. A title was a gift and a weapon: one both the emperor and Mzia could wield. Tariq would need to teach her how to use it well.

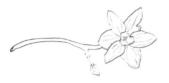

CHAPTER 61
MANY FUTURE DANCES

MZIA CAME TO THREE conclusions in the following few hours. They strung themselves together, not neatly like pearls on a string to be admired, but like words hastily scribbled on a scrap of paper. Even now as the afternoon turned to evening, she internally squinted and mulled over the words. They were truths, but she was having a harder time really knowing them as such.

The first conclusion—Anuva was still missing. She gathered this from the complete lack of mention of her either at the ceremony or the meetings that followed. She sat in with Tariq at advisory meetings and press releases, and not once was Anuva mentioned. In fact, it was brought up often that since Mzia was the only Iaomai Child anywhere close to adulthood, she would need to be strategically used until another could be found and came of age. That was the exact wording—*strategically used.*

The second conclusion came to her at the end of one of those meetings where her opinion was not asked even once. She would be healing people, just not in the way she had ever envisioned. Perhaps it was just a fanciful dream that she had pictured since childhood. Yulia had painted for her a vision of the future where Mzia could go from town to town, healing those who came to her for help. She would stay to fix or mend as long as she needed to and leave in her own time to go on and heal another village.

That silly fantasy had to be set aside when the sheer amount of people in need of a cure was discussed. The numbers and statistics that were tossed around made her head hurt. So no, a leisurely town by town or city by city approach would not work. Her blood didn't keep and had to be given out within 24 hours of being drawn. So, it was decided, before she even entered the meeting, that Mzia would travel to larger cities and the cure would be distributed from there. And, naturally, Mzia was encouraged by the information about how many she would be able to cure. The graphs that showed her potential impact and how many fewer would die pleased her, but it all became very clear to her that she was nothing more than a commodity, a tool for use to get a job done.

And the third conclusion started with something the grand prince had said earlier that day to Tariq and solidified as she met what felt like every noble in the kingdom, or possibly the empire. Tariq had done something, given up something, to be the one who would stay by her side. And not just for the day, but for the years of the tour that stretched ahead of them. In every meeting he was introduced after her as "The Healer's Shield," which she learned meant her head of security. And maybe there was some great honor in that she didn't understand, but she doubted it. His jaw tightened when he thought nobody looked. A guarded wariness garnished his words whenever he was asked to comment on something. He showed a restrained deference to everyone. Mzia couldn't help contrasting this with the authority he had shown on his skyship, where he had been unafraid to even tell the princess what to do. Now he was just a shadow of that: her shadow. And if she was only a commodity, then what did that make him? From what she gathered, no more than her glorified bodyguard.

At some point, the meetings transitioned into a party. She was given an evening dress to wear, this one painted to look like transparent moth wings hanging from her shoulders and wrists with lilac undertones. The bodice had a high collar, real violets somehow grown along the shoulders and sleeves of her upper arm, with more flowers woven into her halo braid like a crown.

Mzia met even more important people at the party held in the throne room. All of them wanted to touch and talk to her like some oddity stood before them, and even spoke about her right in front of her like she wasn't even there. It was all too much. So, when an opportunity arose to slip away, she quickly found an empty balcony off the throne room to hide on.

The night had turned brilliant with the moon hidden so the stars could shine their brightest. To the southwest across the ocean, Mzia saw flashes of lightning. She judged the storm to be far enough off and unlikely to reach her before midnight. So for now, she enjoyed the lights of the city, the stars, and the far-off lighting, allowing her eyes to unfocus and just absorb the blurred patterns as she leaned on the balcony rail and idly bruised the soft flowers on her dress.

A quiet cough sounded behind her. She turned and found Tariq standing in the doorway. Light and music floated out from behind him. "Don't worry," he said quickly. "I am not here to call you away. I just wanted . . ." He smiled and shook his head.

"What?"

"You look lovely."

"You came out here to tell me I look lovely?"

"No." He laughed a little. "I wanted to tell you I posted guards at this door and they will let nobody less than the emperor himself out here to see you. Stay out here as long as you like." His eyes moved to the western sky. "But promise me you will come in before the storm hits." He turned to go.

"Tariq, wait."

He paused.

"Thank you."

"No problem," he said lightly. "You looked like you could use a break."

"No, I didn't mean for the guards." She clasped and unclasped her hands. She couldn't do this now. She would cry if she went on, and she had cried enough today. So she said, "I didn't see Lila at the party. I would have thought this was her thing."

"It is," Tariq said. "But she is a little busy tonight."

"Must be pretty important to keep her away."

He glanced behind him and then took several steps forward. "She isn't here and will have nothing to do with the tour because she is working on a new project." He dropped his voice so that it only just crossed the few feet between them. "She is looking for Anuva."

Mzia gripped the railing behind her, "What? Really?"

Tariq nodded. "Officially, she has returned to her own work, that is the deal. But unofficially," he came another step closer, "they moved your sister, as I predicted. So Lila is breaking into Ezhno's files, which were temporarily easier to connect with during this transition. They are pretty well encrypted. She said a bunch of things I didn't understand, but she assures me it will only be a few weeks at most. I can't promise she will find all the answers, but we are looking."

Mzia fought to control her breathing. So he had a plan for that too. Of course he had. Tariq left no loose ends. Yet one more thing he was doing for her. But how? How had he been able to orchestrate this?

Mzia asked, "I don't, that is to say, politics are not something I am very familiar with, but it seems to me, and I don't want to insult you, it's just that from what I saw this afternoon, and you can correct me if I am wrong, I just—" She huffed a sigh in frustration. "Tariq, what did you do?"

"What's wrong?" He looked rather confused. Of course he was. She explained it all wrong. But the words didn't want to form. The feelings refused to come out as words and instead came out as tears.

"Hey now." He came closer and put a hand on her shoulder. "You can tell me."

"That's just the problem."

"I'm the problem?"

"No." She almost laughed. "You are the opposite of that."

"So . . . I'm a solution?"

Mzia shook her head, smiling despite herself. "Sort of."

"And that makes you upset because . . . ?"

"I'm not upset."

"You're crying."

"I mean, I am a little upset because how all of this happened," she gestured vaguely around them, "was because you did something. You gave up something. And why would you do that? Why would you do that for . . . for me?"

"What makes you think I gave up something?"

"Because I am not blind. I see how they all treat you. And I know being a Marked One comes with obligations. I just—"

He laughed a little.

"What?" Mzia asked, feeling a little indignant.

"Only that I have never met someone so determined to undersell herself. You win, I did give up something—my old way of life, my old command. But what makes you think I didn't want this? Didn't want to be with you?"

Mzia looked at him doubtfully. "Because you loved what you did. I saw that, on your skyship. You fought and worked so hard to be where you were. And you had an opportunity here to get it back and you didn't take it. You can't tell me you aren't going to miss what you had. That authority, that power."

"All right, if it will make you feel better, yes, I will miss my old command and the freedom it came with. Very few Marks ever achieve that."

"There, you see!"

"Mzia."

"What."

"Must I spell it out for you?"

She just blinked.

His smile softened and he brushed the strands of hair from her face. "I want to be with you."

"Won't this tour be terribly boring for you, Skycaptain? I thought you rather liked war games and secret missions?" Her voice was light, but the question was very real.

"Boring?" He stepped in closer so they shared the same breathing space. "I knew from the moment we met and you sassed me about my age, that life around you would never be boring." He pressed his forehead to hers and her heart raced. "I knew that the empire would never again be the same once you touched it. And it is the greatest honor and adventure of my life to stand beside you while you change the world." He pulled back a bit to look her in the eyes. "If you will have me?"

"If?" She didn't understand. How could he ask such a question? Of course, she wanted him there. He had to be there. But she had never told him so. Words felt so inadequate; anything she could say felt so silly and would fall so short of the new and exciting emotion bubbling inside her. Action was needed.

Mzia pushed up onto her toes and kissed him. It was hastily done, a bit awkward owing to her lack of experience, and over in a moment. She felt her face heat as she sank back onto her heels, fearing she had done it all wrong.

But Tariq's smile was delightful. "Is that a yes?"

She nodded and before she could explain more, he kissed her back. His kiss was light and gentle. One of his hands cupped the side of her face, the other slid to the small of her back, pulling her close. After a moment, she felt him smile. A giggle of pure delight escaped her own lips unbidden, and they each pulled back, still smiling. The world and its demands faded away. Mzia wanted to remember that smile, this moment forever.

A soft rumble of thunder broke the tension. They turned to see the approaching storm. A cool wind told them it was not so very far off as first thought. But they still had a little while yet. Mzia leaned her head on Tariq's chest, close to his heart.

"Tonight we celebrate what we have won," he said. "What you have accomplished."

As if on cue, the band struck up a new tune, louder than before, one they both knew. It was the song they had danced to in the desert.

Tariq stepped back and held out his hand to her. "Will you take this dance with me, healer?" It came with the unspoken invitation for many future dances.

Mzia smiled and stepped forward into his arms, a place she never wanted to leave again. It eased one of the tight spots in her heart to know she wouldn't have to face the coming struggles alone.

The music swelled and the dance began.

THE END

ACKNOWLEDGMENTS

Thank you to everyone who supported and believed in me through this endeavor. I spent many years only dreaming of publishing, and it was because of the support I found in the following people that my dreams became a reality.

Thank you to my lovely beta readers: you rock. Thanks most especially to Katie Stover for believing in the book during the rocking first drafts, Angi Resendez for guiding thoughts on the messy middle of the project, and Tiara Blue for wise insights on the tension in the final stages. You all became my cheerleaders and encouraged me to keep going even when I didn't believe in myself.

Thank you to my editors: your critiques were invaluable. Anne J. Hill, I needed to hear the perspective you gave, and you turned my passion project into a manuscript. My rambling thoughts into a book. Crystal Grant and Sarah Harmon, you both provided that end polish and a great second (and third) set of eyes to the final draft.

Thank you to my map designer, Rachael Ward with Cartopgraphybird Maps. You shaped into reality the world I created in my head.

Thank you to my roommate and best friend, Reba Cochran, who made the in-book art while listening to my late-night plot ramblings. Thank you for not telling me how crazy I sounded; I owe you forever.

Thank you to my parents, who have been loving and supportive of this exciting new step in my life.

And finally, thank you to my grandmother, my number one fan and inspiration to keep going when things look difficult.

To God be the glory.

ABOUT THE AUTHOR

Rachael Katharine Elliott is a middle school English teacher and world traveler. She has a Bachelor's Degree in English Education from Grace College and Theological Seminary. Her poetry is published in the anthology, *Sharper than Thorns*. In her spare time, she sews costumes to wear to renaissance fairs and convinces her friends to read classic British literature. She lives with her roommate in Northern Indiana, where they embark on many adventures.

Find her on Instagram: @catching_stardust

CPSIA information can be obtained
at www.ICGtesting.com
Printed in the USA
LVHW050726070623
749062LV00019B/86/J